Praise for *Thornbrook Park*

"Fans of *Downton Abbey* will adore this brand-new Edwardian period romance series set at the grand estate of Thornbrook Park."

—*Edwardian Promenade*

"Browning utilizes the setting and the Edwardian era to her advantage as she crafts her story of a wounded hero and bold heroine who defy the conventions of society."

—*RT Book Reviews*

"*Downton Abbey* fans are sure to enjoy *Thornbrook Park*, where anything is possible... Well written with engaging characters and an intriguing storyline."

—*My Book Addiction Reviews*

"A compelling story that combines emotion, visual imagery, and a sense of the excitement of the times."

—*I Am, Indeed*

"Beautifully written with an eye to the social and political changes of the time period. I thoroughly enjoyed the characters and the author made them all so real."

—*Bookworm 2 Bookworm*

"As a fan of Regency romances, I was eager to try another era and I'm certainly glad I started with this

Edwardian treasure… The mystery kept my attention without overpowering the romance."

—*Bitten by Love*

"[T]he writing is articulate and I did very much enjoy the romance between Eve and Marcus."

—*Romance Historical Reviews*

"*Thornbrook Park* is a delightful installment in the historical romance genre. This is the first Sherri Browning book I've read and I'll be coming back for more."

—*AwesomeSauce Book Club*

"The characters are well developed and multifaceted. It flowed beautifully, so much so, that I read the second half in one sitting… I couldn't put it down."

—*My Gallery of Worlds*

SHERRI BROWNING

sourcebooks
casablanca

Published by Sourcebooks Casablanca, an imprint of Sourcebooks, Inc.
P.O. Box 4410, Naperville, Illinois 60567-4410
(630) 961-3900
Fax: (630) 961-2168
www.sourcebooks.com

Printed and bound in Canada.
MBP 10 9 8 7 6 5 4 3 2 1

For younger sisters everywhere.

One

LADY ALICE EMERSON KNEW EXACTLY WHAT SHE wanted, and it wasn't a husband. She had a whole list of things she longed to accomplish in life, all on her own with no one to hold her back or tie her down.

Her plan had been years in the making, the first step being to get out from under her parents' control. Once Alice's maiden aunt, Agatha, and her father had found themselves more frequently at odds, it had been child's play to convince Mother that accompanying Agatha on an extended visit to Thornbrook Park would be best for everyone, saving Father's health before being around Agatha could make him apoplectic. Had it been anywhere else, Mother might have hesitated, but she had full confidence in placing Agatha and Alice in the capable hands of Alice's older sister Sophia, the Countess of Averford.

Alice knew that her mother expected Sophia to find her a husband, and her sister had been more than up to the task. In her nearly two years at Thornbrook Park, Alice had dissuaded two of her sister's candidates from proposing, and she had faith that she could survive a few more attempts before Agatha was comfortably settled, all Sophia's responsibility, and Alice could announce her intention to depart. Who could stop her once she turned five and twenty, when she would come into the money her grandmother had left her? Just three more years.

On her great list of things to accomplish, Alice had lofty dreams: to travel the world, to climb a mountain, to ride a camel, to captain a pirate ship. And she had simpler goals that she could start on right away, like cornering the fox in a hunt, getting drunk on whiskey, and having a wild affair. She should know love at least once, even if she never planned on marrying. And she had just the man in mind, the same man who could teach her to hunt and to shoot, and who enjoyed a good whiskey—her brother-in-law's estate manager, Mr. Logan Winthrop.

Mr. Winthrop would be no easy conquest. To begin with, he didn't seem to really *like* people, choosing to keep to himself as much as possible. When he did find himself in company, he maintained a cool, all-business demeanor. *Most of the time.* Alice had managed to break through his icy exterior once or twice, enough to fuel her hope that she could manage a seduction.

There were rumors that he'd killed a man, a rival for a woman's affections, and had come to Thornbrook Park to escape his dangerous past. Rumors didn't deter Alice. All men had pasts, and rumors were often far from fact. What made him the perfect candidate, besides his soulful eyes and god-like physique, was precisely that he was not the sort to form emotional attachments. There would be no pining after her or rushing into a commitment.

An estate manager's income wouldn't come close to supporting an earl's daughter in the style to which she'd become accustomed, or so he would believe. He would never expect her to marry him, even if she managed to seduce him. Once she could convince Logan Winthrop to let his guard down again, she would take the opportunity to kiss him.

She'd hoped to run into him that morning when she left the Dower House to breakfast with her sister at Thornbrook Park. The gardeners were preparing the grounds for winter, and it was rare that Winthrop wouldn't be out with the groundskeeper overseeing the efforts. Unfortunately, Winthrop hadn't been in sight. She stood outside the breakfast room, hand poised to turn the beveled-glass knob, when she heard his voice inside.

"Lemon trees? So many of them?" His voice had that raspy edge that signaled his displeasure. Alice knew it from the many times he had told her to stop asking questions and leave him to his work. She smiled. "I don't know much about the care of exotic fruit trees, but I will research the subject."

"Four trees. I can't imagine what the woman was thinking, as usual." Her sister wasn't delighted by the prospect either, apparently. "It's practically an orchard."

Sophia had a tendency toward exaggeration.

"Mother means well. Likely she feared a few might not make the journey safely. She wants you to have lemonade, not exactly a sinister sentiment behind the gift. You could try to be more grateful." The rumpling of a newspaper followed Lord Averford's explanation. Typical. He tended to hide behind the news once he'd had his fill of morning pleasantries, or unpleasantries, as it were.

"It's not that I'm ungrateful. I'll send her a letter as soon as they arrive, of course."

The old Dowager Countess was sending lemon trees to Thornbrook Park from Italy, where she had taken up residence these last few years? Alice, thinking of the hours she could spend in the warm conservatory with Mr. Winthrop, couldn't muster any disappointment. There were roses, sweet peas, and lemon trees on the way. What an ideal setting for a kiss!

"You know who has some experience with lemon trees?" Lord Averford asked, not really expecting an answer. "The Marquess of Brumley. I remember his wife had several trees, oranges and lemons. Perhaps I should invite him to come offer you a hand, Winthrop."

"I wouldn't mind some advice." Winthrop seemed to be none too sure. He might have meant the opposite, that he would mind very much indeed.

"Brumley?" The sound of her sister's teacup clinking in the saucer made Alice jump. "The *widower* Brumley? Your brother's former classmate, the one with the ancient wife who recently passed away?"

"The very one. Eleanor died last year, though, not so recent. He's—"

"Out of mourning." Alice could picture her sister clasping her hands in glee. "And a marquess. I'm sure he's lonely. We should invite him. For an extended stay."

Alice felt the sinking feeling in the pit of her stomach. A widower. Her sister's next candidate to win Alice over to the idea of marriage. Not again. If the aroma of cinnamon toast had tempted her to enter the room, the idea of a marquess being pushed at her changed her mind. She backed slowly away from the door. Perhaps she would break her fast with Aunt Agatha in the Dower House after all. She turned and had begun to walk quietly down the hall when the housekeeper, Mrs. Hoyle, sprung on her from out of nowhere.

"Good morning, Lady Alice. Have you come for breakfast?"

"I thought I left a pair of gloves behind last night. I just had a quick look in the drawing room. No gloves. I'll be on my way."

"But I've just come from the drawing room. I didn't see you come in." The infernal woman cocked an accusing brow. "Perhaps one of the maids picked them up. Come along to the kitchen and we'll have a look."

Alice couldn't imagine a way to decline gracefully, and at least the kitchen wasn't the breakfast room. She would manage to avoid her sister's attempts to present the Marquess of Brumley, undoubtedly a toad, as a charming fairy-tale prince. "Thank you, Mrs. Hoyle."

She followed the old hen to the kitchen, where the few maids at the table jumped to attention to greet her, causing Alice to blush and mutter an apology for interrupting them. The three maids all ran off to attend to duties elsewhere in the house despite Alice's protestations to stay put, and Mrs. Hoyle excused herself to ask Mr. Finch about the gloves, leaving Alice to

stand alone next to the great table where the servants
took their meals.

Off in the adjoining room, she could see Mrs.
Mallows covered in flour as she rolled out dough
and occasionally cursed at Sally, the kitchen maid. A
footman rushed right by Alice with a tray, not even
noticing her in his haste to fetch what he was after and
get back to the breakfast room. Glad to go unnoticed,
Alice stepped into a shadowy corner to wait for Mrs.
Hoyle's inevitable return with the news that her gloves
were not to be found.

"Looking for your next victim, Lady Alice?"

"Mr. Winthrop." He hadn't failed to notice her.
His voice ran over her like one of the velvet gloves
she claimed to be missing, causing her heart to beat
faster. She turned and stepped back into the light.
"I'm not sure I know what you mean. I'm waiting
for Mrs. Hoyle to confirm if she could find something
I've lost."

"Oh, is that the ruse? You've *lost* something.
Meanwhile, you're deciding which of the servants to
trail after all day asking questions to the point of vexa-
tion." He laughed. Laughed! What a rare occasion. Never
mind that he was laughing at her, she was entranced by
the way his eyes lightened ever so slightly from black
to cobalt with his mirth. So dark were his eyes, so
normally inscrutable, that she'd had no idea that they
were actually a very deep blue and not brown at all.
Or maybe they simply appeared cobalt in the light,
drawing from the dark blue of his coat.

Forgetting herself, she took a step closer to examine
them. He seemed to hesitate an extra second, staring

back at her, but he didn't move away. "Naturally, Mrs. Hoyle will come along any moment now to report that she was unable to find the item, for you've lost nothing at all. What really brings you to Thornbrook Park?"

"*Why, you, Logan. I've come to deliver this, just for you,*" was what she said in her mind, as she placed a hand to the silk plum waistcoat covering his solid chest and leaned in. In actuality, she stammered like a fool and clenched her hands at her sides. "Wh—why on earth would you suspect me of having an ulterior motive?"

She *had* lost something after all. She'd lost her nerve. She'd had the perfect opportunity to completely surprise him with a kiss, and she hadn't been able to manage it.

"Why do you do anything, my lady? Because you can. Forgive my impertinence." He cleared his throat. "I've come to fetch a set of keys from Mr. Finch. I'll leave you to your search."

He stepped back, obviously deciding that whatever course he'd been taking with her was the wrong one to follow. Flirting? Could she conclude that he'd been flirting with her? And if so, what had she done to frighten him away? He turned on his heel.

Quick! She had to say something to bring him back. "Mr. Winthrop?"

"Yes?" He turned to face her again. She released the breath that she'd been holding.

"Do I really vex you?" She didn't attempt to hide the concern in her voice.

He sighed. "No, Lady Alice. You do not. I'm sorry to have upset you."

"Oh, I'm not upset." She hazarded a step closer to him, and another one. "I was simply making sure before I tell you that I actually know a little about the care of citrus trees. Mother kept oranges in our conservatory back home. I might be of some assistance to you when they arrive, if you'll allow me."

He quirked a dark brow. "Oranges? Lady Averford didn't mention it."

Alice nibbled her lip. She knew very little about trees, citrus or otherwise. Certainly she would have time to read up on the subject and try to appear knowledgeable. "She wouldn't. She didn't notice. My sister is so often in her own world."

"I see." He stroked his jaw as if considering. "And how do you know about the fruit trees, seeing as the news only came at breakfast and I don't recall you at the table when Lord Averford opened the letter in front of me?"

"You've got me there." Alice blushed. "I was listening at the door. Eavesdropping, can you imagine? What a terrible habit. I didn't mean to, of course. I was about to join my sister for breakfast and then I heard—"

"The mention of Lord Brumley?" He nodded, and his lips curved up in a smile. "The countess enjoys a bit of matchmaking. Before you came along, she tried to pair me with her maid."

"Mrs. Jenks?" She wrinkled her nose at the idea. Jenks was a mousy slip of a woman, no match for a robust, vigorous man like Winthrop.

"No, the one before her. Mrs. Bowles."

"Dear, no." Worse than Jenks, Bowles was a

snip-nosed shrew and certainly far too old for Mr. Winthrop. "I'm sorry. Sophia clearly has no talent for making matches."

"Perhaps not. You were wise to run away instead of sitting through another conversation about yet another bachelor. I don't blame you a bit."

"You—you don't?" Ah, a man of sense. She knew she could rely on his sound judgment, at least. And she appreciated it, though it would make seducing him more of a challenge.

"Any pretty girl in her right mind dreams of a dashing suitor to sweep her away, doesn't she? Alas, Lady Averford's only suitable choice for you so far had eyes for another."

"Captain Thorne." Alice rolled her eyes. "He's better off with Eve Kendal. They're perfectly suited. I didn't care for him much myself, if you must know."

"I mustn't." He shrugged. "It's none of my affair."

Alice bit the inside of her cheek. How she *wanted* it to be his affair. "There isn't a suitable choice. I'll never marry."

"Don't despair, Lady Alice. There's someone out there for you. Your sister simply hasn't found him yet."

"It's not despair." Defensive, she crossed her arms. "I've no interest in marriage. None."

His eyes narrowed as if he tried to peer inside her soul. "I shouldn't have said anything. You might like Lord Brumley. I must go."

"No." She reached out, eager to stop him, and ended up with her hand on his sleeve, over the thick muscles of his upper arm that she had seen in full daylight, bared to the sun, when he'd removed his coat, undid his collar, and rolled up his sleeves while out raking the early autumn leaves. "Please, tell me about Brumley. You know him?"

His gaze went to her hand and trailed back to her face. "We were at Harrow together. I believe he made Lord Averford's acquaintance later, at Oxford. He might have changed considerably in so many years."

"Fourteen years?" She did the math. "If you're the same age as the earl, then it has been fourteen years since you were at Harrow."

"In fourteen years, a man can go through remarkable changes in his life." His full lips drew to a grim line. "In our youth, Brumley was a bit of an oaf. To be fair, I've no idea what kind of man he has become."

"I suppose we're about to find out. Sophia is probably already making out the invitation. But just in case, our mission should be to see the lemon trees replanted and thriving as soon as possible to send him on his way." *Our* mission. She liked the idea of them sharing in something. It was a start.

"Agreed, Lady Alice, on that point. I'm not looking forward to seeing the man any more than you are, I suspect. Perhaps much less."

"No sign of gloves, I'm afraid." Mrs. Hoyle interrupted. Alice had no idea how long the woman had been standing there watching them together. Not long, most likely. Mrs. Hoyle wasn't the sort to wait to be heard. "Will that be all, Lady Alice? There's still time to join your sister at breakfast, I believe."

"I suppose I will take a moment to say hello. Thank you, Mrs. Hoyle. Mr. Winthrop." As much as she hated to pull herself away from him, it wouldn't do to stand in conversation with the estate manager now that Mrs. Hoyle had reappeared. "I look forward to the arrival of the lemon trees. Good day." She delivered a brief nod in parting and willed her feet to walk away.

❧

He'd made a new life for himself at Thornbrook Park. No longer was he a gentleman's son, free to court gentlemen's daughters. Lady Alice made him want to forget, but it wouldn't do to allow himself the liberties he wanted to take with her, a breath of fresh air in his otherwise dreary life. He'd failed to grasp happiness when fate might have allowed it, and now it was beyond his reach.

Alice deserved a young man of fortune and good standing, someone who could give her the kind of life befitting her station, not an estate manager with a tarnished past. But sometimes, when she stood close and studied him with that look of awe in her eyes, he wanted to take her in his arms and remember what it was to be young and in love. He was entirely wrong for her, and he dreaded the day he would have to make it clear to her by behaving in a manner that would frighten her off for good.

For now, he sensed she needed a friend, and it didn't hurt to lend her an ear. How she did prattle on sometimes, drifting from one topic to the next. It made his work go faster when she was near, like a symphony playing on the wind. And when he had a chance to stop and really listen to her, she had some remarkable things to say. The girl had good sense.

Perhaps he needn't have worried that she seemed to be developing an inadvisable interest in him.

It was entirely possible that he flattered himself, imagining that a strong-willed young beauty could be falling in love with him. Likely, her real interest was horticulture, just as she'd often claimed when she appeared at his side as he supervised the trimming of roses, the planting of seedlings, or the tilling of the soil. An estate manager needn't dirty his hands, but working the land helped Logan feel some little bit of hope restored, that he could control what grew from the earth, what flourished, and what faded, after so much time spent out of control in his own world. *His old world.* The life that came before, that he'd struggled to put behind him.

"Are you all right, Mr. Winthrop? You look a little pale." Mrs. Hoyle appeared with a cup and saucer in her hand. He'd been standing in the kitchen where Alice had left him, frozen in place after watching her walk away. "Something to refresh you?"

"Thank you, Mrs. Hoyle. I am a little tired." He didn't want the tea, but he accepted it, drank it down in one gulp, and handed her the empty cup. That he'd been up since dawn without stopping for a meal might have been the real reason for his mental ramblings. "You're very kind to think of me."

"Nonsense, Mr. Winthrop." A blush? From Mrs. Hoyle? "We must look out for one another. If one of us falls ill, who is to look after our family?"

"Our family? Oh yes." She meant Lord and Lady Averford of Thornbrook Park. Their "family." "Must keep up our strength. I'm off to get some keys from Mr. Finch. Good day, Mrs. Hoyle."

"And a good one to you, Mr. Winthrop." She turned to bring his cup to the sink.

With family on his mind, he set off to find the butler, Finch. Logan had a family that was not the Averfords. Logan's father had been the Baron Emsbury, as his older brother had become upon their father's death. Logan hadn't seen his brother much since what they all referred to as "the incident," but he exchanged letters with him and his wife, Ellen, and with Mrs. Leenders, Grace's governess, who assured him that the girl was happy and thriving in the care of Logan's brother and his wife. Grace would be nearly a young woman now, twelve years old, the same age her mother had been when Logan first kissed her.

"Mr. Finch." He turned the corner, glad to find the butler at his desk going over an inventory list so that Logan could put thoughts of family behind him and delve back into his work. "I wonder if you have the keys for the equipment shed. I seem to have mislaid mine."

"Mislaid your keys? How unlike you, Mr. Winthrop."

"I believe I simply left them on my table at the cottage, nothing to fret over. I thought perhaps to borrow yours instead of going all the way back. Not that it's all that far, of course, but I'm eager to bring a few things over to the farm. Tilly Meadow is in need of some new shovels that can handle deep snow. Their current set is ancient, likely to snap under significant weight."

"Snow shovels, good old reliable implements." Mr. Finch nodded approvingly. "I expected you were about to inform me that we've a newfangled steam thingamabob to melt away the snow as it falls. I'm glad to know that some things haven't changed as fast as others."

He gestured to the telephone hanging behind him. They'd had it for more than a year, but Finch was still adapting to the idea of placing and receiving calls through a box on the wall.

"I don't know, Mr. Finch. That steam thingamabob sounds very handy. Perhaps it will come along soon. Mr. Sturridge says it's going to be a stormy season." Winthrop trusted the groundskeeper's instincts in such matters as precipitation. Sturridge had an uncanny sense for predicting what was in store for the upcoming season, as well as detecting oncoming storms before they hit.

"Ah, well, Sturridge is seldom wrong about such things. I should warn Mrs. Hoyle to be prepared."

"Knowing Mrs. Hoyle, she needs no warning. I would be surprised if she hasn't already stocked enough to survive two consecutive winters trapped in this great house."

Mr. Finch laughed. "True enough."

"Thank you for the keys. I'll return them when I'm done." After leaving Mr. Finch, Logan walked the corridor that would lead him up and past the breakfast room instead of going out the back door, in case he might run into Lady Alice again along the way.

Two

ALICE WISHED SHE COULD SAY THAT SHE HATED LORD Brumley on sight as he stepped from the car, but what she felt was more of a marked indifference. Her enmity was reserved for the sharp howling wind that sent her hair every which way and made her skirt cling unflatteringly to her legs under the watchful stare of Mr. Winthrop, standing just across the driveway.

"Watchful stare" was perhaps more hopeful than true, she had to admit. It was more of an occasional glance. And he could have been looking behind her to the potted arrangements of holly and freesia that he had recently placed to frame the steps leading to the front door. But Alice preferred to believe herself to be the object of Winthrop's attention, even under the worst possible conditions. Brumley barely registered a passing thought. Even when he took her hand upon introduction and declared himself "enchanted."

"If I had magical powers, Lord Brumley, I would have made sure that the lemon trees were here to greet you so we wouldn't keep you one day longer than necessary." She smiled sweetly to take some of the sting out of her words. He arrived no later than two weeks after Sophia sent the invitation, some time before the expected lemon trees, which had been held up in a Sorrento port.

He paused a moment as if taken aback. Sophia scowled in her sister's direction.

"What a thoughtful girl." Brumley looked past Alice to speak to Sophia, as if they'd been having a conversation about Alice in the next room instead of standing with her in the infernal wind. "She must realize how hard it is for me to be away from my beloved Brookfield."

Sophia began to extol the virtues of Thornbrook Park, probably to put thoughts of returning to Brookfield from his mind. Brookfield was the glorious house Brumley had inherited from his wealthy wife upon her death, or so Alice had heard from Lucy, her sister's head housemaid. As much as she liked Lucy, Alice suspected the maid had been under her sister's orders to parrot information that might raise Brumley in Alice's esteem. *Impossible.*

Behind his spectacles, his eyes were a watery gray-blue. His russet hair had already thinned to the point that he tried to hide the baldness by parting his hair too far on one side and combing it over the other. He looked like he enjoyed a good meal but disliked the athletic pursuits that might keep his abundant appetites from becoming apparent in his physique.

In short, Lord Brumley was no Logan Winthrop. She glanced over to see the estate manager already taking his leave, making his way around the house, probably in pursuit of a gardener to repot the freesia that had blown away. She had time to admire the way his wool coat stretched across his broad shoulders and to imagine his taut behind under the coattails before he turned the corner. She would have her own money. What did she care for Brumley's status next to Winthrop's godlike physical perfection?

"Enough talk. I'm getting carried away with the wind. Shall we go in?" Alice, to Sophia's evident surprise, took Brumley by the arm and led him to the house.

Once they were settled in the drawing room, Brumley turned to Alice after accepting a cup of tea from Sophia. "It seems we have something in common, Lady Alice. You dislike the outdoors as much as I do."

"On the contrary." She resisted the urge to smooth her hair one more time, convinced that she must look a fright and all the happier for it. The sooner she could scare Brumley off, the better. "I love to be out of doors, just not in so much wind. I thought you were a great enthusiast of flora and fauna, Lord Brumley? Does it not require you to be out in the elements?"

He laughed. "I'm more of an armchair gardener, to tell the truth. I read all about the various growing techniques in agricultural journals and then make my recommendations to the staff."

"Oh, I see." She sipped her tea, uncertain of what else to say. The man couldn't even take up his own rake or spade? What good would he be with the lemon trees? She glared in Sophia's direction.

Sophia seemed to be at an uncharacteristic loss for words. Fortunately, the butler broke the silence with the announcement of new visitors, Captain and Mrs. Thorne.

"Brumley, old man. There you are." Ever the charmer, Captain Marcus Thorne swept into the room and took over, clapping his brother's old schoolmate on the back in greeting. "Have you come to lose yourself in our fine library?"

Alice wished he would lose himself anywhere out of her way. She might have said so, had she not been distracted by a tiny hand reaching out to tangle in her fallen chignon as Eve leaned in to say hello, baby in her arms. "Oh, the darling Miss Mina has come to grace us with her presence. And you, too, Eve."

"I've become used to being ignored in favor of my daughter." Eve laughed. "Even her father fails to notice I'm in the room when Mina's cooing away in her pram."

"An exaggeration," Marcus declared. "I never fail to notice you, my angel wife. I do notice that my brother is missing. Hunting again?"

"Deer stalking," Sophia corrected. "With Lord Holcomb. They'll be back for dinner. My apologies, Lord Brumley, that they didn't wait for your arrival, but perhaps tomorrow."

"Oh dear, no." Brumley shuddered. "I'm more the type to sit by the fire with a good book. As you were saying, Thorne, I used to envy your fine library when I visited, but now I have my beloved Brookfield…"

He went on for the next quarter hour about Brookfield's library, but Alice didn't mind. She made a mental note to take up hunting, or at least to show great enthusiasm for such sport, and relieved Eve of the baby so that Eve could sit and have some tea unencumbered.

"Nurse will come along in a minute," Eve said,

reluctant to hand her sweet bundle off once Mina started to fuss. "She's just getting things settled."

"Nonsense. No need to wait for the nurse." Alice cradled the baby to her shoulder and added a light bounce to her step that seemed to quiet Mina's fussing. "You and Sophia catch up. Mina and I will have a nice little walkabout. Won't we, darling girl?"

Alice never had much interest in babies until Mina, short for Wilhelmina, came along over the summer. Captain Thorne and Eve's delightfully good-natured first child was born a bit too soon after their rushed wedding if anyone cared to do the math, but no one would say so if they did. Alice adored the child as much as anyone, but perhaps more now that Mina provided a distraction from the dreadful Brumley. She walked the baby into the hall, as far as she could get from Brumley's droning on about his exceptional library.

In the hall, she nearly walked right into Logan Winthrop. "Oh. I didn't expect to find you here."

"I didn't expect to find you with a baby." He smiled. "I take it the Thornes have arrived. You look quite natural with the child."

"Ha, I must be doing something wrong. Don't let my sister hear you say it."

"She must have seen you with Mina. She will draw her own conclusion." He drew close enough to lean in to whisper. "Mine is that you already can't stand Brumley to the point where you needed an excuse to escape."

"Will you gloat if I confess that you're right?"

"Not at all," he said, as Mina started to fuss in Alice's arms. "Allow me. We don't want to send you rushing back in right when you've made a successful break of it."

"Allow you?" Mina's fuss turned to a loud cry.

He nodded and held out his arms. "I have some experience with infants."

She handed the baby to him. He turned Mina around to fit in the crook of his arm and offered her his clean, white knuckle to suck. The baby quieted instantly.

"That's remarkable. How did you know?"

He shrugged. "A little trick I picked up. The suckling seems to calm them."

She studied him, feeling the warmth expand inside her until it became a tingle that slid along her nerves. Never had she imagined that the sight of a strong man cradling a delicate baby could be such a powerful aphrodisiac. Instinct drew her closer to him so that she pressed her body right up against his, her head on his shoulder with the pretense of studying darling Mina. She wondered what he would do if she took the opportunity to lean in and kiss him. He would be shocked, but not enough to drop the baby. If anything, keeping a protective hold on Mina would prevent him from pushing Alice away...

"There you are." The nurse appeared from the stairs, stealing Alice's chance. "I'll take our wee little lamb. Her nursery is set, and she's ready to eat from the look of her, aye?"

"Aye," Winthrop said, handing her over. "Yes. She's hungry all right."

"You're verra good with her, Mr. Winthrop," the nurse said in her Scottish burr.

"We managed to get on," he said, seemingly

reluctant to acknowledge what he had readily admitted to Alice moments ago, that he had experience with infants. One infant, many infants? How did a bachelor happen to know about babies?

"I'll let her mother know you've taken her up," Alice said, then turned to Winthrop. "I suppose I should be getting back."

"I'll go with you. I might as well greet Lord Brumley."

"Old schoolmates as you are."

"Former schoolmates. I prefer not to use the word *old*." He placed his hand at the small of her back and escorted her to the drawing room.

❧

Logan dreaded his former classmate's reaction to his appearance in the drawing room. Had Brumley heard of the scandal? Would he act surprised to see Logan at Thornbrook Park, employed by Lord Averford? There was no sense in putting it off since they would be under one roof, working toward the same goal of successfully establishing the lemon trees in the conservatory. At least now he would have the benefit of Lady Alice and her easygoing nature at his side. Everything seemed brighter with Alice in proximity.

His heart had performed a flip when he walked in and saw her with the baby in her arms. There was something so warmly domestic in the scene, so inviting. So forbidden to him, he reminded himself. She would make an excellent mother for someone else's children, never his—and God willing, not Lord Brumley's. A fiery spirit like Alice could never be

content with a dullard like Brumley. Unless Brumley
had changed dramatically since their youth.

Upon first sight of Brumley seated on the divan,
teacup in hand, gut protruding from his waistcoat
and expanding over the top of his trousers, Logan
did not believe the man had changed at all for the
better. As desperate as the countess seemed to see her
sister settled in marriage, she couldn't possibly believe
Brumley to be a match for Alice, no matter his income
or estates.

"Ah, look who is here," Thorne said upon Logan's
entrance. "Another old chum of yours, I believe, Lord
Brumley. Good day, Mr. Winthrop."

"Captain Thorne." He nodded in Marcus's direction.

Logan liked both Lord Averford and his brother
immensely, and he found the younger Thorne to be
an excellent addition to their little community. He
was glad when the Thornes had taken over the old
Markham estate earlier in the year. Brothers should
be close, he thought, and felt an unexpected pang of
remorse that he'd allowed circumstances to keep him
away from his own brother for far too long. But he
refused to be an embarrassment to the family name,
or the source of gossip and curiosity for Grace as she
grew up. One day, perhaps, when she was older, he
could return.

"Winthrop, you say?" Brumley did not get up, but
wrinkled his face into a grimace as if trying to coax a
memory or ease indigestion. "I don't recall a Winthrop."

"Our estate manager, Mr. Logan Winthrop,"
Sophia introduced him.

"The Honorable Logan Winthrop," Thorne

corrected. "His father was Baron Emsbury, as his brother is now."

Alice gasped. Logan looked to see that she was well and hadn't tripped on the Turkish carpet or somehow hurt herself. She looked from Captain Thorne to him, her green eyes wide, and Logan realized that she hadn't known. She'd heard gossip surrounding his past, certainly, but she'd had no idea that he'd been raised in the same privileged circles that she had. At once, he saw her reach understanding and he prayed it wouldn't change her opinion of him. He liked the easy repartee they'd established after months of her trailing after him and him pretending to ignore her.

"I remember now." With some effort, Brumley got to his feet. "Harrow. Yes. Good to see you, man. An estate agent now? Ah, the plight of younger sons."

Captain Thorne, a younger son, exchanged a glance with Logan. "Ah, the bombastic pride of firstborns. Quite satisfied with yourselves for having everything handed to you."

Thorne broke out his wide grin to show he was only joking with Lord Brumley, and Logan laughed, causing Brumley to laugh along. Only an apple-polisher like Thorne could get away with saying such things to a man without causing hard feelings. "When my brother returns, you two can clap yourselves on the back over cigars and brandy for having the good sense to shoot out of the womb before the rest of us had a chance."

"Marcus, there are ladies present." Eve was quick to reprimand her husband before Lady Averford could take offense. The countess had a sense of humor at times, but she tended to be more highly strung than her friend Eve. "And where's my little dumpling?"

"The nurse took her," Alice said. "She's getting settled in your usual rooms. You can relax and enjoy some adult company."

"I mean to do just that, which is why we're staying a few days. I've been lonely shut up at Markham House. And I'm still not sure if there's a ghost. Where's Agatha?"

Aunt Agatha claimed to be in contact with the spirit world, but Logan believed she was simply an old woman who liked attention. Still, she seemed harmless enough. She was Miss Agatha Simms formally, but she preferred for everyone to call her Aunt Agatha.

"A ghost at Markham House? The first Lady Markham, I suppose?" Alice seemed skeptical of her aunt's abilities, and she had told Logan once that she did not believe in ghosts. "I think you're safe. Agatha is resting at the Dower House. She will come over for dinner because she can't resist the urge to read a newcomer's aura."

"What's that?" Lord Brumley, the newcomer, inquired.

"It's supposedly the colors surrounding you, indicating your personality type," Eve explained. "She told me that I have a lavender aura."

"Mine is red," Captain Thorne added.

"And for me, she seems to waver depending on how she feels about me at the moment." Alice laughed. "When I'm nagging her, I'm orange. When I don't pay enough attention to her, I fade to a dull beige. Don't be frightened, Lord Brumley. I'm sure you'll be a lovely shade of brown."

"Is that good? To be brown?"

Alice shrugged. "We'll have to see what Agatha has to say. What color is your aura, Mr. Winthrop?"

He smiled. "I hold the dubious honor of being the first to stump your aunt. She said there's a mysterious shroud obscuring her ability to read me."

If Brumley had heard any of the gossip surrounding Logan, now was the time for the man to mention it. It wasn't so much the shroud as the blood on his hands. But nothing came. Brumley barely seemed to remember Logan, and so much the better.

"I'll be getting back to work, then." Logan began to excuse himself.

"Oh, but won't you be joining us for dinner?" Lady Alice asked. "With your classmate here, I'm sure you have much to discuss."

Normally, Logan made it a point to stay on his own. He rarely even joined the servants for a meal. "I don't usually—"

"Please do, yes," Sophia requested. It was harder to turn down a request from the mistress of the house. "Lord and Lady Holcomb are coming and it will be a lively affair, but better for Lord Brumley with familiar faces around. It's settled. You're dining with us."

Logan nodded, unable to come up with an excuse. "I will see you all later this evening."

He resisted the urge to cast a last glance at Lady Alice as he left the room.

Three

"HAVE A CARE WITH MR. WINTHROP, ALICE." EVE Thorne touched Alice's arm to get her attention once Sophia had gone from the room. They were all gathered in Sophia's chamber to dress for dinner, but some confusion with the dinner menu had Sophia running to the kitchen.

"Have a care? What do you mean?" Alice tried to look unfazed by the warning.

"I've seen the way you look at him. I've been noticing for some time now. Sophia has no idea, I think, but she'll catch on soon enough."

"And what's wrong with Logan Winthrop?" Alice crossed her arms, then dropped them, fearing she presented the picture of a petulant child denied a toy. "Why does she push the Lord Brumleys of the world my way and avoid the one who might hold some appeal?"

"Mr. Winthrop is entirely unsuitable. If not for his past, there's also the age difference and the fact that he's an estate manager. You know that Sophia fancies you will become at least a baroness when you marry."

"As you know, I don't plan to marry." She met Eve's crystalline gaze. "Besides, he's only ten years my senior, hardly an unbridgeable gap. There's nearly seven years between you and Marcus. I believe it was over twenty-five years between Brumley and his dear wife, rest her soul. For that matter, Brumley is of an age with Logan."

"Logan? Are you close enough to refer to each other in familiar terms?" Eve's mouth gaped in alarm.

"Of course not. We're strictly formal. I used his familiar name just between us." She waved her hand, dismissing Eve's concerns.

"Winthrop's life experience makes him much older than Lord Brumley."

"Older than Brumley? The man is an ancient relic, with his armchair gardening and droning on about his great house. Winthrop is active, vital, years younger, no matter his past. And what of his past? Are the rumors true? Did he kill a man? A romantic rival?" Alice tugged at Eve's sleeve, eager for information.

"No charges were ever filed, according to Marcus, so I'm afraid we'll probably never know what really happened unless he tells us, which is unlikely. He never speaks of it. And why would he? Lord Averford hired him on the advice of his father's former land agent, with the agent's word that Winthrop was a good, honest man looking for the chance to work hard and escape his past."

"And that was good enough for the earl to give him a chance and never mention it again. It probably didn't hurt that Winthrop is a baron's son. I had no idea."

"It makes little difference. Mr. Winthrop has made every effort to separate himself from his family and his past, and we must respect that. But it still doesn't make him a suitable candidate for marriage."

Eve had been separated from her family and her past when she married her first husband against her parents' wishes, as Alice remembered. "Marriage?" She laughed at the suggestion instead of insisting, yet again, that it wasn't in her plans. "I simply enjoy looking at him, talking to him. You've no need to worry about me harboring any illusions of permanence."

Eve nodded. "You'll never marry. Yes, I know. But that won't stop your sister from trying, or me from keeping an eye out for you. Marriage or no, you do admit that you have an interest in him. I can understand it. He's handsome. Mysterious. Dark. Mature."

"I thought you were warning me off him."

Eve tilted her head as if considering her next move. She reminded Alice of her mother. When Mother wanted to encourage Alice in one direction, she often pointed her to the opposite, knowing that Alice would rebel and choose against her mother's wishes every time. "Warning? Not so much a warning, but one must be prepared to deal with a man like Winthrop. He's not likely to allow himself to fall in love, and lust quickly burns to ashes without love to fuel the flame. What then?"

"Then? I plan to be moving on. I'm only here long enough to see Agatha happily settled, and then I'll be of an age to claim my inheritance and go. Maybe I'll start with India."

Eve sighed. "I miss India. Maybe we'll go with you. You can't go unaccompanied to India, a young woman on your own."

"Of course I can. Or I can hire a companion. You were there on your own after your husband died, before you came here and fell in love with Marcus."

"It's different. I'd been a married woman. Besides, I had friends in India. You're like a sister to me. You and Sophia both. You can't blame me for wanting to look out for you." Eve placed a warm hand on Alice's cheek, concern twinkling in her bright eyes.

"I don't blame you at all. But I hope you're not working with Sophia to throw me into the arms of Brumley just for the sake of marrying me off."

"God no." Eve looked appropriately aghast. "The man is all wrong for you. For anyone. I don't know what Sophia's thinking, but I'm sure she has your best interests at heart."

"The sooner we can chase him off, the better."

"Chase off whom?" Sophia came back into the room. "Don't tell me that you've already given up on Lord Brumley. Just imagine being mistress of Brookfield."

"Exactly. I've imagined it. Sitting next to Lord Brumley night after night, while he drones on about the wonders of Brookfield or his latest agriculture journal. No thank you."

Sophia took Alice's hands. "Promise me you'll give him a chance."

Alice sighed. "Very well. But I can't promise you that he'll give me one."

Sophia arched a brow. "What are you plotting?"

"I'm not plotting anything. I plan to be myself. If he realizes we're incompatible before I have to let him down gently, so much the better."

"What was the business with the menu?" Eve asked, graciously changing the subject.

"Mrs. Mallows planned to serve trout for the first course, but I heard Lord Brumley mention that fish does not agree with him. I had to ask her to switch to quail before it was too late."

"Cannibalism." Alice nodded knowingly. "Brumley is a big, fat trout. We can't have him eating his own kind."

"Alice, what's to be done with you?" Sophia threw up her hands in exasperation.

"Let's start with a more flattering gown." Eve looked Alice over.

"Not you, too." Alice rolled her eyes. "There's nothing wrong with this one."

Her gown was dreadful, she knew, a plum sheath with a high neck lined in ruffles that came perilously close to qualifying as an Elizabethan collar. She'd chosen it to look ridiculous to Brumley, but she began to realize that Winthrop would be seeing her in it, too. Though he would probably find it a laugh. She imagined him saying, "Lady Alice, what have you done to yourself now?"

"The leaf green velvet, with the lighter green over-lay and the seed pearls along the neckline?" Eve asked. "I saw it in your closet. New?"

"New. From France." Sophia clapped. "It will suit her perfectly. I'll ring for Jenks."

❧

Logan finished his work early so that he would have time to head back to his cottage and change for dinner, but he overestimated the time it would take to prepare and returned too soon, only to wait in the drawing room alone.

He fussed with his bow tie, feeling foolish in his evening clothes. Were they a tad out of date? It had been a great while since he'd attended a dinner. Making conversation with strangers had never been as easy a skill for him as it seemed to be for men like Captain Thorne and even Lord Averford. When he was young, he had Julia, his first love, to speak for him. She knew about his shyness and would introduce topics that might help him along or direct the conversation elsewhere. How he missed her! He didn't mind being on his own, but he never felt lonelier than when surrounded by people he barely knew.

Lord Brumley he knew as well or better than he could hope. Without family wealth, good looks, or personality to recommend him to the women of their own age, Brumley had turned his barely existent charms on a lonely old woman, who happened to be a very rich widow. It had only been a matter of time before frail Eleanor Cavendish succumbed to infirmity and disease, leaving Brumley with a fortune to recommend him to eligible, marriage-minded younger women. Or at least, to their sisters.

Logan had seen Lord and Lady Holcomb visiting Thornbrook Park, though he'd rarely spoken to them. Lord Holcomb loved to shoot the Earl of Averford's birds. Lady Holcomb talked too much and sometimes drank too much at dinner. When Logan stayed late seeing to a crisis, he sometimes witnessed the Holcombs taking their leave. Lady Holcomb would stumble on her way to the car, and Lord Holcomb would admonish her for having that one last glass of claret.

The Thornes, fixtures now at Thornbrook Park despite the brothers not having gotten along for so many years, were easy to get on with, even when Logan was at a loss for words. Eve Thorne wrote books that showcased the same wit and observational skills that fueled her conversation. Captain Marcus Thorne had a certain magnetism and fine manners, which he sometimes chose not to display, only adding to his appeal.

Aunt Agatha always had a kind word and a quirky bit of information or advice. Logan could always see the old bird coming, due to the bright colors she preferred to drape herself in, giving him the choice to engage her or hide in time before she could see him.

Lord Averford, a stern but fair man, shared similar sensibilities with Logan, preferring to weigh his words before speaking due to an inclination to judge too hastily and sometimes speak words he would regret. Averford's wife was the most beautiful woman of Logan's acquaintance, but he believed that her demands for perfection around her masked her own deep-seated insecurities. The woman needed some gentle reassurance, but Lord Averford had no idea how to comfort her following the loss of their son in infancy some years ago.

And then there was Lady Alice Emerson. Fearless, adorable Alice. She lacked her sister's striking beauty, but she drew attention with her fiery red hair. Once heads turned her way, her lack of perfection made her an intriguing study—the indent at the base of her bottom lip, the burst of brown in her green eyes, which lit with a gold tinge when she was excited, and she was often excited. Alice had a uniquely exuberant approach to life. He imagined she woke up each day with a desire to spring from her bed and see what mischief she could manage. Lady Alice Emerson, an earl's daughter, was far beyond his current reach. But neither would Lord Brumley have her. Logan could make sure of that, if she didn't manage on her own.

Perhaps he knew his evening's companions better than he thought. Once, Julia had told him that there were no strangers except for those he chose to alienate in his own mind. She'd been wise beyond her years. Tonight, he would examine Alice's approach to making conversation at the table and try to follow her lead.

Agatha, impossible to miss in a crimson robe trimmed in orange firebursts, swept into the room and claimed his attention. "Ah, Mr. Winthrop. Precisely the man I wanted to see."

"And here I am. Coincidence, or fate?" He knew she would say fate, and not only because he'd heard her declare the person standing in front of her to be "precisely" the one she wanted to see many times over.

"Fate. Always fate. You have a presence around you tonight. She's encouraging you to reach out to those around you."

"An easy conclusion to draw, considering I've come to dinner, something I rarely attempt."

Agatha nodded. "Ever the skeptic. I've delivered the message. Take it as you may. Just remember that you are among friends, not strangers."

"Why would you say such a thing? About strangers?" A chill ran through him.

"Why wouldn't I?" Agatha pursed her lips. "Only the truth."

"Yes, of course." He studied the air around Agatha, as if he might see some glimpse of his lovely Julia smiling back at him. No sign of her. But of course, she'd died at peace, no need for her to haunt him all these years. At least he'd given her that much.

Fortunately, Lord Averford appeared with Lord Brumley not long after, distracting Logan from any further revelations, ghostly or otherwise.

"Winthrop." Averford nodded. "Good to see you. You should join us more often."

"I'm honored to be invited, Lord Averford. Thank you." Having no idea what to say to the idea of coming more often, Logan simply said what was expected of him.

"I say." Brumley fiddled with his tie. "I haven't dressed for dinner in some time. Eleanor was sick for so long that we never bothered with formal dinners, and then to find myself alone at Brookfield, what's the point? I should get used to it, though. A pretty young wife would certainly expect me to put on the dog, eh?" He nudged Lord Averford.

Averford seemed taken aback. Logan found his stomach turning at the idea of Brumley with a wife. "Wives do enjoy their entertainments," Lord Averford said. "We dress for dinner nearly every night here at Thornbrook Park, and we're joined by company most of the time."

"Eleanor detested grand affairs." Brumley shook his head again. "She'd had enough of them in her first marriage, she always said. Oh, I think I hear the ladies about to join us."

They all looked eagerly toward the door nearest the stairs, but it was only the butler coming from the other direction to announce the arrival of the Holcombs, who followed him in.

Averford introduced Brumley to the Holcombs and added that of course they knew Aunt Agatha and the estate manager, Mr. Winthrop. Holcomb asked about the shooting this time of year, declaring his own estate to be woefully lacking in birds, eliciting an invitation from the earl to come and shoot his any time. This was followed by gruff protests from Lord Brumley that he loved to watch the birds, not eat them, and he followed by expanding on the ecologic importance of birds to his gardening efforts.

Lady Holcomb walked around the room, seemingly avoiding Agatha and looking uncomfortable until Lady Averford and Eve Thorne made their appearance. Logan thought he was prepared for the sight of Lady Alice trailing after them, but he found that his breath caught at the sight of her and his heart pounded violently against his rib cage.

"It's our woodland fairy in green," Brumley said by way of greeting her, possibly his attempt at paying a compliment. She looked far too bold and powerful to be a mere sprite.

"She's Artemis," Logan said without thinking. "We have a goddess in our midst."

"But…" Brumley went white. "Goddess of the hunt?"

"I can't think of any woman more suited," Winthrop admitted. "Green suits you, Lady Alice."

"Thank you." She blushed.

"She's not the only goddess present," Eve said with a laugh. "The countess might have been cast down to us from Olympus for rivaling Aphrodite. And of course, I have my very own god of war."

Eve's husband wrapped an arm around her waist. "Only when any other man attempts to steal my spoils, beautiful wife."

"I do mean to take part in your next fox hunt, Lord Holcomb," Alice said, with a pointed look at Brumley, if Logan was not mistaken. "Do say you're having one soon."

"Soon enough. Next month, perhaps."

"Then there's still time for me to practice giving chase."

"You don't really mean to hunt?" Brumley said, taking her arm to lead her into the dining room before Logan had a chance. *And a good thing.* After complimenting Alice so profusely, and publicly, it might look amiss if he followed up by presuming to take her hand.

"I do," Alice declared. "I wouldn't be the first woman to do so. Women have been taking part in the hunt for ages now."

"I'm aware." Brumley nodded. "But I find it so savage."

"Hunting is a necessity. Man must eat, and my appetite is growing savage. Let's go in." Lord Averford tucked his wife's hand into the crook of his arm and led her in.

Captain and Mrs. Thorne should have followed next, but Eve declared her gown stuck in her heel and asked her husband to take Agatha instead while she stayed behind to fix it. The Holcombs followed, then Alice and Brumley.

"I guess this leaves you to lead me, Mr. Winthrop," Eve said, offering her hand.

"It does. My pleasure."

"Is it? Perhaps it won't be once I speak my mind."

Winthrop paused, taken aback. "Yes, Mrs. Thorne? What is it?"

"Just a refresher on Greek mythology. You might want to keep in mind what happened to Artemis's lover."

He sifted through his brain, trying to remember his myths. "Orion, was it?"

Eve nodded. "Orion. Killed by Aphrodite's own hand. An accident? Or did he go too far and get his just deserts? The experts never seem to agree."

His stomach flipped. She meant to issue him a warning? Had his admiration been so apparent? Showering a woman with compliments was hardly a denial of interest. "I appreciate that you're looking after Lady Alice, Mrs. Thorne. But I assure you that I'm in no danger, nor am I a danger to Alice. I know my place. Orion and Artemis are in another orbit, far out of my earthly range."

"I do look out for her," Eve admitted. "But I'm also thinking of you. You have a good place here, and Alice is far from settled in her own mind. She's young, only two and twenty."

"Far too young for Brumley." He chafed watching Alice take a seat next to the man as he entered the room.

"On that, Mr. Winthrop, we're agreed." Eve smiled as he pulled out her chair across the table from her husband.

His own seat was too far from Alice for his liking,

across the table and down one, placing him next to Lady Holcomb and across from Brumley, but he supposed it was better that way with Eve Thorne keeping watch over them.

It wasn't until after dinner, over cordials in the drawing room, that he finally took the liberty of speaking his mind. He helped himself to a cognac from the cart holding an assortment of liquid-filled bottles and cut-crystal glasses and cleared his throat before addressing his companions.

"It is my opinion that Thornbrook Park could use a ball."

"A ball?" Lord Averford straightened up from the mantel he'd been leaning against.

"A ball. Social engagement with dancing, dinner…" Logan swirled the cognac in his snifter.

The countess spun around from the piano, where she'd been perusing the musical selections to choose a song for her sister to regale Lord Brumley with, no doubt. "A ball? Can we do that?"

"I don't see why not. We've got the means. Thornbrook Park used to be famous for your mother's fetes, Lord Averford. The Harvest Ball, the Snow Ball, the Spring Delight." He avoided meeting Alice's gaze. The last thing he needed was for her to question why he would even bring it up.

"She had one every season." Captain Thorne stroked his boxy chin. "Except summer. Then she would have her famous garden party."

"Perhaps it's time we restored some of the gaiety to our old house. What do you think, my lady?" Averford turned to his wife.

Sophia seemed to be considering. On the one hand, she loved to be at the center of a social scene. On the other hand, she hated anything that had her set up in comparison with her mother-in-law, or so Logan knew from the servants' gossip.

"It would bring young people back to Thornbrook Park. What a stodgy old lot we've become with dress-up dinners and then retiring to the drawing room for drinks and conversation. Orchestra music, dancing, that's what we need," Averford said.

Logan didn't want to push too hard. What business did the estate manager have to be declaring how his employers should spend their surplus?

Fortunately, Eve Thorne stepped in with her support. "Imagine it, young women in their finery, young men coming from all over. *Eligible* young men currently out of our regular circle of acquaintance." She focused her attention on Sophia before turning to Alice. "Alice, do young people still enjoy balls?"

Sophia's cornflower eyes widened and lit up as she apparently suddenly made the connection between Alice and bringing in a new batch of eligible young men. Brumley had brought nothing to the dinner table but more dull commentary on his exceedingly fine house. Even the countess had to realize how ill-suited he was for a vibrant woman like Alice.

Alice, seated at the piano, struck a few sour notes, then launched a trill and sighed. "I don't care much for balls. I prefer to be out of doors. Hunting. Shooting." She cast a pointed glare at Brumley that made Logan glad she wasn't currently possessed of a rifle.

"We could turn it into the event of the season."

Lady Averford shrugged. "Hunting parties, tea parties, all leading up to the ball. It will be splendid. Mr. Winthrop, what a brilliant idea."

"I predict it will be a spectacular affair," Agatha added.

"I'm happy to be of service, my lady." Logan gave a short bow.

"Brilliant," Alice echoed without a hint of genuine approval in her tone. "Simply ripping. A ball. I'm in delights."

She seemed far from pleased, but no matter. A ball would bring all sorts of eligible men around— handsome, younger, and capable of sweeping Lady Alice off her feet, killing her interest in Logan Winthrop once and for all.

Logan seldom imbibed, but suddenly he felt the need to have another drink. He downed his cognac, returned to the corner cart, and helped himself to a glass of Lord Averford's finest Scotch.

Four

MORNING COULD NOT COME SOON ENOUGH. ALICE, UP all night plotting her revenge, got out of bed before the dawn and dressed in clothes that she'd pilfered and adapted from Lord Averford's closet. She'd always planned for this day to come, but she'd had no idea it would feel so completely enervating.

Baize trousers tucked into heavy leather boots. A soft, long-sleeved cotton shirt under a scratchy wool sweater, under a thick coat. The boots were her own. The trousers had been taken in. The sweater and coat hung on her like a dress. But no matter. She was warm, and she was ready. It was time to stalk her prey. *If Lord Brumley could see her now.*

She crept out of the Dower House—careful that no one should hear her, and praying that no ghostly spirits had warned Aunt Agatha of her plan—and walked to Mr. Winthrop's cottage on the other side of Thornbrook Park. There was a light in one of the front windows. Perfect. She would catch him awake and preparing for the day ahead, just as she'd hoped. She contemplated ringing the bell, but decided against it in favor of turning the knob and walking in. How better to take him completely unaware?

Fortunately, the brass knob turned easily and the hinges did not creak. Of course the estate manager kept his own cottage in top shape, no dry hinges here. She smiled, imagining him in a dirty apron with smudged hands, seeing to his domestic tasks. She entered a dark hall, just big enough to sit on a bench to remove boots and hang a coat on the way in, and almost tripped on a step up. One step, two, and then she seemed to be in a kitchen. A dim light filtered in from the next room and she could see a small oven, marble-topped counter, and a cozy wooden table by the window hung with gingham curtains. Charming!

She crept toward the light, eager to find Winthrop, but she stopped on the threshold of the next room, feeling a sudden pointed jab into her back.

"Not another step." His voice was gruff, menacing. She felt a thrill course through her veins. "I've killed men for less than robbing me, and I have my rifle ready to rip a hole right through you now."

She heard the cock of the trigger.

"Dear God, Winthrop. So serious. Shoot me for sneaking up on you?" She craned her neck to look back, but he pointed the weapon deeper into her back. "Ow."

"Alice?" The rifle point fell away, and a second later, hazy lamplight flooded the room. "What the devil are you doing?"

She turned. "I've come for my revenge."

"Your revenge?" He arched a brow. He wore only a thin shirt, unbuttoned past his chest, over his trousers. His hair was still rumpled from sleep, and he hadn't had a shave yet. She'd never found him so appealing.

"For you bringing up the idea of hosting a ball. Thank you so much, by the way. There's nothing I want more than to be paraded around a room full of unfortunate bachelors instead of dealing with them at the slow and steady pace of one at a time."

"Sarcasm, Alice?" He set down the rifle, letting it lean against the door frame. "It doesn't become you. Though I daresay it flatters you more than those clothes. What the deuce are you wearing?"

He stood back, framing her with his hands as if to get a better look, and then dissolved into gales of laughter. Hoots, if she were being honest. Staid, stoic Mr. Winthrop actually knew how to laugh. Heartily.

She crossed her arms over her chest, waiting for him to recover. "Just a few borrowed things. I thought they might keep me warm and concealed for hunting."

"Hunting? You look like you've been cornered, trapped, and devoured by Lord Averford's closet." He laughed more, harder, until he had to struggle to get hold of himself.

"Are you quite finished?"

"Alice, you never fail to delight me."

"To…delight you?" Her heartbeat picked up speed. "I delight you?"

"'Surprise me,' I said. You never fail to surprise me."

She shook her head. "I believe you said 'delight.'"

He closed the distance, took her by the lapel, and mocked a shout into her coat. "Lady Alice? Are you in there? Shall I send for help?"

At last, she laughed, too. "I'm right here, Winthrop."

"Oh, I see. There you are." He poked her nose with a finger. "Safe and sound."

"No thanks to you for almost shooting me on entrance."

"It's not loaded. I've never been robbed, but I thought the time had come for some of the village ruffians to find their way through the gates. I confess I did not recognize you in silhouette. Now's the time to tell me what you have in mind, and why you are most improperly in my house." His voice had deepened in tone, the note of levity all but gone.

"Shooting, as it happens. I know how to ride, track, and give chase. I'll do perfectly well in the fox hunt, but that is some weeks away."

He nodded. "Too long. You're hoping to shoo Brumley away long before then. And you think tagging along on an excursion with Lord Averford is just the way to do it."

"Yes! Yes, that's it." She loved that he always seemed to know exactly what she had in mind. "Please teach me to shoot. Or, let me put it this way, you must teach me. You've no choice. After what you've done to me. A ball." She rolled her eyes.

"A ball. It will be the perfect chance for you to remember that you're a young woman. You should be doing what young people do."

"Young people bore me."

"Perhaps you should go ahead and marry Brumley then, eh? No doubt he shares your opinion on youthful activities. Give him a garden manual and a good armchair any day."

"Marry Brumley?" She slapped him on the arm, or she tried, for all she could move in Averford's coat. "Is it me, or is it dreadfully hot in here?"

"I think it a bit chilly. My fire's dying out. I'm on my way to work."

"Work? So soon? No, you must cancel your morning appointments. You have to teach me to shoot." She struggled to loosen her collar.

"Of course. I'll drop everything."

"You will?" She brightened, despite beginning to feel a tad dizzy.

"I will not. I mean to remain gainfully employed."

"You would still be doing your job in helping me. I would speak to Lord Averford if it came to that." She attempted to wave her hands dismissively but her sleeves flopped over, hiding all but the tips of her fingers.

"A respectable young lady speaking up for the hired help?" He stroked his square chin as if considering. She imagined that hand stroking her and she swayed a little on her feet.

"Lady Alice?"

Her vision blurred. Her head felt suddenly heavy, impossible to hold up. She felt herself going down and there was nothing she could do about it. The last thing she was aware of was a pair of strong arms cushioning her before she hit the floor.

She woke up in an unfamiliar bedroom, in a bed that smelled vaguely of pine and leather, a picture of a woman she'd never seen on the table beside her. She sat up.

"Lie back. Don't get up too soon. I've only just got you settled." Winthrop, in an armchair beside the bed, moved to the side of the bed and placed his hand on her forehead. "I think you fainted."

"Fainted?" She put her hands to her chest and realized she was no longer wearing the coat or sweater, just the long-sleeved undershirt and trousers.

"I think it was the heat, and your movement being restricted by so many layers. I'm sorry. I took the liberty of removing a few things in an effort to restore you."

"You carried me?" *You undressed me?* She didn't say that last bit out loud. No harm done, after all. He hadn't undressed her very far.

He nodded. "I carried you in here, to my bed, to think what I'm to do with you. It doesn't look good for me, you being here."

"No, of course not." She started to sit up. With a gentle hand to her shoulder, he urged her back down to the pillows he'd propped under her head.

"Ah, no. Not too soon. Please. If you swoon again, I don't know what I'll do. I'll be forced to send for the doctor, and what then?"

She bit her lip. "What then? I'm so sorry, Winthrop. I bounded over here this morning thinking only what a lark it would be to get back at you and fill you with enough remorse that you would teach me to shoot so I could show that oaf Brumley what a modern, unsuitable woman I am. I didn't think of you at all, or how it would look for you if anyone saw us leaving your cottage together so early in the morning."

"Not that anyone would recognize you in that ensemble, if we'd managed to get you out when it was still dark."

Daylight streamed in through the window. "If only."

"As it is, I'm late for a meeting, and I've no idea how I'll manage to get you back safely and without arousing suspicions."

She sighed. "Well, you've gotten out of taking me shooting."

"Not at all. I mean to take you, but later. After I've completed my business for the day. I should finish up early, with plenty of hours of daylight left before it gets dark."

In her excitement at the news, she sat up quickly and felt her head swim again. "That's wonderful. If only I could stand up."

"You need to drink this. The whole cup." He handed her water. "And when you're done, there's another in the pitcher. I'm going to have to leave you here on your own for a bit. I can't see a way to get you back now. I'll come up with something to tell your aunt in case you're missed."

"Agatha won't be up for hours yet. And the servants always leave me on my own in the morning. No one will miss me until afternoon tea. I'm never late for tea."

"I'm not surprised."

"What does that mean?"

"The way you ate your dinner last night. Like you hadn't seen food in weeks. It's a wonder you stay so slim."

"Winthrop!" She gasped, horrified that he'd been watching her eat and that was the impression she'd made. "You mustn't speak so to a lady. We all want to appear as delicate as sparrows."

"At the dinner table, you're as delicate as a rabid

wolf. That's not the right thing to say to a lady? No wonder I'm a bachelor at my age." He smiled.

She laughed. "Mr. Winthrop, you're cruel."

"I'm also about to save your hide, and mine. I have to finish getting ready in the next room and then I'm off. Stay here. Keep away from the windows. Do not answer the door. Help yourself to whatever you find in my pantry. There's not much, I'm afraid. I'll be back to look in on you in a little while, once I've come up with a plan to get you back to the Dower House undetected."

"Yes, sir. I will do as ordered." She pulled his covers up to her chin, marveling at the intimacy of being in his bed, sharing secrets. "I'm going to sleep for a bit. It might do me a world of good."

"It might at that." He got up to leave her, then turned back. "Oh, and Lady Alice? Stay out of my closets. I'm very particular about sharing my trousers."

She threw a pillow at the closing door.

※

Logan couldn't get Alice off his mind. She'd put him in a dangerous state. Besides what would happen if anyone discovered her in his cottage, the mere act of thinking of her in his bed had brought him to a state of near arousal. He liked her there a bit too much. He couldn't afford to think of a woman in the way he'd begun to think of her. It was more than distracting. It was…an obsession. One that would be cured as soon as her sister could find her a suitable man to hold her interest. Brumley was a hindrance to finding another more appealing candidate. The man had to go.

After a morning with Lord Averford, trying desperately to focus on the conversation while they discussed the financial affairs of the estate, Logan went in search of Lord Brumley to invite him on a tour of the conservatory.

"Brumley, just the man I've been looking for," Logan said, finding him in the parlor, seated at a table, his back to the door. As Logan neared, he realized that Brumley was not alone.

"Greetings, Mr. Winthrop," Aunt Agatha called out. "Would you like a reading, too?" She wore a parrot-green robe trimmed in turquoise that made him wonder how he hadn't seen her right away. She had spread a deck of cards on the table in front of Brumley.

"A reading?"

"Tarot. We're almost done here. You can sit next." She didn't give him time to answer, but flipped a center card. "The Hanged Man, reversed."

"Is that good?" Brumley asked, sounding hopeful.

Agatha placed her hand over Brumley's on the table. "It means that it's time to move on, dear."

"From my loss? Yes, of course. I loved my Eleanor, but it is time to move on. It's what brought me here."

"You might interpret it that way." Agatha cocked her head, a note of skepticism in her tone. "But hadn't you already moved on when you decided to accept the countess's invitation? No, I think it might mean that it's time you went back to Brookfield."

Logan managed to choke back his agreement.

"Back? Nonsense. I've only just arrived. There's to be a ball. What of Lady Alice? Surely I must help to fill her dance card."

Agatha shook her head. The wisps of white hair that had escaped her tight bun shook, too. "Fear not. Alice has never had a problem filling her dance card. Of course, they don't use them anymore. I suppose you haven't been out in a bit."

"No dance cards? How does a girl keep track of whom to partner with next?"

"Women know which men they prefer without writing them down," Agatha explained. "But I suppose it would be beneficial to men like you if the young ones were forced to be held to order."

"Men like me?" Brumley's voice had a wounded edge to it.

"All right, Agatha. I'll go next." Winthrop stepped up before Agatha could do further damage to Brumley's ego. "What must I do?"

"I suggest a full Celtic Cross. You'll need to shuffle the deck as I instruct and choose ten cards…"

"Ten? I haven't the time for ten. How about one?"

Agatha shrugged. "As you wish. It will give us a basic idea. But you must come to the Dower House for a full reading soon. I believe the shroud is starting to lift, revealing a hint of your true aura. I don't want to miss a chance to finally fill in what has been missing when I look at you."

"One card." He would make no promises.

Agatha cleared the cards from Brumley's reading, shuffled them in with the others, and handed Logan the deck. "Move them around until you're comfortable, select a card, and place it facedown in the center of the table."

He followed her instructions.

She flipped the card. "Now, Mr. Brumley, do you see? This is what you needed. This is a very auspicious card indeed."

"Is it?" Logan asked. "What does it mean?"

"The Ace of Cups. Your cup runneth over with good tidings, Mr. Winthrop. In work. In love. In your health. All of it good."

"In love?" He shouldn't have even spoken the word aloud, not while his bed runneth over with Alice.

"The Ace of Cups symbolizes favorable new beginnings. Perhaps there's a young lady you have your eye on? She returns your affection. More than that, you have a fresh go at an extraordinary love. She might be the love of your life."

Logan's throat constricted. He'd already known the love of his life, and she was gone. Long gone. It certainly wouldn't do to entertain thoughts of finding new love. "I think you have your readings mixed up, Aunt Agatha. The Hanged Man most certainly fits my situation best."

"Yes." Brumley was eager to believe Logan's interpretation. "Yes. Doubtless that I was meant to turn the Ace of Cups."

Agatha shook her head, loosening more snowy white tendrils. "It simply doesn't work that way. You may choose to believe what you wish, but there's no denying the wisdom of the cards. You'll see."

"I suppose we will, eh, Lord Brumley?" Logan slapped the other man on the back. "Now if you'll excuse us, I was hoping to give Lord Brumley a tour of the conservatory."

"A tour? That sounds like a fine idea." Brumley

stood and adjusted his spectacles. Logan wished the man had also adjusted his waistcoat, which had strayed up on his rotund stomach and hadn't slipped back down. "I know exactly how to ensure your success in replanting."

"Excellent. If they ever find passage and don't freeze on the journey, we'll be ready for them."

Agatha shuffled her deck and sat back, waiting for her next victim. Nan, feather duster in hand, had the misfortune of walking by the parlor as Brumley and Winthrop made their exit.

"Oh, maid! You there!" Agatha called out. "I have some very important news for you…"

The maid stepped in as Logan walked away with his usual purposeful strides, Brumley, on his short legs, running to keep up. On the way, Logan removed his coat and rolled up his sleeves, preparing for work. "I will show you where we plan to put the lemon trees upon arrival. You can advise me on the size of the plots, their distance from one another, and the ideal conditions of the soil."

But now that Logan had an excuse to show up at the Dower House while Agatha was occupied, he meant to keep Brumley's tour brief. He would tell the maid, Mary, that he'd come to Agatha for a reading and then find a way to get to Lady Alice's closet and smuggle one of her coats and gowns out for her to change into at his cottage. No one from the house would see her if they left from his side door, and respectably attired, she could hasten straight to Thornbook Park in time for tea.

✎

"What on earth is this?" Mouth agape, Alice pulled the gown he'd selected for her from the bag he'd picked up in her closet.

"I only had a moment. I made sure to go when I knew Agatha was out, and then I was able to distract Mary with the idea that she'd made my coffee too weak. The second she returned to the kitchen to brew a second cup, I ran up the stairs to your closet, grabbed the first thing I could, and put it in your satchel."

She held the dress up and he immediately realized his mistake. How could he have missed it? It might take three of her to fill it out, not to mention the bizarre color combination of canary yellow and sapphire blue. "I might eat like a rabid wolf, but there's no amount of food that could increase the size of my bosom to Agatha's ample proportions. Believe me, when I was a girl, I tried."

"What's wrong with your bosom?" He couldn't fathom that he'd asked it out loud.

She held out a flattened hand, then seemed to think the better of it. "Nothing. Um, never mind."

He struggled to avert his eyes from her breasts. Not that he could find them now that she'd put the baggy sweater back on.

"What are we to do now?" she asked.

"The Hanged Man." He took the chair opposite her at the kitchen table, glad to see that she'd listened to him about avoiding open windows and had closed the curtains, not that it mattered now. "It really should have been my card after all."

"No one's going to hang you."

He buried his head in his hands, thought a minute,

then looked up. "Remember last year? When Eve Thorne was late to tea?"

"Back when she was still Eve Kendal?" One ginger brow arched. "And they realized she'd gone missing? And everyone was out looking for her, but she'd been at the mercy of that horrible landlord of hers?"

"Yes. And Captain Thorne organized a search party but…"

"It all ended well. Now they're married. And they have Mina." She placed her hand on his arm reassuringly. The heat seared straight through his coat sleeves and he jumped as if scorched. He feared becoming aroused again in a way that would be all too evident to the young lady in his midst, and what then?

"They won't just sack me if they find you here. They'll think the worst. I have a questionable past."

Fortunately, the thought of prison killed all potential for romance.

"So I've heard. But they know you, Mr. Winthrop. Anyone who knows you couldn't fail to…respect you." She slid her chair closer to his. "To admire you."

"You've no idea."

Her eyes half closed, she moved her head closer to his, almost as if she were contemplating going in for a kiss. Good God! It was the last thing he needed. He pushed his chair back, stood, and began to pace.

"We need a new plan." He pinched the bridge of his nose the way he did when he was worried, an old habit. Julia used to say it helped her to breathe easier and think more clearly in a crisis. He'd tried it and found that she was right.

"Who is she?" Alice asked as if she knew exactly what was on his mind. She couldn't possibly.

"Who?" Julia nearly forgotten, he wanted to reach out and tangle his fingers in the red-brown hair that spilled across Alice's shoulders.

"The woman in the portrait at your bedside. She's beautiful."

"Julia Kirkland." He paused, unwilling to say too much, but he was compelled to add, "The finest woman I've ever known."

"Julia. I see. What happened to her?" Alice stood and began to trail behind him, tracing his steps through the tiny kitchen.

"She chose another. It's all in the past."

"But you've kept her picture. Surely that means…"

"Dammit, Alice." He spun on his heel. "We're in the middle of a crisis. Leave the past alone!"

He hadn't meant to be so hard on her, but she didn't cower at his rage. She stood as close to him as she dared, not backing down. "So it didn't end well. I'm sorry."

"No. It did not." His mouth tensed to a grim line.

"You can talk about her if you like. It must be hard to keep it all bottled up." She even had the nerve to reach out and stroke his arm, a comforting gesture.

"Thank you, Lady Alice, for considering my feelings." He steeled himself, determined to keep stiff formality between them, though she had touched him with such a genuine look of concern in her eyes. He knew she wasn't asking out of curiosity fueled by the gossips, but rather out of her own interest in him. In different circumstances, he would have welcomed the chance to talk with a friend. But she was a member of the family he served, and they'd already gone too far in letting down the barriers that should have been up between them all along. "It's a subject I'd rather not discuss."

She returned to her seat at the table as if nothing had happened. "The solution is simple. There's no reason to fear any sort of discovery. You've done nothing wrong. In my enthusiasm to take up shooting, I sought you out in your private abode to beg you to teach me. No one would think anything of it. I bristle against convention all the time. Why would I see anything wrong with bothering the estate manager at his cottage?"

She just might have a point. "You didn't see anything wrong. You came bounding over here this morning and let yourself in just as you pleased, no regard for my privacy."

"Exactly. It's what I do. Sophia would expect nothing less. Aunt Agatha would hardly be shocked. Even Lord Averford would roll his eyes and wonder what Alice has gotten into now. No one would look at you as having done a thing wrong. I'll simply put on my coat and wait for you to dress appropriately for an afternoon of shooting."

"It's unlikely anyone will see us leave together," he reasoned.

"And if they do, they will simply think I've overstepped my bounds. The truth. We've been far too concerned for nothing. *Incorrigible Alice. There she goes again.*"

Not for nothing, he longed to correct her. Eve

Thorne had her suspicions, and all it took was one person to state the obvious—that the older man was always in the wrong when young ladies erred in judgment with one of them. But there was little else to do. The longer she stayed, the more likely her discovery there and the riskier their situation would become.

"It's the only way." The only hope left to them, really. He had to take a chance.

"I suggest we shoot within sight of the drawing-room windows." She began to pin her fallen hair back up. "When I'm late for tea, they'll see why."

"Brumley will see why. I'm going to get changed," he said, preferring to trade his business clothes for rougher wear. "And then we'll go shooting."

Five

TOO LATE, ALICE REALIZED SHE HAD GONE TOO FAR. She had begun to develop a genuine rapport with Winthrop, and then she'd asked about his past. Alone with the man in his own cottage, and she'd killed her one chance of getting close enough to kiss him. Now, standing beside her, he was all business pointing out the parts of the rifle.

"If you mean to shoot, you're going to have to know how to load and clean your own weapon." He wore a brown coat that made his hair look dark as ebony, when it was really more of a mahogany in full sunlight. The clouds likely also contributed to the darkened effect of his hair and his mood. All the fun had gone out of him. She could hardly believe that he'd been laughing with her only hours ago.

"Ridiculous," she said. "Do gentlemen know such things? Isn't that why we have gamekeepers and grooms?"

He tipped his head. "Some gentlemen know. Lord Averford knows. He would be in full agreement with me when I say that you have no business wielding a weapon you don't understand properly."

"What of Lord Holcomb? Does he clean, maintain, and load his own rifles?" She crossed her arms. All she wanted was for Brumley to get a look at her wielding the rifle. Though killing her own goose for dinner was also on her list of goals, and perhaps she still could manage that if they ever got around to actually shooting.

"That's not the point." He lifted the rifle, held it to one shoulder, and lowered it again. "The downfall of your privileged class will be in trusting all arduous endeavors to the servants. When they all leave, what will become of you?"

"Leave? Why would they all leave?" She widened her eyes at him, aware that some men might respond to the curious twinkle in their greenish depths. But perhaps Winthrop had already developed an immunity to her charms.

"Industry, Lady Alice. The world is ever changing. They would leave for better opportunities, the ability to make their own fortunes instead of relying on the wealth of others."

"Some might leave. Others are like family. Mr. Finch would never leave. Mrs. Hoyle. Sturridge. Mary…" She allowed her voice to trail off. What of Winthrop? Would he leave? Did he not consider himself at home here? She dared not force an answer. "I want to shoot something. That's all. No need to complicate things."

"Shooting is complicated. It should be. There's usually killing involved. Let's start with stance."

"Stance? What's wrong with my stance?" She put her hands on her hips.

"Nothing if you're trying to get a man's attention. Though, in that outfit, it might not be the kind of attention you're craving." A tiny hint of a smile curved his lips.

"I have my regrets. Next time, I'll be properly attired."

"They do have hunting habits for ladies. I've seen them in town at Mrs. Dale's shop."

"I'll pay her a visit. But for now…"

"Mr. Brumley would be disenchanted. If only he could look out and realize who was out here. I doubt he'll recognize you."

"Perhaps I should remove my hat?" she asked.

"Nonsense. The earflaps will protect your ears. The report can be rather loud."

"If we ever pull a trigger." She let the tone of her voice reflect her displeasure.

"Probably not today for you, but I might demonstrate a bit. I did take the liberty of sending word that you were missing tea today in favor of a shooting lesson. That might draw Brumley's attention. Back to stance."

"When? When did you send word?" She didn't recall him telling anyone.

"When we were in the shed selecting the rifles. You were distracted with choosing a suitable weapon. That's when I called over one of the grooms from the stable and told him to get word to the house that you would be having a lesson."

"Brumley knows." She tried not to sound too impressed with Winthrop's foresight.

"He knows. He might be watching, or the knowledge that you're truly an aspiring Artemis might have put him off already." He seemed to be taking great pains to avoid meeting her gaze.

"God willing."

"Mmm. Now, stance. You're too tense."

"Too tense? How so?" She straightened her posture until her spine locked up, and instantly realized her problem. "Oh. Too tense. Yes."

"You need to have balance and control, but you need to be comfortable and fluid at the same time."

"Fluid?" How could she be fluid?

"Try this. Close your eyes. Now imagine that you're by the ocean with the waves rolling in. You've been to the seaside?"

"On holiday." She nodded, forgetting to keep her eyes closed. She shut them again. "In Brighton. Yes."

His hands closed on her shoulders and he began to rub.

"Oh!" She jumped. "No, don't stop. It feels wonderful, but it startled me. I didn't expect your hands… on me."

His hands. On her. She tried not to roll her head back and give in to the wild rumblings inside her.

"Relax. So much tension in your shoulders and arms. Try to let it go."

She nodded. "I'm trying."

"Imagine the ocean washing your tension away, the waves rocking you gently side to side. You're the RMS *Mauretania* about to set sail."

"I might faint again," she thought suddenly with alarm, her eyes popping open.

He sighed and dropped his hands from her shoulders. "It was working. You were just beginning to relax, and now you're tense again."

"I'm sorry. I've never done this before. Why don't you show me how to stand? Perhaps I'll loosen up as we go."

"You're going to part your legs slightly, putting one in front of the other. That's it, left foot front. Your weight is mostly going to rest on that foot. Bend your legs slightly. You don't want to lock up."

"Right." She bobbed a little. "Knees bent, not locked up."

"Good. Maybe not quite so bent." His arms went around her to help physically adjust her position. Her breath caught in her throat. "There. Perfect."

"I'm not sure. It doesn't feel right. One more time?" She wanted his arms around her once more, but he shook his head.

"No, you look good. Nearly ready."

"Nearly?" She would never get to hold a rifle, let alone shoot one.

"Next, we need to determine your eye dominance."

"Eye dominance?"

"Put your arm straight out in front of you and point at that tree."

"Which tree? We're surrounded by trees." They'd positioned themselves at the edge of the woods, far enough away from the house but close enough to be seen at a distance.

"The center tree. Very well." He shook his head and walked up to the tree, then shouted back. "Now point your finger at me and close one eye, and then the other. Not both at once. Look with your right eye. Then look with your left."

"Oh." She'd closed both eyes, confused. "Yes?"

"Which eye lined up with the finger pointing straight at me?"

"My right eye," she said after opening, closing, and opening again.

"And the left?"

"I looked like I was pointing to the tree beside you when I looked with my left eye alone."

"And with both eyes open?"

"I still appear to be pointing straight at you, as with the right eye alone."

"Good." He closed the distance between them. "That's ideal. Some people shoot with one eye closed, but I generally find it a good idea to keep both open. We'll let you experiment a bit to see what works best for you."

"I get to shoot something now?" She had her doubts. It seemed he would put her off with something else.

"Not today. Today, I want you to get used to the feel of the rifle in your arms."

She threw her head back in frustration. "That's it?"

"It's getting dark." He shrugged. "Brumley probably can't see you from the house anymore, and you'll have to be getting ready for dinner soon."

"Dinner is hours away. Aren't you coming?"

"Tonight? I thought I would dine downstairs, then go back to work in the conservatory."

"Downstairs? With the servants?" She tried not to sound so surprised. "You're not one of them."

"I'm not one of you." He looked at her pointedly. "Lest you forget, I am in the employ of the Earl of Averford. And sometimes I like to hear what the servants have to say. It gives me valuable insight into what's needed to keep things running smoothly here at Thornbrook Park. Plus, as you might have noticed, I'm running low on supplies at the cottage."

"I wish *I* could dine downstairs. They seem like a fun bunch."

"The downstairs crew? Some of them are not so bad. Others?" He pulled a face.

"Much like the upstairs lot, I suppose. Some are preferable to others."

He held a rifle to his shoulders, as if he would shoot, and put it down again. "As far as dinner goes, I do prefer the downstairs. They're much lighter spirits."

"The servants, lighter spirits? With all they have to do all day?"

"Their day is closer to over and they're ready to cut loose. The footman Bill plays ragtime on the piano sometimes. Scott Joplin, Ben Harney. The maids like to dance. Sometimes, they partner up with the chauffeur."

"Dale? Dale likes to dance?" She tried to picture the gangly chauffeur twirling a maid around the kitchen. "Now I really wish I could dine downstairs."

"It can be entertaining. They're usually a bit more subdued when I'm present, unfortunately."

"You do have that grave manner about you." She peeked up at him from under her lashes to be sure he wasn't offended. "It wouldn't hurt to smile more."

"I'll take it under consideration. Now, back to rifles." He picked up the weapon.

"There you go. Straight back to business. You can't seem to help yourself, Mr. Winthrop."

"I'm a man of business, Lady Alice. The sooner we complete ours, the sooner I can get on to other tasks. Now, this is the lock…"

She tried to pay attention as he pointed to and named parts of the rifle, but she struggled to hold back tears. She'd thought they were getting on until he casually informed her that she was only another task on his list of things to do. But then, wasn't that exactly what he was to her, just another item on her list? When had it become personal? What made him such an ideal conquest was the lack of emotional involvement between them, she reminded herself. So why was she feeling hurt?

She squared her shoulders, determined. He hadn't said anything that should occasion her tears. He simply had no idea how she dreamed about being in his arms, and he still hadn't entertained any thoughts about her. No matter how intimate things had seemed. She'd been in his bed. Likely, he hadn't even thought of her as a woman in his bed. To him, she was still Lady Alice, nuisance. Would she ever get anywhere with this man?

"Are you paying attention?" Halfway through rattling off the catalog of parts, he paused and looked at her.

She felt a hot tear sliding down her cheek, but she refused to acknowledge its presence. It was a reminder of her failure, and that was all. It certainly wasn't a sign of her emotional engagement. She refused to believe it. "I'm sorry. I find I'm slightly distracted. Hunger, perhaps. All that talk of dinner. Could you start again?"

"Or maybe we should quit for the day. I don't want to overwhelm you. There is a lot to learn."

"Yes. That's probably best," she said quietly.

"I'll leave you with the most important lesson of all. Never point a rifle at anything you don't intend to shoot."

Her heart dropped to her stomach. "You've already broken your own rule. You pointed a rifle at me earlier today."

"But the rifle wasn't loaded. I was sure of it. And you were invading my home. Had you been a robber, I might have intended to shoot you." His lips were drawn to a flat line, no hint of a smile.

"You might have shot me by mistake, and who would blame you?"

"I didn't shoot you, though, Lady Alice. And perhaps you should take it as a lesson not to go sneaking around where you don't belong."

If his words hadn't already cut her, he certainly went in for the kill with that last bit. He might as well have shot her. His words blasted a hole right through her center, and she wasn't sure she'd ever be the same. None of their day together had been a pleasure for him. He couldn't have made it clearer to her. His laughter, his hands on her, sharing details from his past. It was all necessity. Business. She'd become his responsibility for the day, and he'd followed through with what was required of him. Nothing more. She had no idea why it bothered her so. It was a setback, but not a personal affront.

"You're right, Mr. Winthrop," she said, careful to keep her chin up and show no sign of weakness. "I'm learning. I won't bother you again. Thank you for the lesson. Good night."

With that, she turned and marched straight into the growing darkness, not stopping until she reached the Dower House's gate. Then she leaned against one of the iron railings and let the tears fall until she was all cried out.

❧

"Congratulations, old man. You've done it," Logan said out loud to himself, standing in the dark as he watched Alice walk away.

He hadn't expected it to be so easy. Lively, buoyant Alice had proven to be more thin-skinned than he suspected. In his mind, he'd planned to be much more direct and cruel. In execution, he felt that he'd only managed to come off as a bit severe. And still, she could barely contain her emotions when she walked away. Once he saw the tears, it had almost been all over for him. The temptation to take her in his arms and comfort her, to tell her how he'd really begun to feel about her, had been almost overwhelming. Almost. But he'd managed to carry on and get it done, to prove to Alice once and for all that there was nothing but business between them. He was doing his duty, nothing more.

He didn't wake up every morning eager to see her smile. He never went out of his way hoping to bump into her. She wasn't on his mind unless she was directly in front of him, making herself unavoidable. He had no feelings for her at all. She was just another member of the family he served. Or so it had to be.

An ache filled his lungs, nearly cutting off his ability to breathe. He hadn't felt so empty, so alone, since Julia's death years ago. But it wasn't as if Alice had died, he reminded himself. She had her youth and good humor. A little heartache was part of growing up. What young woman hadn't once cried bitter tears for the wrong man?

Had Julia cried for him? He wondered. He'd never known. She'd chosen to marry Stanhope, and it had cost her dearly. She'd certainly cried over Stanhope, time and time again. In the end, Logan had been the one to comfort her, but he'd been all too aware that she'd soaked his handkerchief with tears of pain, sorrow, and regret for the man that the Earl of Stanhope had turned out to be, and not for what she'd given up with Logan. He'd lost her as a lover, but had remained her dutiful friend. Duty kept him centered. His life's purpose had become to serve. There really wasn't anything else left for him.

Once Alice drifted entirely from view, Logan turned back toward the woods, lifted one of the loaded rifles, and shot at the thick trunk of the tree he'd stood in front of not long ago. He couldn't see in the dark, but he knew that his shot hit dead center. His shots never missed the mark, even when words were his chosen weapon, a pity for poor young Alice's heart.

❧

Alice wasn't giving up. Once she'd calmed down and thought things through, she realized that Mr.

Winthrop simply did not understand how much he needed her. Yet.

The truth was that she'd given him reason to laugh again. Whatever he'd gone through in the past was serious and shattering, and no one had bothered to build the man back up. He certainly wasn't capable of doing it himself. He'd buried himself in duty and responsibility and forgotten how to *live*. She meant to remind him.

If he hadn't been such a thoughtless prig during her shooting lesson, he might have had the honor of a visit from her after hours in the conservatory. She might have finally been bold enough to deliver the kiss that would rouse him from his slumber. Fairy tales could be reversed, couldn't they? Perhaps in their version, he was the sleeping beauty, and she would have to fight the dragons of his past that weighed on him and leave him free to live again. She fancied herself in head-to-toe armor headed to battle. It was a good look for her. But tonight, instead of armor, she wore a rose-colored gown that Sophia had once feared would clash with the red in Alice's hair.

Ridiculous, she thought, looking into her mirror. It looked entirely too pretty on her to waste on Mr. Brumley. Suddenly, she wished she hadn't left the plum sheath with the Elizabethan collar in Sophia's dressing room. Perhaps if she left early, she would have time to change? But the Thornes were still in residence. Eve would probably interfere again and agree that the rose looked lovely on Alice, and Sophia would realize that even with Alice's hair, the rose was better than the plum by far. She resigned herself to the rose.

In any event, she wouldn't see Mr. Winthrop tonight. He needed time to himself to realize just how miserable his dutiful life was without Alice to delight him.

"Alice, you never fail to delight me." He had said it in his kitchen just that morning. He could deny it and claim he'd said "surprise" instead of "delight" all he wanted, but she knew the truth. She'd heard him loud and clear. In an unguarded moment, he'd admitted how she truly affected him. He'd never convince her that he was indifferent to her, at least not for long.

"The spirits have been active!" Agatha declared, storming into Alice's room. "We have a poltergeist."

"A poltergeist? Is that why you're not ready for dinner?"

Agatha's white hair, out of her chignon, flew every which way. She wore only her camisole and pantalets. Agatha hadn't bothered with a corset in twenty years. "Indeed. No need for fear, my child. Poltergeists are seldom vindictive. They're more known for mischief and playful tricks. It seems that tonight's playful trick was to hide my canary gown that I'd planned to wear. I've looked everywhere. No sign of it."

"Where could it be? Spirited away?" Alice knew exactly where it was, left behind at Winthrop's, but she could hardly confess that to Agatha. Tonight, she would let the ghost take the blame.

"Exactly!" Agatha wagged a finger. "Whisked into the spirit world until our culprit decides to bring it back. Perhaps if I leave a bowl of sweet milk and crackers on the bedside table, the spirit will take an interest and return with my gown."

"Poltergeists like sweet milk and crackers?"

Agatha nodded. "They adore sweets. Oh, but so does Miss Puss. She might drink it all up before the poltergeist returns. Dear, what's to be done?"

Miss Puss was Agatha's ghost cat, a remnant from Lord Averford's grandmother's time. Only Agatha had seen Miss Puss in recent years. "I suggest you choose another gown for dinner. Sophia's sending the car for us in a quarter hour. I can meet Dale and delay."

"Good child. Yes. That will help. I'll wear my chartreuse instead. If only we could figure out who our poltergeist is and what he wants. Once they get what they're after, they usually fade back into the netherworld."

Alice shrugged. "Perhaps he's a she. She did take your gown. I hardly think a male would do such a thing."

Agatha smiled as if Alice had said something ridiculous. "Sweet, innocent Alice. There are plenty of men who enjoy dressing up in gowns. You wouldn't know about such things of course, but I had a lover once who…"

"You? Had a lover?" Alice had imagined that Agatha had always been single, never married or even kissed. Never before had Agatha mentioned having a lover.

"I've had several. Why do you think I never married? I was ruined before I was eighteen. I couldn't resist Lord Pottersdam, the scoundrel, and he convinced me to run away with him. He refused to marry me, of course, because he had an understanding with Lady Sylvia Mannersly, a much wealthier heiress. After that, there were Lord Fitzharris and Mr. Scottsdale.

Oh, and Lord Beauville. He's the one who liked to wear my clothes."

"You've never said anything. All these years. I thought you were a spinster."

"Well, of course. I never married. Your mother prefers people to think I've been chaste. It has been so long since I've had a lover that everyone's forgotten. Remember that, dear heart, if you're ever in a pinch. Scandals pass. There's always a new one to wipe away the old."

"I'll keep it in mind." She wondered if her aunt had foreseen scandal in her near future. Alice certainly hoped so. "You get ready. I'll go down and wait for the car."

Six

WITH THE ARRIVAL OF THE LEMON TREES TWO WEEKS later, Alice decided to resume speaking to Mr. Winthrop. She'd offered her help with them after all, and it hardly seemed fair to leave the man alone with Brumley, even if Winthrop had behaved wretchedly toward her in pretending there wasn't an attraction between them.

Unfortunately, Brumley wouldn't be put off, no matter how she'd tried to dissuade him. She believed in equal rights for women. He believed wives should be subservient to their husbands. She enjoyed outdoor activities. He preferred to sit inside with a book. Every time she pointed out a departure of sensibilities between them, he seemed to take it as encouragement to further press a courtship.

She had a feeling that he was getting dangerously close to proposing, putting her in the awkward position of having to say no and explain the refusal to her sister. Sophia would never understand why Alice would turn down such an opportunity, leading to arguments between them, and what if Sophia threatened to send her home to Mother? It would be far easier to simply convince Brumley that there could never be any love between them.

She paused outside the conservatory. What if Brumley were there, but Winthrop wasn't? She couldn't risk being alone with Brumley when he seemed to be waiting for the chance to request her hand. Winthrop would never appreciate how vulnerable a position she had put herself in for his sake. Still, she decided to hazard a walk downstairs, target the first available maid, and insist that she needed assistance. She would ring for one except that they were all so carried away with preparations for the ball that most of them had stopped responding to bells unless they could be sure the earl or countess was ringing.

At the bottom of the stairs, Alice bumped straight into Winthrop, who was carrying an enormous pair of gardening shears.

"You seem intent on impaling me," she quipped. True to form, he didn't even manage a small smile. Why did she put herself out for him?

"The sharp end is facing my way. I would never risk carrying shears point-out. It would be madness."

"Relax, Mr. Winthrop. I was joking."

He raised a dark brow. "Do you find something funny in safety hazards?"

"Says the man who pointed a rifle at someone he did not intend to shoot, or so he claims." She would not lose her sense of humor, no matter how stone-faced he chose to remain.

"We've been over that. The rifle wasn't loaded. You might have been a robber. But speaking of rifles, why haven't you turned up for your next lesson? Capricious Lady Alice, her interest proves short-lived once again." His eyes flashed with a challenge.

She would not be cowed. "I thought you had enough duties in running Thornbrook Park without taking on the burden of one more. I'll learn to shoot. Eventually." She hadn't been near a rifle since her ill-fated afternoon with Winthrop.

"Soon." His eyes narrowed. "Or you'll forget everything I already showed you and our efforts will have been a waste of time."

"Not a waste, Mr. Winthrop. I have a sharp mind. I'll not soon forget the lesson I learned." She smiled, smug. "To further prove I'm not capricious, I've come to offer my assistance with the lemon trees. I'd told you I would, and here I am. How did they fare on the journey?"

"We lost half, one to the cold and one to disease."

"That means two trees survived the journey, which seems fortunate considering the recent drop in temperatures."

He nodded. "If they'd stayed in port any longer, we'd have lost them all, most likely. Mr. Brumley is very excited to supervise their replanting."

"He's in the conservatory now?" She let go her sigh of relief that she hadn't gone right in. "Alone?"

"Alone with his books. He has brought three manuals with him, and he's trying to decide which soil composition will be most suitable. Shall I congratulate you?"

"On what?" She felt the color drain from her face, fearing the worst.

"Your happy change in circumstances? The impending nuptials?"

"To Brumley? Good lord, I would rather impale myself on your shears."

"So you haven't accepted him?" Finally, a note of happiness in his voice. "A wonder he stays around."

"He hasn't asked. I have a feeling he's waiting to get me alone, which is why I came in search of a maid to accompany me into the conservatory. I prefer not to be alone with him, if I can help it."

"Be warned. He has been speaking of you as his future bride. I think it's only a matter of time. Perhaps at the ball."

"The ball!" She smacked her forehead with her palm. "Of course. The perfect opportunity to whisk me out into the moonlight and propose. I don't want to dance every dance, but I have to be sure I have partners to avoid being alone with him."

"It sounds like an impossible task."

"Help me." She placed her hands over his on the shear handles. "Keep watch and dance with me every time I look to be without a partner. Please, Winthrop." Her eyes held his gaze, and she hoped he could see the urgency in them.

"I would love to be of assistance to you, Lady Alice, but I'm not attending the ball."

"Not attending? You must. It's a ball. At Thornbrook Park. Which you oversee."

He shrugged. "It's not a requirement for me to attend. I do what needs to be done and step back. I could attend, of course. Lady Averford has invited me to join the festivities. But I tend to avoid such affairs."

"Avoid? But it was *your* idea."

"That doesn't mean I have to attend. I've seen to

it that everything is in order. The overnight guests begin arriving tomorrow. The rooms have been readied. The ballroom floor has been uncovered and mopped. The wall separating the dining room from the parlor will be removed today, which is why you'll be dining on trays tonight, or at the Dower House in your case."

"You took down a whole wall? Just for an event?"

"It folds up, to be concealed in a space between the rooms. It was constructed so that it could be removed to enlarge the space for parties. The hinges had to be repaired, however, due to the length of time the wall has been left in place."

"Oh. You've been busy."

"Overseeing the stocking of the pantry, the menus, the budget, and the preparations of the house and gardens."

"It's so cold in the gardens at night."

"Not cold enough to deter guests from seeking a late-night stroll. It gets stifling in a crowded ballroom, or haven't you noticed?"

"I have. I suppose you're right." She hadn't been to many balls, and none of them recently.

Still, she could remember the heat and the excitement, getting carried away with the feeling of triumph when a handsome man asked her to dance, and defeat when a better-looking one asked one of her friends. It all seemed such a part of her past, her dazzling youth. She was a woman of the world now, or so she preferred to think of herself.

She supposed she wouldn't truly be a woman until she'd properly made love with a man. Nibbling her lip, she absently studied Winthrop's solid jaw. What it would be like to drop kisses, soft as butterfly wings, along his jaw and down his neck?

Suddenly he dropped the shears, snapping her to attention, and wrapped his arms around her. He felt it, too! He was overcome.

"Logan." She spoke his given name before crushing her lips to his.

❧

Her mouth covered his before he realized what was happening. But once he tasted her sweetness, he couldn't stop. He drew on her tongue as she boldly slipped it between his lips, urging her to explore before he took the lead and showed her the pleasure created when two tongues met and tangled. He kissed her until he lost all power to breathe, and then he backed away, prepared to apologize profusely.

"Lady Alice. I'm sorry. I reached out because I thought you were going to faint again. You were so still for a minute there, and your eyes became heavy-lidded."

"I may yet," she said, looking up at him, eyes wide. "But I'm not sorry. I've wanted to kiss you for a long time, Logan. I think we could have something wonderful."

"Something wonderful," he repeated, lost for a minute in her hazel eyes. How could eyes have so many colors? Green, brown, gold. Her eyes were bewitching. He could study them all day long. But he remembered himself in time. Not quite in time. He'd kept an arm around her waist, resting on her backside, for a few seconds too long. He pulled it back.

"Lady Alice, you know I admire you. You've become a dear friend, and I've had precious few of those, honestly. But we can't have anything like you're suggesting. Please. Be my friend. Expect nothing more from me."

He held out his hand, hoping she would shake it, cementing the bonds of friendship. She closed her eyes a moment, then popped them open and tilted her head. "Friends. Yes, of course, Mr. Winthrop. I'm delighted that you count me among your friends, and I hope you continue to do so."

Relief was what he expected to feel on such news, but disappointment weighed on him heavily. Something wonderful was within his grasp, and he'd left it on the shelf. What choice did he have? He could only give her temporary pleasure at best, a season's diversion, and she deserved a lifetime of wonderful. She was just young enough to think living for the moment a fine idea, unaware of how quickly such moments pass. And then, a lifetime of emptiness ahead, a trail of moments that ended too soon and led nowhere.

Lady Alice deserved so much more. He knew her well enough to know that no one could turn her against something she'd set her mind to. The key was in subtly convincing her that she'd wanted something else all along. He prayed that the right young man for her would be at the ball, ready to sweep her off her feet. She would forget all about him, he reflected with a pang.

"The lemon trees, and Mr. Brumley, await. Shall we face the challenge together, my friend?" He laced fingers with hers, though it pained him to do so. To let himself get close to her even in friendship, only in friendship, fed the hungry ache in his core. He was a man, after all, and she was a desirable woman.

"Stay with me," she begged. "At all costs. Don't leave me alone with the oaf."

"I won't leave you to Brumley," he said, stooping to retrieve the shears. "I promise."

At the top of the stairs, he conveniently let go of her hand to open the door for her, and he didn't reach for it again. It wouldn't do to be seen hand-clasped with a member of the family. Down the hall in the conservatory, Brumley sat, book in his lap, on the bench next to the trees in their pots.

"Lady Alice." At their approach, he shot to his feet. "A pleasure to see you again. I'm so glad you've joined us."

"Lady Alice has experience with citrus trees," Logan explained, flashing the barest hint of a smile at Alice. He suspected it had been an exaggeration. "She has promised to share her knowledge."

She wrung her hands, probably to avoid holding one out to Brumley, who looked eager to grab on. "What little knowledge I have, that is. I watched my mother tend our trees, but I provided little assistance to her, to be honest."

"Of course. Leave the men to the work and you can look on admiringly. It's a woman's job to orna-ment the room."

Logan watched Alice's face go red until he thought her pretty eyes would pop out of her head. But instead, she took a breath and offered a sweet smile. "I'll stand here and watch until I have worthy advice."

"I'll be waiting for your wisdom. Meanwhile, it's time to transfer our prizes from the confines of their travel containers to their more spacious plots. I do believe I've dug deep enough. What say you, Lady Alice?" Logan deferred to her for advice before turning to Brumley.

"Yes. It looks sufficient." She agreed, taking a moment to study the six-foot-square, four-foot-deep box he'd constructed for the trees. "They'll be lovely there as they grow taller, with the other greenery filling in around them."

It would suit while they were small, before their roots spread wider. Provided they survived a year or two, he could devise a new plan for their continued growth. Once the trees were replanted, he would ornament the boxes somehow, hide them with a row of shrubbery, paint them, or affix stones. He hadn't decided, but the goal was to incorporate the trees seamlessly into their garden-like surroundings.

"I beg to differ, Lady Alice. They might be too close, both in the one box," Brumley said.

Logan knew she took a second calming breath, because his eyes were drawn suddenly from her face to the tops of her breasts, just barely visible through the diaphanous blue material that covered her décolletage and the darker blue bodice of the gown. Blue was more her sister's color. Green suited Alice better. Or the rose color he'd seen her wear on occasion. Her breasts were small, but not as flat as she supposed. They were ripe little apples waiting to be picked. Or lemons perhaps would be more apt, considering the trees… Why was he thinking of her breasts? He had to stop thinking of her as a woman and remember that she was only his friend.

"But Mr. Brumley, we consulted on the planting, and you thought the proportions ideal. Changed your mind, have you?" Logan turned his attention from Alice. "One box, six feet square to give the roots room to spread, and three deep. I added some depth, just in case, and I've ensured for adequate drainage."

"I suppose it looks different in execution than I'd imagined. Smaller, somehow. But of course, I referred to Edith Wharton's *Italian Villas and Gardens* for such a recommendation. I'll consult Howard's *Garden Cities of Tomorrow* to see if he has anything to add." He returned to his bench and book.

"I might need Sturridge's assistance." Logan wouldn't ask Alice to dirty her hands with stepping into the box to hold the trees upright while he shoveled the soil around them, and Brumley clearly couldn't be relied upon. "Lady Alice, could you go after him for me?"

"Of course. I suppose he's out of doors where he won't hear any ringing of bells. Shall I look in the gardens?"

"Yes, he should be tending the walks to ensure a clear path for any dancers who go out wandering."

"I'll accompany you," Brumley announced, rising again. "A young woman shouldn't have to walk about the gardens alone on a lovely day, though it is a bit cold for my liking."

"Stay inside where it's warm, Lord Brumley. We wouldn't want you to catch a chill," Alice urged.

Logan could see the man wouldn't be deterred.

Brumley probably thought he had his chance to corner Lady Alice and propose. It was time for drastic measures. Logan stuck out his foot and kicked over one of the pots, knowing full well it might cost him the life of a tree. The tree began to topple, and Logan called out. "Crikes! Mr. Brumley, a hand?"

Brumley looked over to see Logan struggling to keep the tree upright. "Oh dear."

The trees were young and Logan wouldn't have any difficulty holding one of them up on his own, but he pretended to struggle. As soon as Brumley, obligated to lend a hand in crisis, came to assist him, Logan nodded at Alice to slip away.

Moments later, when Sturridge came in, he did not have Alice with him. It was as Logan had expected, but he felt the sorrier for his loss.

⌒

Once she fled the room, Alice broke into a run down the hall. Thanks to Winthrop, she'd made a narrow escape. As much as she wanted to return to help him, she wouldn't risk being too close to Brumley again. She knew Winthrop would understand. They were friends.

Friends! She laughed with the joy of it, an unexpected triumph. He might have felt he was doing the right thing, letting her down gently. To Alice's way of thinking, he'd opened the door. Winthrop didn't have friends. It was an intimacy he almost never allowed himself. Alice had become the closest person to Logan Winthrop in the entire world, next to perhaps Julia Kirkland. And Julia had chosen another.

Winthrop was far too principled to carry on with a married woman. Wherever she was, Julia was out of his sphere. And Alice was in. Being friends could most certainly lead to more between them. It was an enormous step in the right direction. Friendship could lead to friendly seduction…

"Mr. Sturridge," she said, crossing the lawn into the garden, where the man was pruning back errant branches. "I hate to disturb you, but Mr. Winthrop says you're needed in the conservatory at once."

"At once?" He looked up from his shrubbery. "Thank you, Lady Alice. I'll go straightaway."

She watched as he handed his lopping shears to an under gardener and headed for the house. Her work was done. She supposed she should look in on Sophia, a safe enough risk with Eve Thorne still in residence, to check Sophia's urges to get Brumley alone in a room with Alice. With the ball only days away, Alice figured she would try on her gown for one last fitting. Sophia would probably insist, and so she resigned herself. At least, it would keep her out of Brumley's way until she could find someone to accompany her back to the Dower House.

But first, walking by Lord Averford's study, she had an idea. She stopped at his door and knocked. To her surprise, he called out. She'd expected he might be stalking deer.

"I only need a moment, Lord Averford." She peeked her head around the door to see that he'd been in conversation with his brother. Informally, she usually referred to him as Gabriel, his given name, but she couldn't be sure he wasn't with more important company until after she'd spoken. "Good day to you, too, Marcus."

"Shall I leave you alone?" Marcus stood.

"You can hear what I have to say. I'll only be a moment. Please sit." She stepped in and closed the door. "It's about Mr. Winthrop."

"Winthrop?" Gabriel's face registered some surprise. No doubt he wondered what she had to do with his estate manager.

"I've been informed that he does not plan to attend the ball. It struck me as a shame, since it was his idea. And of all people, doesn't it seem that Mr. Winthrop could use a spot of fun? He's so severe and alone so much of the time. I think it would be good for him to attend."

It would be good for her. She remembered his kiss, the way his lips melted into hers, the feel of his tongue questing. The heat deep inside her, making her tremble with the need for more.

"What brings on this sudden concern for Mr. Winthrop's welfare?" Marcus asked, a note of suspicion in his voice. No doubt he'd picked up on gossip from that meddling wife of his. Not that Alice didn't love Eve Thorne like a sister, but one sister interfering in her affairs was quite enough.

She tried not to give herself away with a blush. "I was talking to him about the lemon trees, which led to a mention of the ball and of course his refusal to attend. To be perfectly honest, I asked him to dance with me when he saw me unoccupied with other partners. Anyone but Mr. Brumley. You should know, Gabriel, that your wife has horrendous taste in men that are not for her."

He laughed. "As long as she had the good taste to accept me when I asked her."

"Not to be indelicate, but I believe I was one of those men that you suggest reflects Sophia's taste," Marcus added.

She blushed. Sophia had tried to pair her with Marcus before it was obvious that he had eyes only for Eve. "I'm sorry, Marcus. You were another exception. But you must understand what I mean about Brumley. No one can possibly like the man."

"You're talking about my former schoolmate. If I didn't like him, he wouldn't be here," Gabriel defended.

"Yes. I see." Alice felt like she was making a muddle of things. "But I don't like him, and that's the point, isn't it? She wants me to marry him, but would she have me marry a man I don't even like?"

"And what does this have to do with Mr. Winthrop again?" Gabriel narrowed his eyes, confused.

"She doesn't want to dance with Brumley. She prefers Winthrop," Marcus summarized.

"Should we be concerned about you and Mr. Winthrop, Alice? You know I find him a very capable estate manager, but he's not right for you."

"I don't prefer Winthrop to Lord Brumley. Well, actually, I do. We're friends, and I prefer almost anyone to Brumley. But, the point is, I just want you to be sure Winthrop makes it to the ball."

"You consider Mr. Winthrop a friend?" Marcus pressed the issue. "I didn't think the man had friends."

She was becoming more and more flustered. She should have asked to be alone with Gabriel after all, but it was too late now. "All I want is to be sure that

I have plenty of tolerable dance partners that are not Mr. Brumley. Gabriel, please, could you see that Mr. Winthrop attends?"

He tented his fingers on the desk as if considering and slapped his hands down flat once he'd made a decision. "I'm sorry, Alice. I can't force the man to go to the ball. If he doesn't want to go, so be it. I don't interfere in the private lives of those who serve me."

"Isn't it his job to attend, though?" She crossed her arms. "You can make sure he's doing his job."

"He has done his job as far as I'm concerned. Attending the ball is not part of his duties. Frankly, I'm growing a bit alarmed at your apparent personal interest in Mr. Winthrop. Has he given you any reason to take such interest?"

Now she'd really done it. She'd made Logan an object of suspicion to his employer.

"Of course not. You know Mr. Winthrop. He's strictly professional at all times. I've an interest in horticulture and I might have made myself a bit of a nuisance to him on occasion, but he has never been rude or overly encouraging. He's simply…Winthrop." It was mostly the truth. She wasn't about to reveal that she'd thrown herself at him. "I suppose I can count him out for the ball. But don't think this leaves you off the hook, either one of you."

"What do you mean?" Gabriel seemed taken aback to be at the end of Alice's pointed, accusing finger.

"I mean that I expect both of you to be watching over me, helping to make sure that Lord Brumley doesn't get me alone. I would rather not have to refuse a proposal. I would prefer to not be asked at all.

If you're not going to do everything in your power to force every eligible, non-objectionable male into attendance, then you had better be prepared to dance with me yourselves."

Giving them no further chance to object or raise questions, Alice turned on her heel and stomped out of the room.

Seven

ONCE THE LEMON TREES WERE SAFELY REPLANTED, Logan went in search of the one person he wanted to see before the grand ball, Eve Thorne.

He found her walking in the garden, pushing her sleeping baby in a pram. Fortunately, she was alone and not attended by her nurse, husband, or Lady Averford.

"Mrs. Thorne. I've been looking for you," he whispered, anxious that he should wake the baby.

"Looking for me? I'm honored. No need to whisper, Mr. Winthrop. Mina sleeps through anything, as evidenced by her remaining in dreamland despite the bumpiness of this path."

"I'll look into it. Sturridge was supposed to be checking into it today, but I called him away to other tasks."

"Heavens." She laughed. "Quite the perfectionist, aren't you? It's supposed to be bumpy. It's only a path, not a major thoroughfare."

"Yes, well, we don't need any ladies complaining of twisted ankles from going on midnight assignations with their lovers in the gardens, do we?" He shrugged.

"It's important that what I want to talk to you about stays between us. It regards Lady Alice Emerson. You've been direct with me regarding her attentions in the past, so I feel I can be direct with you."

"Of course. Speak your mind, Winthrop."

"It's very important to me that she commands attention at the ball. I want her to draw the eye of every suitable bachelor in town. When I say suitable, I mean someone appropriate for Alice."

"Not the Lord Brumleys of the world." She nodded, clearly in agreement.

"Exactly. I'm not sure being relegated to our quiet corner of the country here at Thornbrook Park has done our lovely young lady any world of good. Lady Averford likes it because it's home to her. She has a husband. What does she need with social engagements and parties?"

"Sophia loves a good party, Mr. Winthrop. No one loves being at the center of attention quite like my dear friend the countess. But I can see why you would have the impression that she doesn't. She has been quiet these last few years, surrounding herself with dear and trusted friends and forgetting the rest of the world. We can't blame her, after what she's been through."

"Losing her firstborn was very hard on her." He knew that Lady Averford made frequent visits to the grave of her infant son. She didn't make a fuss about it, preferring not to call attention to her mourning perhaps, but he had seen her head that way with clusters of blue forget-me-nots in her hands. Once the flowers lost their luster, he would clean them off the grave only for her to bring more. He'd added forget-me-nots to the window boxes outside her bedroom windows and more in the conservatory so that she would always have them around.

Her husband never left flowers. Once a year, he placed a colorful kite at the grave of his son who was buried next to Lord Averford's father. Logan supposed it represented the activities they would have shared together, had the boy lived. All of the servants in the house pitied them for their loss and prayed for the still-young couple to have another child. "No one could blame her. But…"

"Your concern is for Lady Alice. It's not fair that she's here with little to no society to hold her interest. Looking after Agatha is certainly no task for a young woman. Do you know that she wants to travel the world? India, Africa, America…"

"Lady Alice? In India?" He had no idea what she had planned for herself. He'd assumed, perhaps foolishly, that she was like most young women, eager to marry well and happily. "Is it safe?"

"Safe enough, I suppose, if she's accompanied. Captain Thorne and I have thought about going with her. I would love to show my husband where I lived for many years. If we happen to be leaving at the same time, so much the better for Alice."

"Yes. I hope you can arrange it. I hate to think of her all alone on such an adventure."

"I'm sure you do." She smiled. "So what is it, Winthrop? Has Alice finally thrown herself at you? I've seen the way she looks at you. I've expected it would happen one of these days. Alice is not easily deterred."

"I did my best to discourage her, Mrs. Thorne. I had my own suspicions of her interest that I had discounted as the egotistical musings of an aging man. Until this morning."

"This morning?" She looked at him, the question in her eyes. She didn't ask. "I see. So you let her down gently, and now your ideal solution would be that she becomes infatuated with someone else. Someone closer to her own age? Or really, anyone but Brumley, whom you've deemed unsuitable because…"

"Look at the man. Try to engage him in conversation. He's a boor. She deserves so much better."

"If it makes you feel any better, I went over the guest list with Sophia and then gave it a second look with Mr. Finch."

"Mr. Finch?"

"Precisely. Finch has been at Thornbrook Park for decades. He knows the families that used to come for the Dowager Countess's balls when she was mistress of the house. He knows other butlers at other houses, which ones have young men, what their expectations are. He knows so much. I relied on that knowledge to be sure that Lady Alice has a number of wealthy, eligible, handsome men her own age to dance with at Thornbrook Park's first ball in seven years. A pity if she were forced to rely on Lord Brumley for entertainment. Sophia sees his title, and that he was left a fortune and a house that could rival Thornbrook Park, and she thinks Alice would be lucky to have him. She forgets that Alice isn't looking for fortune or position. Alice only wants to have fun."

"As befits a women of two and twenty. Thank you,

Mrs. Thorne. You have set my mind at ease. Do your best to see that she is the loveliest, most breathtaking creature in the room, even over her sister."

"Her sister? Sophia is extraordinary, yes, but none of the young men will look twice at a married woman."

He laughed. "You would be surprised, Mrs. Thorne. I have no doubt that Lady Alice can command her share of attention. Still, I would feel better with you looking out for her, making sure she shines her brightest with no one to block her light."

"You know I will, Mr. Winthrop. I look after Alice all too attentively for her liking."

"She's in good hands. Good day, Mrs. Thorne."

◆

"Be careful what you wish for," Alice said too quietly for anyone to hear as she held her place in the receiving line next to her sister. The night of the ball had finally arrived, and her parting words to Lord Averford and his brother came back to haunt her. She'd demanded that he do everything in his power to force every eligible, non-objectionable male into attendance, and he'd most certainly done it beyond her imagination.

She'd never seen so many attractive, well-heeled young men in one place. Each one that came in the door was better looking than the last. Solid prospects, all of them. According to what she'd said to Gabriel and Marcus, she should be over the moon. Yet, as she'd expected when Winthrop had suggested a ball, she'd ended up in one of her worst nightmares come true. Eligible bachelors everywhere, so many that it

would be a struggle to come up with reasons to turn
them all down.

She wouldn't turn any down tonight, with the
exception of Brumley. He was the only one at risk
to ask for her hand in marriage. The rest would need
time to work up to that, if any of them had an interest
after tonight. She tried to tell herself they wouldn't.
She would prove to be capricious Alice, incorrigible
Alice, prideful, determined Alice and scare them all
away. She was tolerably pretty for a dance or two, but
no one wanted an outspoken whirlwind for a wife.
Again, with the exception of Brumley, who seemed
to believe that marriage would transform her into a
docile, library-dwelling hermit.

Brumley, she huffed under her breath, and as if she
were a witch uttering an incantation, he appeared—
poof!—straight in front of her, next in line.

"Lady Alice," he drawled, dropping suddenly to
one knee and taking her hand to deliver such a sloppy
kiss to the back of her hand that she swore she could
feel it dripping through her kidskin gloves. "You must
save me a dance or two."

"I don't know, Lord Brumley. I've already promised so many." Embarrassed by his display, she looked
to Sophia for help, but her sister was engaged in conversation with the next in line and would no doubt be
more of a hindrance than a help. She looked to Marcus
on her other side to hurry Brumley along.

"Lord Brumley." Marcus, the dear man, took
Brumley's hand and shook it vigorously, as if he'd
been waiting hours for the chance. "Good to see you.
I wasn't sure a ball was quite your kind of event."

Alice wished that Winthrop would come. She imagined the fun they would have off in a corner, whispering to one another about the dancers. And later, once the lights were low and the mood was right, she could lure him into an alcove and try to get another kiss.

"Lady Alice." A seductively low voice lured her from her reverie. She tipped her chin up to see one of the handsomest faces she had ever looked upon, next to the godlike Thorne brothers. He had a straight nose, high cheekbones, large brown eyes, pale skin, and chestnut hair with just a hint of auburn to it, not as much red as in her own hair but enough that they might pass for siblings. "Forgive me. I am Lord Ralston. We haven't been properly introduced, but it is a reception line. I'm known to take liberties."

"Liberties?" She arched a brow. "I've been known to take a few myself."

He broke into a grin so wide that any other man would appear comically altered, but this one's perfectly aligned shiny white teeth added to his appeal. "I had a feeling we would get along. I've been trying to get your attention since my arrival yesterday."

"Yesterday? I think I would remember seeing you. I can't imagine that you have trouble getting anyone's attention when it suits you." It only just occurred to her that he'd been holding her hand the entire time, his enormous palm enveloping hers so that his fingers toyed along her wrist. Through her glove, it only felt slightly scandalous.

"I rode in on a white horse, your typical fairy-tale prince sort of entrance. I thought it might set me apart. You were with your sister greeting a carload, the Sentledens, who came in ahead of me."

"Ah yes," she recalled. "The Sentledens. You were with others on horseback. I thought you might have been with the earl's hunting party, with most of the guests coming in by automobile these days. Forgive me for not staying to greet you properly."

"Automobiles, a means to an end perhaps, but there's nothing like the bond between man and horse. We're sacrificing romance for convenience, and I'm sure we'll all come to regret it eventually."

"You're a romantic, Lord Ralston?"

"A romantic, yes. A traditionalist, perhaps. In time, I'll be a relic. I don't see anything wrong with our fine old ways, but I suppose times change. They call it progress. I see it as a loss of our humanity." He laughed. "But I'm drawing perilously close to making you think I'm a much older man."

"You don't look very old." Perhaps thirty if she were to hazard a guess. It shamed her a little to think that if Brumley looked more like Lord Ralston, she might have given him a chance.

"I waited for you yesterday. You went in to get the Sentledens settled and never came back out. Didn't your sister tell you I asked after you?"

She shook her head.

"Lady Averford," he admonished, looking over to Sophia. "How could you forget to give your sister my regards?"

"Forgive me, my lord." Sophia blushed like a schoolgirl under the man's watchful gaze. "Lady Alice, may I present the Earl of Ralston. He did, in fact, ask after you and it completely slipped my mind. But now you're acquainted." She turned to greet the approaching Lady Holcomb.

An earl? And a handsome one at that. Sophia must really be caught up in the idea of Alice marrying Brumley if she forgot to mention a man who might actually command notice.

"And again, in the drawing room when you were having tea with the ladies. I strutted like a peacock back and forth for a quarter hour and you didn't look up once." He might have attempted to look stricken, but he only managed to make himself all the more adorable. She guessed he was not unaware of his effect on the opposite sex, and possibly on some of his own.

She laughed. "Perhaps I could ask you to do it again. I think I missed quite a show." Alice recalled that Brumley had come in with the gentlemen when she was pouring tea with Sophia to entertain the newly arrived guests. No wonder Alice had averted her gaze and missed his entrance!

He bowed slightly, never taking his gaze from hers. "I'm at your command, Lady Alice. A shame that all your dances have been claimed."

He must have overheard her telling Brumley. "I think I can make an exception, Lord Ralston. Pleased to make your acquaintance."

"Ralston dear, move along. You're holding up the line." Lady Holcomb urged him onward and took his place in front of Alice. "My nephew seems quite taken with you."

"Your nephew?" Alice couldn't contain her surprise. Ralston seemed far too dashing to be a relation to the Holcombs, though she supposed it helped to explain his traditionalist views. The Holcombs were notoriously reluctant to embrace change.

"My sister's son." Lady Holcomb nodded. "He's always in demand in London, but I've finally convinced him to come breathe the country air. He's with us for three weeks, until just after the hunt, unless I can convince him to stay through to Christmas."

"The hunt? The fox hunt? At Holcomb House?"

"Yes. Will you be joining us?"

"I had been thinking of it." She'd wanted to participate for the sake of the adventure, but the idea of possibly putting off Brumley had aided in her determination. And now she found that having the company of Lord Ralston might not be so intolerable, either.

Lady Holcomb moved down the line, her husband trailing after her. Once there was a brief lull between guests, Alice turned to Sophia. She didn't want to appear too eager, but perhaps showing interest in Ralston would keep her sister from encouraging her to accept Brumley, should he ever succeed in getting her alone. "The Earl of Ralston? How old is he? Have you met him before?"

"He has dined here. Years ago, when his father passed away, he spent some time with the Holcombs. I don't know his age, but he's not yet thirty, and he's a bit older than you."

"I see." An earl under thirty? Showing her some interest? Alice thought that Ralston's presence might take some of the sting out of Winthrop's abandonment for the evening.

Once in the ballroom, she found her first partner.

She hadn't seen Robert, Baron Shermont, since they were children in Delaney Square and he'd gone off to school. Clearly, he had grown into his looks, no longer a husky boy with buckteeth.

"Good to see you again, Lady Alice." He swept her into his arms. She felt no romantic stirrings, but she wouldn't mind a second dance with him.

"And you, Lord Shermont. May I call you Robert? You still feel like a friend. How are things in Delaney Square?"

"Of course, Alice. Your parents send their regards. They're sorry they couldn't make the journey."

"I understand. I'm not sure what's worse these days, Father's temper or his gout." She'd been home for a few weeks over the summer to visit and had witnessed her father's growing discomfort firsthand.

"He is having trouble getting around."

"Poor Father. I know how he detests sitting still."

"He doesn't seem to mind it so much lately. He has taken up a hobby, building ships in bottles. It keeps him occupied."

"Ships? I don't recall Father ever being that impressed by the sea. He complained the entire time we were at Brighton."

"I guess we have no idea what will interest us once we're older. We'll all change as we age. You dance well, Alice. Almost as well as you bake mud pies."

She laughed. "I hope better than that. I haven't made a mud pie in years."

"You were the best mud-pie baker in Delaney Square. Mine could never hold a candle to yours."

"But I think you might be the better dancer,

Robert." Effortlessly, he guided her across the floor, keeping perfect time to the music. She almost regretted when the song ended and her next partner found her.

She'd lost count of dances and partners when Lord Brumley finally found her. Her dance with pleasantly forgettable Mr. Danleigh had just come to an end when Brumley appeared before her.

"Lady Alice, I believe our time has come." Instant dread snaked through her. She wondered if she could manage an excuse. Her feet hurt? She needed to sit down? He was beginning to take her in his arms when Lord Ralston came from seemingly out of nowhere.

"I'm sorry, old man." He clapped Brumley on the back and stepped in. "The lady has promised this one to me."

Before Brumley could protest, Ralston put his arms around her and swept her into the throng.

"My hero," she said when she could finally catch her breath. "You have no idea how perfect your timing was."

"I have more idea than you know. Isn't he the man who has been trying to get you alone so he can ask for your hand? We can't have that. I'm just getting to know you."

She didn't mean to like Lord Ralston, but a thrill coursed through her at his words. "How could you possibly know that?"

He shrugged. "Servants talk. A smart man knows which servants will have the most to say and takes advantage of the situation."

"Which one of them betrayed my secrets?" She

pretended to be shocked, her eyes widening. She was, in fact, delighted that he'd been asking after her, but she reminded herself to remain aloof. A man like Ralston might take her interest all too seriously.

"One of the maids. I believe her name was Mary? Flattery will get you everywhere."

"I won't admonish her for gossiping since she has actually done me a great favor this once." Her hand felt small in his as he expertly guided her around the room.

"I do feel a little bad. We were rather rude to the poor fellow. I'll have to make it up to him by letting him win at cards."

"I don't think Mr. Brumley plays cards. He doesn't seem to do much of anything but read gardening manuals."

"Before his marriage, he played cards, badly I'm afraid. Lady Cavendish settled all his debts after the wedding and made him promise not to gamble anymore."

"And how do you know all this? Do you flirt with the footmen for stories, too?"

He laughed. "You are a delight, Lady Alice. No. I heard it from my uncle."

A delight. He wasn't the first man who had complimented her so, though unlike the other, he hadn't taken it back. She felt suddenly disloyal to Mr. Winthrop for having such a good time with Lord Ralston. Of course, Winthrop had made it clear that they were "friends" and to expect nothing more. Ralston, on the other hand, seemed to have an interest in her, and he was available and perfectly acceptable.

He might expect marriage, though, and she would be in a spot to convince him that she didn't want to be proper about things. She only wanted a wild affair.

"Your uncle, Lord Holcomb?"

"Lady Holcomb wouldn't know anything about Brumley's gambling. Or, she wouldn't say anything if she did. Not to me. It would be indelicate." He suddenly changed course and began to direct them to the opposite corner of the room, perhaps due to another sighting of Lord Brumley.

For once, she welcomed a strong male lead and followed him willingly. "And yet, you've told me. Do you have the wrong impression of me?"

"On the contrary." He smiled and raised a brow. "I think I have a very good impression of you, Lady Alice. And the right one. You're the one who confessed to taking liberties."

"Touché, Lord Ralston."

As the sound of the music faded, she realized she had allowed him to dance her out of the main ballroom into a gallery, and then out into the dimly lit hall.

"He won't find you here," Ralston said by way of an excuse. "The dance was ending. I didn't want to take the risk that he would accost you again."

"Thank you," she said, still in his arms. She gestured toward the bench across from the windows overlooking the garden. "I could use a minute to sit down. I've been on my feet since this afternoon."

"By all means," he said, twirling her gracefully away from him and helping her to a seat. "Shall I fetch us some refreshments? A glass of champagne?"

"Not right now. Unless you want something. If not, sit here by me." She patted the cushion beside her and pointed to the window. "We can spy on lovers sneaking off into the shrubbery."

She saw Robert headed down a path, holding hands with a young woman she didn't recognize, another of the ball guests. "There goes my friend Baron Shermont."

"With Lady Symon's middle daughter, Jane. I'm glad. You had your first dance with him. I was seething with jealousy, but now I know he won't be a rival."

"Seething? It's a bit early for that, Lord Ralston. Though I'm flattered." She smiled at him.

"You're right. Perhaps seething is a bit too strong. Still." He laced fingers with hers. "There's one out of the way."

"Robert, Baron Shermont, and I are old friends. We used to bake mud pies together."

"Lady Jane Symon gave me my first kiss. There. Our friends have found each other."

"For tonight, anyway. Sometimes these things don't go much further, do they?"

"For our sake, I hope that's not true. I'll be in West Yorkshire for another few weeks, at least, and I was hoping to call on you."

"I would like that," she said quietly, meeting his mysterious gaze.

"Lord Averford has invited us to come shooting in a few days."

"Lord Averford does love his excursions." A pity she hadn't really learned to shoot. "When Lord Holcomb comes for birding, Lady Holcomb usually joins him and they stay for dinner. She doesn't hunt, of course. She visits with Sophia."

"Then I will be seeing you again soon, though I'm not sure it could possibly be soon enough."

At the edge of the garden lane, she spied Winthrop. He stood back, almost blending into the hedges, and looked up at the windows. She couldn't see his face, but she knew him from his posture and his walk. She knew him from the shape of his head, the width of his shoulders. She knew him. And she was a little surprised to find that she missed him tonight. Even in the company of Lord Ralston.

"I should be getting back. I'm promised for more dances and I think I can find my next partner without running into Brumley. But thank you again, for saving me." She stood.

He brought her hand to his lips and kissed it before letting go. She was sorry now that she still wore the gloves. "The pleasure was all mine. You go ahead without me so it doesn't look like we were off on an intrigue. I'll follow in a few minutes."

She nodded and started to walk away.

"Alice." He called her back. "Know that I mean to find you again before supper."

"Until then, Lord Ralston."

In the ballroom, she stayed along the windows overlooking the garden as she crossed the room and then lingered on the other side, being careful to avoid Brumley. Once she saw that Ralston had reentered the room, she stepped into the adjoining parlor and out through the door to the garden in search of Logan.

Eight

HIS BREATH CAUGHT WHEN HE FIRST SAW HER THROUGH the window, gliding across the room in a young rake's arms. As much as Logan hated not to be the one holding her, he was relieved that she wasn't with Brumley, and that her partner seemed completely captivated by her. Or perhaps he imagined it. From the distance, he could barely discern their facial expressions, but he envisioned Alice laughing and having a good time.

He knew her at once, spying her through the crowd, her auburn hair piled in a mass of curls on her head, her shoulders bare. She'd chosen lavender for her gown, and he thought it a splendid choice for contrast to bring out the green in her eyes. God, he was a fool. A fool to fall in love with her, a fool to let her get away. But he would be a bigger fool to saddle her with an unsuitable husband, a rumored murderer, and expect her to handle the gossip that he'd learned to shrug off.

Perhaps it was a duke holding her just now or a marquess, at least an earl? She could avoid Brumley's advances and fall in love with the right man tonight.

And then she would realize that what she'd had with Logan had truly been friendship and nothing more. He would be alone again, no one to trail after him chirping like a magpie, teasing him, asking endless questions to distract him from his work.

"I thought you weren't coming tonight. And here you are."

Alice. He closed his eyes. A wave of longing went through him at the sound of her voice. He wanted to turn around and kiss her, hard and fast, claiming her for his own, never letting her go. Instead, he steeled himself, opened his eyes, and turned around slowly.

"Lady Alice. You should be inside. They're playing a waltz. Surely, you're promised for this dance?" His voice did not betray him, though he felt like he'd been punched in the gut when he saw her up close, hit with the full force of his sacrifice. Her beauty overwhelmed him.

"This one is for me," she said, holding out her hands. "I get to choose my partner. I came to dance with you, Mr. Winthrop."

He stepped from the shadows into the courtyard. He wore the same navy blue suit he had worn all day. "I'm not dressed for it."

"I don't care." She laughed. "Please don't deny me one dance. I won't force you to come inside. We can hear the music from here."

She placed her hands, encased in gloves that went up past her elbows, on his shoulders.

He took her by the waist and began to move. "You look exquisite tonight, Lady Alice. Truly. The sight of you takes my breath clean away."

"Thank you," she said quietly. "I saw you from the window. You looked lonely. I wish you had changed your mind and come to the ball."

"I am at the ball. With the fairest partner." She felt right in his arms. "What more could I ask?"

She didn't answer, but lowered her head to his shoulder. She smelled like the roses that were no longer blooming in the garden, with an extra hint of something sweet, like baking biscuits. The bare skin of her neck glowed in the moonlight, and he fought back the urge to taste her, to drop kisses along her neck and her shoulders, along the low neck of her gown that exposed more of the tops of her breasts than he had yet seen. He imagined having her alone in a room, tugging the gown lower…

"I could stay out here forever," she said. "It's a beautiful night. Not even that cold."

"It's colder than you realize when you're out for a while." He knew from experience. His hands had been ice until he touched her.

"Then I'll stay until I'm chilled to the bone. You dance well, Logan."

"I have a skilled partner. It helps."

"We're suited, you and I. I've missed you tonight."

"Surely there are other young men to command your attention."

"But they're not you." She looked straight into his eyes. "They can never be you."

"I'm not going to kiss you again, Lady Alice. No matter how much I want you." He'd never been so painfully honest with her, but tonight she deserved the truth.

"You do want me. I can feel it. Why do you deny me? We can be good together. I don't expect you to marry me. I just want—"

He placed a finger to her lips. "We can't always have what we want. I learned that as a young man, and I've been paying for my mistakes ever since."

"What mistakes? What did you do? Tell me. I want to know everything."

"Not now. Tonight is for enchantment, not reliving the pain of my past. We can have this dance. For now, it's enough."

She shook her head. Tears glittered in her eyes. "Never enough."

"It's all we can have." He pulled her closer, placing a hand on the back of her head and urging her to relax against him. "Let's enjoy it while it lasts."

They swayed in each other's arms, no longer dancing, but responding to the music and the feel of each other. White specks dotted his vision. For a minute, he thought he was crying, until she said, "It's snowing," with a laugh. "Look, Logan, it's really snowing."

"The first snow of the year. Sturridge said it was coming, but that it wouldn't amount to much. It should be safe enough for guests to leave when the time comes."

"Ever dutiful, Mr. Winthrop. Forget your responsibilities. Look around. It's like a dream world," she enthused. "An enchanted fairyland just for us."

That's when he couldn't hold back any longer. He had to give in to his urge, just this once.

"Alice." He breathed her name against her shoulder as he tipped her face up to his. "My Alice."

He kissed her gently at first, afraid to overwhelm her, then grew more urgent as she responded and drew his tongue between her lips. One hand tangled in her hair, unmindful of her undoubtedly elaborate arrangement, while the other found the curve of her backside, cradling her against him. She moaned softly.

"This is madness," he said, breaking away from her.

"If it is, let us lose our minds together." Her hands raked over his back. "I want this, Logan. I want you."

"No. Nothing more can happen. We've risked enough. Go back to your ball, Lady Alice."

"I don't want to. Not now. I want to stay here with you."

"You'll catch your death of cold." He stroked her arms. "You're already shivering."

"Not from the cold."

"Alice," he said, sliding his palms down her arms to her hands and giving a gentle squeeze before letting them drop. "I must go. Good night."

Before he could change his mind, he turned and slowly walked away.

❧

Alice watched him go, torn between returning to the ball and running after him. She knew if she went after him, he would probably just run faster to get away and her feet were already aching. Not quite as much as her heart. For him to admit that he wanted her, and then walk away? After that kiss? Her hand flew to her lips, reliving it. It was progress, she reassured herself. She was breaking down his defenses.

Eventually, he wouldn't be able to force himself away from her.

She walked back toward the house and stopped when she saw Lord Ralston standing in wait for her. How much had he seen?

"Lord Ralston, what a surprise. You've found me."

"Instinct brought me here, Alice. Somehow, I just knew where to find you."

"Fate, my Aunt Agatha would say. There are no coincidences."

He slipped an arm around her shoulders. "You're frozen. Here. Take my coat."

"No, I couldn't. I'll warm up inside." But he'd already slipped free of the sleeves and draped it around her.

"Nonsense. I won't have you catching your death."

"Well, thank you. It's nice to be looked after." She cast a glance back toward the courtyard, but there was no longer any sign of Winthrop, only the angel statue that had been keeping watch over them while they danced. Stifling a sigh, she followed Ralston inside.

"Maid, you there," he called to Nan once they'd walked through the door. "My lady's hair seems to have fallen. Please take a moment to tend her."

"Of course, my lord." Nan barely managed to conceal a smile.

Alice's hands flew to her tumble of loose curls. She hadn't realized what a mess she must look.

"Go on," he urged Alice. "I'll wait right here."

Alice stepped into the parlor and allowed Nan to pin her hair back up. When she emerged, Lord Ralston was waiting as promised, but he was engaged in conversation with her sister. They were sharing a laugh and didn't even notice Alice had joined them until she interrupted.

"What's funny? I hate missing out on the joke."

"Alice. Lord Ralston is a bit of an impressionist. I had no idea. He does a perfect imitation of Sir John Bradley attempting to dance."

Ralston performed a stiffly exaggerated waltz with one leg out and straightened. Sophia lost herself in a second fit of giggles.

"Sir John was injured as a young man at war," Alice observed, not finding Ralston funny. "I think it admirable that he insists upon taking a turn on the floor with his wife, who adores dancing. He could shift her off to a more capable partner, but he won't have it. He says he can't bear to see her in the arms of another."

"Yes, and all that romantic nonsense." Sophia waved off Alice's explanation. "What's a ball if you can't have a little fun?"

"A little fun? At a very kind man's expense? That's not like you, Sister. Thank you. I've warmed up." She handed Ralston back his coat, but in fact she'd only begun to feel the chill.

"I'm sorry. The fault is all mine. I didn't realize about the injury." Lord Ralston smiled and cast a sidelong glance at Sophia even as he apologized to Alice. He slipped into his coat. "Your sister is right, Lady Averford. Let's not be cruel."

Sophia blushed with apparent shame. "I'll go see about the supper service."

Lord Ralston buried his face in his hand, seemingly distraught. "I've really done it now."

"What have you done?" Alice asked.

"I've put you off." He dropped his hand and met her gaze. "I like you and now you probably won't agree to go riding with me tomorrow. I always do this."

"Do...what, exactly?"

His perfect teeth gnawed his full lower lip. "I'm awkward in social situations. I become nervous when I can't make adequate conversation and I play the fool. Suddenly, I found myself standing with our hostess, and I was at a loss for words."

"So you mocked poor Lord Bradley?"

"I suppose I do it to take the attention off my own shortcomings. There. I've said it. I'm sorry to show you the ugly truth, Lady Alice. You deserve so much better."

"Nonsense." She placed her hand on his arm consolingly. "You've been perfectly natural with me so far."

He nodded. "I find it easier to get on with you. You bring out the best in me."

"Well, then I suppose we've found the answer. It's settled. You will have to stay by me until you feel more comfortable to face the masses."

"I would like that." He took her hand and pressed it warmly between his. "You're very kind to take on a charity case."

She laughed. "Now you've gone too far. If you expect me to believe that any of the women in this room wouldn't gladly take a poor fool who looks like you under their wing? With your name and position, too? You have every advantage in a crowded ball-room, and you know it."

"I wish that was enough to bless me with easy manners and a silver tongue. Alas, even such advantages can't help me to overcome my anxieties."

She rolled her eyes. "Come along, Lord Ralston. Let's get to the table before all the good seats are gone. I don't want to have to wait until a space clears." With so many guests at the ball, supper started at one in the morning and would be served in a continuous rotation until three, with new diners taking the places vacated by the previous ones.

"I meant it about riding tomorrow," he said, pulling out a chair for her after they entered the expanded dining room. "There's a great stretch of land between Thornbrook Park and Holcomb House that's worth exploring. There's one very pretty lagoon in particular that I wanted to share with you."

"A pretty lagoon? Perhaps it had better wait for spring."

He shook his head. "It's a wonderland in winter when the pond freezes over. The perfect place for ice skating. Do you skate?"

"I haven't in years but I used to enjoy it."

"One day, we'll go skating then."

"I think it a tad early for that." She held a hand up, gesturing to stop him before he got carried away.

"You're right. The temperatures have only started to drop below freezing. In a few more weeks perhaps. The sight of the flurries got me excited. I love winter."

"What I mean is, riding, skating. You're getting ahead of expectation. You know how this goes. You're supposed to call on me first. I won't be available, of course, so you'll leave your card."

"And then come back another time, where you

will receive me oh-so-formally in the drawing room. Properly chaperoned."

She nodded. "And then perhaps you can ask me to go riding. Do you see? There's an order to these things. We can't just go skipping ahead."

"Of course we can. We're unconventional." He laughed and took her hand under the table. "Let's skip the bouillon and go straight on to the Newburg. Or we'll start with the pudding. Footman, bring my lady one of those cakes."

There weren't any cakes out yet. James, the footman, looked at Lord Ralston in confusion. "Let's not befuddle the man, Ralston. Bouillon will do, James. Thank you."

"There are always cakes. How can there be confusion?"

"Behave yourself, Lord Ralston," she chastised. "We don't want poor Sophia to get out of sorts. She likes everything to be in proper order."

"Does she now?" He looked across the table to where Sophia stood in animated conversation with one of the Sentleden girls. "I suppose she would. Let's not upset Lady Averford by any means."

"Let's not. Believe me, it's not worth the trouble."

❧

It felt like the crack of dawn when Alice finally opened her eyes the next morning, but she supposed it was past noon. Her legs ached. Her feet were still burning. How she'd danced! It was dangerous to her reputation to be the girl who kept the same partner occupied for an entire event, but she couldn't seem to chase Lord

Ralston off, no matter how she'd tried. Admittedly, she didn't put in much effort. After supper, there was no being rid of him.

On the other hand, she didn't mind his company, and he did keep Brumley away. She was safely, and most definitely, not engaged to be married. She did seem to remember that she'd finally agreed to go riding, though. Riding, not driving. She still couldn't decide if he was that much of a sportsman or merely old-fashioned. Her head still swam from the champagne. And in the fog, she remembered Winthrop's kiss.

He'd kissed her. On purpose. It was all his doing this time. She wanted to dress quickly and go off to look for him. What would he think when he saw her riding out with Ralston? Perhaps it was best that Logan did see her out with another man. He might realize that it was time to encourage her affections. Getting up too early in the day left her vulnerable to Brumley, of course. He might still be skulking about, lying in wait. She rang for Mary. Or Lucy. She'd stayed the night at Thornbrook Park and couldn't be sure if Mary had stayed to tend her or if she were to rely on Sophia's head housemaid. She supposed she would see who turned up.

A minute later, Lucy came into the room with a basket of fresh linens.

"Lucy, you're a gem. I hope you were able to get some sleep last night. How do you manage?"

"We're used to the hours, and it's always a treat to see how your lot lives, the glittering finery, the music and pageantry. Such excitement! We do get to have some fun downstairs, you know. It's not all endless drudgery."

"I'm glad. I wasn't even working last night and I feel like I'm half dead." She dropped back down to her pillows and shielded her face dramatically. "Are most of the others up?"

"Of the ones who stayed? Yes, mostly. Some are still abed." She paused. "Lord Brumley is gone."

Alice sat up. "Gone?"

Lucy's pause indicated that the maid knew the reaction her news would have. "Gone. He packed up early this morning and requested a ride to the train station. Apparently, his trip was not a success. Entirely."

"Entirely? What do you mean? Lucy, tell me."

The maid pursed her lips, seemingly reluctant to gossip, then shared the rest. "The eldest Sentleden girl got up to see him off. They seemed very friendly. I believe Lady Sentleden asked Lord Brumley to come visit them at home to help restructure their library. Brookfield isn't all that far from Forreston, after all."

"Forreston?"

"The Sentledens' estate." Lucy nodded.

"Expert on libraries that he is. Well, that ends well for Lord Brumley after all, doesn't it? I needn't worry about putting him off. June Sentleden can have him, and may she be very happy with her prize."

She could tell from Lucy's expression that there was more gossip making the rounds, but nothing that Lucy could share. Likely it involved her scandalous behavior in keeping Lord Ralston by her side all night. Not that she could help it. Why did they always blame the female in such situations?

"I need my riding habit from the Dower House,"

Alice said, changing the subject. "I've an appointment this afternoon. Can we send for it?"

"I'll get word to Mary to pack it up and have one of the footmen fetch it."

"Is Mary back at the house?"

"She returned to the Dower House with Aunt Agatha last night. Agatha expressed concern for Miss Puss with a poltergeist still in the house."

"Ah, yes." When Agatha's canary gown appeared back in the closet two days after it went missing, Agatha declared the poltergeist must be playing games with her. She claimed to have had more things go missing and suddenly return, but Alice believed it to be Agatha's usual forgetfulness and nothing more. "The poltergeist. A perfect excuse for things not being found in their usual place. I think Miss Puss could handle her own against any otherworldly being, though."

"Have you ever seen Miss Puss?" Lucy suddenly seemed uncertain.

"Only Agatha has ever seen her, as far as I know. I'm not sure she'll ever agree to leave the Dower House unless she can convince her ghost cat to follow where she goes." It was one of many problems that Alice would have to solve before she could embark on her worldly adventures—how to convince Agatha to move into Thornbrook Park, with or without Miss Puss.

Nine

SHORTLY BEFORE LORD RALSTON WAS TO ARRIVE, Alice made her appearance in the drawing room. She was surprised to find Sophia sitting alone.

"I thought you would be entertaining," Alice said, pulling on her gloves. She wore her riding habit, all black except for the white blouse that showed just under the collar, with a smart top hat. "Where is everyone?"

"Only the Sentledens were left, and they've just gone home. They're preparing for a houseguest." She turned a sharp gaze on Alice. "You can only guess who."

Alice grinned. "I wonder."

"You had an opportunity. He was yours for the taking." Sophia got up to pace. "And now we'll be wishing June Sentleden all happiness at her own wedding."

"I didn't want him." Alice shuddered at the thought. "Why would you think I would? And good for Junie, off the shelf at the ripe old age of six and twenty."

"You're not getting any younger." Sophia stamped a foot.

Alice laughed. "Darling, why does it bother you so? Do you fear I'll be a lifelong burden? I have my inheritance. There's no need for concern."

"But I want you to be happy. And close to me. If I don't find you a suitable man in Yorkshire, you'll go off to London and be so far away."

"Not so far by train. If only you could stand London."

"By train? After the Shrewsbury disaster, you think I would risk travel by train? Eighteen poor souls killed in a derailment, lest you've forgotten."

"An accident. It doesn't mean the railway is unsafe. Any excuse to avoid London." Alice knew her sister too well.

Sophia waved Alice off, not bothering to make further argument. "Or worse, you could end up in Paris. Or Italy. What if you fell in love with an American?"

Alice placed a hand to her chest, mocking horror. "The idea!"

"Laugh if you must. Mother has taxed me with seeing you comfortably settled, and I don't mean to disappoint her."

"I, on the other hand, live to let her down. Or so you would think by hearing her talk. All three weeks I was there this summer, nothing but complaints about my posture, my clothes, my disposition…"

"She only wants the best for you."

"The two of you should leave it up to me to decide what that is. Now, I'm expecting Lord Ralston, if you don't mind. We're going out for a ride."

"I'm aware."

"I don't recall telling you." She found her reflection in the window and adjusted her hat.

"He did. Last night. When you came in from the garden and stopped to fix your hair, we had a talk."

"At Sir John's expense." She turned to glare at her sister. "That talk?"

Sophia had the sense to blush. "You took longer than you realized. Your hair was a complete mess. We talked about a good many things."

"I hadn't even agreed to go riding with him yet." She began to recall the order of events. "I don't think he'd had the chance to ask."

"Nonetheless, he informed me that you would be riding out today. It gave me time to make proper arrangements."

"Arrangements? What arrangements?"

"You're an unmarried woman, Alice. An innocent. I can't let you go traipsing all over the country with a reputed rake."

"A rake? Lord Ralston?" According to him, he was too shy to be a rake. Awkward in social situations. Ha! She'd known not to believe him.

"He's too handsome not to be." Sophia shrugged. "I'm sending you out with a chaperone."

"A chaperone? To ensure I stay chaste? What harm is to come to me on the back of a horse? I don't recall you having any trouble when it came to leaving me alone with Lord Brumley. I finally find a man that I like, and you insist on making me look like a coddled young schoolgirl."

"You like Lord Ralston?" Winthrop appeared in the doorway. Her heart hammered her rib cage on sight of him.

She struggled to get hold of herself. "He's tolerable, at least."

Sophia looked from one to the other.

"Good." Winthrop said. "You should have something to talk about on your ride. I can keep a comfortable distance from the two of you without having to facilitate conversation."

"You? You're the chaperone?" She turned to Sophia. What could she say? They'd already risked looking too close.

She realized that he was dressed for riding in his dark coat and tall boots.

"No one else was available on short notice," Sophia said. "And you know I'm a terrible rider. Mr. Winthrop agreed to step in."

"Surely you have other duties, Winthrop? Tending the lemon trees? Is it safe to leave them alone?"

He laughed. "Quite safe. They're trees. It's not as if they're going to fight or eat each other. I have to ride out and survey the property anyway, as I told the countess. I do so twice a week or more to be sure that everything's in order and take an inventory of what needs to be done. I'll be killing two birds with one stone, so to speak."

She'd wondered about piquing Winthrop's jealousy. Now she would find out just what effect her flirting with another man would have on him. Unfortunately, he seemed all too pleased that she was riding with Ralston. Perhaps she'd imagined that she had any power over him. She'd never seduced a man so she hadn't any idea of her progress, or if she'd truly made any at all. Sometimes a kiss was just that—a kiss, and nothing more. Though it had felt like more. Lost in thought, she reached up to stroke her lips. A good deal more.

"Thank you, Mr. Winthrop, for taking the time," Sophia said.

"I'll be in the stable seeing to the horses." He tipped his head and strode purposefully from the room without a glance back at Alice.

A short time later, Ralston arrived, looking even more attractive than the previous night in a brown riding coat and buff trousers tucked into dark boots. After Finch announced him, he strode into the room.

"'Beauty is certainly a soft, smooth, slippery thing and therefore, of a nature which easily slips in and permeates our souls. And I further add that the good is the beautiful.'" Perhaps more pleased with his quote than with Alice and Sophia, Ralston performed a bow.

"Marvelous," Sophia mused, too easily impressed. "What an extraordinary greeting."

Alice recognized it at once as Plato. "'Beauty is a mute deception.'" She answered with Theophrastus.

"Ah, a fellow student of the Greek philosophers." He approached, took Alice's hand, and put it to his lips. "You've already donned your gloves. Will I never get to kiss your bare flesh?"

Alice snorted, a very unladylike response. "You are quite something, Lord Ralston."

For a fleeting moment, he looked hurt. She hoped he wasn't so thin-skinned. Perhaps he was merely confused by her response. Alice wondered if anyone had questioned his overtures before her.

"I thought you did that last night," Sophia said most indelicately.

"Sophia!" Alice couldn't hide her shock. Sophia, of

all people, embraced decorum. How quickly she'd let down her guard around Lord Ralston.

"I suppose you're referring to our mussed appearance in the ballroom last night when we came in from the garden? You might be surprised to learn, Countess, that I am quite the gentleman. Your sister is certainly safe with me."

Alice's eyes widened in alarm. Had he seen her with Winthrop? Was he about to expose her?

"It was the wind. Only the wind that created our startling appearance. I wouldn't take such liberties. At least"—he cast a glance at Alice—"not so soon."

"Shall we go?" Alice said, taking his arm. The sooner she got this over with, the better. Only a few hours ago, she had been looking forward to her ride with Ralston, but now with Winthrop following along and Ralston spouting philosophical quotes...her stomach turned. She doubted anything good would come of the afternoon. With her luck, she would end up alienating Ralston and putting off Winthrop for good instead of securing the temporary affection of either man.

❧

Lord Ralston, in Logan's estimation, was everything a woman could dream up as her romantic ideal— tall, strong, alternately brooding and jovial, heir to a fortune, pleasant to look upon, and titled. Why, then, did Logan feel he should warn Alice off the man? He wanted Alice to find happiness, didn't he? If Alice couldn't be swept away by such a prodigious example of a man as the Earl of Ralston, what hope did she have?

Logan straightened as he saw them striding side by side across the lawn toward the stable. He would let them set off first, give them some privacy, and follow at a safe distance. He'd promised Sophia to keep watch over them, but he hardly felt his presence would be conducive to building a rapport between them. He busied himself with examining the bridle of his own horse while the two of them prepared to ride.

Was he imagining it, or did Ralston bristle uncomfortably when he caught sight of Logan across the stalls? Logan was certain they'd never met. Grady, the stable master, led Lord Ralston's white stallion to him, paying all his attention to the earl and ignoring Alice as she struggled to swing herself up. Logan had no idea how ladies managed to ride sidesaddle. He imagined that it was deuced uncomfortable and a little dangerous, all for the sake of appearing demure. He pictured her sitting astride instead, his own Artemis, with her skirt riding up to bare a hint of her shapely legs. Keeping his distance might be more trying than he'd thought.

"Let me help you, Lady Alice." He approached and offered his hand to help her mount Brutus, the gray stallion she favored. Brutus was a good horse, not the swiftest ride but a capable jumper with a steady gait.

"Thank you, Mr. Winthrop. You're most kind." He couldn't tear his eyes away in time when she met and held his gaze. His pulse raced, remembering the feel of her in his arms.

"Lady Alice." Ralston abandoned Grady and his

horse to shoo Logan out of the way so that he could help Alice himself. As much as Logan hated to be swept aside, he liked that the man had paid attention to Alice in time. "Let's get you settled."

Logan attempted to fade into the background, but Alice looked around for him once she was properly seated. He shook his head as if to warn her off, even while he secretly delighted in her inability to ignore him.

He watched them ride out of the yard, keeping up with each other and chatting amiably. Alice was a good rider, he knew from watching her these last few years. She handled Brutus well. Once they were halfway to the orchards, Winthrop mounted Fergus, an older horse who still had some charge in him, and set off in their direction.

He wondered what they discussed, especially when Lady Alice tipped her head back in laughter and nearly lost her hat. Possibly, they'd made a solid connection at the ball last night. It seemed a bit soon for Ralston to be calling on Lady Alice for an afternoon of riding, but perhaps men like the earl could do as they chose without adhering closely to society's rigid expectations.

They turned off the path that would have taken them to Tilly Meadow Farm, which was a shame because Logan had hoped to get a look at the fence Brandon Cooper was building along the west side of the property. The lad had become indispensable to Mrs. Dennehy, the old tenant farmer's widow, in the year since she'd taken him on. Logan liked to see the farm thriving again. They had some new lambs in the pasture.

Instead, Ralston's route would probably take them across the expanse of land that separated them from Holcomb House some miles away. If Logan guessed right, Lord Ralston would bring Alice by the old McGinty place and the small pond through the woods around it, a picturesque little spot that some of the locals referred to as the Fairy Pool, popular for swimming in summer and, when the pond froze solid, a likely spot for skating.

At the urging of Lord Averford, Logan had been spending a fair amount of time at the McGinty place. The land adjoined Thornbrook Park, and Averford had bought it once McGinty died and the farm came up for sale. At a time when most estates were selling off land, Thornbrook Park was adding on. Over the summer and autumn, Logan and his crew had made repairs on the old farmhouse in case a prospective new tenant happened along. It was almost in habitable condition.

As other landowners began selling out to industry, more and more tenant farmers were being displaced. Some of them would give up and look for factory jobs, but what of others? Why not encourage one to come to Thornbrook Park and take over the old McGinty place? Demand for farm-fresh food and goods would not die out as industry took over. In fact, textile mills needed farms to supply wool or rapeseed oil. Mrs. Dennehy at Tilly Meadow kept sheep and cows, but she was bringing in profits by supplying establishments with her fine cheese and apples from the orchards. A new farmer might cultivate crops that could also bring a profit to the estate.

Try as he might to divert himself from the sight of Lady Alice riding with another man, Logan's attention kept straying back. If the riders slowed, he wondered if Alice were deliberately waiting for him, eager to lure him into the conversation. If they sped up, he assumed that Lord Ralston wanted to leave him behind, perhaps for nefarious purposes. When they took an unexpected direction, he tried to guess where they might be headed or if they were trying to stray out of his sight. It was madness. He should have insisted that Lady Averford find another chaperone.

As predicted, they ended up stopping at the Fairy Pool, dismounting, and having a look around. He didn't want to discourage the budding romance… Well, he did. But he knew he shouldn't. Instead of stopping with them, he decided to ride to the McGinty house and back. It would give them just enough time alone to charm one another, but not enough to take any regrettable actions.

෴

On their ride back, Winthrop had trailed at an even greater distance than on the way out. When Ralston broke into a charge, taunting Alice to keep up, they left Winthrop well behind.

After the ride, Ralston tried to beg an invitation to stay by insisting his horse needed a rest. Eager to regain her upper hand, Alice informed him that Averford's groom would care for his horse—predictably named Goliath, as all men seemed to suffer from the need to gift horses with names that implied size—and return him to Holcomb House once rested. Meanwhile, she whistled for Dale, the chauffeur, to give Lord Ralston a ride home.

"Thank you for the lovely afternoon," she said, seeing him into the car. She thought he might try for a kiss, but she hadn't given him the chance. When he leaned in, she held her hand out and forced him further away.

"Will I see you again? Tomorrow?" he asked hopefully.

She shrugged. "Perhaps later in the week. I'll check my schedule."

Dale lingered, giving them more chance to talk, until she met his gaze and widened her eyes at him. He got the message, sliding behind the wheel and whisking Lord Ralston away just as she spied Winthrop rounding the last hill. She hadn't spoken with him alone since their kiss. Not that she minded Ralston, but what she wouldn't give for some time alone with Winthrop. She hastened back to the stables in time to greet him on arrival.

"Was everything in order?" she asked, as he reined to a stop and dismounted.

"Lady Alice." He removed his hat and raked fingers through his dark, damp curls. "Mostly everything was in order, thank you. I hope Lord Ralston was in order as well."

"He behaved perfectly, if that's what you're asking. A gentleman."

"I should hope so."

"You know so. You saw most everything that went on, thanks to Sophia."

"Most everything. I didn't want to intrude. I tried to give you some privacy."

"I noticed. Out by the McGinty place? It looked like someone's been working on it. Do you know Lord Averford's plans?"

"Tilly Meadow has become such a success in the past year, doubling profits with the addition of the Cooper family to help Mrs. Dennehy, that Lord Averford and I thought we might put more of the land back to use. Farmers are losing their places all over England. Perhaps we can lure one here."

"Lure? You sound like you're plotting a trap. It's beautiful out there. I think any farmer would be happy to take over the land and make a home there."

"There's still work to be done."

She hazarded a step closer. "Is that where you go when I can't find you? I look for you all the time."

"You find me quite a bit." He smiled. "I'm going to have to see to my horse."

"Grady," she called out, "please see to Mr. Winthrop's horse. I believe he's wanted inside."

"I can manage…" He started to protest but Grady had already sent a groom to lead Fergus away.

"There. Now I have you all to myself." She took his arm and walked with him toward the house, wondering which way to detour so that they wouldn't have to go straight inside. The garden path?

He didn't take his arm back right away. "I'm wanted inside. You said so."

"You're wanted. I want you, Logan. We have unfinished business."

"Lady Alice, I told you, no more. In the garden, I lost my mind. With the snow falling and the amount of time I'd spent out in the cold…"

"The cold stripped you of reason? A shame. What were you doing out there? You never told me."

He looked away. "I was checking Sturridge's work, making sure the walk was safe for midnight amblers."

"That shouldn't have taken long. Sturridge is thorough in everything he does. I think perhaps you regretted not attending the ball. You came looking for me."

"You are full of yourself, Lady Alice." He must have tried to keep a straight face, but the urge to smile overwhelmed him.

"Since you're clearly going to pass up the opportunity to get me alone and take advantage of me, I guess we'd better head back inside." She dropped his arm and walked a little ahead of him. Once they were at the door, she turned back. "You'll regret this one day, Winthrop."

They were inside, about to greet Mr. Finch, before she heard his whispered answer. "I already do."

Ten

LADY ALICE EXPECTED LORD RALSTON TO VISIT THE next day, but he didn't come calling or send word. Much to her relief, he was absent the next day and the next after that as well. Perhaps he had truly taken offense at the way she'd rushed him off. She began to feel a tad remorseful that she hadn't treated him better. Not that she wanted to marry the man, but it would serve her to have a suitor that she could seduce in the event that Mr. Winthrop never came to his senses.

He would come to his senses, she assured herself. They'd become closer than she'd expected in so short a time. Not very short, she supposed. She had made her home at Thornbrook Park's Dower House for almost two years, though she'd only really been pursuing the man since last summer. What did men do when they were trying to woo ladies? They penned letters or poems. They took them on outings. They sent flowers and bought gifts. Ah, yes. She would buy Mr. Winthrop a gift. Sending flowers was out of the question, since he was around them as much as he could possibly desire and he seemed to prefer them in the ground growing, rather than out in a vase.

What would a man like Winthrop want? He didn't gamble or play cards. He worked almost all of the time. He had a watch, a very fine gold one on a chain that she'd seen him consult from time to time, usually when trying to find an excuse to be rid of her, which hadn't happened as much lately. She would have to think of something, not just anything that anyone could buy, but something to show she cared and paid attention.

But she wasn't supposed to care, she reminded herself. She was supposed to be able to walk away once she'd made her conquest, but Mr. Winthrop had declared them friends. That changed her plans a bit. Friends cared. It still didn't mean they had to marry, even if they had a little something more between them.

"Where's Agatha, and why aren't you dressed for dinner?" her sister asked as soon as Alice entered Sophia's room. Alice, bored and hoping to run into Winthrop, had come to Thornbrook Park in the late afternoon, as she often did.

"It's a little early to be dressed for dinner." Alice raised a brow. "I thought you would still be napping."

"Then why did you come if you thought me unavailable? What other reason would you have to be here?"

"Boredom." Alice threw herself down on her sister's neatly made bed. "What else?"

"You wouldn't be bored if you had a husband." Sophia dismissed Alice to turn back to her own reflection at the dressing table. She patted a puff of powder on her thin, straight nose.

Though she'd never wanted to be the beauty of the house, Alice had to admit that she still harbored some jealousy for the perfection of Sophia's nose. Alice's nose had a slight bump on the bridge, not to mention a smattering of freckles, and it turned up a smidge at the tip. She propped up on her elbows. "You're bored, and you have a husband. Or why else would you be playing with powders and spending so much time worrying over my marital prospects?"

"It's my duty to see you comfortably settled." She didn't bother to turn around, but Alice could see Sophia's reflection staring back from the mirror.

"Why not see Agatha comfortably settled? She's older and could use more help. Wouldn't it be lovely to see Agatha find true love at last?"

"At her age? I think she's a little past her prime."

Alice sat up and shrugged. "I don't know. There's probably a lonely old man out there somewhere. Agatha is nothing if not interesting. Do you know she's had lovers?"

With that news, Sophia actually turned around in her chair. "No! Agatha?"

"She says she has had quite a few. It's why she never married. She was ruined before the age of eighteen. A Lord Potters-something-or-other whisked her away to elope, but never married her. Then she rattled off a list of men who came after him."

"A list of men?" Sophia's jaw dropped. "I had no idea. I'm astonished. Truly amazed. Aunt Agatha! I thought she'd been left on the shelf."

"So did I, but apparently not. I wonder if it's why Father finds her so objectionable."

"I always thought it was her dabbling in the spirit world, but perhaps you're right. Perhaps it was her promiscuity. It's a wonder Mother let her in the house, let alone around us as impressionable girls."

Alice felt a sudden pang. "They share the unshakable bond of sisterhood. Would you cast me out if I had an illicit affair?"

She was not encouraged by the fact that Sophia took a minute to answer. "Of course not. You would always be welcome at Thornbrook Park."

"Thank you." Alice was greatly relieved when her sister answered as Alice had hoped she would.

"Not that it would ever come to that." Sophia laughed and turned back to her own image. "You'll be married before you have a chance to create a scandal. Lord Ralston is coming to dinner."

"Ralston? You didn't tell me. Now I see why you were eager for me to be dressed. You want to see what I'm wearing to have time to make a change in case you don't approve."

Sophia smiled and did not deny it. "Ralston went out this morning with Gabriel and Lord Holcomb. They'll return when they've shot enough birds. No doubt Lady Holcomb will arrive shortly for tea."

"Let's send for Agatha. It's always so much more fun to entertain Lady Holcomb when she's trying her best to keep her distance from Aunt Agatha. Perhaps Agatha can bring her tarot deck."

"You are incorrigible, Alice."

"So I've been told."

❧

At her sister's insistence, Alice wore a black satin skirt that gave her the appearance of a tiny nipped-in waist, paired with a low-cut ivory lace blouse draped in translucent cranberry silk. The overall effect flattered her figure, enhancing her meager bosom so that she hardly recognized herself, but she liked what she saw. Sophia's maid piled Alice's hair on her head in a mass of russet curls.

"For the finishing touch." Sophia handed her a tube of lip rouge.

"Oh, I don't think so." Alice waved her off.

"Trust me. He won't be able to resist you." Sophia meant Lord Ralston, of course, but Alice imagined Mr. Winthrop finding himself inexplicably drawn to her.

"All right." She sighed. "And perhaps a necklace. Do you have one I could borrow? Maybe the garnet?"

"No necklace. It will become an unnecessary distraction. Perhaps a bracelet." She gestured to Alice's bare neck and shoulders, and bowed her head to look her collection over. Finally, she handed Alice a thick diamond cuff.

After sliding it on her wrist, Alice immediately dropped her hand low, a slight exaggeration. "How much does this thing weigh?"

Sophia shrugged. "It was a gift from Lord Averford to make up for one of our arguments last summer."

There'd been so many that Alice doubted her sister could pinpoint the exact one.

"I hope you forgave him appropriately."

"Alice." Sophia shook her head. "You have much to learn about marriage."

Sophia's maid laughed. "I think Lady Alice has it

right. Perhaps one day soon, she'll be handing advice to you."

Sophia pursed her lips in disapproval. "That will be all, Mrs. Jenks."

Jenks's eyes widened with the realization that she'd overstepped her bounds. She curtsied quickly and left the room.

"Shall we?" Sophia asked. Alice nodded and followed her sister.

Alice's heart picked up speed when she noticed Mr. Winthrop among the gentlemen when she reached the drawing room. He stood facing her, in conversation with another man. When he caught sight of her, his eyes lit with a purely sexual charge she could feel clear across the room. His companion must have noticed, because he turned to see what had occasioned such a response. It was Lord Ralston. Alice stifled a wave of panic. What must the two of them have to say to each other? She ignored them and found her place among the ladies.

Aunt Agatha, wearing her favored canary and blue, regaled them with the tale of the poltergeist, and how that playful spirit had taken and finally returned her gown. Lady Holcomb's hands shook with what Alice supposed might be terror.

"Surely, you misplaced the gown," Lady Holcomb said, her voice wavering.

"Misplaced? I always hang it in the same spot. It was there in the morning and gone by afternoon. Tell them, Alice. You saw it, too."

"I saw that the gown was gone, yes. And Agatha told me she found it sometime later, hanging right where it was supposed to be."

"A poltergeist. I've never heard of such a thing. But I do believe I've had some items go missing through the years. I've always blamed the maid." Lady Holcomb gripped her long string of beads tightly, probably to stop the shaking.

"They're tricky little spirits," Agatha explained. "I tend to think they're the ones who have died young, perhaps in the teen years. No malevolence, all play. I've researched the family history, and I believe this one could be young George. He supposedly drowned in a vat of wine when he fell in trying to sneak a taste."

"Horrible," Lady Holcomb muttered. "Simply horrible. His poor mother."

Sophia put an end to Agatha's storytelling. "Let's go in."

"Aren't we waiting for the Thornes?" Alice asked.

"They're in London. Eve had a meeting with her publisher."

As if on cue, the gentlemen approached to lead them in, but Alice was chagrined to see that Winthrop was no longer among them.

"No nursemaid for you tonight, Lady Alice." Ralston offered his arm. "I have you all to myself."

"To yourself in a crowded dining room. I believe I'm quite safe."

"Exactly where I want you, feeling safe so that you'll let your guard down." He smiled.

"I'm ever on my guard, Lord Ralston. What did you mean by my 'nursemaid'?"

"That fellow Winthrop. The one your sister sent to follow us. He couldn't stay for dinner. He has business

to attend. The man says we're due for snow. A storm.
It seemed perfectly clear outside to me."

"The temperatures have dropped. It has been
very cold these past few days." She tried to appear
completely disinterested in Winthrop. "I'm surprised
I haven't seen you. I thought you meant to make a
nuisance of yourself."

He helped her into a chair. "Exactly why I haven't
been around. You seemed all too eager to be rid of me
after our ride, and I wanted to give you a chance to
miss me. Did you?"

"I probably shouldn't confess that I did." It wasn't a
lie. With Winthrop keeping himself scarce, she'd been
bored. She hadn't realized just how much she'd come
to rely on the estate agent's companionship. "Did you
find it easy to stay away?"

"I filled my time with activities so I wouldn't be
bad company to my aunt and uncle. No one likes a
morose lover." Their conversation was temporarily
halted as he found his seat across the table.

"A shame about the Thornes," Lady Holcomb said.
"I always enjoy their company."

"Jilting us for London." Sophia shuddered at
mention of London. She hated the place. "I hope it's
productive for them."

"I do look forward to her next book." Lady
Holcomb reached for her wineglass.

"She couldn't put the last one down," Lord
Holcomb said. "I begged her, 'Darling, come to bed.'
She would always answer, 'But one last page.'"

Alice looked across the table to find Lord Ralston's
gaze trained on her.

"It was quite a romantic story." Lady Holcomb blushed. "I do like a good romance. Speaking of romance, my nephew has been spending quite a lot of time at the Furbish estate. Is it their horses you find so fascinating, Harry, or is it the company?"

Lady Matilda Furbish, age eighteen, was pretty enough, Alice supposed, though she had never seemed very bright when Alice had spoken with her. Perhaps Ralston was hoping to make Alice miss him after all. She arched a brow in his direction.

"The horses, of course, Aunt. As you know, I'm making a fair number of changes at Kenterly. I would like to add to the stables. Lord Furbish has some fine stallions, but I was looking for a gentle mare suitable for a lady to ride."

"Ridiculous," Alice declared. "Do you imagine that a lady can't manage a fiery stallion?"

"I doubt I could if I were expected to ride sidesaddle. I don't fault the women riding, but the style in which they are forced to ride."

She nodded. "You make a good point. It does make riding a challenge."

"Why, Alice, I'm astonished." Lord Averford paused, fork in air, before diving into his trout. "I don't think I've ever heard you concede an argument so easily. Not even a counterpoint for Lord Ralston here?"

Sophia coughed into her napkin. Alice suspected she might have kicked her husband under the table. "Alice is a very agreeable girl. She has such a good nature."

"This Alice?" Lord Averford went on. "Are you mad? Alice is—" Ah, that must have been the kick.

Averford recoiled. "Very sweet. Of course. Yes. I must have been thinking of someone else."

"The Furbish girl, Lady Matilda, she is the best-natured young woman I've had the pleasure to meet. Such manners. They came to dinner twice this past week, and each time I found her more agreeable than the last. I daresay you noticed her, too, Harry?" For the second time, Lady Holcomb seemed to go out of her way to push Matilda Furbish as a match for Lord Ralston. Alice began to wonder what Lady Holcomb had against her.

"She's a lovely girl," Ralston acknowledged, his gaze trained on Alice. "But she's so young yet. I believe she's lacking the kind of irrepressible spirit and confidence that a woman gains with age and experience."

"Lady Alice," Averford observed, "I believe Ralston has just called you old."

Again, Lord Averford jumped a little in his seat. Sophia narrowed her eyes in her husband's direction. Alice wondered if her brother-in-law might soon be in the market for another bracelet. "I'm beginning to miss the Thornes myself," he said. "I can usually count on my brother to say the wrong thing before I do."

Ralston laughed along with Lord Averford, and Lord Holcomb joined in. The women turned their attention to the arrival of the next course.

After the very quiet second half of the dinner, the ladies followed Sophia's lead and passed through to the drawing room. Before the men could join them, Mr. Winthrop came into the room. His hair was damp from being out of doors, even though he'd probably worn a hat, and he still wore his gloves and overcoat.

Heat rushed to her core when Winthrop fixed an intimate stare on her, but abruptly he turned to face her sister instead.

"Lady Averford, a word please." Together, they went to the far side of the room. He held the window curtain open and gestured outside. Sophia nodded along. Then he dropped the curtain and walked away, increasing Alice's disappointment. She'd hoped he would join them for cordials.

The men came in the room and Lady Averford addressed them all.

"Our agent just came in to inform me that the snow promises to be deep. It has only been falling for a little while, but it's accumulating quickly. The wind is beginning to pick up. You're all welcome to stay the night. If you choose to turn the invitation down, I must insist you leave before it gets much later and the roads become impassable."

"We should stay," Ralston said. "Let's stay. We'll have a jolly good time snowed in. How cozy." He looked at Alice and winked.

"Dear, no." Lady Holcomb protested immediately. "My little Dinkums is home. He gets so afraid during storms. I can't bear to leave him. If it's safe to go now, let's go. Before it's too late."

"Darling, of course," Lord Holcomb agreed. "She dotes on that little dog so."

"I'll have the driver bring your car around." Sophia smiled.

"Your maid is with Dinkums." Ralston waved his hand dismissively, clearly irritated with the news. "He'll hardly know you're gone."

"Oh, my silly nephew." Lady Holcomb placed a hand on Ralston's cheek. "Nothing soothes quite like a mother's love. No, we must go. I'm only glad your man came in to warn us before it was too late. Good night, Lady Averford. And thank you."

Ralston held back while the others walked to the door. He cradled Alice's elbow in his palm. "I mean to see you again soon. I've missed you too much these past few days."

"I'm certain that Lady Matilda helped to lessen your pain."

"She's nothing to you. You must know how I feel. Snow won't keep me away. Good night, my sweet dove."

He leaned in, kissed her forehead, and walked away quickly as if by hesitating another moment, he would be lost. Alice remained in the drawing room. The others could see him off. When she turned, she saw Winthrop standing in the opposite doorway across the room. But before she could call out to him, he disappeared.

Eleven

For two days, the snow came down hard and fast, and Logan had barely a moment to stand still and breathe. Keeping the walks and roadways clear was a monumental job, and he was the one maintaining the schedule around the clock. Many times, sensing the crew was tiring, he went out with a shovel and worked alongside them.

After midnight, he rode over to Tilly Meadow to make sure they were all well on the farm. They proved to be a merry lot, well-stocked and ready to manage with the storm brewing. The animals were all fed and in their stalls, and the boys were out shoveling when he'd arrived, a task they'd evidently kept up through the night. He had to leave his horse in Brandon Cooper's care and take one of theirs back to Thornbrook Park, fearing the labored horse wouldn't survive both ways through the increasingly deep and drifting snow.

Once back in the safety of the house, he didn't dare return to his cottage before thawing some before the fire.

"You look like a snowman," Alice said, appearing in the room as if she could sense him there. "I'm glad you're safe. I was worried."

"What are you doing out of bed, Lady Alice? It's two in the morning." She wore only a nightgown, albeit what looked to be a thick flannel one, under her heavy cotton wrapper.

"I can't sleep with the snow. It stirs a liveliness inside me. I wish I could go out in it. So beautiful."

"Not tonight. The wind is brutal." He could still feel the ice clinging to his hair. "It's not fit for man nor beast."

"And yet you went riding all the way out to the farm."

"It's my duty to check on the tenants."

"It's not your duty to get killed in the process. You might have been stuck out there."

"Believe me, I know the dangers." He shook, unsure if it was the chill from outside or the fact that she kept stepping closer.

"Look at you. You're soaked." She thought to ring for a footman, then reconsidered with the lateness of the hour and the idea that she could keep Winthrop all to herself. "Tell me you wore gloves."

"Of course." He rubbed his hands near the fire. "I'm not daft."

She nodded. "Very well. Remove your clothes."

"Somehow, I always knew you would get around to saying that, but I didn't imagine it would be quite like this," he joked inappropriately, the cold making him careless.

She fetched a blanket, a decorative knitted thing

from the back of a couch. "I won't look. I'll turn around. Right now, I'm only interested in keeping you warm. By no means do I intend to let you return to your cottage alone."

"Yes, my lady," he said obediently from between chattering teeth. How was it possible that he felt even colder? With Alice standing so close, even barking orders, one would think he would have instantly warmed. Even love had its limits, he supposed.

Love? Did he love her? What madness. He must have frozen his brain.

Only because the hour was late and he was so wet and cold, he stepped into the corner, stripped off his wet things, and wrapped up in the ridiculous excuse for a blanket. Once he'd wrapped in it, he realized the thing was full of holes, deliberate gaps in the lacy pattern, but holes nonetheless. Her gaze was drawn to his cock, and he realized that part of him was getting warm. Very warm. He hunched over in an attempt to protect her from the unseemly sight. "You said you wouldn't look."

"When you were undressing. By now, I assumed you were properly covered." She flashed a shy grin, a blush heating her cheeks. "I think I'm in danger of becoming unraveled."

He curled into a chair, the blanket bunched up around him. "You can leave me now, Alice. I'll find my own way back once I'm warm enough."

"You'll do no such thing. There are a number of guest rooms at the ready, and Captain Thorne has left some clothes behind that I'm sure will fit you well enough. I must insist that you stay. Don't force me to alert the others." She crossed her arms over her chest. "You must promise me you'll stay the night here. There's nothing more to be done until morning. You're no good to anyone if you don't get some sleep. At last. I believe you haven't had a wink since the snow started."

"Are you keeping track of me, Alice?"

"I confess that I do pay attention to your comings and goings, yes. I like to think that you're all too aware of me, too. Admit it, Logan. You can't help yourself when it comes to me."

"That's where you're wrong," he said, managing to be serious at last. "I can. I will. It's not always easy, I'll grant you, but I am a man of honor, reputation be damned, and I will not tarnish you. I will not be the one to ruin your hopes with my own carelessness."

"Ruin my hopes? The only thing I hope for is to be free. Always. The only way you could ruin my hopes is to imprison me."

"Love can be a prison, Alice. I know it more than most. One day, perhaps, you'll understand. Now go to bed. I can see myself upstairs. I promise you that I will. Think of the consequences if anyone else were to see us like this…"

"You're right, of course. Now that I know you're safe, and you've given me your word, I will go. But only because I know you must be exhausted, and I really do want you to get some sleep. Good night, Logan."

"Good night, Alice. Sweet dreams."

❧

Her dreams had been sweet. She recalled every inch of his body that she could see and committed them all to memory. The broad chest, the rippled abdomen, his arms corded with thick muscles still throbbing from overexertion. And lower, the sight of him growing erect beneath the blanket's loose-woven strands. She dreamed of him all night and into the next day. She fantasized about him making love to her at last.

The fantasy might be all she would ever have, a harsh fact she faced in her waking hours. Despite whatever had happened in his past, he was too principled, too good, to do anything she might regret. Her only hope lay in convincing him that she would never, ever regret giving her innocence to him. Who dared to tell her otherwise?

In her heart, she knew he would be gone before she woke up. There would be no bumping into him at breakfast, no chance meeting in the hall. The snow had stopped. The sun was up. Thornbrook Park buzzed with activity, the workers intent on restoring the grand house to business as usual. Winthrop had probably already gone to the farm again and back. She pictured him out in the snow, ordering men here and there, jumping in and doing some of the harder jobs himself. It's the kind of man he was, and she… admired him. She admired him greatly. Of course she did. They were friends.

Once dressed, she went to see what was happening in the rest of the house. If she were at the Dower House, she would be enjoying a quiet breakfast, with Agatha trying to predict what the rest of the week would bring and slipping bits of bacon to Miss

Puss that would remain on the floor until Mary swept up. Agatha was probably driving Thornbrook Park's servants wild with requests to read their auras or give them a tarot spread. But when Alice got to the breakfast room, she realized that no one was up yet. Mrs. Hoyle informed her that the countess was still in bed. Agatha had yet to arrive. Even Lord Averford, usually up early to hunt, had remained in his room.

"Snow puts people in a lazy frame of mind," Mrs. Hoyle said, glowering at one of the footmen who scurried by with a tray of silver. "I don't expect any of the family to be up for a few hours yet."

"Snow inspires me to be active," Lady Alice explained. "I want to make snow angels, go sledding, have a snowball fight. I don't suppose you would spare any of the servants for my amusement?"

Mrs. Hoyle shook her head. "They all have more important duties, Lady Alice. You wouldn't want to keep them from their work."

"No, of course. Wouldn't want that." She rolled her eyes. Asking about Winthrop wouldn't do, she supposed.

"I almost forgot." Mrs. Hoyle reached in her pocket and turned over a slip of paper. "Mr. Finch took a message for you earlier this morning."

"A message for me?" She opened it. It was from Ralston, up early in pursuit of her, or up early and managing to appear to be in pursuit. He asked her to meet him at "their little lagoon" at three and to bring her skates. "Did he telephone?"

"He rode here. Perhaps Lord Ralston shares Mr. Finch's mistrust of modern conveniences." Hoyle flashed a rare grin. "Or I suppose he was on his way somewhere. He didn't stay more than a moment."

"I'm sorry that I missed him."

"If you'll excuse me, I have duties to attend. Bill will be along with pastries and fresh hot water for tea."

"Thank you, Mrs. Hoyle." After breakfast, Alice had a few hours to kill before heading off to the lagoon. Doubtless, it would be a long walk in the snow.

Hours later, she was dressed for skating in her woolens and a becoming violet coat and hat, and on the way. Her skates still fit, a miracle. Alice was glad she'd thought to bring them along to Thornbrook Park, though she hadn't had an opportunity to use them in her years there.

She found her way to the lagoon with surprising ease considering how different the woods looked all caked in snow. Lucy had told her of a short cut through the Tilly Meadow farmland that made for a picturesque scene. It had started snowing again, adding to her good cheer. At least she had someone to enjoy activities with her. She would rather it be Winthrop than Ralston, but Winthrop had the enormous responsibility of managing a large estate. Ralston was a man of leisure, and he wasn't there yet. She looked around. No sign of him.

She sat on a snowbank to lace her skates while she waited, and then decided to test the ice and warm up. The pond was indeed frozen solid, and she still possessed the ability to glide across the ice gracefully. Her ankles had grown weak, though, and she decided to wait for Ralston before she tired herself out. No doubt he would be along at any moment.

~

It was growing dark by the time Logan got back to the house. The new snow required him to offer encouragement and motivation to Thornbrook Park's overtaxed grounds crew. They'd barely had enough time to recover from the previous storm, and this one looked to be worse.

Inside, he meant to check on the lemon trees in the conservatory. Sturridge had been doing his best to keep them warm and would have sent word if they'd started to decline, but he thought it best to have a look. Along the way, he passed Lord and Lady Averford sharing tea in the drawing room and stopped to give them news on the storm's progress.

"It looks to be a bad one, worse perhaps than the last. The crew is prepared, but I told them to be sure to rest in turns and to remember that we can catch up with it once it slows down. We don't need any injuries or health risks. It's even colder tonight than it was yesterday."

"No indeed," Lady Averford agreed. "Let it snow. Be sure Mrs. Mallows prepares a hearty stew to feed them."

"Done. She has stew simmering and fresh bread in the oven. I've told them to come in within the hour to rest and eat."

"Very good, Winthrop," Lord Averford said, looking eager to get back to private conversation with his wife.

It was encouraging to see them getting on well. Logan knew that the staff wished for another baby in the house, an heir. As much as everyone liked the earl's brother, Captain Thorne, the idea of a new baby and more direct heir held a great deal of appeal.

As soon as Logan took his leave, he headed for the conservatory, but ran into a befuddled Mr. Finch along the way.

"What's wrong, Finch?"

"We've had a curious call on the telephone, that infernal machine. With the static on the line, I couldn't hear well but I believe Lord Ralston meant to beg forgiveness from Lady Alice for canceling their plans. She had a message from him this morning to meet at their 'lagoon' at three o'clock. You don't suppose…"

Winthrop's heart dropped like cannonball to his gut. "Did she go? Has she been out all this time?"

"What lagoon?" Finch looked puzzled. "We have no lagoon."

"He means the Fairy Pool, I think. The servants enjoy bathing there in summer, and they call it the Fairy Pool. It's a secluded pond near the old McGinty farm."

"Yes, I know the one. As far away as that?"

"It's not a bad walk when you know the short cut through Tilly Meadow lands but quite a bit longer than I would like for someone who has been out for hours. It's just past five. The snow has picked up, along with the wind." Logan fought a wave of fear. If the pond hadn't quite frozen solid…"She's out there alone."

"Maybe she's at the Dower House."

"She could be."

Mr. Finch tipped his head, considering.

"I'll check on the way out, but I wager she's

not," Logan said. "She would have gone. This was her chance to be out in the snow. I'll go after her. It won't take long on horseback. I'll be sure that she's safe. Please, not a word to her sister. I don't want the countess unduly upset."

"But the snow's getting deep."

"She'll be cold, but likely unharmed. If she's out, I'll get her back to the Dower House to warm up as fast as I can."

Logan left at once. The car could get him close, but not if the roads were bad. He would be more successful on horseback. Grady had kept one of the big plow horses saddled in case one was needed for an emergency, and Logan declared his purpose to be of urgent importance. His stallion might have been quicker, but the plow horse could progress through the heavy snow without tiring as fast.

As he passed through the woods, he searched for signs of her, but any footprints in the snow had been covered over or blown away. At the Fairy Pool, he breathed a sigh of relief to see the ice intact, no sign of anyone falling through. He was about to leave when he spied skates left at the edge of the pond. He retrieved them. She'd been there. If she had headed home, he would have passed her on the way. There was a slim chance that she'd thought to go to the old McGinty house for shelter. He had told her that he'd been working on it. He headed there, hoping he was right and refusing to consider any alternative.

Once he arrived, he jumped from his horse and ran in, a tremendous weight lifting off his chest when he saw her there, huddled under a tarp in front of the fireplace and a fire she'd apparently given up on starting. Her teeth chattered and she struggled to warm herself, but she seemed none the worse for wear.

"Good God, Alice. I was worried sick."

She looked at him, taking a minute to find her voice. "I'm not an idiot, Logan. I had the sense to seek shelter when I lost feeling in my hands."

"You were fool enough to wait too long for Ralston." In two strides, he was at her side. Without a word, he pried her arms from the tight wrap and examined her fingers. "It looks like circulation is coming back. No frostbite. Good thinking to come here."

"You said you'd been working on the place. It was my nearest hope."

He looked into the fireplace, recently redone in stone, where he'd left some stacked wood. "I'll light this. A moment."

He bent to retrieve more of the wood he'd meant to build with—he could get more—and stacked it nearby for burning. He'd left a flint on the mantel, but she must have overlooked it. Within minutes, he had a full, burning blaze.

"Oh, that's heaven. You're an angel," Alice said.

He was a man in love. He recognized the symptoms at once now that fear of losing her had been added to the mix. Damn, how had it happened? How could he stop it? If it was confined to a limb, he would cut it off in one fell swoop before the contagion spread. But it ran through him, his very lifeblood, and he could no more drain himself of love for her than end his life itself.

"You stay here by the fire. I'm going to tend my horse."

"What will you do with him?"

"The barn has been boarded up well, no loose holes. I've got some old blankets there. I'll dry him, brush him down, and cover him up. Without the wind howling in at him, he should survive the night comfortably enough."

He went and returned as fast as he could, bringing some extra blankets back with him.

"They smell of horse, but we should be able to ignore that soon enough. It really doesn't matter as long as we're warm again. The snow is falling faster, and the wind has whipped up to a frenzy."

"What will we do?"

He shrugged. "Stay the night here. At least through the worst of it. Finch knows I've come out to look for you, but I advised him not to tell your sister. It wouldn't do to have the whole house out on a night like this."

"Which is exactly what Sophia would do if she feared for my safety. She'd send out every last available man and possibly some of the women."

"Exactly. But you're safe now. Together, we'll brave the elements. Or, whichever elements threaten us in here."

"It's a sound structure. I can see where you've been passing the hours when I couldn't find you anywhere on Thornbrook grounds."

"Not enough time recently. Roof, windows, walls. This is the original floor." He gestured to the smooth stones beneath their feet. "I rebuilt the hearth, planning to keep warm enough while I worked through the winter. The top level is barely framed, the kitchen is gutted, and, well—you can see there's still much to be done."

"But we're out of the wind and snow, and we have a fire. Tonight, it's all I could ask. Well, maybe not all. Those horsey blankets are certainly warmer than this."

She tossed the tarp at his feet. He was concerned to see that she still wore her wet clothes. He should have a noticed when he took her hands earlier, but he had been more concerned for her immediate safety.

"Lady Alice, what's this? I thought you were the authority on thawing snowmen. You're soaked. Remove your clothes."

"I beg your pardon?"

"It's what you had me do. Remove your wet clothes immediately. We can't have you catching your death."

She met his gaze, all too eager to accept the challenge. She didn't cower or try to hide. She stood ramrod straight in front of him and undid her buttons one at a time. Once her coat was undone, she tossed it aside and started on her blouse, never taking her gaze from his.

"I'm so frozen. You'll have to help me." In only her underthings, she crooked a finger and beckoned him nearer. When he was close enough, she took his hand and placed it on her stomach, over her corset. "Is this damp, or just cold?"

"Damp," he answered, his voice hoarse. "It will have to come off. All of it."

She nodded agreement and turned, her back to him, her pert backside tempting him. "Unlace me, please."

His hands trembled as he obeyed her, the confining

garment finally falling away, leaving only her chemise and petticoats, woolen stockings, and pantalets, he saw, once she turned to face him and slid the petticoat down her narrow hips. The pantalets lasted only a second longer, and then her russet thatch was exposed, glowing like a flame against her snow-white flesh. His breath caught. Then she gripped the bottom of her chemise and slowly peeled upward until her breasts bounced free, two peach-tipped mounds of glory.

"You're beautiful, Alice. Exquisite."

"And you're going to catch your death. Your turn. The snow that covered you has melted and now you're a wet mess, too. Off with your clothes, every last stitch."

He could hardly deny the naked goddess before him. Holding her gaze, he stripped, losing his overcoat and coat, unbuttoning his shirt and his trousers, and letting them ease down his hips. She watched, eyes wide, while he removed every last stitch and finally stood facing her, as naked as she was.

"This won't do," he said, stepping toward her and taking her in his arms. "We need to warm each other." Her skin felt so wondrous against him, her breasts, the nipples pebbling to scratch his chest. He wrapped a blanket around them and eased her down in front of the fire.

"Better," she said. "I'm feeling very warm now."

Facing each other, his gaze held hers. And in that moment, he was lost.

He kissed her. Softly. Slowly. Savoring the feel and taste of her. The kiss grew more insistent, and his senses came back to him. He stopped.

"Stay here, in the blanket. I'll be right back."

He extricated himself to lay their clothes out closer to the fire so that they would dry faster. He draped the tarp over the blanket for extra warmth, and slid back in beside her.

"Necessity," he said, more to himself than to her. "It's necessity."

Deep down, he wondered: If he'd tried to get her home, would they have safely reached their destination? Chances are, they would have. But there was an equal and worse chance that the snow had fallen too deep, the horse would tire too quickly, and the bitter cold would overwhelm them. They could have arrived home without perishing along the way, certainly, but what of the horse? And there was an honest risk of lost limbs from frostbite. He was doing the right thing, he tried to reassure himself. But it was impossible to trust his instincts when every urge drove him toward the woman in his arms. Alice. So close, and yet...

He turned, his back to her. It was the only way he could control his desire. But she curved her body around his, embracing him.

"I know you're trying not to touch me, Logan, and I admire your restraint. I'm sorry if being so close to me is testing you. But I need your warmth. You understand. Necessity, as you said."

"Necessity," he agreed. "It's best if we try to get some sleep while our clothes dry. With any luck, the storm will let up and we can dress and try to get home."

"In the dark? It's probably best we stay the night."

"I can find my way in the dark. I know these woods like I know my own home."

She laughed. "I managed to invade your space there, too. Try as you might, you can't get away from me, Logan."

"God knows, I've tried, Lady Alice." He laughed along with her. "Good night."

He prayed he would find peace enough to sleep with the feel of her body against him.

Twelve

ALICE HAD NO IDEA WHAT TIME IT WAS WHEN SHE woke. It remained dark and the fire still blazed, leaving her to doubt she'd slept long. But she had slept. Logan's breathing remained steady.

"Are you awake?" she whispered, propping up on an elbow and leaning over him. She doubted he would answer if he were. His eyes remained closed and his mouth slightly open. She was used to seeing it in that hard, grim line. He wasn't a conventionally handsome man, but his rough-hewn features appealed to her all the more for his lack of perfection. At rest, he looked almost angelic, all the tension drained out of his features.

He'd done an admirable job of keeping his hands off her against all temptation. She knew he was tempted, or else she would be beside herself with the impossibility of her situation. He'd kissed her, and he'd turned from her. She doubted it was easy for a man to deny himself, but Logan was nothing if not determined and dutiful. She admired him for his tenacity. She might even be more than a little in love with him, but she knew the impossibility of that situation. Even if she loved him more than life itself, she could never marry him, an estate manager, and live in the cottage on her sister's estate. For eternity.

She had complete respect for the man and his position. It didn't matter what anyone thought. If her choosing an estate manager would be nothing more than a shock or disappointment to her parents, she would probably resign herself to making it a reality. But to be rooted in one spot? It would never do. She had her dreams of adventure, and she wasn't prepared to sacrifice them for anything or anyone. Not even for love. There could be no love, only the physical act. She wouldn't get a better chance than this, a naked man at her side, and she wasn't about to let it slip away.

Of course, she would have to convince him that his job was not at risk. No one need ever know. There were ways to be careful about things. She'd read about them in Eve Thorne's *Kama Sutra*. Two consenting adults alone in the wilderness, what was the harm?

She got up to put more wood on the fire. Once she woke him, she wanted nothing to disturb them. She shifted the blankets so that she could get in on the other side, facing him. With one arm around him and leaning on the other, she raked her nails lightly along his back, enjoying the intimate contact. Nothing had ever felt as good as Logan's skin flush against hers. How much better would it feel to have him inside her?

But first, there might be some pain. She'd steeled herself to the possibility. He was larger than she'd imagined. If she hadn't read up a bit on the subject, she might be afraid that he would never fit. Armed with knowledge and a faith in nature, she jostled him a little to wake him up.

"Logan," she said, her face so close to his that their noses touched. "Logan, I'm cold."

Her breasts were flush against his solid chest and her nipples reacted to the contact, becoming hard as pebbles. She wrapped a leg around him so that they were as close as they possibly could be everywhere. His cock hardened against her hip, but she stifled the urge to trail her hand down and explore. For now. Though, if he failed to wake…

"Logan?"

His eyes shot open, but he didn't back away. His arm curved around her and he pulled her closer, perhaps a protective instinct. "What's wrong? Are you unwell?"

"I'm cold. I thought I would be warmer if we got closer."

"Closer." More awake now, he eased away from her. "I think we're close enough. I—"

"Logan." She cupped his whisker-roughened cheek in her hand. "I want you to make love to me. Please."

He sat up suddenly, baring his sculpted torso to the night. "No. We can't."

"We can. Why not? I want to. No one needs to know." Her gaze trailed over his broad shoulders and down his rippled abdomen.

He ran a hand through mussed dark hair. His every muscle tensed. "You will know. I will know. Your future husband—"

"There won't be one. I don't want to marry. I've told you." She sat up, too, damn the cold. She had to plead her case. "But that doesn't mean I don't want to know what love is. Physical love. I should get to experience it once, at least. And I want you, Logan."

"Why, Alice? Why me?"

She reached for his hand and laced her fingers with his. "Because you're wise and responsible, and you're my friend. I wouldn't trust just anyone. But I know I can trust you. And I know you like me, despite your attempts to push me away."

"That hasn't happened in far too long. My mistake, perhaps. I should have made it clearer to you, Alice, that—" He looked in her eyes and he froze. Whatever he'd planned to say, he lost his words for a moment, and then averted his eyes and forced them out. "It can't be like that between us. I'm a man and you're a girl, and we've already gone much too far."

He propped his elbows on his knees and buried his face in his hands.

"I'm not a girl." She kneeled next to him, her hands at her sides. "I'm a woman. Look at me."

"I'm not looking." He kept his head down.

She laughed, not out of humor but from sheer nerves. "You can't say that you don't want me. Please, don't lie to me. We've been so close."

"No need for lies. You're beautiful, Alice. Exquisite. If circumstances were different—"

"Circumstances are in our favor. Don't you see? We're alone. No one will ever know, and why should they? I would never speak a word against you, and there's no need for any further attachment between us. We're friends. It's enough for me, and I suspect quite enough for you. And I want to do this. I really, really want to make love to someone I know and trust. You wouldn't have me go to someone else with such a request, would you? One of the stablehands or a footman? A stranger at a tavern?"

"You wouldn't." He looked up at last, concern in his narrowed gaze. "It would be foolish, possibly even dangerous."

"Exactly. But I will know what it is to make love, and I won't choose someone who would only insist on marriage first. You know how determined I can be."

"God, Alice." He reached for her, tangling his fingers in her tousled hair. "Lovely, foolish Alice."

Sensing her victory, she leaned into him, pressing her body against him. "Logan, yes. Please."

"Alice." All tenderness gone, he took her roughly by the arms and rolled her under him on the blankets. He shook his head. "I should have scared this out of you a long time ago. I'm not a man to be trifled with."

"Of course not. I'm not trifling." She wrapped her arms around him and brought her lips to the tender vein that pulsed at the base of his neck, kissing him there as she shifted her hips beneath his weight.

"Dammit, Alice." Savagely, he jerked her arms up and pinned them over her head. Losing control, she bucked against him, desperate to feel him at the core of her, spreading her legs around him and pulling him tighter against her.

"Please, Logan," she begged. He couldn't hold her arms and push her legs off him at once, though she could see him trying to find a way in his mind. "Take me. Ravish me."

The need inside transformed her into a monster—greedy, fierce, and desperate. She'd always imagined lovemaking to be tender and sweet. The ferocity rising inside her took her by surprise. She wanted him to do his worst. She fed on the roughness. God help her.

She wiggled under him, the limited movement excruciating.

"You're testing me." He bit his lip, his struggle to control her proving futile. He could hold her arms, but he couldn't stop her from moving her hips.

"I'm needing you. Inside me."

He let go of her hands and extricated himself, a sigh escaping him as he sat beside her. She sat up, refusing to be put off. On her knees, she rose up to meet his lips, kissing him with all her might until he kissed her back, his tongue in her mouth, questing. She sucked his lower lip and rose up taller on her knees, offering her breasts.

His hands found the small of her back and urged her to him, his lips closing on a nipple. He slicked his tongue around the tip and drew it into his mouth and out, his teeth nipping the bud so that she felt the sharp tang of pain that she craved. A hand slipped between her thighs and he rubbed her in a steady rhythm that she matched, riding his hand until he slipped a finger inside her.

"Yes," she called out on a moan, urging him deeper. He added a finger and continued to stroke her fiery nub with his thumb. She fell to the blankets and spread her legs wider. He fell atop her, his hands parting her wider.

"Remember, this is what you wanted," he said before lowering himself, his gaze never moving from her. "It might hurt."

He was all tenderness now, entering her slowly. Welcome as the pain had been only a moment ago, the intensity of it took her by surprise and she gasped. He froze.

She cupped his buttocks. "No. Go on. Please. All the way."

"All the way," he repeated, easing completely inside her.

She released her breath, the pain more bearable until it was barely anything at all. Her muscles clenched around him. "Yes. Oh, yes."

He stroked her cheek, her forehead, her hair, until she began to move with him again, savoring the feel of him, every inch. Their urgency increased as they rocked faster, in unison. His fingers laced with hers. The fire flamed up inside her, spreading and filling her with overwhelming heat, lightning in a bottle.

He called her name and the bottle broke, shattering around her in shimmering fragments that danced behind her dazed eyes.

"Logan." He remained atop her, fingers laced with hers, until their ragged breathing steadied.

With a sigh on his lips, he rolled off her to sit beside her as his breathing returned to normal. She placed a hand on his back. He hadn't wanted to do it, she knew, guilt starting to rise. She'd pushed him until he'd had little choice. For a man who valued his principles, he must feel some sense of disappointment in himself. Her temporary feeling of triumph dissolved to remorse.

"It is what I wanted, Logan. I thank you. One day, you'll see that you did me an incredible honor. I'll always treasure the memory."

He turned to her with a smile that did not look at all forced. "I hope you never regret it. I wish I could say that I did, but...I find that I don't. You've reminded me what it is to be truly alive. I think I'd almost forgotten."

His candor surprised her and flooded her with relief. No regret. No remorse. He got up and walked to the door.

"Logan?" she called after him, worrying when she heard the sound of the door opening and relieved when it closed again a minute later. He padded back across the floor with bare feet, his hands full of snow. He placed it in a small pile by the fire, then ripped a corner off the blanket with his bare hands. She had no idea what he had in mind until his hands were on her, gently smoothing over her feet and legs with the damp cloth. He inched up toward her mound and tenderly rubbed between her legs, cleaning all traces of him from her. The simple act was so stirring, so achingly sweet and considerate, that she found herself on the brink of tears.

This was Logan Winthrop, the kind of man who would always care for others before he took time for himself. And she loved him. But she had to let him go. Nothing could change the fact that he would always be her first lover, and she was glad. She'd chosen well.

He covered her with the blanket, wrapped himself

in the tarp, and stood to check on their clothes. "Almost dry. Another hour or so."

"Come back to bed." She patted the blankets beside her. "Even with the fire, it's still cold. We'll be warmer together."

"I'm not the kind of man who can take intimacy lightly." He sat beside her. "You said that you don't want to marry, but I will marry you, Alice, if your sister grants her approval. I know she was hoping for a title and a grand estate, but she'll always have you close, at least."

She smiled and reached out for him. "Ever dutiful. Of course you would marry me. Thank you for saying so. No, Logan. I'm sorry. It's a lovely offer, and if I ever planned to marry, maybe. But I meant what I said. I have no intention of ever marrying. I have an inheritance, not large but quite enough, and I plan to see the world."

"You really don't plan to marry?" He sounded honestly surprised, like her choice had never occurred to him as a genuine possibility. "Never?"

"I don't want a husband. I have my independence, so why would I? It's why I wanted to do this. I really wanted to know love once, and I'm so glad I've done it with you."

He still looked shocked. "I see."

She laughed. "Am I too modern for you? I'm sorry. But you don't want to marry me, either. Not really. We're much alike that way, happiest on our own."

"Are you? Are you really happy?"

"I am."

"I'm glad for you, then."

"We're still friends?" She raised a brow. "Your friendship means the world to me. I hope that in doing this, we haven't lost that."

"Friends." He nodded and slipped into the blankets beside her. "Though, I've never had a friend who felt so good beside me."

"Get some rest, Logan. I have a feeling you'll be very busy come morning."

❦

Rest? As if he could rest knowing he'd taken her innocence, and she had no intention of marrying him. Not that he wanted to get married. Did he? No. She was right. She was better off on her own. He didn't rule out the fact that she would find someone more suitable and change her mind. But perhaps he could breathe a little easier knowing he hadn't damaged her, to her way of thinking. Alice was the kind of woman who would not rest until she got what she wanted. She wanted to make love to him, but she didn't want his love. So be it.

It was a beautiful dream, though, Alice in his bed every morning, greeting each day with her ebullient laughter. She'd given him a reprieve from the darkness he carried inside him. It was time that he stopped letting the terrible weight of his past drag him down. But how could he see Alice every day and resist the urge to pull her into his arms and kiss her senseless? He turned to face her, sweet Alice, her back to him, already asleep. He put an arm around her and pulled her close, determined to make the most of the little time they had left.

He woke some time before dawn and went to

the window. All was dark and quiet. The full moon reflected off the snow. Deep, but not impossible. He dressed in dry clothes and then woke her.

"Sweet Alice, the time has come."

"Mmm." She tugged the blankets tighter around her. "Can't we stay a little longer?"

"I dare not. I would like to get you home before morning, when Finch will certainly sound the alarm if I don't report back on your safety."

She sat up. "The last thing we need is a frantic countess. How much snow did we get? Will we be able to get back to Thornbrook Park?"

"Come, it's quite a sight." He held a hand out to her. Not as lovely a sight as his Alice rising from sleep, her glorious red hair hanging loose about her pale white shoulders. He thought of the Botticelli painting he'd seen in books, *The Birth of Venus*. But she was more Artemis than Venus to Logan. She would always be his huntress, and he her very willing prey.

"It's extraordinary, Logan, every branch heavy with snow, the world done over in pure white. How deep do you think it is?"

"We had over a foot the other day, and it looks like we have another eight inches on top of it. It will have compressed down. We'll manage. I'll tend the horse while you dress. I hope he stayed warm enough through the night."

By the time he got her back to the Dower House and headed for Thornbrook Park, the sun was beginning to rise. Grady didn't ask many questions when he returned the horse, but Logan had a feeling Mr. Finch would be more curious.

"Good morning, Mr. Winthrop." Finch met him in the kitchen. "I trust all is well? I expected to hear from you before bed last night. I confess, I was a tad uneasy about you and Lady Alice."

"Lady Alice is well. She was at the pond, but she had the good sense to seek shelter at the old McGinty place. I stayed with her there through the worst of it. Thank goodness I had the hearth repaired. We were able to build a fire."

"Thank goodness indeed."

"No need to mention it to anyone. I believe the young woman was embarrassed at her lack of judgment, waiting too long for her suitor to show up. She will be relieved at your discretion in not alarming the whole house."

Logan was surprised at how easily he lied, but it was more that he wasn't telling everything than that he was dishonest. What had happened between him and Alice was no one's affair but their own.

"Have some breakfast, Winthrop. You look tired. Perhaps take the morning off."

"I will take some time once I check on the lemon trees in the conservatory. They were looking worse for wear after the drop in temperature, and I have my doubts they're going to survive through the winter."

He allowed Mrs. Mallows to make him some eggs and coffee, though it was early for the servants to eat. Up with the dawn, they usually worked until eight in the morning before having a chance to sit down briefly. Logan was shocked by his own hunger. He ate like a man who couldn't get enough. He ate like Alice, he thought with a laugh.

"Mrs. Mallows, thank you. Your eggs have never tasted better. I'm a man restored."

She smiled at the compliment and went on about her work. Expecting that disaster awaited him, Logan went to check on the lemon trees.

✌️

Alice was careful not to wake Agatha on the way to her room. She was grateful that Mary was not yet up and about for the day. Her plan was to sleep a bit, give Mary time to start on Agatha's breakfast, and then request a bath. She ached in places she'd never ached before, but it was a delicious secret pain. She was truly a woman, able to check off one of the things to accomplish on her list.

But doing it once and moving on was not as easy as she'd supposed. Logan stayed on her mind. To see him again would be to want him again, and she couldn't afford for him to get caught. She would not be responsible for Logan losing his position.

And now she had Lord Ralston to contend with. On the way home, she'd finally asked Logan how he'd known where to find her. He told her about Finch's message. He knew Ralston had taken Alice to the pond on their ride, and he could only assume that was where they'd planned to meet. Good sense led him to check the only possible nearby shelters, and there she was. Alice wasn't sure anyone else would have known where to look. Logan was attuned to her fate, as Agatha would say.

Alice had taken a lover. She imagined how shocked

her sister would be. She wondered if she should seduce Lord Ralston next, to know how one man compared to another in making love, but she couldn't bring herself to do it. Not so soon after Logan. Logan was the only one she wanted now, and she would consider herself lucky if they could find a way to be together again.

She supposed she would have to turn Ralston down gently. Then again, perhaps he had already rejected her. He'd made a date and then hadn't turned up. Had he been stuck in the snow? Or perhaps he had made plans with another. Lady Matilda Furbish? Alice had already decided to ride with Ralston in the Holcomb fox hunt, provided they still held it with all the snow, but Matilda could have him after the hunt. Alice didn't want to take any more of the earl's time without intending to marry him. It wouldn't be quite fair.

It seemed equally unfair to leave a catch like Ralston in the hands of a mousy, boring girl like Matilda. She had no conversational skills and nothing to mark her as interesting besides her family name and money. Obviously, Ralston's aunt preferred the match, but why? Why did it matter to Alice? Ralston could handle his own affairs.

She knew her sense of competitiveness was rearing up and that would be her undoing, as Agatha had once predicted. Alice couldn't bear for people to think Ralston preferred another woman. She wanted to be the one to turn him down, and she wanted everyone to know she'd been the one to turn him down. The idea of being jilted left a sour taste in her mouth. She would use the fox hunt to at least build the reputation of being in demand.

Thirteen

IN A WEEK, SHE HADN'T MANAGED TO BUMP INTO Winthrop once. It was as if he remained two steps ahead of her at all times. Could he be avoiding her? Alice supposed she couldn't blame him if he was. But the truth hit her unexpectedly when she was talking to Sophia at breakfast one morning.

"With Winthrop gone home, who is to say what will happen to the lemon trees? Sturridge says they're hanging on, but I would much prefer that Winthrop return to tend them. Gabriel's mother will blame me if they don't survive."

"What do you mean, gone home? Thornbrook Park is his home. I thought he had some dark secret in his past that prevented a return to his family." Suddenly, Alice wished she knew where Logan's family home was. They'd never talked about it.

"His brother has taken ill, poor man. Winthrop rushed home to be at his side. I had no idea he had a brother to rush home to, but Gabriel says they have kept in occasional communication all these years."

"How long has he been at Thornbrook Park?"

"Five, maybe six years. The previous agent retired and recommended him. His brother is a baron. Did you know?"

"I've heard, yes." She wondered why he hadn't at least told her that he was leaving. They were friends, were they not? "How long will he be away?"

"Until his brother is out of the woods, I imagine. If his brother doesn't improve, I suppose Winthrop will become Baron Emsbury and we'll have to look for a new estate manager."

"Is it as bad as all that?"

Sophia shrugged. "I imagine it can't be all that good. It's the first time Winthrop has left us in all these years."

"I suppose," Alice agreed. Winthrop, a baron? She knew he had the ability to live up to any title, but did he have the desire? She'd never bothered to ask what he dreamed for himself. Did he wish to leave Thornbrook Park? Was he not happy with his lot? She could have been a better friend. "I hoped he would be here for the fox hunt. I wanted his advice in hunting etiquette."

"Gabriel will stay by you, and Grady will be on hand as well. Poor little fox. Do you suppose it will be easier for him to hide now that most of the snow is melted? Red fur would certainly stand out in all the white."

"It will be easier on the horses without the snow. I care more that we avoid injuries among the riders and horses than that our fox gets away unharmed. What's one fox to dozens of men and horses? And women," she corrected herself. Matilda Furbish would be riding, or so she'd heard from Lady Holcomb. And probably the Sentledens. They welcomed any opportunity to show off, except perhaps for June, who no doubt was eager to cater to the wishes of her fiancé, Brumley, poor thing. She was cornered more surely than the fox.

"Speaking of the hunt, be sure Mary packs your things," Sophia reminded her. "We're to leave this evening."

"The hunt isn't for two days yet."

"Did I forget to tell you?" Sophia smiled, clearly pleased with herself. "When the Holcombs were here for dinner, they invited us to stay for a few days. I agreed for us all, of course."

"Knowing this would keep me in proximity to Lord Ralston. Oh, Sophia, really."

"He's a good match. You said yourself that you like him. Why should Matilda Furbish get all the advantages?"

"The Furbishes are staying over, too?"

Sophia nodded. "Unfortunately, yes, but don't worry. Mattie is such a droll, toady little thing. She's nothing to you."

"Perhaps Lord Ralston likes droll." Alice had always found Miss Furbish more dull than droll.

"Lady Holcomb likes her, for some reason. I suppose it's the enormous Furbish fortune, but Ralston doesn't need it. He has plenty of his own."

"I don't care about his fortune."

"You shouldn't. Leave that to me. Your job is to just relax for once and allow yourself to fall in love with the man. He has much to recommend him. I don't know what's taking you so long."

"Taking me so long to fall in love with him? I'm

sorry. I'll move it up on my list of priorities." Alice couldn't possibly fall in love with Ralston when she remained preoccupied with Winthrop.

Besides, Ralston freely admitted that he'd allowed himself to be distracted by his aunt and a luncheon with Matilda Furbish instead of meeting Alice at the appointed time for a date that he'd made with her. She could have died out in the cold if not for Winthrop. She hadn't quite forgiven Ralston for his neglect, and she wasn't sure she ever would. Even if she did secretly thank him for putting her in a position to get exactly what she wanted with another man.

❧

Winthrop was at his brother's side when the fever broke. He'd hardly left John's room the entire time he'd been at Stratton Place, and not strictly out of devotion. Logan had a strong desire to avoid running into young Grace, or any circumstances that would require him to explain his role in her life or his absence.

Better she had no idea that he'd come. John and Ellen had adopted her as their own, and they were far better parents to her than anyone could be—with the exception of her own mother who'd died giving birth to her. Through Mrs. Leenders, the nurse, Logan had made sure that Grace knew about Julia and how much she'd loved Grace even before she was born. As far as he was concerned, Grace didn't need to know the rest. No doubt she'd heard of him as the villain in her parents' story, and he didn't mind assuming the role as long as it kept her from the unfortunate truth.

"John." He refreshed the cloth on his brother's clammy forehead and waited for some sign of recognition. John's eyes were open but struggling to find focus.

Eventually, he pinned his gaze on his brother. "Logan? Is that you?"

"It is. Let me ring for Barnett to inform Ellen that you're awake." Uncertain what had caused John's sickness, Logan had tried to keep Ellen and their daughters from the room as much as possible. No sense in all of them becoming sick. The doctor had finally declared it to be a very strong case of bronchitis and had started John on the proper medication.

"It's good to see you, Brother, but you're a scary sight."

Logan ran his hands through his hair. "I haven't had a proper bath. I didn't want to leave you."

"Not like that." John laughed until it became a wheezing cough. "I mean, I must be in sorry shape for you to have come. You haven't been home in years."

"Eight years." Logan nodded. "Nice to see the place hasn't changed much. And you're right. You were in sorry shape. Ellen thought she was going to lose you."

"John." Ellen came bounding into the room. "Of course I knew I wouldn't lose you. I finally saw our chance to get your brother home."

"Do you see how married people lie to one another, Logan? She's sparing me from knowing I was on the brink. What do you think now? Will I live?"

Tears glistening in her eyes, Ellen placed her hand on her husband's cheek. "Dr. Hall will be here shortly. He'll have a better idea. But I'm thinking yes."

The doctor did deliver good news. With the fever breaking, John had a strong chance of full recovery. Logan had planned to stay only long enough for John to recover, but it seemed only fair to spend some time with his brother before setting off again. Eight years was a long time to be apart, and Logan had to admit that he'd missed being part of a family.

On the third day after John's fever had passed, Logan happened to run into Grace in the garden where he'd been walking. She looked remarkably like her mother, with long, fair hair and rosy cheeks, as opposed to John and Ellen's younger daughters with their dark Winthrop curls and pale skin.

"Hello." She looked up from her book to greet him.

He'd contemplated turning around and walking the other way, but she had already seen him. He might arouse more suspicion in fleeing than in blustering on with it. Her younger cousins pushed their dolls up and down the walkway in matching miniature prams. Mrs. Leenders, knitting while she watched over the children, sat on the garden bench by Grace.

"Hello," he said quickly, meaning to walk on.

"You're the one who knew my mother," Grace said boldly, making him stop in his tracks and turn. "I remember you."

Mrs. Leenders looked stricken. "I'm sure the man is busy, Grace. We must mind our manners."

"You remember me?" Logan asked, intrigued. "I haven't seen you since you were a very little girl."

Grace disregarded authority as surely as her mother once had. She put down the book and approached him. "My mother, Julia. Julia Kirkland. I recognize you from her pictures."

"Her pictures?"

"I have her sketchbook. She drew you all the time. You're the same man. She was a brilliant artist."

"Yes." He had to admit that she was. "She had a very sure hand, but I think I might have changed some in twelve years." In Julia's sketches, he had been a love-stricken boy of eighteen at the oldest. Julia had been drawing him since they were children.

Grace cocked her head, as if studying him through an artist's eyes, and her expression was so like her mother's that Logan might have at last wept the tears he had not cried so long ago, if only they would come. "Your nose and chin. Such a broad nose and pointed chin. Some things change, but the structural lines give you away."

"Are you an artist like your mother?"

She straightened, clearly proud. "I'm an artist, not like her. I'm my own sort of artist."

"Well, of course. And so you should be your own sort of artist."

"I'm going to study painting at the Royal Academy."

"Is that what you would like to do?" He remembered Julia sharing the ambition. "I'm sure you will. Best wishes to you, Grace."

She crossed her arms. "You're my uncle. Well, not my real uncle. You're Uncle John's brother, which would make you my uncle if Uncle John were my real uncle, which, of course, he's not."

"No." He followed along, knowing enough to avoid becoming confused.

"Did you know my real father, too?"

"Yes. I'm sorry for your loss. Losses."

"It was an accident." She took his hand, peering up at him with Julia's eyes as if she knew the truth. "A terrible accident. I wish I had my parents, but Uncle John and Aunt Ellen are as good as the real thing. You could stay longer and tell me more about my parents, maybe? No one seems to know them as well as I could hope, but your face is all over Mother's sketchbook."

"That it probably is. I did know your mother very well. Your father, not as much. I was there when you were born," he confessed, eager to give her some sort of happy information on the parents she never knew. "You cried. A lot."

She laughed. "Oh, that's what you remember?"

He nodded. "Your mother was delighted by it. She said it meant that you were healthy and strong, like her."

"And then she died." Grace said it so matter-of-factly. *And then she died.* But of course, Grace had never known her mother and didn't have the memories that still haunted Logan.

"In fact, yes. Not long after she remarked on your health, her own gave out and she died. She was sorry not to be able to watch you grow. She'd been very much looking forward to raising you."

They both had, Julia and Logan. The plans they'd made. They were going to go to France and on to America, far enough away that her husband could never find them. Logan would raise the child as his own. Julia would take his name. Logan's greatest mistake was in allowing Julia to convince him to wait until she'd given birth before they could slip away.

Stanhope wouldn't hit her while she was expecting a child, she'd said. Julia had wanted her ailing father to see his grandchild before he died. If only Logan had trusted his instincts and spirited her away sooner.

"Thank you." She squeezed the hand she held, surprising him. "It's good to know. I'm sorry that she died."

"So am I. Quite sorry. You should have had the chance to know each other better."

"If you stayed longer, you could tell me so I would know." Those eyes! Her mother's eyes, blue as the summer sky, looked up at him.

All these years, guilt had driven him away. Now guilt made him consider returning to Stratton Park for a longer stay. He was probably the only one who really could tell her about her mother. Messages he passed through Mrs. Leenders clearly hadn't been enough for the girl. "One day, Grace. One day, perhaps I will come back and stay a while longer. As it is, I have duties to return to at Thornbrook Park."

He had Alice, though not really. He had to let go, but he found he wasn't quite ready to leave the dream behind.

❧

On the day of the hunt, Alice woke with an ache at her core that could only be attributed to missing Winthrop. When she'd planned to join the hunt, she'd thought to impress him with her style and ability in the saddle. He'd once called her Artemis. With her new hunting whip, a gift from Ralston, she looked the part. But Winthrop wouldn't see her jumping her horse over hedges or commanding her place in the field. What if he never came back?

She needed to focus on the hunt. Sophia came with Jenks to help her dress.

"I have something for you." Sophia presented a small enamel box.

"A present for me?" Alice took the box, hesitant to open it.

"For luck. It will go beautifully with your hunting habit."

She looked inside. It was a cabochon ruby with seed pearls set in gold. "Sophia, it's extraordinary."

"It was a gift from Grandmother on my coming-out. She said it would bring me luck in finding the right man, a husband. I should have given it to you sooner. Grandmother passed away before your coming-out, and I think she would want me to pass it on."

"I'll wear it to remind me of Grandmother," Alice clarified. "And nothing more." Their grandmother had also given them each a sizable inheritance in case the right man never came along. Alice wanted to point that out to Sophia, but she held her tongue.

"As long as you wear it."

Once Alice was dressed, Mrs. Jenks helped her fasten the pin at her throat, just over her cravat.

"Perfect," Sophia said, and she sent for Gabriel to go down with her.

"Follow the huntsman's lead and you'll be fine," Gabriel recommended. Alice nodded, pretending not to be nervous.

"She can follow *my* lead." Ralston joined them as

they stepped out to the yard. "I don't plan on leaving her side, Lord Averford. She's in good hands with me."

"I hope so," Alice said, hazarding a glance at Ralston from under the brim of her hat. He flashed that wide grin of his, reminding her somewhat of the fox they would be hunting.

"First, the master of hounds sounds the horn and looses the hounds to follow the scent. We follow the hounds," Ralston explained. "Simple as that."

"If it's anything like last year, we'll end up spending half the day seated around coverts waiting for the fox to come out and run again," Averford said. "Ah, here comes Winthrop leading out our horses."

"Winthrop." Alice's head shot up. "When did he arrive? I thought he was going to miss the hunt."

"Miss the hunt? He wouldn't dream of it. Winthrop's been at my side these last six Holcomb hunts at least."

"Don't worry, Lady Alice," Ralston whispered. "Mr. Winthrop will stay with Lord Averford. We'll find our own way through the crowd."

"I'm not worried, Lord Ralston. Thank you."

"It's a crowded field. More ladies than usual. Over thirty." Was Ralston suggesting that he could have his pick? Did he expect her to be grateful?

"I'm glad of it. Some men think women have no place in sport. I would love for a woman to take the prize this year."

"Perhaps it will be you, Lady Alice."

"It won't be Junie Sentleden." Alice nodded to June on the sidelines, where she stood with Lord Brumley choosing refreshments from the buffet. "Sadly, she's not dressed to hunt."

"Your horse awaits, Lady Alice. Come, let me help you mount." Winthrop appeared at her side and bowed dutifully. "Lord Ralston, your groom requests a word with you."

"I'll join you in a moment." Ralston headed off.

"Thank you, Mr. Winthrop. A surprise to see you here." Alice followed him to Lord Averford and the horses. "I hope all is well with your brother, not that you informed me you were going. I heard it from my sister."

"I left in a hurry, Lady Alice."

"Still, you could have said something. I thought we were friends." She felt he owed her some little bit of courtesy, even though he owed her nothing.

"I hope we are."

"And yet, you also didn't send me word that you were coming back. I haven't heard from you since…" She shook her head. "What was I to think?"

"I'm sorry. I hardly know what to think of it myself, if that helps any. And then there was the letter from Ellen with word of my brother's rapid decline. Please, if I've offended you, forgive me." He placed a hand on her shoulder. He could hardly do much more without arousing suspicion. "You must know that I never intended to avoid you on purpose."

She softened. What was he to do, really? He couldn't very well go looking for her or be caught sending her notes. And if his brother had been as sick as all that…"There's nothing to forgive. I really do hope your family is well."

"My brother has recovered, thank you. Bronchitis, not contagious. At least, no one else in the family seems to have come down with anything like it. I arrived at Thornbrook Park last night and headed to Holcomb House this morning."

As they drew nearer to Lord Averford, she tried to appear as though they were having a simple conversation. "Brutus made the journey well?"

"The horses came with Grady days ago. He's rested and ready. I hope you got more practice in taking him over hedges and fallen logs."

"There wasn't time. I hope my skills will suffice." She hadn't ridden since her day out with Ralston, and there were few reasons to lead Brutus over obstacles then. Their path had been mostly a clear one. "Brutus makes up in agility what he lacks in speed."

"You are skilled, but have a care riding with Ralston. Rumor has it the earl likes to show off and will go out of his way to leap obstacles when he could easily go around."

"He informs me that there are thirty women riding today. I'm sure some of them will be impressed with Ralston's skills, but I won't be among them."

"Because you don't wish to marry? You might want to rebuff him a little before he finds the opportunity to ask. I see the way he looks at you, Alice. It's only a matter of time. And you don't seem to be in a hurry to be rid of him, despite your protestations."

At last, was she to see a hint of jealousy from Winthrop? Her nerves tingled with hope that he hadn't entirely vanquished his affection for her after all. She risked meeting his gaze and became instantly flooded with desire. His heavy-lidded eyes mirrored her own intense attraction.

"Logan," she said suddenly, daring to stroke his whisker-roughened cheek. "Why must everything seem so impossible?"

"Anything is possible. Just not as likely as we might wish. Please, stay focused on the hunt. Don't take any foolish risks."

She already had, risking her heart to the estate manager. He helped her into the saddle, lingering beside her until Gabriel, on horseback, joined them.

"Mount up, Winthrop. They'll be starting soon."

"Yes, my lord."

Before he could return to them, Ralston rode over to Alice's side. "Should we make a friendly wager?"

"A wager, Lord Ralston? Of what sort?"

"If I'm the one to corner the fox, you'll kiss me."

It seemed a safe enough risk. At worst, it would cost her a kiss. At best, the hounds would corner the fox and the huntsman would be the first to get to it. "And if I corner the fox?"

He shrugged. "You could choose the same prize, a kiss."

She laughed. "But that's a pointless bet. If either of us is victorious, we get the prize."

"Exactly."

"What if I choose a different prize?"

"Preposterous. Why would you want anything else?" He winked and jerked the reins, charging ahead of her before she had a chance to protest. She caught up a minute later. "Get ready, he's going to sound the horn."

She looked around for Logan and Gabriel, but had lost sight of them in the crowd. The master sounded the horn, and the dogs sprang into action. There were supposedly two hundred riders, but they were easily outnumbered by fox terriers, foxhounds, and little scruffy dogs she couldn't name but that she understood were famous for bravely scurrying right into the fox-holes after their prey.

From the middle of the pack of hunters, Alice and Lord Ralston followed the incessant woofing and howling to the first covert. Within minutes, before the back of the pack had even caught up, the hounds snuffed out a red fox so gorgeous and sweet that Alice had a moment's hesitation. How could they frighten such a lovely little thing? Even worse, to stand back and watch the hounds tear into her. But as the rest of the pack caught up and the hounds raced on to the next covert, excitement bubbled in her veins. The thrill of the hunt! A feeling she knew at last. It was perhaps livelier than her pursuit of Winthrop had been, but every bit as jolly.

Catching Winthrop had been more rewarding, alas, but she wanted him again, perhaps all the more when she finally spied him not far behind the master of the hunt. Winthrop had fine form on a horse. She suddenly didn't know if the tingling in her veins came from hunting or from her memories of lovemaking, but she charged Brutus into pursuit so that Ralston had to try to keep up with her. The next covert was some way off. The fox had outstripped the pack and burrowed into a dense thatch of greenery.

The dogs, noses to the ground, sniffed everywhere and seemed a little confused at being eluded.

"Stay alert," Ralston assured her, catching up.

"The grounds crew was out at dawn making sure the burrows were all filled in."

"The poor thing has nowhere to hide."

"Exactly. Any moment now."

"It seems a bit unfair."

"We don't want the riders getting bored, now do we?"

A little tuft of red appeared in the brush and suddenly the dogs were over the other side, charging ahead. Horses followed.

On it went for what seemed like hours. Ralston rode dutifully by her side, commanding his horse to make graceful leaps over any object in the way, while she rode easily around most of them. Every time she thought she would be close enough to speak to Logan again, he charged ahead after the pack.

A surprising thing happened at the next covert. The dogs went in sniffing and two foxes appeared. Much confusion ensued, with the master and half the hounds going one way and some dogs and riders trailing off in the other direction. By the next few coverts, the pack had thinned to only a few riders, and Alice began to think they'd set off after the wrong fox.

"Follow me," Ralston said. "I think I can see where all this is headed. We'll beat the fox to the next covert and perhaps force it into the open together."

"I—" She was about to protest when Ralston's horse charged off. She wanted to end the hunt with Winthrop. If only she could find him again. "Here we go, then."

She braced herself and went off after him, leading Brutus over a tall fence that she wasn't sure he would clear. When he did, she wanted to stop and compliment him on his performance, but Ralston hadn't looked back or slowed down. She raced ahead, following, more pleased by his plan when she thought she saw Winthrop and Lord Averford joining in from the opposite direction, perhaps after the second fox. Ralston's horse leaped some fallen logs, clueing Alice to prepare Brutus for a similar feat. Brutus cleared the logs and stumbled, possibly not expecting the puddle that followed. Alice held on, but the momentum drove her forward even after her horse had stopped.

The wind was knocked clean out of her. She lay flat on her back, trying desperately to catch her breath, when she heard her own name through a fog. "Alice! Good God, Alice!" Winthrop's voice, and suddenly he was at her side, leaning over her.

The last sight she had before losing consciousness was of Winthrop's very anxious cobalt eyes peering down at her. Eyes like the midnight sky, she thought, and drifted off into their darkness.

Fourteen

LOGAN WINTHROP, NO STRANGER TO MURDEROUS thoughts, had never wanted to kill a man more than he now longed to murder the Earl of Ralston. And this time, he felt capable of doing it with his bare hands. Sitting at Alice's bedside, waiting for her to wake up, he imagined his hands closing around Ralston's throat and popping his Adam's apple like a chicken egg. It was the only distraction that kept him from throwing himself on Alice and begging her to be all right.

The man had no business leading Alice to certain danger. Ralston knew of the water hazard and had led his horse from right to left to avoid being mired in it. He certainly should have anticipated that someone following him closely would have had no ability to react in time. Now Alice, lovely Alice, was paying the price.

Logan insisted on staying by Alice's side, only leaving to allow her sister to be alone with her for a short time and for the doctor's examination before pleading to be let back into the room. On her own, Alice had moved her hand once her attendants were through changing her for the doctor's examination. It was an encouraging sign, according to Dr. Pederson. She would probably not be paralyzed. The main concern was that she should regain consciousness, which she hadn't yet. Outside, Logan could hear the doctor mulling options with Lady Averford. Brain swelling. Coma. Words that Winthrop did not want to hear, especially after being with his brother during the recent crisis. None of it was good.

"Alice." He squeezed her hand. "My sweet, you have to wake up."

He loved her, he knew beyond a doubt. The way his heart had constricted when he saw her tumbling from the horse, the agony of not being able to reach her in time. The bitter roiling in the pit of his stomach from his fear and worry. He loved her. She wasn't just a woman to him anymore. She was life itself.

She remained as if asleep, eyes closed, not a bruise on her. A sleeping angel. But Alice was no angel. "You're a rebel, Alice," he reminded her. "You have to fight."

He heard the door open behind him and a soft hand on his back. He stood to give his chair to Alice's sister, the woman who rightfully belonged at Alice's side.

"She can't be moved," Lady Averford said. "The Holcombs are very understanding, of course. They've invited us to stay as long as Alice is here."

"Charitable of them, considering. Damn that fool Ralston!"

"Logan." Lady Averford sighed and accepted the chair. "If I may call you Logan, considering the closeness you apparently share with Alice?"

"I'm sorry, Lady Averford. We never meant for it to become public knowledge."

"I'm her sister."

"I know. That's why I'm trying to explain to you how I feel about Lady Alice. It came upon me suddenly. One day, she was trailing after me as usual, annoying me as I tried to work. The next day, I couldn't find her and I began to miss her chatter. Not long after that, we became friends, and from friendship—"

"It's why she couldn't bear to consider any of my other candidates." Sophia nodded.

"Not exactly. Maybe. I tried to step aside. She's persistent. And when we found ourselves alone together… I understand you will want me to resign. I will, effective immediately. But please don't force me to leave her now." The ache inside him went so deep that he had no idea how to root it out.

Lady Averford pursed her lips. "You have to understand what it looks like. The minute it happened, you leaped from your horse. Some say you flew, but I think they might be exaggerating. You were at her side in less than an instant, and some worried that you and Lord Ralston would come to blows."

"I was mad with concern, Lady—Sophia. Mad." He ran his hands through his hair. "I'm still nearly out of my mind. It's what caused me to realize the full depth of my love for her. Because I love her, I'm willing to walk away. She deserves better. I kept telling her."

"You're a good man, Logan. We all think very highly of you."

"But I'm not the right man, am I? You're

sympathetic now, and I appreciate it, but you don't want me to be the one for her. I offered."

"Marriage? You offered Alice marriage?"

He nodded. "Of course I did. What would you expect me to do? But she wanted nothing to do with a marriage she felt I offered out of duty. I never told her that I love her. What I wouldn't give to say the words, to see how she feels, if it makes a difference."

"If it were up to me, I would let you stay. I've seen the way she looks at you, and it has worried me. Eve warned me. We both thought if I insisted that Alice stop trailing after you, that it would be the very thing she would do. So we said nothing. I said nothing. And now, letting you stay might do her some good. But people talk, Logan. Your reaction was more than an estate manager would feel for a mere member of the family he serves. I can only explain it as duty or a reaction from your own past trauma so often before people begin to think otherwise."

"Before people begin to think that there's something between Alice and me." He nodded, knowing exactly what she was getting at but not quite saying. "You think I should go."

"Alice is going to wake up. I don't know when, but she will. She's tenacious."

"I know." He smiled.

"Exactly. But if you stay much longer, people will expect a wedding. Ralston told me he was about to propose. I fear she will look damaged somehow."

"You fear they will believe the truth, that Alice and I were lovers."

"Lovers. We live in a modern age, but I'm not sure most men are ready to accept a lightskirt for a bride."

He fisted his hands. "She's your sister. You know she's not like that. It wasn't like that."

"What people believe is often far from the truth, Logan. You know it better than most."

People believed him a murderer. Sophia was right. "Alice doesn't care what people believe."

Sophia shook her head. "She does not, indeed. And perhaps you will stay by her side until she wakes, lean over her with tears in your eyes, and tell her how glad you are to have her back, how much you love her. And she will agree that she loves you, too, and that she'll marry you..."

"No. It's not what she wants. Not that way. I won't have her feel forced to accept me."

"I don't think it is what she wants." Sophia raised a brow, as if considering. "But if you stay..."

"She doesn't want any of your candidates, either, you should know. Whether I'm here or gone. She wants freedom."

"What kind of freedom does one have when ostracized from the only society one knows? Believe me, I know it sounds cruel. But you can tell me. You've been there." Harsh as Sophia's words were to hear, he knew she spoke out of love for her sister. And she was right. Deep down he knew. If he stayed, he would tell Alice he loved her, and it would change everything, perhaps not in the best way for Alice. She had to be free to make her own choices when the time was right.

He nodded. "In a way, I'll always be there, on

the outside, not fitting in with one set or the other. Alice taught me what it was to want to live again. I won't take that chance from her. Could you give me a moment to say good-bye?"

Sophia stood to leave. "Not much longer, Logan."

"I'll be quick." Once the door closed behind Sophia, Logan took Alice's hand and leaned over her. "I love you, Alice. I should have told you as soon as I realized it. I love you. When you open your eyes, I won't be here, but know that my love remains. Come back to us, Alice, and forgive me for what I'm about to do."

It nearly ripped his heart out to walk away from her, looking so fragile in the bed. Even the red in her hair seemed to have dulled. He wanted so badly to stay and bring her color back to her. Sophia had a point, though. If he stayed and Alice woke, would she feel compelled to say she would marry him? Would she regret it afterward? He knew her dreams, and he couldn't stand to hold her back. On his recent visit, his family had made it clear that they would welcome him back. Now it seemed best that he leave Thornbrook Park and return to his family.

His next step was to explain himself to Lord Averford. He found his employer in the drawing room and asked for a word alone.

"I've been expecting you," Averford confessed, leading Logan to a small parlor where they could speak privately. "It's clear that you're a man in love. I've seen that look. I've worn it. She'll pull through this, Winthrop. Alice is as strong as they come."

"So is her sister, and you know the countess would

never approve of us together, Alice and me. Not really. She might give her permission, but I'm not sure she would ever really like the idea. As for Alice, she doesn't mean to marry. I offered, and she turned me down."

"Well. That is a surprise." Averford poured two glasses of whiskey and held one out to Logan. He took it. "She's a spirited one, our Alice. You don't think she would change her mind? The girl says a lot of things she doesn't mean, or so I've noticed through the years. She likes to watch the effect her words have without really thinking through the impact on herself."

Logan tilted his head. "That might have been true when she was younger, and she does have a flair for the dramatic."

"It runs in the family." Averford paused mid-sip to wink over the edge of his glass.

"Yes, but I find she has changed some in the few years I've known her. She has grown into herself, and I believe she's a remarkable woman."

"Then stay, Winthrop. Stay and marry her. Who cares what people think? Lord knows she doesn't care much for public opinion."

"Your wife reminded me that Alice might care if it took her away from the only people she has known and cared about her whole life. You know what happened to Eve before she married your brother. She still hasn't reconciled with the family who disowned her over her first husband. And then there's my past to consider. I've become used to the rumors and questions. But could Alice?"

"It would be to your credit to wait and ask her. Find out."

Logan shook his head. "No. I've made my decision. I think there's some part of her that needs more time to be on her own. I was just a step on her journey. A good step, I hope. But she'll get past me and on to other things. She might have already done so, or why would she have come to the fox hunt in the fine company of the Earl of Ralston? Alice is an explorer. I'm going to give her the freedom she deserves to explore."

"That's it, then? I've lost my trusted estate agent?"

"I'll head back to Thornbrook Park and work with Mr. Finch and Mrs. Hoyle to see that a replacement is found. I won't leave before I know that you have someone. It will take me some time to pack up my belongings in the cottage. And of course, I can't bring myself to go as far away as Stratton Place without knowing how Alice is recovering." He brought his hand to his forehead, more to hide his concern than to ease his tension.

"I know, Winthrop. I know. And I thank you. I'll be sure you get word of her progress daily. You know you're always a welcome visitor at Thornbrook Park. I hope we'll all be back within the week."

"I hope so, too. Good night, Lord Averford. And, I suppose, good-bye as well." He held out his hand.

Averford shook it. "Don't say good-bye. Let's just say until we meet again."

～

When Alice opened her eyes, the first thing she saw was a genuine look of relief on Lord Ralston's face.

"Alice, you've come back to us." Were those tears

in his eyes? How long had she been unconscious? She tried to sit up.

"That's it, try to sit. Your body has been through a bit of a shock."

The whole scene reminded her of when she'd fainted and had woken up in Winthrop's bed. Only Winthrop's eyes had held the look of concern, and he'd urged her not to sit up too soon. In fact, Logan Winthrop's eyes were the last thing she could remember, like a midnight sky, and she was floating toward it...

"What happened?" Her hand went to her head as if to steady it. It seemed to weigh ten times more than it should, and she found she could barely hold it up. And the pain, sharp shooting pain. "Ow."

"Some pain is to be expected, I suppose. You've had a sharp knock to the head."

"I think I went down on a log when I fell off Brutus."

"Ah, that explains it," Ralston said. "It's good that you remember."

He looked uncertain about whether it really was a good thing. Where was Logan? She'd expected to find him at her side when she woke, if only out of his unerring sense of duty. Of course, she expected more than duty to keep him close. And yet...

Sophia came in. "You're awake. Oh, Alice." She ran to the bed as if she hadn't seen Alice in a year.

"How long was I unconscious?"

"Two days. Well, two and a half, if you count the day it happened. And on the third day, Alice opened her eyes." Sophia clapped as if Alice had just performed a miracle or at least a brilliant tune on the piano.

"Two days? As long as that? And you're treating me as if you thought I might wake up a mental invalid?"

Ralston had the nerve to laugh. "We did wonder a bit about your memory recall."

"My recall is perfectly fine, thank you. Except that two days seems a long time to be unconscious." Who had changed her clothes? She prayed it was Jenks or her own sister, people she was familiar with, and not the Holcomb maids.

And she was dying to ask Sophia what had become of Winthrop. They weren't exactly engaged, but she couldn't help but think he would stand by her in a traumatic crisis. He wasn't the sort to run away, was he? But wasn't that exactly what he'd done in his past?

"Dr. Pederson is on his way in."

After a brief examination, the doctor declared her well, but not ready to be moved. He recommended that she slowly begin resuming her usual activities and said she should expect to tire easily. He added that she was very lucky it hadn't been worse. She might have broken her back or become paralyzed instead of suffering several days' unconsciousness and a stinging headache.

"That settles it." Ralston came back in as soon as he was allowed. "I'm not leaving your side. I'm to be your constant companion and personal servant until you're completely recovered."

Sophia had come back in as well. "He stayed by your side the entire time."

"The entire time?" The thought made her a bit uncomfortable. What if she'd talked in her sleep? She supposed she hadn't actually been asleep, but if she had any sort of awareness, she might have asked for Logan. She wanted to ask Sophia about him now.

"You heard the doctor. I'm going to be fine. I'm certainly capable of being left alone. In fact, I am feeling tired. Perhaps you can take some time to yourself while I sleep?"

Ralston laced fingers with hers, lifted her hand to his lips, and kissed it. "I hate to leave you even for that long."

Please leave me, she thought. She wanted to speak with her sister, and then she really did want some time alone to think about what had happened.

"Thank you, Lord Ralston," she said, trying to be at her most charming. "But I do need some rest, and there's really no point in staying by my side and watching me sleep. How dreadfully dull!"

"Yes, Ralston," Sophia said, taking the hint. "She's bound to have a parade of visitors soon, now that word is out that she's back among the living. Let's leave her for a little while. But we'll be back."

Ralston agreed. "A short separation. 'Parting is such sweet sorrow…'"

Alice rolled her eyes. At least Winthrop's thoughts were all his own and not borrowed quotes. "Sophia, a moment. Could you fluff my pillows?"

Sophia came back to Alice's bedside and fluffed. "There. Anything else?"

"What happened to Logan Winthrop? I expected he would be here." She didn't care if she was giving herself away. He had been her last vision before closing her eyes and her first thought upon waking.

"Mr. Winthrop?" Sophia appeared to be surprised.

"Why, he went back to work at Thornbrook Park. Someone had to tend the horses and get back to manage the tenants. He is a man of duty above all, isn't he?"

"Yes. Still, I thought he might be concerned about me."

"He did see that you were settled before he left. But Alice." Sophia nibbled her lip in the way that said she was about to say something she didn't want to say, but actually meant that she was usually quite delighted with herself for being the one to share the news. "He's leaving."

"Leaving Holcomb House? You said he already had."

"Leaving Thornbrook Park. He has decided to go home to his family. Isn't that wonderful? For him. We'll have to find a new land agent, of course, but... I suppose when he was home tending his brother, he realized how much he was missed."

"How lovely for him." She tried to hide her disappointment, mostly because she sensed it was exactly what Sophia had expected Alice to feel at the news, disappointed. "I never got to ask him about his time there. He must have been gone a long time to lessen the impact of what happened in his past."

"I suppose. Gabriel has already hired a replacement, a cousin of Mrs. Hoyle, as it happens."

"How convenient."

"The new estate manager starts in a week."

A week? Alice tried not to startle at the news. She would never even get to say good-bye. How could Logan rush off without saying good-bye? Maybe it was easier for him, a man. A man used to running when things went wrong. But she was being unfair. He'd never gotten around to explaining his past. Alice forced a yawn. "Thank you for the news. I really should get some rest."

"Ring if you need anything."

She needed Logan. She'd never seen it more clearly. She missed him. She missed his laugh almost as much as she missed his scowl. Why would he leave her? She'd always thought that she would never marry, but what if she had fallen alone? What if no one had been there to see her go down? Could she have died in a field alone? Rotted to a corpse before anyone noticed? Or worse, died alone in a foreign country without anyone realizing who she was or where she belonged? She might have been on her own and hit her head and lost her mind. What then? To think of strangers tending her, bathing her? Undressing her?

But Logan had his own family, his responsibilities. He'd left without saying good-bye. And Ralston was here by her side. Perhaps she should give the man a chance. She couldn't be sure she would ever marry, but she realized the importance of having a partner in life, someone to rely on, someone who knew everything about her. She had been given a second chance, time to think about what she really wanted in life, and she wasn't going to be too hasty in making decisions this time around.

Fifteen

His last week at Thornbrook Park passed in the blink of an eye, although the first few days, when he was uncertain of Alice's recovery, had dragged on endlessly. Hearing that she'd opened her eyes and seemed the same sweet Alice, his Alice, had been a balm to him, but a balm that could not heal his wounded soul. To leave without saying good-bye? He knew she would be hurt by it. But how much harder would it be to stay, only to leave her forever? She would forget him. She had plans to see the world. He would always be in her memory, the first man who'd physically loved her, but he would fade from her heart with new experiences over time.

When he'd lost Julia, he'd thought he could never love again, never as intensely or as fully as he'd loved her. Alice had proven him wrong. He was thirty-two years old, far too young to consider his own life at an end. The past twelve years had been wasted in burdening himself with guilt over what had happened. Alice had lifted that weight from him, showing him that he had so much left to offer the world. His family had forgiven him for his crime so many years ago. It was time he forgave himself.

"Do you know I killed a man, Mr. Finch?" he said to the butler without warning. One minute, they were going over the inventory, and then the next, he'd blurted it out.

Finch paused a moment to adjust his spectacles and went right back to the next item on the list before adding, "I'd heard something to that effect, yes. Always assumed it was self-defense. You're not a cruel or rash sort of man."

Logan tipped his head. "Not self-defense, and it wasn't an accident. I've always considered it a worthy crime. What wouldn't any of us do to save someone we love?"

"You were never arrested for the murder, to my understanding. Were you?" Finch asked. "It seems there must have been some question of your guilt."

"Extenuating circumstances." Logan nodded. "Witnesses contradicting one another. In the end, there wasn't enough evidence that I meant to kill, even though I willingly confessed. Some people believe I avoided charges because of who I am, a beloved son from a noble family. People have wondered about the truth for years. I've heard the whispers."

"And this is the first you've ever spoken of it. People grasp on to all kinds of nonsense when they don't know the whole truth, and even sometimes when they do. People are odd, Winthrop. Deuced odd. I've seen it all in thirty years of service. But I've also had time to develop a keen set of instincts about people, who to befriend and who to avoid. I consider you a friend, Mr. Winthrop. I never bestow the honor lightly." He held out his hand. "It has been an honor working with you."

"You say this now, knowing that I am a confessed murderer?" Logan held off a moment before taking the offered hand.

"I say this knowing that you're a man who loves deeply enough to protect his own at any cost."

"Thank you, Finch." Logan shook the butler's hand at last. "I'm going to miss Thornbrook Park."

Once he arrived back at Stratton Place and settled his things—or the ones he could fit in his suite of rooms, the rest going into storage—he thought back to his last conversation with Mr. Finch. How long he had kept it all buried, never confirming, never denying, knowing he was a murderer and letting himself be judged. No one could judge him as harshly as he'd judged himself. And oddly, in all the years, he'd never blamed himself for killing Alexander Blythe, Earl of Stanhope. Instead, he blamed himself for not having killed the man sooner.

He'd shut himself off from the world for far too long. He had a lot of living to catch up on.

"Finally back where you belong," his brother said as they settled into their places at the table in Stratton Place's enormous dining room for dinner. "By Jove, man, I've missed you."

"I've missed you, too. All of you." Was that a tear glimmering in his brother's eye? "For the first time, I finally realize that staying away wasn't protecting you all from my infamy. It was merely being selfish in denying you all my company when you were hurting for me, too."

"Selfish? Perhaps." Ellen smiled, even as John gasped.

"Ellen, no," John said, trying to stop his wife from possibly sending Logan scurrying again.

"It's better that she speaks her mind, John. Go ahead, Ellen. Give me the lashing I deserve."

"If the two of you would let me talk." She shook her head, clearly exasperated. "What I was saying is that yes, you were selfish. Grief is selfish, isn't it? We don't really grieve for the dead. We grieve for ourselves, for who we are missing. You needed time to grieve. We knew. In your selfish grief, you denied us, your family, the ability to support you in your time of need. But we love you. We understood. We left you alone for as long as we could, as long as you seemed to need. But now, Logan, we're glad you're back."

"All this time, you thought you would be a burden on us, Brother, but in fact, we needed you, too." John picked up his napkin and coughed into it.

"How long before you're fully recovered? Has your doctor said?" Logan suddenly realized how frail John still looked, but it had only been a little over a week. Perhaps it was to be expected.

"I'm getting better every day. Sometimes, I still wheeze a little, and I cough a bit here and there. I'm really very much improved."

"He tries to do too much," Ellen said with candor. "Running an estate this size, you know what a lot of work it is."

"Ah, of course. I can be useful, then." Logan liked the idea of being a help to his brother, at least until John recovered. "I might go mad all day in the country with nothing to do, but perhaps I'm needed, as you say. I know all about running a large estate. You still have Chalmers?"

"Yes, though he is getting on in years. I really could use your assistance and advice in keeping the place going. I wouldn't have asked while you were happily ensconced at Thornbrook Park, but now that you're here…"

"It would be my pleasure, John. More than a pleasure, actually. It's my family home as well, our shared history. Not that I'll inherit, of course, but the old place still means a great deal to me. More than I ever realized."

"Good. Then it's settled." John cast an uncertain glance at his wife.

"You just tell me when you feel strong again, and I'll step aside," Logan added, suddenly concerned that he'd overstepped his bounds.

"It's not that at all," Ellen said. "It's just that you will still inherit. You're John's heir. There won't be another. After Laura was born, the doctor said that I am unable to bear more children."

"I'm sorry. I had no idea."

"Don't be. We're very lucky. We have so much more than some people ever dream of having, three beautiful, intelligent daughters. When I think of the Countess of Averford, losing her only son…" Ellen's voice broke. "Tragic. We're blessed. So very blessed. We don't need a son to complete our family."

"When you say three daughters, I confess that I'm relieved to hear you add Grace as one of them with Sarah and Laura."

"Why wouldn't we? We love her as our own.

We've always made sure to tell her about her parents, though, in case she ever wants to know. It would seem wrong to deny them. Grace knows she's special, and she knows she is loved. She doesn't want for anything as far as we can tell, except perhaps to know a bit more about her parents. She's at an age to be curious and start to wonder how she might resemble them."

"And the rumors? She has heard them? How is it that she doesn't blame me?"

"Blame you? When she sees love in every sketch of you drawn by her mother's hand?" Ellen didn't bother hiding her astonishment. "She's too innocent to believe that anything evil could come of that kind of love. I doubt she's ready to believe ill of her father, but I know she thinks the world of you. You two could help each other heal at last."

Ellen and Grace could see Julia's love for him in her sketches, something he'd never been able to see so clearly in all those years. He'd always wondered about her love. If she loved him, how could she have chosen Stanhope? But she had loved him in her own way, perhaps not the way he'd hoped. If only he could have understood it then.

It took Alice to open his eyes to love, to allow him to be able to see it all more clearly. He loved Alice. Now he knew how Julia must have felt. He loved Julia, but not in the way that he loved Alice. Julia had loved him, but not in the way that she'd loved Stanhope. If only her beloved had not taken her trust and her love and thrown it all away. If only Stanhope hadn't treated her like his own porcelain doll and then broken her, smashed her to bits.

Right at the table, tears formed behind his eyes and threatened to spill out uncontrolled. And then it happened. He cried. In front of his brother and his brother's wife, in front of the footmen. He cried big ugly tears, not only for the woman he'd been unable to save, though he'd tried, but for the woman and the love that he'd lost, possibly forever. For Alice.

❧

Nine days after her accident, Alice still saw the world as if through a veil, fuzzy around the edges, and there was a constant buzzing at the base of her brain. She wondered how much longer it would last. Would it always be this way? It made it impossible for her to enjoy being alone. She could only stand to be around people or things that could provide an adequate distraction, something to fill her mind.

In the past, she'd appreciated occasional moments on her own for quiet reflection. Now, she needed loud sounds, bright colors, anything to hold her gaze. Aunt Agatha had become a favorite companion, dear Agatha, when Alice wasn't with Sophia or Lord Ralston, which was almost all of the time.

At least Ralston hadn't abandoned Alice in times of trouble. His loyalty and devotion surprised and impressed her. He'd been by her side throughout her convalescence, and he'd even insisted on seeing her home to Thornbrook Park.

"I promise I won't leave you," he said. "Not until you're comfortably settled, and even then I think you might have to chase me away. I'm growing attached to you, Lady Alice."

She smiled. "I seem to be attached to you, Lord Ralston. Physically, perhaps. It's so rare that I find myself without you. And I'm grateful to you. Your company soothes me, and I find that I don't like to be alone."

She thought of Winthrop often, the one man she'd thought she could count on to be nearby in her time of need. And now, he was gone.

"We're all here for you, Pumpkin." Standing over her, Sophia slipped her hands around Alice's shoulders protectively. She'd reverted to calling Alice by the childhood nickname she'd had for her, Pumpkin. To be honest, it scared Alice more than it comforted her. It told her that Sophia didn't even think Alice was quite right in the head, and what if it was true? She didn't feel right, not anymore. "Always."

Always. Sophia and Ralston always. Sometimes Agatha, too. Or Lord Averford, even more occasionally. Alice missed the Thornes. They hadn't been around much.

"It hurts, doesn't it?" Alice said to Sophia, out loud. She hadn't meant to say it out loud, had she? Why couldn't she control herself?

"What, love? Are you getting another headache? Shall we go lie down?"

"No." Alice laughed. For the first time in a week or two, she had no idea why. But she laughed, and she loved the feel of it. "Not getting all the attention for yourself, Sophia. It hurts you."

"Alice, what's gotten into you?" Sophia asked.

"I'm only speaking the truth." No, she wasn't. What was she saying? "I'm so sorry, Sophia."

"I know, Pumpkin," Sophia said brightly. Too brightly. "It's the head injury. The doctor says to give it some time."

❧

In time, just over a week, living at Stratton Place began to feel normal again, as if Logan had been there all along. Except, even with three young girls in the house, it was far too quiet. Not a one of them could compete with Alice in keeping a running commentary going on his every action. God, he missed her. He loved her, and he missed her.

He began to think that Lord Averford had been right all along. It was Sophia who'd wanted Winthrop to keep away. But Averford had said to wait, to ask Alice how she felt about him and his past and their future, if they had a future together. He needed to at least tell her that he still thought about her, that he hadn't wanted to leave without saying good-bye, that he missed her. That he loved her.

He had to tell her. It was up to her what she did with the information. He excused himself early from his afternoon meeting with Chalmers and John, and began to write Alice a letter telling her that he had so much to say to her and asking her to agree to meet him and let him finally explain.

❧

Struggling to focus, Alice looked at the calendar hanging on the wall across from her. Christmas was circled in red. One week away. She had been recovering for nearly three weeks, so why did she feel like she was getting worse, and not better?

"Alice, my dove, pay attention," Ralston urged. "Your sister is trying to show you something."

"Pretty," Alice said, looking over at the bow her sister had tied from gold velvet ribbon.

Sophia rolled her eyes. "Now you do yours."

"Mine?" Alice looked down. She held a red ribbon. Red, like the circle around Christmas. Then she noticed something sparkling on her left hand. A diamond ring. Vaguely, she recalled Ralston slipping it on her finger as she nodded yes. Yes? She looked at Ralston, trying not to sound surprised, like it was occurring to her for the first time, when she'd obviously already said yes. "We're getting married."

"Very good, Pumpkin," Sophia said. "We're going to have a big party to celebrate your engagement just as soon as you're feeling better."

"A diamond," she said. "Like one of the stars falling to earth from the sky."

"That's what I said when I put it on your finger." Ralston, the fox, flashed his toothy grin. The fox had won the hunt after all. Crafty beast.

Did she really want to marry him? Why shouldn't she? She could barely string two thoughts together and yet the man still loved her. He stayed with her. Why wouldn't she marry him? She needed him.

"Ralston," she said. "My loyal knight in shining armor. Or, in a black coat. It will do."

"It had better." He took the seat next to her at the work table in the back parlor and patted her hand.

"Armor is heavy, but I'm willing to wear it every day if that's what would make you happy, Pumpkin."

Pumpkin? From Ralston, too? Her head hurt. As if for the first time, she noticed the twined ring of branches on the table, the basket of holly, and the ribbon, and she made the connection at last. "Wreaths. We're making wreaths for Christmas. How lovely!"

It had always been her favorite thing to do as a girl, making the Christmas wreaths to decorate the house, next to making mud pies. But she couldn't shape mud pies at Christmas time. The ground was too frozen.

"Do you want any fruit for your wreath? Or just flowers?" Sophia asked.

"Lemons," Alice said. "Have we any lemons yet? Winthrop planted them so long ago."

"Not so very long ago," Sophia said, sharing a glance with Ralston. "The trees haven't borne fruit yet. But soon enough, if we wait patiently."

Alice nodded. It was a full minute before she realized she was still nodding. She had to stop nodding. Why couldn't she stop? Lord Averford came in. She stopped. Thank goodness, a distraction just in time. "Gabriel, we're making wreaths."

"I see, Alice. Very pretty. Perhaps I can hang one in my office to remind me to come out in time for Christmas to see my wife. Getting Kenner used to the estate is taking more time than I imagined."

Mr. Kenner, the new estate manager, Mrs. Hoyle's cousin. Alice started nodding again. He was no Winthrop. No one ever could be. God, she missed Winthrop. He would never stand for everyone treating her like a child. There was a time that she wouldn't have, either, but she was so tired. Too tired to protest. She said terrible things to Sophia when she got tired. Sophia always said it would pass, but Alice wasn't getting better. Why wasn't she? Her head started to ache again.

"I'm out of wire," Sophia said. "There's another roll in my writing desk. I'll just be a moment."

"No, I'll get it," Alice said. "Please. I would like to start feeling useful again. You can't imagine what it's like inside my head. I need to be useful."

Sophia flashed her a look of sympathy. "You go on. It's…"

"I know. It's in your desk. In the drawing room. I can find my way alone." In the desk, of course. She knew. Her mind seemed to be a little clearer, even if her head did hurt.

She got up carefully. It wouldn't do to make a mess of things. She walked across the room, staying focused on the doorway and then on the pictures on the wall, and before she knew it, she was in the drawing room. She'd done it! Though she wasn't sure it was an occasion to celebrate, simply getting from one room to the next.

She fumbled with the latch on the desk but managed to open it, and she reached for the wire. But then, her eyes found focus on an envelope bearing her name. Why did Sophia have a letter addressed to her? Alice had probably known about it and just forgot. Sometimes she forgot things, like being engaged to Lord Ralston.

But things came back to her, too. Seeing her ring reminded her that she had said yes. He'd asked her in the drawing room one evening after Agatha had left for the Dower House and Sophia and Gabriel had left them alone in front of the fireplace. Ralston had asked her if she wanted a blanket, and he'd covered her lap with the same blanket that Logan had worn that night after the storm. How she'd laughed! She couldn't explain the joke to Ralston, so she simply said she was so happy to be with him. And then he'd said he was glad to hear it and pulled out the box with the ring.

She still couldn't remember having seen the letter. She slipped it into her pocket and planned to ask Sophia when she handed her the wire. Alice had managed to focus and had formed a plan. The world was slowly becoming less fuzzy around the edges. The doctor said she would make progress, if a little slowly. And here she was, progress.

She walked a little faster, filled with a little more confidence, as she returned to the back parlor.

"Here is your wire, my lady." She even performed a little bow.

Sophia thanked her. "You seem to be in good spirits. Are you beginning to feel a little better perhaps? Do you still have the buzzing in your head?"

"It's still there, but it seems a little quieter. I think the walk did me some good, actually. Maybe it helped clear my head just a little." She decided to ask about the letter later. If it had been bad news, maybe she did not want to know just now.

"Tea, Alice?" Ralston poured her a cup. "Drink up. It might help clear your head further."

"Worth a try." She smiled over the edge of the

cup, taking a sip. "Ooh, hot. I'll just let it cool down a moment."

She set the cup in the saucer and looked over to watch Sophia putting the finishing touches on her wreath.

"It's beautiful, Sophia," Ralston said, looking it over.

"It is," Alice agreed, though she thought it was nothing to the ones she used to craft and would make again once her head got better.

"You're an artist, darling." Averford did not even look up from his newspaper.

"She is," Ralston agreed. "I like the way you've put a cluster of poinsettia on this side and echoed the pattern on the other side with ribbon."

He smiled at Sophia, baring his large, white teeth. His fox grin, as Alice had come to think of it. Alice sat a little straighter in her chair. Was he flirting with her sister? She knocked the teacup over with her elbow. Fortunately, cup and saucer landed on the rug without making a sound. While Ralston and Sophia were distracted by Sophia's handiwork, Alice simply picked the cup up and put it back without saying a word. She didn't want to call any more attention to her failures. It was time to show everyone that she could beat this thing. Her mind would be whole again.

"Your tea cooled enough to drink it?" Ralston asked, looking over at last to nod at the empty cup. "Another cup?"

"No. I think I've had enough. Perhaps I should go lie down."

Once Sophia finished tucking Alice in for a nap and left her alone, blessedly alone at last, Alice got up again. The buzzing had stopped. She could see the objects in her room clearly, no longer through a haze. It was happening at last. She was getting better. The doctor had given her the impression it would happen slowly, a little at a time. But this was more sudden. First, she couldn't stop nodding and could barely remember her own engagement, and in the next hour or so, she felt almost completely back to herself. Thank God. Sophia would be so relieved. Ralston would realize he wasn't marrying an idiot. Lord Averford might even look up from his paper to congratulate her.

But first, she remembered the letter from Sophia's writing desk. Why did her sister have a letter addressed to her that did not appear to have even been opened? She looked. It was from Winthrop. Her heart beat a frantic tattoo.

What might he have said? She wanted to rip into it right away, but no. She decided to go to the conservatory to read it next to the lemon trees, to feel like he was with her again, if only for the moment.

Sixteen

ALICE'S HEART SANK WITH EVERY WORD. LOGAN *HAD* wanted to say good-bye. He'd written! How could Sophia have kept it from her? He'd asked Alice to meet and let him explain, and she'd never answered him because she'd had no idea he'd written. In Alice's mental state, could she blame Sophia for protecting her? She supposed she could. She did.

She paced in front of the lemon trees. If only Logan could see how well the trees were thriving under the gardener's care. She would tell him. She would pack and leave at once and tell him. It was too risky to wait. If Sophia had been deliberately keeping Alice from Logan, she would prevent Alice from seeing him. If Alice wrote a letter, she couldn't trust Sophia to post it. Sophia would convince Alice that she was too unwell to make a journey. Alice didn't even know where Stratton Place was, exactly, but she would find out.

In less than an hour, Sophia would return to Alice's room to check on her. They seldom left her alone for long. She had to hurry. She had to get away, to get to

Logan. She returned to her room to pull on a warm coat, her hat, and gloves. Her more sensible walking boots were at the Dower House. Agatha would help her, wouldn't she? Agatha would never choose to side with Sophia over Alice. Before leaving, Alice grabbed one last thing—the pin that Grandmother had given Sophia, and Sophia had given to her. If she ever needed luck in finding the right man, it was now.

At the Dower House, Agatha had proven more than helpful.

"They kept saying you were wrong here"—Agatha tapped a finger to her temple—"but I knew you were right. The only thing that wasn't right was you letting them tell you what to do all day. I'm glad you've snapped out of that."

"Head injuries can take time to heal, Auntie," Alice said. "But I seem to be feeling much better."

"Head injuries? Bah. It's Lord Ralston. He's a wizard who cast his spell on you. You're feeling better because you're away from him. The further, the better."

"You don't like Lord Ralston?" Alice ignored the wizard accusation, but she did feel better than she had in a while.

Agatha shuddered. "He's most impolite. Mary agrees with me."

Alice hadn't counted on the maid being part of their conversation, but she supposed Agatha considered Mary a confidante. Alice would just have to trust the maid, too, or take care in how much she revealed.

"There's something off about the man. I can't think what. He has fortune and birth to his credit, but he lacks a certain…" Mary sighed. "Give me time, I will think of it."

"Time is exactly what I haven't got. It will be less than an hour before Sophia discovers me missing. It's not that I mean to run off without a word and worry her, but I do need to get away and she'll stop me if she can. She wants me to marry an earl."

"Where do you mean to go? Home to your parents?" Agatha looked concerned. "Your mother would certainly report to Sophia the minute you arrived."

"I have somewhere else in mind."

"You're going to see Mr. Winthrop." Agatha folded her hands across her chest as if enchanted by the idea.

"How do you know? Have you seen something in the cards to make such a prediction?" Alice couldn't doubt supernatural interference when Agatha became certain of something.

"I've seen things out my own windows, dear. Or out Thornbrook Park windows, as it were. The two of you together, more than once. No one could mistake your attraction."

Ah, it wasn't the paranormal at all that had given them away, but simple human interaction. If they'd been so obvious about it, it was a wonder no one had put an end to it sooner. "You must help me by redirecting Sophia's suspicions. It will certainly occur to her that Stratton Place is where I will have gone. I'll buy a ticket to London and change trains at the next stop. Be sure she thinks to look for me in London, with an old friend perhaps.

"Yes, tell her I planned to stay with Millicent

Fields. Millie's brother studied medicine. It would be natural for me to seek out Millie for help and advice. The London ruse should give me enough time to at least see Logan before Sophia arrives to drag me away. He wanted to talk to me, and I believe he deserves a chance to have his say."

"He does." Agatha smiled as if she'd known something all along that had eluded everyone else. "You do. You both do. You two will be very happy together at last!"

"We're simply going to have a conversation, Agatha. Don't go reading anything into it. I will let you know when I've arrived safely so that you won't have to be concerned."

Agatha waved a hand. "I'll know, my dear. I will know."

Alice didn't dare linger long enough to pack more. She'd gotten what she came for—sturdy shoes and a look at the map—and she wished Agatha and Mary luck in keeping up their end of the deception, for her sake. As much as she hated to have to ask them to lie for her, Alice supposed it was more important that someone knew where she had really gone and that she was safe. A quick good-bye and she was off on foot to the train station.

She left for London in the first-class car. If Sophia checked on her ticket purchase, it would only make sense for Alice to travel as she'd been accustomed. In Teckford, just off the train, she meant to hire a car, but a shop with sparkling jewels in the window by the station drew her notice. There was a pair of cuff links in the window, onyx with a small diamond set

in each, that looked like something she could imagine
Logan wearing. Suddenly, she had to have them. She
remembered when she'd considered courting him
with a gift, and she'd looked for just the thing to no
avail. Here it was before her eyes, exactly what she'd
hoped to buy him.

She went in. The price was more than she could
afford at the moment. She hadn't brought that much
money with her. But she had her engagement ring, and
she had her grandmother's pendant. Something told
her she had better hang on to the engagement ring.
She put it in her pocket for safekeeping and prepared
to offer the ruby pendant in exchange for the cuff links.
It seemed a fair trade, and the shopkeeper was agreeable. He even promised to put the pendant aside for a
reasonable amount of time so that she could return and
buy it back. Pleased with her bargaining skills and her
purchase, she returned to the station to look for a cab.

❧

The sun had gone down by the time she arrived, but
she could see that Stratton Place was almost as grand
an estate as Thornbrook Park. Her nerves skittered as
the car left her and she walked to the door. Perhaps
coming here had been a mistake. She would arrive
unexpected. They were probably getting ready for
dinner. She should have told the car to wait. But it was
Logan, she assured herself. He would never be sorry to
see her, would he?

A butler of about the same age as Finch—which was
to say a stately, formal, older man—answered the door.

"Lady Alice Emerson." She gave her name, trying to appear authoritative and in command when her insides were quivering like aspic. "I'm here to see Mr. Winthrop. He's not expecting me."

"Come in." The butler welcomed her into the hall. "One moment."

In that moment, her own heartbeat echoed in her ears so loudly that she feared her heart was about to explode. When Winthrop, elegantly attired in white tie and black tails, appeared from around a corner and stepped into the hall, she was nearly convinced that her heart did actually burst. It was all she could do to stand on her own accord and not run and collapse into his arms.

"Mr. Winthrop," she said, more coolly than she felt. "You're looking well. I hope I'm not interrupting your dinner."

"Alice." His jaw dropped. He made no effort to keep up an act of formal politeness between them. He closed the distance and took her in his arms. She nearly sobbed with relief.

Returning his embrace, afraid she might have half strangled him, she stayed in his arms a moment too long to be certain she had regained her composure. At last, he held her at arm's length.

"I wasn't sure I would see you again. You never answered my letter. I thought perhaps you were holding a grudge for my leaving without saying good-bye."

"I am holding a grudge." She smiled and stripped off her gloves, prepared to stay a while. "You know me too well. But I'm willing to give you a chance to explain. We are friends, after all."

"Yes. Of course we are." He took her hands in his and gave a gentle squeeze. "I'm sorry. I'm—I'm still astonished by your presence. You're really here? I'm not imagining?"

"I'm here." She suddenly became aware of the butler standing off to the side, no doubt waiting to see if he could take her hat and coat. "I got your letter at last, and I came at once."

"I'm glad you did." He held her gaze, perhaps still a little dazed by her sudden appearance.

She couldn't take her eyes off him. She knew Winthrop, the estate manager, but she was meeting Logan Winthrop, the gentleman's son, for the first time. His hair was neater, smoother, perhaps combed into place with pomade, and his clothes were posh, much more so than his estate manager's business suits. He stood straighter, taller, and he had replaced his brusque stoicism with a certain rough elegance.

The difference was in his demeanor and mostly in the area of his mouth, she realized. His lips seemed fuller and more inviting now that he'd softened his mouth from the usual tense, grim line. This man could be a baron, though of course he was a second son. His brother was around somewhere, possibly sitting at the dining table wondering what had become of Logan.

"Your house is lovely," she said at last to break the awkward silence. "You grew up here?"

The butler, growing impatient now, gave a little cough.

"Barnett, why don't you take the lady's coat? Inform my brother that we're to have a guest for dinner."

"I'm not dressed for dinner." She shrugged out

of her coat, feeling suddenly awkward in the simple emerald frock she'd worn all afternoon. "I didn't plan to stay."

"But you've traveled a bit. You don't mean to head right back to Thornbrook?"

She shook her head. "I've no idea. I didn't really plan much at all. I saw my chance to get away and I took it. I suppose I should explain."

A beautiful woman with golden hair pinned into a chignon stepped into the hall. Julia? Alice hadn't even thought that Logan might have reconciled with his first love. Of course, that would explain why he couldn't say good-bye, and why he'd left Thornbrook in such a hurry. Perhaps they'd met again when he'd come to visit his brother and somehow it all came together for them at last.

"Logan?" the beauty said. "Are we to have company?"

Heat rushed to Alice's cheeks. "I see now. I'm sorry. I shouldn't have come. Just call the butler back and I'll ring for a car…"

"What are you going on about, Alice? Let me introduce you to my family, please." He took her by the arm. "Ellen, this is Lady Alice. Lady Alice, this is my sister-in-law, Ellen, the Baroness Emsbury."

Ellen. His sister-in-law. She breathed a sigh of relief.

"Call me Ellen, please, Alice. We're not very formal here at Stratton Place, all present appearances aside." She gestured to her gorgeous gown of pale yellow silk dotted with diamond-like crystals. "We're having a dress-up night. We do it now and then when the children join us for dinner instead of eating in the nursery. They do enjoy making a fuss."

"You don't dress for dinner every night?" She looked to Logan.

"We're not quite as elegant as the Thornbrook set, I suppose." He smiled, then turned to Ellen. "I hope I'm not holding things up. Are the girls ready to go in?"

"They're still with Mrs. Leenders. I can just imagine what delightful princess ensembles they're putting together for us. I know it involves pink tulle. I saw Mrs. Leenders carrying a basketful into their room. They do like to go all out. I think it's important to indulge their imaginations, don't you?" Ellen turned to Alice.

"Yes, of course. My sister was the princess in our house. I went through a phase in which I was determined to be a pirate. I wanted to come to dinner in trousers tucked into boots and with a red silk cape and a patch over one eye, but Mother absolutely refused to allow it. I'm still suffering from the effects of deprivation." She mocked a swoon.

"Don't let her fool you, Ellen. Alice has never been deprived in her life. She wouldn't allow it." Winthrop laughed, a sound all too rare to hear at Thornbrook Park. Was she to believe that he was both relaxed *and* jovial in his own home?

She felt out of sorts, uncertain of what to do or say. Her head felt right. It wasn't that she was still ailing. Perhaps if she'd dressed appropriately…

"Alice, come with me." Ellen held out her hand. "We're about the same size. Who says grown women can't have a little fun with dress-up?"

"Oh, no need to trouble. I don't plan to intrude—"

Logan took her other hand. "Alice, you're a welcome guest at Stratton Place, never an intrusion.

I would be honored for you to join us at dinner. Afterward, we can talk."

She didn't want to be rude. If Ellen was anything like Sophia, she had closets full of gowns, more than enough to happily share. "Thank you. I *would* like to freshen up."

"I'll be waiting with John in the drawing room."

"John is your husband?" Alice asked once they were upstairs. "Logan's brother?"

Ellen nodded. "I can't tell you how pleased John is with Logan's return. We missed him terribly. And of course, John is still weak from having been sick and welcomes Logan's advice on running the estate."

"There's no one better at management than Logan. Lord Averford has had a trying time doing without him these past few weeks." Alice wondered at Logan staying away so long with such a warm and welcoming family missing him at Stratton Place. She wished they'd had time to talk alone before dinner, but she supposed it would take Sophia at least a day to figure out that Alice wasn't in London and catch up to her. They would have their chance.

❧

"She's here," Logan told John upon his return to the drawing room. "Lady Alice, from Thornbrook Park. She has come to see me."

He'd told John and Ellen about Alice, briefly, but enough that they had formed some idea of what she meant to him. "A wonder that she didn't call ahead. But you said she was impetuous."

"Did I? I thought I said tenacious. But she is also impetuous." Unable to contain his nerves, he paced in front of the fire. "Just seeing her again… I had no idea what effect it would have on me. I'm glad she's well. She looks well. You'll see. She's with Ellen. They're dressing up. Alice didn't bring any bags. I don't know why. We've hardly had a chance to talk."

"You're making up for it by talking at me." John laughed. "Sit down, man. You're making me nervous."

"Sorry." Logan flexed his hands and straightened them, trying to release tension. "It's just that—she's here."

"Yes, you've said so."

"Why did her sister let her come alone? It's odd, so soon after Alice's injury. I guess it has been nearly three weeks now."

"You could put in a call to Lord Averford," John suggested.

"Not until we have a chance to talk. After dinner."

John gestured to the doorway, causing Logan to turn around. He'd barely recovered his ability to breathe from when Alice had suddenly appeared in his entry hall. Now he felt the wind knocked out of him again at the sight of her in a gown of shimmering rose silk that clung to her slight figure, accentuating her few natural curves. The hem was split to tease the barest hint of leg from ankle to knee under a petticoat of glittery gold netting, the same gold netting that formed a shawl-like collar over her pretty white shoulders. A diamond tiara sparkled in her elaborately styled auburn hair.

He went to her, bent on one knee, kissed her silk-gloved hand, and rose. "A princess stands before us. Two princesses." No sense in leaving out Ellen, who had adorned herself further with showy jewels, aquamarines glistening on her tiara, her choker, and a matching bracelet.

"I prefer to think of myself as the queen." Ellen drifted over to stand by her husband, who was perched on the corner of the sofa.

"You are my queen, darling." John rose to kiss his wife on the cheek.

"This is my brother, John." Logan led Alice across the room. "John, Lady Alice Emerson."

"A pleasure to meet you." John folded her hand in his. "I'm glad you've come to visit. I hope you're feeling much better."

"Much better than I was three weeks ago. Thank you for asking. And you? You had your brother worried." She and Logan had hardly had a chance to talk about his homecoming, but Alice knew him well enough to imagine what it must have taken to get him home.

"I'm much better, too. I tire easily, but I suppose that's to be expected."

"Recovery can be slow, or so I've heard." Alice nodded sympathetically. "No need to rush into anything."

"I hope we can rush into dinner soon. I'm getting hungry." John looked at Ellen. "Any word from the girls?"

"Ah, I think I hear them now." Ellen stood with John, Logan, and Alice, all of them turning expectantly to the open double doors, waiting for the children to make their grand entrance.

The butler introduced them as if they were esteemed visitors from enchanted foreign lands.

"Princess Laura of Lillyhampton." The youngest, age five, came in draped in yards of tulle, pink as her mother had warned. She wore a sable stole over her shoulders and a crown fashioned from flowers over her ebony curls.

"Princess Sarah of Sweetenburg." The middle girl, seven years old, used the pink tulle as a veil that cascaded from a cone-shaped hat of pink silk. Her dress had most likely been one of her mother's old ball gowns, cut down to size and with an added lace collar.

"Princess Grace of Gleeshiredale." Julia's Grace floated into the room on a cloud of billowing white lace and ice blue velvet. She had apparently opted against a crown, letting her golden hair flow loosely around her shoulders, her only ornament. Growing up fast, she wouldn't be content to play with the younger girls in the nursery for much longer.

"Well done." Their father clapped.

"Such beautiful princesses. Thank you for gracing us with your presence." Their mother curtsied.

"My name is Grace. I'm gracing you." Grace spun in a circle and laughed.

"Allow me to introduce another visiting princess, a friend of mine from Thornbrook Park, Lady Alice Emerson."

"*Lady* Alice?" Laura contorted her face in confusion. "You said she was a princess."

"She's a princess to me."

Sarah laughed behind her hand. "Uncle Logan is in love."

He turned to Alice, but she'd focused her beaming smile on the girls and didn't seem to be aware of him.

"Sarah, don't be impolite," her mother corrected her.

"I'm very glad to meet you all." Alice dipped to her lowest royal curtsey. "I had no idea I would be in the presence of royalty. I hope that I will remember to mind my manners."

Laura got as close to Alice as her tulle would allow and whispered loudly, "We're not really princesses. It's just an act."

Alice nodded. "Thank goodness. The last time I dined with a princess, she wanted to throw me in the dungeon for eating too fast. Your uncle says that I eat like a rabid wolf."

Now she turned her attention to him, and it was his turn to blush. "I'm sorry, Alice. I should never have said such a thing, a lie. You pick at your food like a delicate bird, a sparrow."

"I value your honesty, Logan. The wolf reference will suffice."

"Oh dear, what shall we do?" Ellen mocked horror. "We have more ladies than gentlemen present. Who is to escort whom into the dining room?"

"I'll take two princesses, Laura and Sarah," John volunteered. "One on each arm. You take Grace, Ellen, leaving Logan to escort Lady Alice."

"That will do the trick." Ellen offered her arm to Grace.

Logan tucked Alice's hand into the crook of his elbow. "You look exquisite, Princess."

The last time he'd called her exquisite, she had been stark naked in the glow of a roaring fire. He preferred her naked, but the pretty gown was an admittedly better choice for mixed company. Still, he hoped he would have another chance to get her naked. His memories could only get him so far.

"Thank you. I have my fairy godmother to thank. You look a bit like you might have fallen under an enchantment yourself, Logan. I admit that seeing you again has had an overwhelming effect on me."

"Not too overwhelming, I hope. I do still worry about your health." He pulled out the chair next to his. He wasn't about to risk having Ellen work up a seating arrangement that would take Alice too far from him. They had too much to catch up on, and he was eager to get on with the meal and then excuse them to go conduct a more private conversation.

"I've never felt better," she said, placing her hand meaningfully atop his.

⤜◦⤛

After a dinner that featured a few too many cloyingly sweet courses to please adult palates, they spent some time with the family in the drawing room before Ellen declared it bedtime for the princesses. After they said their good-nights, Logan led Alice to a small parlor where they could speak privately. She took a seat on the sofa, and he pulled an armchair closer to her.

"I'll get to why I'm here in a moment," she said, her mouth going dry. "But first, a question. I'm curious. Grace calls Laura and Sarah her sisters, but yet she refers to Ellen and John as uncle and aunt."

Logan nodded as if he'd been expecting the question. "John and Ellen agreed to adopt her at birth."

"Your family is wonderful, Logan." That John and

Ellen had adopted the girl confirmed her suspicions. Grace was his daughter. Somehow Julia had agreed to let them raise her as one of their own. "The girls all seem to adore you, and it's clear that John and Ellen have missed you all these years. I can't imagine what kept you so stubbornly away, though I know you're about to tell me. But first, let me tell you that I didn't get your letter until today."

"I sent it not long after I departed from Thornbrook Park, once I knew you were conscious and recovering. When I didn't hear from you, I'd assumed you'd given up on me."

"Given up? Certainly you know me better than that. I don't give up easily." She smiled, wishing it was easier to bridge the gap between them. Why did she suddenly feel so distant from him? "I simply didn't know. I woke up and was told that you'd gone, and that you planned to leave Thornbrook Park. I had no idea what to think, and I was barely able to consider it. Apparently, I wasn't quite right when I woke up."

"Wasn't right?" He moved to the couch next to her and took her hand. "What do you mean? The doctor didn't think there would be any permanent damage."

"Not permanent, fortunately. I feel better at last."

"At last?" A dark brow shot up. "How long did it take for your recovery? Sophia lied to me. She said you were yourself right away."

She shrugged. "I think I was. I remember that when I first regained consciousness, I felt clear-headed, though there was slight pain and a buzzing in my ears. And then…"

"Then?" he prompted her.

"I seemed to get worse. My mind grew fuzzy. I had trouble remembering details. Even just this morning, I found myself nodding my head and being unable to stop."

"Unable to stop nodding?"

"It sounds odd, I know. I felt trapped in a fog, and suddenly it just lifted. The doctor said my progress would be gradual, and I thought he meant it could take days or weeks. Instead, it happened over the course of a day, today."

"Just today? Alice, I could have waited. You needn't have rushed out immediately. Are you sure you're well?" He placed a hand to her forehead, and the contact drove her to long for his touch elsewhere, all over her.

"I am. At last, I am."

He stroked his jaw as if considering. "That doesn't seem quite right, does it? I've seen a few head injuries in my time, though nothing as serious, and I assumed that being clear-headed when you woke meant that you were on the way to a full recovery."

"On the way, yes, but not quite there, I suppose. But I feel better, and that's the main thing, isn't it? Earlier today, in my determination to finally regain some independence, I stumbled across your letter and I knew I had to see you. I came at once."

"Stumbled across? Did someone hide it from you?"

"Sophia. She has become an overprotective hen, always right at my side." She couldn't bring herself to bring up Lord Ralston or her engagement, not yet. She'd left the ring in her coat pocket with the cuff links. "I think she might have thought I wasn't ready to hear from you. I didn't tell her what happened between us, exactly, but I asked for you when I woke. I believe that's what gave her cause for concern. At that time, I didn't care what she thought. I only wanted to see you." She watched him for a reaction.

"She knew before you woke," he said, surprising her. "She asked me to leave. My concern when you were thrown from your horse was too apparent, and she worried what people would think, rightfully so. I didn't want to leave your side. I had to be reminded of my duty and yours."

"*My* duty? To marry to her satisfaction?" Hope flooded her. He'd wanted to stay. She placed a hand on his cheek. "I knew you wouldn't leave me. We're friends."

"Friends," he repeated, a slow smile spreading on his lips, and then fading fast. "I hope you're still my friend when I tell you that I confessed to Sophia that we were intimate. I was mad with worry, Alice. I told her that I'd proposed to you. It explains why she felt the need to protect you from me, I suppose."

"I'm perfectly capable of protecting myself. Logan, she had me in a prison. At least that's what it felt like. I'm free. I'm myself again at last. But why didn't she tell me she knew? Why didn't she ask me about you?" If Sophia knew Alice had been intimate with a man, wouldn't she feel the need to lecture Alice about being ruined?

His eyes narrowed with concern. "You said you were having memory problems. Perhaps she thought you'd forgotten."

"I could never forget. Our night together is emblazoned in my mind. It will be with me forever, and it means more to me than I could ever express."

She placed her hands on his arm, longing for more intimate contact.

"You can't blame Sophia for wanting to protect you, especially if she thought you had a chance with Ralston. You could be a countess, her social equal. Blame is a terrible thing. It can warp your perspective. I held myself accountable for my own actions for far too long. I've finally been able to forgive myself, but it hasn't been easy, especially being here with so many reminders."

"I've been protected for far too long. It's time I took matters into my own hands." Reminders? Alice wondered if he meant reminders of Julia, or the woman herself. "Are you ready to tell me what there was to forgive?"

"Tomorrow. It's late. You've had a long day and I don't want to exhaust you. You're still healing."

Tomorrow. She expected she would hear about Julia tomorrow. Perhaps he was engaged as well and there would be no need for her to fear telling him that she'd accepted Ralston. "I don't want to be away from you. I've missed you."

"I've missed you as well, Alice. At least we're under the same roof. I'm so glad that you've come."

Logan rose to escort her to her room, but she stopped him at the door.

"Wait, please." There was only one thing that could ease the ache that had risen from deep inside her. She stood on her toes and gently brushed her lips to his. When he didn't recoil, she traced the outline of his lips with her tongue.

One strong arm curled around her waist and pulled

her tighter to him as his mouth opened hungrily on hers. Her knees weakened. Without the strength of his arm around her, she might have stumbled. The fiery curl of desire licked at her core, replacing the hollow ache. She wanted him. She would always want him. And as soon as she could free herself of her unfortunate entanglement with Lord Ralston, she meant to have him.

"Good night, Logan. I think it best I leave you here and find my own way to my room."

Seventeen

She woke early the next morning, far too early. Sleep had eluded her. The comfort of the bed, luxury of the room, and quiet of the night did not matter next to her endless thoughts of Logan. Did he love her like she loved him? Did it matter? They couldn't be together. He had his family and his home again. Perhaps he had Julia back, too. What would he need with Alice anymore?

If that was the case, she might as well marry Lord Ralston. As soon as Sophia found her and insisted on her return to Thornbrook Park, they would announce the engagement. But perhaps she needn't think of marriage as a prison. As a married woman, she would be more freely able to travel alone, not less. Perhaps she and Ralston could come to some sort of agreement on what their marriage would entail. She would be willing to share his bed and give him heirs, as long as she were free to embark on adventures once the nursery was filled. A modern marriage. Why not?

She knew why not. Her heart was engaged elsewhere. Would she bare herself to Ralston, picturing

Logan in his place all the while? Now that she knew what it was to love, could she be intimate with a man for whom she held no genuine affection? She supposed women did it all the time, but she couldn't be one of those women now that she knew real love. Not at all. Instead of lying in bed wondering, she got up, washed, and dressed. It was early, too early to ring for a maid. She managed on her own and set out to explore Stratton Place.

In one of the small parlors, she ran into the house-keeper. "I was having a look around," she explained. "It's too early for breakfast, so I thought I might explore."

"I'm Mrs. Morrison, Lady Alice. My apologies that you were not properly shown around yesterday, but I understand it was late when you arrived."

Mrs. Morrison, a little on the plump side, had a round face and wispy white hair that reminded Alice of Aunt Agatha. She inspired confidence, and Alice took a chance to ask her about Logan.

"I'm interested in Mr. Winthrop." Alice came right out with it. "Have you been with the family long enough to know what he was like as a boy?"

"Oh, yes." Mrs. Morrison nodded. "Logan was a quiet boy, very shy. He kept to himself most of the time, though John, six years older, doted on his younger brother when John wasn't off at school. Logan came out of his shell a bit once he became friends with Miss Julia Kirkland. The Kirkland family lived in a manor house across the green. You might have passed it when you arrived."

"It was dark." She'd been concerned only with getting to Stratton Place safely.

"Of course. It was just Julia and her parents, an older couple. Her father ran a textile mill over in Bainsbridge. They say his lungs went bad from inhaling all the fine fibers that fill the air at the mill. He was ailing most of the time. Julia was a lively child, a beautiful girl with long, blond hair."

"Like Grace's."

Mrs. Morrison smiled. "Grace is the very image of her mother. Those two, Logan and Julia, were always underfoot in the house when they were not running wild outside. From the day they met, the two of them became inseparable companions, but of course the time came when Logan had to go off to school."

"The separation must have been hard on them. Especially Logan, suffering from shyness." Alice could picture him, a brooding boy with dark eyes and tousled hair.

"I believe it was." Mrs. Morrison paused as if considering how much to reveal, but fortunately she went on. "While he was away, Julia became enamored of the Earl of Stanhope. The earl was off at school when Logan and Julia were younger and had returned to Wenderton, his estate not far from here, upon the death of his father. He met Julia at one ball or another and swept her off her feet. He was a man. Logan was yet very much a boy. Still, when Logan came home from Harrow, he proposed to Julia expecting to be accepted."

"He must have been devastated when she turned him down." Alice could imagine the crushing blow to a shy young man who trusted and loved as completely as Logan would have. "She did turn him down?"

Mrs. Morrison nodded. "She hoped they would

remain friends, but he went months without speaking to her. He refused to attend her wedding."

"How could she have expected him to? It must have felt like a betrayal." Poor Logan, rejected and alone, isolated from his only friend—his closest friend, anyway.

"At some point, they became friends again. I couldn't tell you how it happened."

Alice suspected Mrs. Morrison knew exactly how. Servants always did. Out of respect, Mrs. Morrison would hold back that part of the story.

"And shortly after, Stanhope was killed?" Alice asked.

"Such a scandal. He was a powerful man from a respectable family. Some say his downfall was in loving the wrong woman. Those are the ones who blamed Logan."

"But Logan didn't kill him. Not really. He must have been covering for someone."

"I've said too much. It's his story to tell."

"I'm sorry. I've kept you far too long. Thank you for everything, Mrs. Morrison."

"You're welcome. Can I get you anything?"

"Yes. I left something in the pocket of my coat. If you could get my coat for me and direct me to Logan's office or study, if he has such a nook in the house?"

"He does. He shares it with his brother, but I believe Logan is there now. Like you, he was up very early."

The news didn't surprise her. "Excellent, Mrs. Morrison. I will be grateful if you lead me to him."

Logan hadn't slept. How could he get a moment's rest knowing that Alice was under the same roof, that she'd slipped away from her likely disapproving sister just to come and see him? He wanted to spend every waking moment with her, but she'd had a long day and she'd barely regained her health. Reluctantly, he'd watched her go off to bed. In the morning, his heart picked up speed when someone knocked on his office door and he saw that it was Alice.

"Come in, Alice. Good morning. I trust you slept well?" He rose to greet her.

No one else was up yet, as far as he knew. Not even the girls, and they usually scampered through the halls at the crack of dawn with the nanny chasing after them.

She started to smile and nod, then shook her head instead. "Not a wink."

"I'm sorry. Is your room sufficient? I can have another prepared…"

"The room is ideal." She placed a hand on his arm. "I simply had too much racing around in my head. A good thing, really. It has been too long since my thoughts have been clear enough to keep me awake."

"You're dressed for walking?" He noticed she held her coat. "It's a beautiful day, especially for this time of year. The sun is shining and I daresay it's even a little warm outside. Let me call Barnett for my coat and I will join you for a walk." He rang for the butler.

"In a moment. First, I've got something for you." She took a small box out of her pocket and placed it on the desk between them.

"For me?"

"I wanted you to have something to remind you of me."

"I don't need reminders, Alice. You're on my mind all the time. I could never forget you."

"Still." She shrugged as if that was to be expected, but it was news to her. She was on his mind all the time? "I first had the idea to get you something a while ago, when I was trying to seduce you. But then I—well, things went along as they did, and I never got around to it. On my way here, I saw these in a window while I was passing a shop, and I knew I had to buy them for you. I just knew. Go ahead. Open the box."

He opened it to see a matched pair of onyx cuff links with diamond studs in the middle, tasteful but extravagant. He felt heat rise to his cheeks. "Alice, it's the man who is supposed to buy jewelry for his lady. This is most unusual."

"But do you like them?" Her eyes widened expectantly.

"I do. Very much. But I'm sure they were too expensive."

"Don't say you can't accept them. I won't bear it. I need you to have them. Please."

"All right, Alice. But I wish I had something for you. It's not even my birthday." Her lips began to form a slight pout, and he realized he was saying all the wrong things. He changed his tone. "Thank you. I love them. I will treasure them forever, as I treasure you."

She applauded his gracious performance of acceptance. "Well done. You're welcome. I'm so glad you like them."

"But you shouldn't have, you know."

"I did. It's almost Christmas. A gift is hardly out of line, and you can't give them back now."

He laughed and stepped around the desk to take her in his arms, where he felt that she belonged. It was good to have her back. "I never could stop you, Alice, when you set your mind to something. I'm not sure anyone could."

Before Logan could kiss her, as he so badly wanted to, the butler interrupted, appearing at the doorway with Logan's coat as if he'd anticipated Logan's request. Once Logan helped Alice into her coat and donned his own, he held out his arm to escort her to the grounds. They ambled to a lane that wrapped around the back of the house and wandered through the three garden hedgerows that were carved into arches along the way.

"I thought about doing something like this at Thornbrook Park." He gestured to the hedges. He couldn't remember having so many silences with Alice in the past. She'd been a veritable magpie. And now, so quiet. Had her feelings changed so much? "Sturridge changed my mind. Too much upkeep, he said."

"I find them rather charming." She let go of his arm, walked through one arch, and spun around the outside to go through again. "It's a shame that Sturridge lacked the bravery to execute the idea. The lemon trees are thriving, though."

"At last? Truly? When I left, I worried we would lose them both. They were dropping brown leaves by the hour."

"All green now with some buds. Perhaps we'll have lemons by spring."

"Probably not. They can take a few years to bear fruit. I read one of Brumley's books on the subject. I wish I'd read a book on you instead," he said, stopping to take her hands. "What's going on with you, Alice? Are you really well?"

"Of course. I'm much better now. I know I'm quiet. The accident left me quite shaken. Afterward, I didn't know what to think. I knew I wanted to see you. That was the one thing of which I'm certain. And then everything dissolved into the fog."

"The fog has lifted, though? It hasn't come back?"

"No. I'm free of fog. I am dying of curiosity, though. Where are you taking me?"

"We're reliving some of my past."

She stopped in her tracks. "If you're taking me to meet Julia, Logan, let's turn around now. I don't want to go. I can barely stand the thought of losing you, but I won't be able to meet the woman who will share your life instead of me."

Her words racked him so that he felt physically shaken. He managed to remain on his feet, but he felt as if her hand had reached right into his chest and gripped him by the heart. In two strides, he was at her side, pulling her into his arms and holding her as tightly as he dared. "Alice."

"Logan?" She remained in his arms, waiting.

"Alice, you'll never lose me. Not unless you want to, and even then…you'll always be a part of me, deep down." He took her hand and placed it on his chest, inside his coat. "You're in here, rooted like a weed. You've tunneled your way in and I can't rip you out."

"A weed?" She tilted her head, examining her hand

on his chest. "At one time, I thought your heart was made of stone. But perhaps it was only frozen earth, now melted."

"You melted it to damp, fertile soil."

"A weed, though? You could have at least said, 'Like a tree.' Rooted like a tree. It sounds a tad more romantic, doesn't it?"

"I'm no romantic. Maybe with a little more work. You do bring out the best in me. Although, 'My heart is made of damp soil' wouldn't exactly inspire poets, either." He laughed with her. The feeling of laughing with Alice again sent his spirit soaring. She could barely stand the thought of losing him? She thought Julia was still alive. "Trust me. Come with me. We're taking a walk through my past, not my present."

She nodded. "I trust you, Logan."

They walked past the brook, half frozen, and the tree he used to climb and sit on top of for hours all alone.

"You climbed way up there? Could you still climb it?"

"I'm not inclined to try. I was a bit more agile in those days."

"You're still very agile. I've watched you climb the eaves to clear clogged storm drains."

"Aha, I always felt like I was being watched." He turned to her, one eyebrow arched. "I supposed it one of Agatha's ghosts."

She tapped his arm playfully. "You've somehow grown a sense of humor since you've come home. It becomes you."

"If I've grown a sense of humor, it's something else you planted in my damp soil heart."

"We'll have to be careful with that. It's remarkably fertile."

"Or you're that remarkable a gardener. You've never tried your hand at it enough to know."

"Touché, Logan. I confess that I watched you all last summer. I could hardly take my eyes off you."

"I wasn't exactly blind to you. Even before you made yourself unavoidable. I noticed you when you first came to Thornbrook Park, though I convinced myself that I was an old man with no business ogling such a beautiful young creature."

"Now I'm a creature." She pretended to be offended. "But you didn't think me beautiful back then. Like everyone, you compared me to Sophia and found me wanting."

"Not at all. Alice, you've no idea how striking you are. When the sun hits at the right angle to bring out the red glints in your hair, we're all like moths to your flame. Your sister might be compared to Aphrodite, but you're my Artemis, a far more interesting goddess, one who hunts versus one who swans around looking pretty."

"I'm not much of a hunter, as evidenced by my fall from a horse. And to her credit, Sophia does far more than swan around. Especially once I gave her a purpose. She took to caregiving with an unexpected fervor. I didn't think I would ever manage to get out of her sight."

"But you did, and I'm delighted to have you with me. One can't help but notice you, Alice, even with your sister in proximity. But of course, it's your conversational skills that held my attention. I've missed our talks."

"As have I." She tucked her hand into his as they walked on. "And if by conversational skills, you mean my ability to talk until you have no choice but to listen and respond, then yes. I'm very skilled."

He led her along the bank of the brook toward the Kirkland house. He stopped at the edge of the woods, where the brook curved before it turned into the marsh and the slate roof of the manor house was just visible over the treetops.

"This is where I met Julia." He gestured at the clearing all around them, drab brown with the winter, but green with new life in the spring. "I suffered from shyness when I was a boy."

"Not exactly hard to believe."

"She found me here one afternoon, by that tree." He continued walking to where he pointed, leading Alice by the hand, and stopped to lean against the trunk. "We were eight years old. I'd gone for one of my long walks. Mother had died the previous year. With John off at school and Father always so busy, I spent a lot of time out of doors on my own. And I had quite an imagination, as children do. When she came across me, I was knee deep in the water, trying to catch a fish with my bare hands like a bear would."

Alice giggled. "Did you frighten her with your mighty growl?"

"I jumped when my hands actually made contact with a fish and fell in the water, and she roared with laughter at me. It was humiliating."

"Poor Logan. Your ego was bruised." Alice rumpled his hair.

"Until Julia got in the water with me. She claimed

to be an expert on bears, that she had seen them fishing in the brook on numerous occasions, and she knew exactly what to do."

"Oh." Alice blushed. "Like another woman who claimed to know what do with lemon trees. You keep running into females with vast experience in your topics of interest."

He brushed a wisp of hair from Alice's eyes. "Yes, it's my good fortune. For her part, Julia said that fishing all came down to knowing how to use one's claws to spear the fish at just the right moment. The fact that neither of us had claws didn't occur to us. We got very wet, and of course we caught no fish. But we became fast friends that day and remained so for many years. We would often meet here, at this very spot, and hatch our plans for the day's adventures.

"Years passed. I went away to school. Julia became bored waiting for me to come home and met someone else. It was inevitable. She was a beautiful seventeen-year-old girl, and some other man had the advantage of winning her heart in my absence. I'd had no idea. I came home and proposed right here on this spot with a ring that had been my grandmother's, a moonstone, not the most expensive stone but one that would mean something to us. We'd stayed out as late as we could when we were together in the summers. The nights with a full moon were our favorites because we could see at night almost as clearly as during the day.

"I used to tell her I would capture the moon for her, if I could, and here I was presenting it in a platinum band set with tiny diamond chips, like twinkling stars, on either side of it. She looked at me, astonishment widening her eyes, and said it was a lovely ring that I should save for the right girl."

"She didn't understand what you were asking? That you thought she was the one?" At Logan's side, Alice relaxed, leaning against the tree to hear the rest of what she'd rightfully decided was going to be a longer story.

"She understood perfectly. When she turned me down, though she did it as sweetly and gently as she could, I was angry. Hurt, but that came out as anger. I said things I regretted instantly. I threw the ring in the brook." He stomped to the water's edge and mimed the toss, reenacting, and turned back to Alice. "We didn't speak for a year. She married her earl and became Countess of Stanhope.

"Unfortunately, her marriage was not the fairy tale she'd dreamed. As she later told me, Stanhope spent much of his time gambling and drinking, and his estate was deeply in debt. When Julia accepted Stanhope's proposal, her mother had been dead for two years and her father's health was in steady decline. Stanhope proposed believing that Julia's father would be dead soon, leaving Julia his sole heir and enabling Stanhope to pay off his debts."

"How awful for her. I'm so sorry." Alice's brow furrowed with concern.

"The longer William Kirkland lived, the angrier and more resentful Stanhope became. He took it out on Julia. He would stay out gaming too long and drinking too much, and come home raring to tear into someone. It started as a slap here, a push there, and escalated to knocking Julia unconscious and even breaking bones. For her father and for the doctor who treated her, she always had a ready excuse."

"But she finally came to you. She knew that you would still do anything for her."

He shook his head. "It wasn't like that exactly. I happened upon her here one day. As I walked up"—he gestured to the path they'd followed—"I could see that she was soaking wet. I thought perhaps that she'd fallen in the brook, but she threw herself in again. And again. She kept throwing herself back into the water only to emerge a minute later.

"I thought she was trying to drown herself and going about it badly, and I ran all the way to try to stop her. That's when I saw her black eye, and I realized that she wasn't just wet from the brook, that she'd been crying. I said she had to stop whatever she was doing and talk to me. She said she was done, that she had finally learned to fish like a bear, and she held up her catch, shining in her palm."

"Your grandmother's ring." Alice's mouth gaped. "Fate. That's what Agatha would say."

"It felt like fate." He nodded. "She told me that she'd made a mistake in turning me down, and that she missed me. I held her while she cried. Finally, she told me about her marriage. I was ready to kill Stanhope right then with my bare hands. Of course, she convinced me to step aside. She was expecting his child. Her father believed her happily married, and his fondest wish had been that he could hold his first grandchild before he died. I should have protested. I should never have let her go back home to that monster, but I…"

"Whatever happened, Logan, you can't blame yourself."

He went on. "I believed her when she said that

telling Stanhope about the baby would make all the difference, that he wouldn't do anything to her that would hurt the child. She was five months along and she hadn't told him yet. At first, she'd said she was hoping he would beat her so that she would lose the baby and be free again, no trace of him remaining with her. Then, once she'd first felt the baby move, she realized how desperately she wanted to be a mother."

"My apologies, Logan." Alice placed her hand on his back consolingly. "I thought perhaps that Grace was your daughter, and that was why John and Ellen had agreed to raise her."

"I wished she could be." He had to inhale deeply to calm himself and keep the tears from his eyes as he thought about what happened next. "She was right, though. He didn't touch her for months after hearing they had a baby on the way. She continued with her pregnancy in good health, but she'd lied to Stanhope about when the baby was due. She hadn't wanted him to get angry with her for keeping things from him. She thought when she went into labor, she would say it was an early delivery and he would simply believe their child a miracle.

"In the meantime, we planned to run away together after the birth. Once we got to France, we would go on to America. I would claim her as my wife and the child as our own, and Stanhope would never find us. Again, I started to worry, and I told her that it might be easier for us to get away before the baby's birth. But Julia wouldn't hear of it. What would happen to her father? He wouldn't live much longer, and he deserved to hold his grandchild at least once.

"One afternoon, I was waiting here for her. She stayed with her father when Stanhope went to London on business, and she would come out to meet me. When she came riding up on a horse, I was overcome. She was heavily pregnant, too far along to be riding. Then I saw him chasing her on another horse, charging up behind her." He gestured to the clearing between the trees in the opposite direction from whence they'd come. It was as if he could still see Julia on her horse, approaching, looking behind her desperately to see how close Stanhope had gotten.

"A week earlier, Stanhope apparently had stumbled on a list she'd made herself, a list of things to pack. She'd tried to explain it away, but he'd apparently followed her undetected and had watched her with me. Our meetings were innocent. Sometimes I held her hand, but nothing more. Still, Stanhope concluded that the child was not his. He didn't snap right away. Instead, he coiled in wait to strike, the snake that he was.

"He pretended he was going off to London as planned and then surprised her at her father's house with the truth of his suspicions. When he started hitting her, she believed, rightfully so, that he didn't plan to stop until he'd killed her and the baby. She somehow managed to grab hold of a fire poker and hit him with that, knocking him unconscious long enough for her to get to the stable and mount the horse that she found saddled there.

"Stanhope came after her. He didn't even saddle a horse, just rode bareback all the way, and he caught up to her. On foot, I couldn't reach her before he did. He pulled her from the saddle and jumped on top of her and kept swinging. I ran and pulled him off and let the punches fly, telling her to run for help. Instead, she ran and grabbed my rifle from where it leaned against this tree, and pointed it at us. It had been John's birthday, and my excuse for getting out of the house was that I'd wanted to catch his birthday dinner—rabbit, John's favorite.

"I warned her not to shoot, afraid she would hit me by mistake, and fortunately, I managed to hit Stanhope with a good right hook that laid him out. Julia put the rifle down. We had just enough time, I believed, to get out of there before Stanhope could come after us again. But I was wrong. Julia had started to bleed and she was having contractions. I thought she might deliver her baby right there with Stanhope clinging to consciousness only feet away. He did, in fact, start to get up. I'm not sure he had the energy to come after us again, and I wasn't about to find out. I grabbed the rifle, and I shot him. He never got up again."

Logan paused, leaning against the tree with one arm for support and wiping his brow with the other. The high emotion of that fateful day came back to him in a rush—the worry, the fear, the joy, and the pain.

"But you had to. He would have killed Julia, or you both." Compassionate tears sparkled in Alice's eyes, and Logan had never loved her more for understanding the situation immediately. "He was a despicable man, and you were only protecting the woman you loved."

"At that point, I might not have been protecting anyone. I'm not sure he was in any condition to come after us, but I would not take the risk. I shot him. I only wished I'd done it sooner. But before I could get help for Julia, she was too far gone, about to give birth. With my own two hands, and plenty of sweat and tears, I delivered Julia's baby girl. I'd never been so scared, and I had no idea what I was doing, but that baby cried the loudest cries I'd ever heard at her birth.

"Julia and I smiled at each other, so relieved, because we knew the cries meant that the baby was strong and healthy. Julia wanted to name her Grace, after her mother. I had to leave them long enough to ride for help. The doctor came with a rig, and we were able to get Julia back to the house. She insisted on watching her father hold his granddaughter for the first time before she would agree to let the doctor have a look at her."

Alice looked puzzled. "Stanhope had been waiting at her father's house, beating her. Didn't her father know? The servants? How could no one have come after her?"

"Stanhope had arrived earlier that morning and dismissed all the servants with the exception of the one attendant who looked after Julia's father. They both somehow napped through Julia's arrival and Stanhope's first outburst. I suspect Stanhope might have actually drugged them."

"Drugged them?" Alice's eyes widened and she nibbled her lip, as if she'd thought of something, and then shook it off. "Horrifying. And Julia?"

"She'd lost too much blood. I thought, at first, that I'd done something wrong with the delivery, but the doctor suspected she had internal injuries from Stanhope's beating. She died hours after giving birth, and her father died the next day. Stanhope finally would have had what he wanted, but it was too late."

"I'm so sorry, Logan. I thought—"

"That she'd lived? How I wish. I lost her all over again, and I lost our dream of raising her child together. I went directly to the constable and turned myself in for the murder of Alexander Blythe, Earl of Stanhope. Despite my admission of guilt, witnesses came forward. The doctor testified about how badly Julia had been beaten. William Kirkland's servants testified about Stanhope arriving at the house and sending them away. Stanhope's own servants testified about his history of abuse and his debts. Stanhope's reputation suffered.

"Our family attorney was building a strong case for self-defense, but it wasn't self-defense. I wouldn't declare that it was. I insisted on sticking to my story, the truth, that I shot Stanhope to save Julia's life, and that my biggest regret was that I hadn't killed him sooner. It remains my biggest regret."

Alice shook her head. "But you would have been convicted for certain, and Julia would be the one unable to live with the guilt. He was a terrible man who acted reprehensibly. You did the best you could."

"I felt dead inside. Numb. My life was over. The woman I'd believed to be the love of my life was gone. John and Ellen adopted Grace. I had nothing left to live for, or so I believed. Instead of acting to save myself, I practically begged to be put on trial for the crime, but the constable refused to charge me with murder. No matter how much I tried to tell them otherwise, they ruled the death an accidental shooting and said I was free to go.

"At Stratton Place, John and Ellen were struggling to raise a new baby, and I was bringing bad attention to the house. Some people, our friends, supported me. An equal and louder number of people called for my arrest and trial, proclaiming that the law worked differently for the nobility. I couldn't bear the notoriety I'd brought to my family. I didn't want it to haunt Grace growing up. Mostly, I wanted to escape from everything and everyone I knew. I wanted to wallow in self-pity and grief. And I did.

"I spent years in France, Spain, Italy. I came home for the funeral when my father died and meant to head right back to France, and on to Morocco. One of my father's friends knew of a position, managing Thornbrook Park. When I was home from Harrow, before the tragedy, I assisted my father in managing the estate with Chalmers, our agent. John didn't have much of a head for business affairs. He still doesn't. But I thought I could learn to do the job, and do it well. I was tired of running from my past but still not ready to return home. The job at Thornbrook Park seemed the perfect solution."

"And there you stayed," Alice said. "And as sorry as I am for all that you've been through, and for your loss, I'm selfish enough to be glad that you stayed so that I had a chance to know you."

"Alice." He took a deep breath and held her hands in his. "It shattered me inside when Julia rejected me. I was young enough to believe that what we had was romantic love beyond the bonds of friendship. She chose someone else and begged for me to understand. She loved me, but not in the way that she loved

Stanhope. She truly thought him to be the missing part of herself. At the time, I didn't understand the way she described her feelings for him. I thought they were the same feelings I had for her, but they weren't quite. I didn't know it until I made love to you, Alice. That feeling, it's not like any other. It fills you. It was you, Alice, who showed me I had so much life yet to live. I want to live it with you."

When she stood looking at him for several seconds without speaking, a look of earnest confusion in her pretty hazel eyes, he feared that he'd lost her for good.

Eighteen

AFTER EVERYTHING HE'D JUST TOLD HER, ALL HE'D BEEN through, how could Alice do exactly what Julia had done and tell him that she planned to marry someone else? She had no desire to break his heart, and in fact, she felt her own heart beginning to splinter and crack around the edges.

"You know I never wanted to get married," she said, squeezing his fingers like she never wanted to let go.

"I'm aware, and I would never ask you to give up your dreams, Alice. We don't have to rush into anything. John needs me here for now, and you have your family. I'm sure Sophia is worried about you. Should you call her?"

"Not yet." She shuddered at the thought. "I have things to tell you, too. When I was recovering, and not quite myself…"

"The brain fog?"

"The brain fog." She nodded. "I thought you'd left me. I knew we were friends, but I thought you had come back to Stratton Place, never to return to

Thornbrook Park. I didn't know what to think. I was…Logan, I was lost. And so alone."

He embraced her. "I'm so sorry. I never meant to abandon you. I did, of course, at your sister's urging, and I'm very sorry for it, but I also thought I was doing the right thing for you. I didn't want to remove all of your options. Once people started drawing conclusions, you would have had to marry me to save your reputation, and it wasn't my choice to make for you."

"I love you for it, Logan. I do. I love you." The ache at her core at the thought of losing him confirmed it. "You know me like no one else, and you would never force me into a corner, trapped like a poor fox in a hunt." Or trapped like the fox's prey. Ralston was the fox, and he'd emerged victorious with her between his gleaming teeth. How could she marry such a man? But she'd given her word. How could she not?

"Never, Alice. You're made to be free."

"You did the right thing in leaving, I agree, as much as it hurt me to wake up and not find you by my side. But I was vulnerable. What if I had been damaged permanently? My head grew increasingly fuzzy. My ability to remember things that had just happened was sometimes there and sometimes gone. When it was time to leave Holcomb House and return to Thornbrook Park, Sophia invited Lord Ralston to accompany us. He has been there ever since."

"Staying with you, a guest at Thornbrook Park?" Logan's cobalt eyes darkened a shade.

"Staying with us. He looks after me with Sophia, always there, always right at my side. Sophia seems to welcome him as one of the family. And finally, I remembered something. Something awful, Logan. I'm so sorry."

"Good God, did he hurt you?" Logan held Alice closer and placed a kiss on her forehead. "If he did, Alice, I know what I will do. Perhaps I haven't changed that much after all."

She shook her head. "He hasn't hurt me. On the contrary. He has been doting on me. He said he loves me, that he will never leave me. And in a moment of weakness that I barely remember, to be honest, my head was so full of fog…"

"Alice, no." He closed his eyes as if to shut out the painful reality. "Tell me you haven't accepted him."

"I don't remember thinking I had any other option." She didn't bother to hold back the tears that filled her eyes. "I felt so scared, so alone. I've always loved being alone, but suddenly, it became the thing I dreaded most. In the quiet darkness, the buzzing in my head became louder and nearly unbearable. There were shadows in the fog. I wanted people around me all the time, noise and colors, anything but empty silence. I wanted so badly not to be alone, never to be alone."

"Sophia wouldn't ever cast you out. You must know that."

"But she wanted so badly for me to accept him. I knew it, though I hardly remembered my name. He presented a diamond ring, and he asked me to marry him, and I accepted him. I'm engaged to Lord Ralston, Logan." She placed her hand on his rough cheek. "I'm so sorry. But I mean to break it off as soon as I return to Thornbrook Park. I never would have accepted him in the first place if I wasn't so impaired."

He took her hands and clung to them. "Of course not. You weren't in your right mind. You can't be held accountable for your decision. He couldn't possibly expect you to stand by a promise made when you were not quite yourself. The bastard!" Suddenly, Logan's face contorted to rage. He dropped her hands, turned, and punched the tree trunk so forcefully that the blow echoed in the woods. His hand dripped blood, but he shook it off unconcerned and wrapped it with a kerchief from his pocket. "How could he take advantage of you at such a time? How could your sister allow it? Lord Averford?"

"I—" She held her hands out at her sides. "I'm at a loss. I don't know. Lord Averford has been tremendously busy with the new agent, who isn't catching on very well, by the way. He's hardly ever around lately. Aunt Agatha has been exiled to the Dower House. I don't think Ralston likes her very much."

"Who doesn't like Agatha? She's a delight."

Alice loved him all the more for loving her dotty old aunt. "She is. I know. Sophia has taken to Ralston like they're fast friends, co-conspirators in caring for invalid me. Only now I'm better. They won't know quite what to think of me."

"They should never have underestimated you, Alice. I'm sorry if I scared you with my anger." He embraced her again. "I just—I can't bear men who take advantage of weakness. It's like Stanhope all over again."

"Lord Ralston's not that bad. I do believe he means

well, and for some reason, he seems to love me. I remember thinking that anyone who wanted to put up with me in my addlepated state must truly care for me."

"No." Logan shook his head. He released Alice and began to pace up and down the brook's bank, head down in contemplation "No, there's something he wants. There has to be. Men like Ralston are not attracted to infirmity."

Now she was a little insulted. Was she not a beauty? Flame to moths? Artemis and all that? "Why not? The doctor assured him I would get better in time. If he found himself attracted to me, he might have been simply acting on his best chance to secure my affection for himself."

Logan's head shot up. "Really? You don't think he has any ulterior motives? Lovely as you are, Alice, I'm not sure it's enough to entice a man like Ralston."

"Excuse me? I'll not stand here and be insulted." She turned away.

"I love you"—he placed a hand on her shoulder, gently urging her to look back—"in any condition. Sick, well, completely mad. I love you no matter what. But…"

"But another man couldn't possibly love me enough to make a commitment to me without some ulterior motive?"

"He's a vain man, Alice. Shallow. Surely you could sense it."

"I know he has been at my side since the accident, even when I've been far less than at my best." She strode with purpose back to the path that they'd followed to this spot.

"You don't love him, Alice." He walked quickly to catch up and take her arm. "You couldn't possibly. You're nothing alike."

She nudged away from him. "I don't see that you have any right to judge. He did swear his devotion to me."

"Very good." Logan threw his hands in the air, exasperated, clearly not thinking it very good at all. "Go on and marry the man, if you're so determined to see only the best in him."

She stopped and crossed her arms. "I never said I saw only the best in him. He's arrogant. Presumptive. He hasn't made much effort to get to know me. Worst of all, he's not you. You're the one I want by my side."

"I didn't mean that you were undesirable, Alice. I'm sorry that my words came out all wrong. I'm upset and unable to expressly myself clearly in my distress, apparently. Forgive me. You're engaged," he repeated as if the news was slowly sinking in.

"For now. I hope you can forgive me."

Really, she simply felt foolish. She knew what he meant. She'd known all along. In her heart, and in her now-clear mind, she harbored her own doubts and suspicions about Ralston's motives. She'd noticed little things, like his insistence that she drink her tea. "Drink, Alice. Drink up." His shared glances with Sophia. Their treatment of her, acting like she'd reverted to childhood. Something wasn't right, and it wasn't all in her head. It would have helped if Logan hadn't jumped to the same conclusions so quickly. He might have taken a little time to be jealous first. But no.

When Logan had been telling her his story, he'd mentioned Stanhope drugging the servants. It was then, for the first time, that she realized that she'd felt exactly like these past few weeks, as if she were being drugged. Her speech had been thick, perhaps thicker than even her mind. Her head had always been filled with the fog, unable to form a lucid thought. Even her movements were slow and unsteady. Could all that have been simply a result of a brain injury, or had it been something more? Would Ralston have been drugging her? And if so, why? What did he have to gain from their marriage?

"Alice, please." He reached for her again, his large, warm hand closing on her shoulder. "Look at me. There's nothing to forgive. You were unwell. He was there, ready to take advantage. How will he take the news?"

"He has to understand that I have no intention of marrying him. He can't hold me to a promise I made while impaired, as you've said." With a sigh, she directed her gaze up at his and nearly melted on the spot. His eyes were filled with love and concern, all for her. She had to force herself to breathe. Merely looking at him had such a powerful effect on her that her knees began to quiver.

Without another word, he pulled her into his powerful embrace and kissed her again—deeply, passionately, with every ounce of his soul. It was more than just a kiss. It was a promise between them, the promise of a love that would never falter or fade away.

"I can accept that you might never want to marry me, or marry at all," he said, his voice raspy and low.

"But I could never stand back and let another man hurt the woman I love. Never again. Do you need me to come with you to give him the news?"

"I think it best I tell him myself. He will be hurt, but the sooner I tell him, the better. Doubtless, Sophia has discovered me gone and is racked with concern as well. I should make arrangements to return to Thornbrook Park."

"But how will I bear to let you go?" He stroked a tendril of hair from her forehead.

"I guess you'll have to come back and visit as soon as you can manage it."

"As soon as I can manage," he agreed, taking her hand as they walked together back to Stratton Place.

      ∽

He realized his time with her had come to an end as soon as they entered the house and he could vaguely discern the sound of Ellen's voice mixing with another distinctly feminine tone. Sophia. His gaze darted to Alice's.

"Oh dear," she said, apparently realizing it at the same time he did. "I underestimated the speed at which she would find me. Too soon, but it will save me the trouble of making arrangements."

"She was worried about you. I'm glad you have her to look after you."

"That she does. She looks after me very well." She gripped his hand and let go only briefly as Barnett came to take gloves and coats, and then, bare handed, she laced fingers with his again. "I suppose it's time."

Would she confront her sister? Be coolly polite? Tell her right away that she meant to break her engagement? She did mean to break her engagement? They hadn't exactly had a chance to settle things. He would just have to stand back and give her a chance to deal with her sister as she saw fit.

"Ellen, I see you've met Lady Averford. Lady Averford, welcome to Stratton Place." Logan got the greeting out of the way and looked to Alice.

"There you are, at last. I was worried we would have to send a footman out after you." Sophia stood at once, her eyes drawn to their clasped hands. "We've all been worried about you. I was just telling Lady Emsbury how you've been unwell. She had no idea. I'm astonished."

"I've been perfectly well." Alice said, not letting go of Logan's hand. "Completely back to my senses at last. I had some things to discuss with Logan, so I found my way to Stratton Place."

"Well, you could have told me where you were headed. I had no idea you even planned to leave. Thank goodness for Aunt Agatha, or I might have been scouring London for you fearing the worst."

"Agatha told you?" Alice's eyes widened in apparent shock. She'd trusted Agatha.

"I had to coax it out of her, but yes. She gave in once she realized I would probably come calling here, anyway, once I realized…Well, we can discuss it on the way home, Pumpkin."

"Once you realized I'd found Winthrop's letter? And please, don't call me Pumpkin." Alice waved a finger at her sister with her free hand. "Not ever again. I'm not a child, Sophia."

"Of course not." Sophia flashed a sympathetic pout. "Adult enough to make your own decisions, in fact. I'm sorry. But you were sick only so recently that you can't blame me for my concern."

"I don't blame you entirely." Alice softened her tone. "I know you were concerned. You can see that I'm safe. I'm a welcome guest here. They've treated me like family." She smiled warmly at Ellen. "Possibly better."

"Your fiancé is worried as well," Sophia said, with a pointed glance at Logan. "Lord Ralston wanted to come with me, but he dared not risk it as you have yet to announce your intentions. We're planning a party to celebrate. You're all invited, of course. It will be a grand affair…"

"There will be no grand affair. I don't mean to marry Lord Ralston. But as you say, we can discuss it on the way home. I'll gather my things."

She hadn't arrived with many things, so it was a matter of moments before Logan rang for Barnett to bring Alice's coat and, with Ellen, he walked the sisters to the door.

Alice turned to him, tears shimmering in her eyes. "Thank you, Logan. For everything."

He wanted nothing more than to kiss away the sadness in her eyes, but he knew it would take a lot more than just a kiss to improve her situation. She had to let Lord Ralston down gently, or forcibly. Logan suspected it would take more than a gentle refusal.

"Please, Alice. Do keep in touch. Lady Averford, thank you for coming."

"You're welcome, Mr. Winthrop. You have a lovely place here with your family. I'm glad to see you back where you belong." With that, she hustled Alice out the door to the waiting car without even allowing Alice a glance back until she was seated. Logan's last glimpse of Alice was one of her sweet face, drawn with worry, as she waved out the rear window of the car.

⤜⤝

"I'm so sorry, Sophia," Alice said, as soon as they were out of sight of Logan and the house. What if it was the last she ever saw him? She worried for a moment before pushing such concerns from her mind. "I know you must have been fearful about what had become of me."

"Fearful is an understatement. In your condition? I'm so glad I found you." Sophia reached for her sister's hand. "Lord Ralston was out of his mind, too."

Good, Alice thought. He should know what it feels like. "I simply didn't believe that I could trust you to let me go once I found the letter in your writing desk. Why did you hide it from me?"

"Why would I have allowed you to read it, in your condition? You weren't equal to it. I was waiting for the right time, when you were well again."

Alice wasn't ready to forgive so easily. "I'm well again. I finally regained my mind, no thanks to your coddling."

"My coddling? Nursing you back to health was a twenty-four-hour-a-day mission. A mission of love, because you're my sister and I love you, which you seem to forget."

"I seem to forget? I wonder why that is… Oh yes. Because my lovely fiancé was drugging me."

"What? Ralston drugging you? That's ridiculous. I was with you all the time. If he was drugging you, I would know about it. You can't think I would let a man hurt you. Where do you come up with these ideas? Did Winthrop suggest such a thing?"

"Winthrop did not. I came to the conclusion on my own." Alice tapped her chin as if to think. "I seem to recall your back turned in many instances when he could have slipped something into my tea. Or perhaps you were in on it."

"In on it? Why would I drug you? I thought I would lose my patience having to take such care with you all of the time. I wanted you to be better, not worse."

"All I know is that I woke up in good condition, not great condition, mind you, but I was in possession of my mental faculties. And then gradually they began to slip away. I don't think it's supposed to be like that, Sophia."

"Dr. Pederson said it would be a gradual recovery."

"But I had recovered. And only after that did I begin to slip into the fog and get worse. Something is very wrong there, Sophia. And I think it has to do with Lord Ralston. Don't you think it a little odd that he refuses to leave my side, except for sleep and the obvious reasons?"

Sophia tipped her head, considering. "He cares about you. He's very much in love."

"If he's so in love with me, why is he always looking at you?"

"At me? I'm married. He knows I'm married. His only interest in me is a sisterly one. He looks to me for advice on how best to look after you."

"Hmm." Alice had no words.

"What purpose would it serve for him to drug you? He doesn't need to marry for a title or for money. There are a number of eligible young heiresses interested in him. Younger than you, so long on the shelf."

"Sophia." Alice shook her head. "And you call me incorrigible."

"It's true. You're not getting any younger. And you finally have a wonderful man overcome with love for you…"

"And you made me leave him behind…" She looked over her shoulder again, though Stratton Place had been long out of sight.

"I don't mean Mr. Winthrop. For Jove's sake, Alice, you're engaged."

"Engagements can be broken." She flashed a challenge in her grin. "I don't love Ralston, Sophia. I don't know what I want, but I need some time on my own to figure things out."

"You have some time. You'll be home for Christmas and then we'll have our big party after the New Year, and we'll tell everyone. I can't wait to see Matilda Furbish's face. She thought she bagged the catch of the season."

"Bagged? We're not hunters. And she can have him. I'm telling you, Sophia, there's something off about Ralston. You're blind to his faults. It makes me wonder."

"Wonder? About what?" Sophia arched a brow, suspicious.

"Gabriel hasn't been around much lately. Is everything going well between you?"

"Gabriel and I are perfectly well. We've been busy. He has been occupied with getting Winthrop's replacement settled, and I've been looking after you. We'll have more time to ourselves after Christmas. Sooner, perhaps, now that you're better." Sophia patted Alice's leg, softening. "I was honestly worried about you when you went to nap and then were not there. You can only imagine what I went through, Alice. You're my sister. I love you. I only want you to be happy. There was no need for running away."

"And if I'd asked you about the letter, you would have told me?"

"Reluctantly, once I realized you were well enough to be reasonable. But yes, I would have told you. I didn't burn it or toss it away. Honestly, I was saving it until I deemed you well enough to hear from Mr. Winthrop."

"I was always well enough to hear from a…friend. A good friend like Logan. There was no need to hide correspondence. And if you truly want me to be happy, you will help me be free of this engagement."

"Alice, no." Sophia turned to her. "Please, give him a chance. He'll be a good husband to you. You'll be a countess, like me."

"I don't care to be countess. And I've given him a chance. I don't love him, Sophia. I'm not even sure that I like him. I know Mother has taxed you with the gargantuan task of finding me a husband, and you've made an admirable effort, but perhaps it's just not in me to be a wife."

Sophia shook her head. "Like Agatha with her lovers. She really has been a bad influence on you. What kind of life is that?"

"Agatha seems perfectly happy."

"And at our mercy. Without our providing a home for her, where would she go?"

"Grandmother left us money. Perhaps she left Agatha a share, too. Agatha couldn't bear to live all alone, though. She thrives on interaction. She needs people to spook."

"I suppose." Sophia seemed unconvinced.

"And you seem to forget that I do have money."

"Not yet."

"In three more years. I can lead an independent life if I choose. I have no need for this husband you seem to want to push on me. None at all."

"You don't even mean to marry Winthrop?" Sophia asked, incredulous.

"He would have me if I wanted him. I'm fairly certain of that. But I'm not sure what I want. I meant what I said. I need some time to think."

"You'll have your time," Sophia said with a sigh. "I got you into this mess, so I will help get you out of it."

"The engagement? You'll help me speak to Lord Ralston?" Alice took back every horrible thought she'd had about her sister in the past hour. Except for one in which she wished for an enormous pimple to appear on Sophia's chin. It really wasn't fair for a woman to be so beautiful, with an enviable figure, lustrous black hair, and perfect ivory skin. It wouldn't hurt Sophia to have to deal with the occasional imperfection, just like everybody else.

"I will help you. The poor man. It's going to break his heart. I don't know why, but he really seems head over heels for you, Alice."

Alice started rattling off her attributes. "My eye-catching red hair. My scintillating conversational skills. My adorable sense of humor. My natural grace. What else…"

"Humility." Sophia shook her head. "Your strong sense of humility, to be certain."

"Yes." Alice nodded along. "Poor Lord Ralston, indeed."

Nineteen

"STOP PACING AND GO AFTER HER," JOHN SAID. "YOU know you want to go."

Logan gnawed his lip. "It's not that easy. She's engaged."

"Engaged?" John sounded incredulous. He hadn't been in the room when Sophia pointedly mentioned Alice's fiancé. "How could it be? It's obvious that she loves you. The two of you belong together."

Ellen didn't say a word, but she nodded her agreement.

"I tend to agree." Logan sighed. "But the fact is that she accepted Lord Ralston when he asked her. Of course, she was under the influence of a head injury at the time."

"She can't be held accountable," John said matter-of-factly. "It's unconscionable that he would even ask her at such a time."

"I thought so, too. A wonder her sister didn't stop him. Unless…she wanted Alice to say yes, too, and she knew it was her only chance. I can't blame her entirely. Sophia has wanted Alice to marry and stay close to Thornbrook Park for quite some time, and marrying her sister to an earl would be ideal."

"An earl, bah. To marry for love would be ideal," Ellen said. "Without love, what is there?"

"We can't expect everyone to see the world as we do, my love," John told his wife. "Though I quite agree."

"I'm not sure Sophia married her husband for love. They've had some trying times. But I know Lord Averford loves his wife beyond measure, and I know that love is strong enough for the both of them. But it is possible that Sophia doesn't understand the power of love, the necessity for it, any more than she truly understands her sister. She would never do anything to hurt Alice, not on purpose."

"But would she have encouraged the Earl of Ralston to propose at a time when she suspected her sister was more or less powerless to object to him?" Ellen wondered.

"I won't let her marry him out of duty or obligation. If she loves me, she should be with me."

"Hear, hear!" John raised a fist. "So get on your white horse and charge! Or have Evans drive you."

"Perhaps I'll pay a social call on Lord Averford's brother and his wife. Eve Thorne was quick to warn me off when she thought I had an interest in Alice, but I think she would be equally quick to help me once she realizes that Alice really loves me in a way she could never love Lord Ralston. Yes, I'll visit the Thornes. One can never have too many allies in such a situation. If all goes well, Alice will have broken her engagement before my return to Thornbrook Park."

"And if not?" John looked concerned.

"I'll just have to convince her to make haste. I'm the only one for her."

⁓

When they arrived home, Gabriel informed them that Lord Ralston had left.

"He said that there was no sense in him pacing the floor with worry when he could be at Holcomb House placating his aunt. Lady Holcomb keeps asking after him. Now she has him back. But he means to return to celebrate Christmas with us."

"So much for his broken heart. Clearly, he wasn't all that concerned with my welfare after all." Alice turned to her sister, hands on her hips.

"Nonsense. The poor man probably needed a distraction to keep him sane until he could hear what became of you. It's good that he's catching up with his aunt. He will be back for Christmas, after all. We'll have to send word that you're back where you belong and feeling better."

"Must we? Perhaps we could simply tell him I died."

"Alice!" Sophia gasped. "What a terrible thing to say. We were all so worried about you."

"I'm sorry for causing a panic."

Lord Averford shrugged. "Aunt Agatha said that you were safe and well. I wasn't worried at all. If anyone would know, she would."

Sophia narrowed her eyes at her husband. "I thought you doubted Agatha's abilities."

"The woman is uncanny sometimes. But mostly, I believed that Alice wouldn't run off without giving

Agatha word of her intentions." He kissed Sophia on the cheek. "Now that you're all safely home, I've got to ride with Kenner out to the McGinty place. We're meeting a prospective new tenant."

"A new tenant? Logan's plan worked? What I mean to say is, what you planned with Mr. Winthrop, to attract a new tenant to the old farm. That's wonderful news." Heat flooded her, rushing to her cheeks and elsewhere, at the very thought of the McGinty house.

"It seems that it has. Mr. Higgins is a promising candidate. He had a farm over in Teckford but the estate was broken up and the land sold. He's looking for a new situation, and we're happy to welcome him."

"It's a shame that Mr. Winthrop isn't here to see it. I believe he would be very pleased."

"He would." Gabriel nodded. "He worked very hard to restore the house to habitable condition, and I'm grateful to him. Some repair and maintenance remains, but it's nearly ready. I'll be back in time for dinner."

"The long ride has made me so sleepy." Sophia yawned and stretched. "I'm going to have a nap. Alice, you should try to sleep, too. You must be exhausted."

"I'm strangely enervated. I think I'll go for a walk."

Alice needed time to reflect. She didn't even mind that the temperature had dropped. Being on her own in the cool air boosted her spirits. No Lord Ralston waiting for her. She was free! She spun in a circle on the grass and laughed.

And what would she do with her freedom? She felt obligated to put it to good use. Hadn't Logan told her that she reminded him of all the life he had yet to live? What of her own plans, her own life? She had a whole list of things she meant to accomplish, but she'd given up on her first chance to learn to shoot. No time like the present. There was no reason to put anything off.

She headed right for the storage shed and asked Patrick, the first groundskeeper she came across, to help continue teaching her to learn to shoot. She meant to do things properly, the way Logan would have taught her. If she was to consider herself a modern woman, she could hardly be reliant on servants for all things. Times were changing, as Logan had rightly observed. She would learn to do for herself.

They stayed out until dusk. First, she learned to name all the parts of the rifle and their functions. Next, Patrick showed her how to clean and load her weapon. It would take a little more practice, but she was surprised at how quickly she'd learned. By the end of the day, before the sun began to set, she'd actually had a chance to shoot at targets. And she'd hit one dead center.

"Thank you, Patrick, for taking the time with me. You're a wonderful teacher."

"It helps to have an attentive student." He bowed to her. "Good evening, Lady Alice."

She felt an overwhelming sense of pride and accomplishment as she returned to the Dower House to prepare for dinner. She could put a check next to another of the goals on her list. Strangely, though, it didn't seem quite as satisfying without someone there to share her triumph. Patrick had been a good teacher, but learning from Logan would have been so much better. He had his special way of laughing with her, teasing her, and encouraging her at once.

Would she find herself in an exotic locale, ready to turn to a partner and share an observation, only to realize that she was alone with no one to care? If she saw all the wonders of the world but had no one to discuss them with, would it be as if she'd never seen them at all?

She sighed. She didn't want just anyone along on her adventures. She wanted Logan. She missed him. There was no doubt that he loved her, and she him. Making love with him had been her most amazing adventure so far, and she didn't think it would be that way with just anyone. She didn't want to make love with anyone else. Her body longed for Logan's touch, and her heart was in full agreement. It meant having to admit that she'd been wrong all along. She *wanted* to marry. In fact, she'd felt more freedom in Logan's arms than she had ever felt on her own. Needing Logan didn't make her any less of a woman. He was part of what made her the woman she was, a part of her. How could she ever have thought that she could live without him?

She wished she'd never left him, but she had to rid herself of any obligation to Lord Ralston. Then she could return to Logan and tell him how much she needed him. Her happiness had been in her own hands all along. Perhaps Logan's as well. Now more than ever, she was convinced that Ralston had been drugging her. But with what powerful stuff to have had such an effect on her? She would find out for certain, and she would have her revenge.

"I'm sorry they found you so quickly, my dear." Agatha embraced her upon her return. "I tried to throw Sophia off your trail, but she would not be deterred. I think she had you all figured out from the start."

"You did your best, Aunt Agatha. Admittedly, Sophia would have been an idiot to believe I'd gone anywhere else. It's good to see that she has some sense to be relied upon."

"Did you have time to talk, at least? Did you do what you set out to do?"

"I did. I wish we'd had more time, but perhaps another day."

"He'll come back for you. Romance is in the air. I can feel it." Agatha held her hands up in the air as if commanding the winds to blow romance into the room.

"Are you sure it's not simply that Miss Puss has got into your perfume again?" Alice teased her aunt.

"You'll see," Agatha waved a finger. "Fate has a grand surprise in store for you. You can always count on fate."

"The only thing I can count on is that we're going to be late for dinner if I don't get in the bath."

❧

Later that night at Thornbrook Park, Alice discovered that fate's grand surprise was perhaps only a cruel trick on her, the early reappearance of Lord Ralston.

"Darling." He took her hands in his as soon as she entered the drawing room. "My love. You're looking well. How do you feel?"

"I feel much like myself." She pulled her hands back. "Completely restored."

"I had to rush back. I've been too long without you. You gave us quite a scare. Didn't she, Sophia?"

"Yes." Sophia stopped gazing at her own portrait long enough to respond. "We were overcome with worry. For a time, it seemed that you would never be yourself again, Alice. And here you are back to us."

Sophia had commissioned a portrait for over the central fireplace, one to replace the painting of Gabriel's mother, the Dowager Countess, that Sophia had never liked. It was Sophia posed as the goddess Aphrodite, a suggestion of Gabriel's brother one night after dinner. Eve and Marcus had shared a laugh at the idea, as if there were a private joke, but Sophia had embraced the notion. She'd been posing for it all summer, and just over a month ago, it was finally finished and hung up. The Dowager Countess had been put into storage.

"If only it could have been the real one pack-aged up and put away," Sophia had commented on the occasion.

"She's in Italy, far enough away that she shouldn't bother you." Alice didn't see that Sophia had any cause for concern. Rumor had it that the previous Lady Averford was involved in a tempestuous affair with an Italian count, which meant that she wasn't rushing home any time soon. "You're the mistress of your own house."

"About time." Sophia had folded her arms over her chest, only looking away from her own portrait once Gabriel walked into the room. She'd waited all day for him to notice. He'd had the nerve to not even realize there had been a substitution until long after dinner, when Eve Thorne had begun to admire it. Ah, Alice remembered now. That was what had occasioned the gift of the diamond cuff, Gabriel's ignorance of his wife's new portrait.

"Yes, I really am quite well," Alice said, about to add that she would like to speak to Lord Ralston privately, no time like the present. Except that before she could speak, she was interrupted.

"This calls for champagne!" Ralston cheered. "Finch! Finch, my good man, pop open a few bottles from the case I brought."

"You know which to open, Finch. Stick with ours. You brought a case?" Gabriel responded immediately, surprising Alice. Perhaps he, too, had finally begun to realize they'd let a fox into the henhouse. "No need for that, Ralston. We've plenty of champagne."

"Consider it a gift. I'm very particular in my tastes."

"If by particular you mean wanting, I completely understand." Gabriel adjusted his cuffs, giving the appearance of remaining calm. But Alice noticed the golden licks of flame dancing in his dark brown eyes. "You can't get better champagne than I have in my cellar. I bought the last of it before even Bertie himself could snap it all up."

"Champagne fit for the king? I suppose I'm not that particular. We'll go with yours. I'll make a present of mine to my aunt and uncle. They'll be delighted with it. My apologies, Averford."

Gabriel nodded coolly. Alice hadn't seen him look so dangerous since his brother's reappearance at Thornbrook Park during the previous year. There was definitely some unspoken war being waged between the men. Alice's evening suddenly became more interesting. She wondered if it had something to do with Ralston's departure for Holcomb House during Sophia's absence.

As if sensing the very wrong thing to do to placate his host, Ralston took a sudden interest in Sophia's portrait.

"It's an uncanny likeness." Ralston framed Sophia with his fingers and turned back to the portrait. "Down to the last detail, from the perfectly shaped bow of your lip to the mysterious gleam in your cornflower-blue eyes. I confess it draws my gaze even from my lovely Alice."

"Even from me? What a thing to say, my dear Ralston." Alice hated to even speak to the man, suspecting him more strongly of foul play by the minute, but she felt it her duty to keep the peace between him and her brother-in-law. Sophia seemed unaware of any tension between them. "Nothing should command your attention from the woman you're to marry. Am I right, Lord Averford?"

"Absolutely, Alice. And it's not often I will allow you that." Gabriel smiled in her direction, though she could still see a hint of menace buried beneath his jovial surface. Gabriel was not a man she would dare to cross. She'd always been glad he was on her side, more or less. His brother, Marcus, was the only man she could imagine successfully standing up to him, and that for no other reason than she'd seen it with her own eyes. Once, Marcus had knocked Gabriel unconscious over a disagreement concerning Eve.

"My husband took nearly a whole day to even

notice my portrait." Sophia flashed a glance at her husband. Did she know she was playing with fire, adding to the tension that simmered between the men? That Alice believed Sophia to be aware of her actions concerned her all the more. "When we first hung it up, he didn't realize I had removed his mother's portrait and replaced it with my own until Eve Thorne mentioned it that evening."

"It commands me to look." Ralston's lips curled back from his teeth in a predatory grin. "I can hardly look away."

"Aren't the Thornes coming to dinner?" Alice grasped at any potential change of subject. "It feels like the longest time since I've seen them. I miss them. Mina must be getting so big."

"It has only been three weeks," Sophia said. "Maybe a month. They were going to come tonight, but they sent another excuse. Eve promised me that they would be here for Christmas. They're coming tomorrow."

"Christmas Eve." Alice laughed, thinking of Grace and her gracing them with her presence. "How fitting. Eve, on Christmas Eve?"

Sophia nodded, not welcoming the interruption. "With Mina. And they're staying through the New Year. It will be a merry week of celebrations."

"I'm happy to hear it. Christmas is so much better with children in the house." Sophia and Gabriel exchanged grim looks that told Alice she had been the one to say the wrong thing this time. They hated to be reminded of their childlessness, and especially of their baby's untimely death. Their only son had died the night he was born. Still, perhaps their grief bonded them in ways that nothing else could. "Mina is always a delight," Alice added, hoping she was not too late to save the situation.

"That she is," Gabriel said. "I can't wait until she sees the rocking horse Winthrop restored for her."

"Winthrop?" Instantly, Alice lost all ability to think of anyone else. "When did he have time for that?"

"He found it at the old McGinty place, in the attic. It was in good condition, just needed sanding and staining to be shiny as new. Girls love horses, do they not? Sophia being the exception, of course. A toast to my wife," Gabriel said, taking the first glass from the tray as Finch appeared. He waited until everyone had a champagne saucer in hand. "My wife, an extraordinary woman. I don't always say it enough, but you are the love of my life, and I'm grateful for every minute we have together."

"Gabriel." Tears were shining in Sophia's eyes. She'd been rendered speechless, a rare occasion.

Well done, Lord Averford. Alice turned to Ralston, her eyes narrowed as if to say, "Just try to compete with that."

Not to be outshone, Ralston made his own toast. "Plato said that 'wonder is the feeling of a philosopher, and philosophy begins in wonder.' To the wonder of the woman I'm to marry. To Alice."

She smiled, raised her glass, and sipped, certain he hadn't had the chance to poison it. Ralston did enjoy his Greek philosophers. She had suspected he was going to raise a glass to Sophia. Even after he said Alice's name, she felt like a last-minute substitution, a poor comparison to her sister in his eyes.

Sophia moved across the room to join hands with her husband as they lifted their glasses. Ralston watched them before turning to Alice. "Might we be as happy one day?"

"We might," she said. If they managed to part soon enough. Alice now had a theory as to why Ralston wanted to marry her so badly. The true object of his affection was taken. Being married to Alice was the next best thing to winning her sister's heart, putting him in proximity to Sophia as often as he liked. And maybe one day, he would drug *Sophia's* tea and try to take advantage of *her*.

Alice could not allow it. "Lord Ralston, I wonder if I could have a word with you in private."

His eyes narrowed shrewdly, then widened again with relief. "Ah, no, my dear. It will have to wait. My aunt and uncle have arrived to join us for dinner."

She turned, disappointed to see Finch about to announce the Holcombs. "After dinner, then. I'll just have to wait."

Twenty

DINNER, A TEDIOUS AFFAIR, LASTED FAR TOO LONG, and the Holcombs were unfortunately aware of the engagement. Of course Ralston had told his aunt, but the more people who were aware that Ralston and Alice had an understanding, the harder it would be to get out of it. It didn't stop Lady Holcomb from chattering on about Matilda Furbish as often as she liked. For her part, Alice spent most of the meal imagining her fiancé's wedding to another woman. Matilda Furbish would make a fitting bride for him.

Alice's main conversational contribution at dinner had been to inform the gathered company that she had learned to shoot, with a pointed look in Ralston's direction. He failed to take the hint. Logan would have been proud of her following through at last.

The gentlemen passed through to the drawing room almost directly after the ladies had gone, telling Alice that Gabriel had no desire to linger with Ralston any longer than necessary. Alice took the opportunity to try to get Ralston alone. The sooner she could tell him, perhaps the sooner the Holcombs and Ralston would decide to leave.

"Lord Ralston," she said, taking his hand to tear him away from the selection of music at the piano. Alice suspected that Sophia had asked him to play. "I need a word with you. It can't wait."

"Perhaps you would like some tea first." He pressed the back of his hand to her forehead as if testing for fever. "I'll ring for Finch. I think you still tire easily. You can't rush recovery."

"I don't care for tea, thank you." She took his hand and led to the small parlor down the hall. "As you know, Lord Ralston..."

"Alice, why is it that you refuse to use my given name? We're to be married, darling. Please, call me Harry."

"Harry," she said. "As you know, I was quite compromised when I consented to marry you."

"Winthrop, the bounder." He nodded knowingly. "I suspected as much. He got there before me. I understand. But Alice, it doesn't bother me. I'm willing to accept that you come to the marriage in a compromised state..."

She stifled the urge to slap him. He wasn't worth it. "I meant compromised as in mentally off. In a fog. Still recovering from a head injury."

"Oh. Oh, that. Of course."

"Of course," she echoed, wishing she could accuse him point-blank of having kept her in such a state on purpose, but how could she without proof? "I don't think I can be held accountable for anything I might have said when I wasn't quite myself."

"No. You said some terrible things, especially to your sister, but we were willing to overlook them."

"There is no *we*, Lord Ralston, when it comes to you and my sister." He was trying her patience now, and she suspected he did it on purpose. She pulled his ring out of her pocket. She'd chosen a skirt with pockets for just such a reason. "I'm returning your ring. I no longer wish to marry you. I'm not sure I ever did. I think it best we part as friends."

He refused to take her hand or the offered ring. "Part? Don't be ridiculous. Of course you'll marry me. I'm an earl."

"And? Am I supposed to be impressed by that? My sister is a countess, but she hasn't changed from the sister I've always known. What's in a title?"

"Everything. Besides, we're engaged. You said yes. There's no going back on it gracefully. I won't accept it." He turned and walked toward the bookshelf, leaning with his back to her.

"Be reasonable. We haven't told anyone outside family. It's not too late for us to part without anyone being the wiser. I'm sorry to hurt you, but you were right about Winthrop. I love him, Lord Ralston. I'm not in love with you."

He laughed bitterly and turned back to face her, closing the distance between them. "I told you, I don't care about Winthrop. He'll never have you. Or, not again."

This time, she slapped him. Square across the face.

"I'll let you get away with that now." He rubbed his cheek. "But once we're married, don't think I won't take my rights over you. I wouldn't hurt you on purpose, but I certainly wouldn't avoid retaliating."

The answer would have disturbed her if she had any notion to stay with him. "We'll never marry. It's what

I'm trying to tell you. Take your ring back or don't, but I'm not going to marry you." She placed the ring on the table next to him, walked to the door, and held it open. "I suggest you all enjoy a quiet Christmas at Holcomb House. I'm sorry things didn't work out."

"Alice, please." He dropped to his knees. "Please reconsider. You don't know how much I love you. I was willing to have you even when we had no idea you would be yourself again, when other men had run off."

There was only one man to whom he referred, and Alice knew Logan's reasons why. She would not be swayed. "I think you liked me that way. Docile. Obedient. That's not who I really am. I'm not sure you even really know me, Ralston."

He rose, came forward, and took her hands. "And you don't know me. We rushed into things perhaps, but I see no reason to punish me for my haste brought on by my earnest desire to be with you always. Alice, please, give me a chance. Get to know me."

"I don't think we should waste any more of each other's time. I've already told you that I love another man."

He shook his head. "I don't accept it. You might still be more damaged than you think. The doctor said healing would take time. I'm not going to allow you to cast me off when your judgment is likely compromised."

"A laughable suggestion." But she wasn't in the mood to laugh. "You had no trouble accepting me when my judgment *was* compromised."

"Because of the great love I bear you. Alice, trust me. I know what's best. I'm an invited guest for the holidays, and I plan to stay. You needn't say another word of our engagement. I'll consider it off for now. Hold this for safekeeping." He placed the ring in her hand. "And when I think you are ready, I will ask you again."

"Please, Lord Ralston. I would rather that you leave."

"You don't know what's good for you, darling. I can't disappoint my aunt and uncle who have gone to great pains to arrange to spend the holiday here. And by the end of the week, you'll be glad I stayed. Now then." He took her hand. "Let's go rejoin the others."

She followed him down the hall. Her head was quite right, she was certain, but she began to wonder about his. What madness had overtaken him? Jilted lovers weren't supposed to stay for Christmas. How desperately she wanted him gone! And she sensed that Gabriel was in full agreement. But with the Holcombs invited as well as Lord Ralston, the chances were that they were stuck with the lot of them and would have to make the best of it.

❧

Alice and Agatha had planned to abandon the Dower House in favor of Thornbrook Park for the festive week ahead, but Alice wished to rethink that plan. The thought of meeting Ralston's gaze across the breakfast table made her nervous. And what if he tried to slip something into her food? Unfortunately, their plans had been made and Mary had moved their things over to Thornbrook Park with Agatha. It would be too much trouble to expect Mary to pack it all up and head back.

By the next morning, Alice was disappointed to find Lord Ralston hadn't left in the night. He remained lingering over his coffee, watching Sturridge direct the footmen in erecting the tree in the corner of the drawing room. Mr. Kenner, the new estate manager, tried to help. At home, her parents had never bothered with a tree, but Sophia loved the grand Victorian tradition. Alice was surprised that her sister was willing to settle for one large tree and didn't insist on one in every room.

"It's leaning too far to the left," Kenner said, as the men attempted to straighten the tree.

Even Alice could see that the cross of wood nailed to the bottom of the trunk was too small to support all the weight of it, and how was the tree to get water? If Sophia wanted candles to light the branches, and Alice was certain she would, they couldn't risk the tree drying out in the night. For now, she watched the men and said nothing. Logan would have valued her opinion, but she didn't feel the need to make her voice heard with Logan so far away. She had little interest in the new Kenner fellow.

"Too far right, you mean," Ralston interjected. The adjustment nearly sent the tree toppling. Of course, Ralston had an opinion on the matter.

"No, no," Sturridge said. "Just line it up with the ceiling and—"

"Tie it up?" Ralston suggested. "Secure it to the wall and it should stay put."

"Tie it?" Alice was about to question, and then

stopped. Let Mr. Sturridge handle Ralston and his silly suggestions. The room smelled of pine and the idea of Christmas put Alice in a brighter frame of mind. In light of the holiday, she supposed she could be more charitable to Ralston, or simply pretend he wasn't there.

"Merry Christmas," he said quietly, turning his attention from the tree. "I've been looking for the mistletoe, but it seems they haven't gotten to hanging it yet."

"Merry Christmas, Lord Ralston," she answered, making an attempt to add some warmth to her tone. "I hope you don't find the holiday too disappointing. It's not too late to return to Holcomb House."

He laughed. "I'm sure it isn't. Lord Averford hinted at it a little more strongly than you, until Sophia reminded him of his manners. I'm here as a guest, Alice. Invited. I'm not out to hurt you."

She softened a bit. "We can be friends, Lord Ralston. I see no harm in it." Though why anyone would want to stay on when it was clear he wasn't wanted, Alice couldn't begin to fathom.

As she reached out to shake his offered hand, the tree teetered and began to fall directly at them. She shrieked and Ralston tossed his cup in time to take her in his arms and leap aside.

"Thank you," she said, breathless, still in his arms when she heard the voice behind her.

"Ah, I see the problem. The stand is too small, and you'll need to place the tree in a tub to help support it, with some water in the bottom to keep it from drying out. Wilson, run out to the hothouse and fetch the small tub. We have just the right one. You know where it is." A voice of reason at last!

"Yes, Mr. Winthrop. At once, sir."

She shrugged out of Ralston's hold. "Logan. I didn't expect you."

"I can see that." The tension had returned to his face, his mouth in the grim line. She couldn't decide if it was being back at Thornbrook Park or the sight of her in Ralston's arms that had effected the change in him.

"The tree was falling. It almost landed on me."

"But it didn't, because I was here to catch you," Ralston said. "Mr. Winthrop, returning to your duties?"

He shook his head. "Old habits are hard to break. Like you, I'm here as an invited guest." He raised a brow, his reference to being invited like Ralston indicating to Alice that he had been on the sidelines watching them for a moment before letting his presence be known.

"Lord Averford invited you?" Alice did a poor job of hiding her disbelief. Gabriel was a genius. If one couldn't get rid of the unwanted fiancé, invite the competition. "For Christmas?"

"Lady Averford did, actually. I happened to drop in on the Thornes when they were getting ready to journey here, and she extended the invitation to include me. Lovely of her, don't you think?"

"Very." It was the least Sophia could do, she supposed, after allowing Ralston to worm his way into their intimate circle. "I hope your family won't miss you too much. The girls must have been looking forward to the holiday with you."

"They're looking forward to holiday treats. They will hardly notice I'm gone."

"I doubt that. But I'm very happy that you could join us." Now that she was over her shock, she wanted to throw herself into Logan's arms. She couldn't tell what he was thinking, though, or if he felt the same. He seemed distant. Finding her in Ralston's arms couldn't have helped matters. She longed to reassure him, privately, that she had spoken to Ralston and ended their engagement.

"Are the Thornes here as well? With Mina?"

He nodded. "They're getting her settled with the nurse upstairs. The car ride seems to have upset her. If you'll excuse me, I would like to make myself helpful to Mr. Kenner in getting this tree up. Lady Averford can't have Christmas without a tree."

"You can't have Christmas without your loved ones close." Ralston stepped forward and boldly took Alice by the hand. She opened her mouth to protest, but what could she say without making a scene? She went along with it, for now. "I'm glad I'm here. Alice, shall we go for a walk to get out of the way while the men get to work?"

He dismissed Logan as if he were a lowly servant and swept her out of the room. She went without protest, if only to get Ralston out of the way and avoid a scene between the men. But she tugged away from Ralston as soon as they left the room. "Logan Winthrop is also an invited guest. It would serve you well to try to get along with the man, in the spirit of Christmas."

"I'll try, darling." He placated her. "But it's hard to be nice to the man who holds your heart in his hands. Deep down, you must know that I'm the better choice."

"I know nothing of the sort," she said. "I'm going to look for Eve. I haven't seen her in so long."

"I'll be here waiting for your return."

&

Perhaps coming back to Thornbrook Park had been a mistake. He hardly knew what to do with himself as a guest. As a manager, he could cope perfectly well. Work took his mind off almost everything, and there was plenty of work to be done with Christmas coming and the Kenner fellow not quite up to the task. When he entered the room to see Alice in Ralston's arms, though, he nearly lost his sense of purpose, and his mind along with it. He had come to secure her affections. But had she changed her mind about breaking her engagement to Ralston?

The Thornes could not have been more welcoming when he appeared at their door. Eve had been instrumental in eliciting the invitation from Sophia for Logan to join the family for Christmas. Suddenly, Eve Thorne had gone from warning him off getting too close to Alice to becoming his greatest champion in winning Alice over. What had changed her mind? She didn't have a bad word to say about Ralston, but he suspected she didn't much like the man. Or, in his bravest dreams, he hoped perhaps Alice had confided something to Eve about her own feelings for him, meaning that he still had the right to believe in the best possible outcome.

"Mr. Kenner." He clapped his successor on the back. "Let's show you how things are done around here, shall we?"

"I welcome your advice, Mr. Winthrop. Everyone speaks so highly of you. You've been missed." His brown eyes were wide as a doe caught in the crosshairs.

"But you might be just the breath of fresh air an old estate needs to meet the demands of changing times." Besides his youth, part of the man's problem might be that he looked generally nervous and not up to the task. Averford was a good sort, but Logan knew him to be exacting and impatient, which probably hadn't helped the new man to catch on. All he needed was a little confidence, and Logan hoped to inspire him. "Let's start in the kitchen. Mrs. Mallows should be preparing baskets for our tenants. We'll check to see how she's progressing."

Once they were in the kitchen, Mr. Kenner had been temporarily swept aside by some of the staff eager to greet Logan and welcome him back. It was good to know that he had been missed. He'd had no idea he was so beloved a figure while he worked at Thornbrook Park, but perhaps his absence had made them all fonder.

"Here we have the baskets, all prepared." Mrs. Mallows looked proud of her work, two large baskets stuffed full and trimmed in ribbon. "Mr. Finch will bring them up to Lord Averford shortly."

"We do this every Christmas? Bring baskets to the tenants?"

"The day of Christmas Eve. What do we have this year, Mrs. Mallows?"

"Venison haunches, a fat goose, a pudding, and some candies and cakes for the children."

"There's a new family at Tilly Meadow Farm," Logan explained. "It used to be just Mrs. Dennehy left after her husband passed on, but Captain Thorne..."

"Lord Averford's brother?" Kenner asked.

"Yes. Captain Thorne introduced Mrs. Dennehy to his friends from London, the Coopers, and now they live and work at the farm with Mrs. Dennehy. I understand they have some new lambs. With the addition of extra hands, Mrs. Dennehy has expanded her cheese trade and her revenues."

"She's reaping sound profits, which is good for us all." Kenner nodded.

"As long as we keep up our end of the bargain and don't let her buildings fall into disrepair. We helped with some construction and repairs last year, and she bought a new cider press. But there are two baskets. Have we a new tenant at the McGinty place?"

"We do." Mr. Kenner nodded enthusiastically. "I welcomed him just last week, but I won't say more. Lord Averford was eager to share the news with you."

"Excellent." Logan was pleased to know that their work on the old McGinty place had paid off. But he couldn't think of the McGinty house without feeling a flush spread over him.

He could still see Alice leaning over him, the beauty of her pale skin glowing in the firelight, her red hair spilling down her shoulders...The need to see her again overwhelmed him. He had to finish his business with Kenner so he could rejoin the family back upstairs, where he now belonged.

"Mr. Winthrop." Mrs. Hoyle clapped her hands together at the sight of him, probably the most excited he had seen her in all his years at Thornbrook Park. "How lovely of you to come back to help Cornelius adjust. I hope he's doing a good job of it. I know it has been trying to learn so many new things at once."

"Cousin"—Cornelius Kenner rolled his eyes—"you must stop treating me like a child."

Logan had forgotten that Kenner was Hoyle's cousin, and he had more respect for the man for taking the job with his ever-present relative. Logan saw no need to correct her notion as to why he'd actually returned.

"He seems to be fitting right in," Logan said, to be encouraging. "It's good to see you, Mrs. Hoyle. Merry Christmas."

"Merry Christmas. I'll let you go back to your work." Mrs. Hoyle left them, and Logan escorted Kenner back upstairs before any other maids or footmen could accost them. Lord Averford met them at the top of the stairs with Mr. Finch.

"There you are," Averford said. "We're just about to visit the farms. Would you like to come along, Winthrop?"

It depended on Alice. If she was going, he would go as well. But usually, just Lord and Lady Averford went with the estate manager. "I'll let Kenner have the honors this year. You're doing a great job, Mr. Kenner. Keep up the good work."

"Are you sure? I wanted you to meet the new tenant, Higgins. A good man. He's just about all settled with his wife and new babies, twins. Some people have all the luck." Averford smiled, clearly good-natured and excited at the prospect of new tenants.

"Perhaps I'll ride on out later. It's Mr. Kenner's turn to enjoy this special part of the holiday season. But I'm glad to hear there will be a new farmer in the area, a welcome addition to our little Thornbrook community. Or your community, as it is. I can't quite get used to the fact that I no longer call it my home."

"Ah, but you are back where you belong. Enjoying life with your own family at last?"

"Truly, I am. I worried about bringing unnecessary drama to Stratton Place, but enough time has passed that people have forgotten or, at least, no longer bring it up as a regular topic of conversation. I am very glad to be of use to my brother. He's still recuperating from his illness."

"Well, old man, don't be a stranger. It's not all that far from here, and I hope you'll come back and visit us through the years."

"I'll try to do that." He would especially make a point to do it if things went as he hoped with Alice.

"I have a feeling he might be back sooner than expected." Captain Thorne joined them. Logan had already told Thorne and his wife of his love for Alice and his hope to convince her to marry him. "Eve and I are heading over to visit with the Coopers at Tilly Meadow. Lady Alice is currently cooing over Mina in her pram out in the gardens, if you would like to come have a look. I've created the most beautiful daughter known to mankind, and I'm always at my most delighted when people pay her the proper attention."

"Admittedly, I'm not much of an authority on

babies, but I could probably summon the appropriate compliments on sight." Logan smiled.

"You too, Brother. And Mr. Kenner. Everyone should be admiring my baby. Finch is sending footmen out with the tenants' baskets. We can meet him out by the cars."

Logan breathed a sigh of relief to see no sign of Lord Ralston out with Alice, Sophia, Eve, and the baby. Marcus Thorne leaned in to kiss his wife.

"I let the nurse have a rest," Eve informed her husband. "She might be up late with Mina while we're at Christmas Eve Mass tonight. Alice said she would keep an eye on the baby until we return."

"Isn't that kind of her? Thank you, dear Alice." Marcus bowed to her, and Logan felt a ridiculous twinge of jealousy.

He could not forget that Sophia had intended Marcus and Alice to fall in love when she'd first invited her husband's brother to return to Thornbrook Park. But of course, Logan had no need for concern. Alice had professed no interest in Marcus, and it quickly became all too obvious that the man only had eyes for Eve. Now they were married, with a child. Why would Logan be jealous?

"It's my pleasure. Mina and I have so much fun together, don't we?" Alice bounced the baby on her hip, looking so natural that Logan felt another twinge that was far from jealousy. It was more a biological reaction to Alice's proximity. He wanted to sweep her into his arms and kiss her madly. Without the baby present.

At the very least, he had to get closer to her.

Being so near and not able to touch her was driving him out of his mind. He crossed the walkway to stand with her, waving as the others got into cars and drove off.

"Will she be going to sleep soon?" he asked. "Perhaps if you put her in the pram? I'm dying to get you alone."

She stopped bouncing the baby and met his gaze. "She's nowhere near ready for a nap, I think, though I'm no authority on the matter. Besides, it's going to be quite a challenge finding time to be alone with such a houseful. Lord and Lady Holcomb stayed over with Lord Ralston, and Agatha's inside. I suppose we should go in and make sure they're all getting along. Agatha doesn't like Lord Ralston."

"I knew I loved her. Did the ghosts fill her in on his flaws, or was it something she read in his aura?"

Alice laughed, a sound he hoped to hear for the rest of his life. "I believe she's just going by her instincts. He's dismissive of her free-spirited nature. Lady Holcomb is a bit afraid of Agatha, too, from what I've seen. She might be concerned that Agatha is actually in command of the supernatural instead of merely being in communication."

"If that were the case, I'm sure we would have a bit more paranormal activity around Thornbrook Park. Agatha would certainly enlist a mischievous poltergeist or two to do her bidding in chasing Lady Holcomb and Lord Ralston away."

"And Lord Holcomb?" Alice asked

"He's a good sort." Winthrop shrugged. "He can stay. When we go shooting, he always has a joke, a smile, and a little something extra in his flask to keep the chill off."

"Aha. If I weren't holding a baby, I would dazzle you with my new skills. I took your advice more seriously to heart, and I had Patrick teach me how to shoot."

"There's more to it than simply aiming a rifle and…"

"I know." She placed a hand on his chest, shooting a tremor through him as surely as if she'd pulled a trigger. "I had him show me properly how to load, clean, and shoot a rifle. I can name all the parts. And I hit a target dead center. Only one, but I'm sure I can improve with practice."

"Alice." He embraced her, though that meant dodging Mina's sticky grasp. "I'm so proud of you. That took real determination. You can even load?"

She nodded, pride shining in her hazel eyes. "I wanted to check another accomplishment off on my list. And now I have."

"This list of yours, could I see it sometime? I wonder if there are any more goals I might help you with."

She nodded. "I have a few I want to add. I realize nothing is written in stone. It's a list that is sure to see changes through the years, as often as I change my mind."

"I had the impression that you never changed your mind once you made it up."

"That might have been true in the past, but you've brought out a whole new side of me." Mina fussed in her arms and reached for Logan, to his surprise. "Look, she wants you. How sweet."

"She probably thinks I'll be the one to free her from

that silly bow in her hair. What were they thinking?" The red bow was barely clinging to her little blond wisps, and she was wrapped in a red bunting to match.

"That it's Christmas, and she's adorable? Here." Before he could protest, she handed him the baby.

He juggled her until she felt right in his arms. He'd missed out on his nieces Sarah and Laura in all their infancy and toddlerhood. "All right, Mina. If we're to be friends, I must beg you not to spit up on me."

The baby cooed and resumed with sucking her own fingers.

"You are a natural with her. How long were you with Grace before you fled to Europe?"

"She was about six months old when I left, just a little older than Mina. She was four when I returned for Father's funeral."

"Do you ever think about having children of your own?"

"I didn't. Not for years. I thought to never have them. I had my well-ordered life and my work, and that was all. And then something happened to change all that. You happened, Alice. But I don't expect to have children. I'm not against the idea, but I'm not resigned to it, either, as some are. I spent too long living my life in a box. I'm out of the box now. I'm learning what it is to live, and I find that spontaneity is part of my brave new world."

"Mr. Winthrop, spontaneous? Who would believe it?"

"Just about anyone watching me hold a baby right now, I suppose."

Alice laughed again, and he let the sound wash over him, a balm to his soul.

Twenty-one

"THIS IS WHERE YOU FIRST KISSED ME," ALICE INFORMED Logan, settling a drowsy Mina into her pram. "Here near the fountain during the ball, with the snow falling down."

"I remember, but we kissed before that. Don't you remember? When I was coming up the stairs with shears in my hands."

"Yes, but that time I kissed you. I prefer to consider the time that you took matters into your own hands, right here."

"It's starting to snow again." He brushed some flakes from her hair. "If we didn't have the care of an infant, I would take you in my arms and dance with you again. I might be daring enough to kiss you, even with the possibility that your fiancé could be watching from a window. Be warned, I've made sure to hang mistletoe in some out-of-the-way spots."

"So if you begin to lure me away from the crowd, I should know that I'm in danger of being kissed?"

"Even worse. I'm not sure I can control myself

around you, Alice. I might not even need the excuse of mistletoe."

A thrill coursed through her veins. How she wanted to be in his arms, swept away. "I want you to know that I told Ralston I have no intention of marrying him. I've broken the engagement."

"That's wonderful news." He put his arms around her. "I'm happy to hear it, overjoyed if I'm being honest."

She stared into his midnight eyes and remembered the feeling of drifting away into them, the peace she felt becoming a part of him, even if it was only a hazy dream as she lost consciousness. The euphoria had felt so real, so overwhelming, that it was a wonder she ever woke up again. But looking into his eyes as he stared back at her, she began to feel it again. This time, it was real and not the effects of an injured daze. She loved him.

"I'm happy being with you. What made you decide to come?"

"Being away from you. Thornbrook Park is no longer home. Once you left, I realized that neither is Stratton Place. My home is with you, wherever you are. And that's where I had to spend Christmas."

"Logan." She placed a hand on his cheek. "Let's get the baby in out of the snow so we can find a place to be alone."

They rolled the pram inside, prepared to hand the sleeping baby over to her nurse.

"Ralston didn't take it well," she confessed as they walked. "He's determined to change my mind."

"And how does he plan to do that?"

"He wouldn't exactly say how. Why would he?"

Alice had some idea, but she didn't want to alarm Winthrop with her suspicions. He'd been on the brink of facing charges over murdering a romantic rival once. There was no need to tempt him to it again.

She knew he wouldn't be capable of it without good reason, but that she suspected Ralston of sedating her might be reason enough. After all, the thought of it made her own blood boil. But first, she had to be sure she was right. Unfortunately, that meant keeping a close watch on Ralston when he was around, a tricky endeavor when she didn't want to give Logan the wrong idea that she had any interest in Ralston.

Inside, the nurse was waiting for them.

"There's my wee charge. I hope she doesn't take ill from the cold."

"She's well bundled up," Alice said. "Look, only her little cheeks are red and will undoubtedly be quick to warm."

The nurse nodded, not quite approvingly. "I'll take her from here."

Logan and Alice didn't get far before Aunt Agatha, draped in a flowing, royal blue robe trimmed in silver, caught up to them.

"Mr. Winthrop! The veil has lifted. I can see your aura at last."

"Oh?" He lifted a brow. "And what color might it be?"

"It's a sunny, happy yellow. You have a yellow aura, which goes very well with Alice's orange. Together, you look like a bright sunburst. It reminds me of springtime. What a perfect omen! I do love the spring. It's all about new life. Together, you have new life. You see, Mr. Winthrop? The Ace of Cups was always meant to be yours. New beginnings."

"I should have never doubted you," Logan said. "What does this yellow aura reveal about me? Should we be warned?"

"You are prone to leading with your head instead of listening to your heart. You have a tendency to keep to yourself, and you do not suffer fools gladly. But when you love, you love deeply and loyally. I don't know how I didn't see it before, because yellows love to garden and watch things thrive under their care."

Logan stroked his chin, considering. "Very astute. And what of the orange aura?"

"Oranges are impatient. Their main flaw is a tendency to act first and think later. Capricious!"

Alice blushed. "I think we have that covered, then, Agatha. Thank you."

Agatha went on. "They are quick to anger, but quick to forgive. But also absolutely charming, nearly impossible to resist. Thoughtful, generous, honest, and genuine. You always know exactly where you stand with an orange."

"Insightful. This aura reading seems to be quite an accurate science," Logan said.

"I wouldn't exactly call it a science." Alice took Logan's hand. "You'll have to excuse us, Agatha. I believe Mr. Winthrop had something to show me down the hall."

"Of course, my dears. I'm trying to locate Lady Holcomb. I've never met anyone as badly in need of a tarot spread. She is in for a rough time of it if she keeps ignoring warnings from the spirit guides."

"I'm not sure she's up yet. The Holcombs might be sleeping in to prepare for a late evening with Mass."

"Perhaps I'll wait in the breakfast room with another of Mrs. Mallows's divine cinnamon twists. Carry on."

Logan and Alice exchanged glances, watching Agatha drift away as if floating on a cloud.

"I wonder what color her aura is," Logan asked, after she had gone.

Alice laughed. "Probably all of the colors of the rainbow, or she can summon the one she wants at will."

They walked through the house as of one mind. Alice didn't have to ask where he led her. The conservatory's double doors were open, beckoning them. He barely waited until they were inside before he tucked her into a corner behind the ficus trees, with the heady scent of orchids all around them, and enveloped her in a kiss. His tongue seared her like a branding iron, marking her as his own.

"I've missed you. God, how I've missed you." His forehead pressed against hers, his hands ran over her body and slowly gliding up her corseted waist to her breast, then pausing there, his palm flat over her hardening nipple, his thumb grazing the rounded curve through the delicate silk of her blouse. "I need you, Alice."

"I need you, too." She caressed his rough cheek, the slow growth of beard scratching her hand and flooding her with desire. She wanted to tug him to the floor and roll atop him, but it was too dangerous. They could be caught. Her hand trailed down his neck to toy with the buttons of his shirt, eager for contact with bare flesh.

He caught her fingers in his hand. "Not here, Alice. Somewhere proper. I want to take you in a bed this time."

"A bed?" She arched a brow. "You have put me in a mind for anything but proper. And how could we manage it?"

He shook his head. "We might have to test our patience and wait for a more opportune time. I'm willing to wait for you, Alice. I'm willing to do anything for you. I want to give you…"

"The moon?" She didn't mind that he'd confessed to saying the same to another woman. She knew he'd loved Julia, and she knew that he loved her more intensely.

"No, Alice. The entire universe. I want to give you everything."

"All I need is you. I want you, Logan. Nothing else matters."

They kissed again, his hand pressed in the curve of her backside, urging her flat up against him. It was how Ralston found them when he walked in.

"I knew the mistletoe was hidden somewhere. It seems some other man has found it before me." He gestured up to the arch above the doorway. "But you're a bit misplaced. It's over here."

"Ralston," she said, breaking the kiss, but not backing away. If she stayed in Logan's arms, he would have a harder time attacking Ralston, and she was certain it might come to blows. She could feel the heat of Logan's anger rising within him, the vein at the side of his neck pulsing furiously. "I'm sorry you've come upon us in a private moment. Perhaps you could leave us alone?"

"Leave you? In the arms of another man?" He walked further into the conservatory. "I assure you that ignoring the situation is the last thing that crosses a gentleman's mind when he find his fiancée in a compromising position."

"I've told you, Lord Ralston. I will not marry you."

Ralston shook his head. "It's Harry, darling. Why are you being so formal?"

Alice could feel the tension taking over Logan's body, his muscles turning to steel beneath her fingers. She stepped out of the circle of his arms to stand in front of him, keeping hold of his hand. "Because we're not engaged any longer, Lord Ralston. You know I was mentally impaired when I agreed to the marriage in the first place."

She admired Logan's restraint in standing back to allow her to try to handle matters with Ralston on her own. She could only imagine how trying it was for him not to throttle the man on the spot.

"'Love is a serious mental disease.'" Plato, again. Ralston placed his hands over his heart. "And we're all just sick over you, Alice. I can't blame a man for losing his head. Lord and Lady Furbish have sent word of their congratulations, by the bye, on behalf of the family, of course. I daresay Matilda is devastated."

Alice tried to remain unfazed, but her panic increased when she realized he'd gotten the word out. "She will be overjoyed, then, when I tell her you are back on the marriage mart."

Now there could only be a scandal, or one of them scrambling to save face. Of course, it would be her. Her family's reputation could be on the line. Logan snapped. She hadn't expected she would be able to hold him back forever.

"How dare you take advantage of a woman and then act as if you had every right? How could you possibly allow word to get out? Have you no honor?" He stepped perilously close to Lord Ralston.

Alice began to look around and calculate how many plants could be irreparably damaged if they should come to blows. Not the lemon trees! She had to get Logan and Ralston out to the parlor, at least. What were a few damaged antiques next to living things that had taken so much of Logan's love and care to grow strong and lush?

"How dare I?" Ralston gave a sharp laugh. "Have I no honor? That's rich coming from the man who had his arms around my fiancée."

Alice stepped between them. "Why do you insist on being ornery, Ralston? There's no reason to be indignant. Disappointed, perhaps. Embarrassed, most assuredly. When you interrupt a private moment between two other guests in the house, you should know to bow your head and walk away, or at least cough to alert us of your presence. But it's preposterous that you should stand here and claim any rights over me. You know we were never truly engaged. My heart was never in it. And if you believed otherwise, I've taken pains to set you straight."

"Allow me to set the both of you straight. As far as I'm concerned, I walked in to find my fiancée with her tongue down the throat of another man." Ralston held up a hand. "Pardon me for being crude, but I could see with my own eyes. And if word gets out of our broken engagement, everyone will know what I saw, and that I am the wounded party."

Logan dropped his hands, unable to figure Ralston out. "Why would you want to emasculate yourself so, to appear jilted? You could just walk away. Have some pride." It was both a last chance to reason with the man and an attempt to figure him out. Logan was clearly at a loss.

"Because I am an earl, Mr. Winthrop. Not a simple estate manager. And I get what I want. I want Alice to be my wife, and it will be so—or her reputation and her family's reputation will pay the price. You might have been out of our world long enough to forget, but that's how it works. Reputation is everything."

Alice poised on the tips of her toes, ready to jump between them again, desperate to avoid a terrible situation. She had no concern for Lord Ralston, who would certainly take the brunt of the blows, but she dreaded Logan putting himself in any situation that might leave him vulnerable to judgment or censure. He had already been deemed a murderer once. The last thing he needed was for people to believe him at it again, over yet another romantic rival. She had no doubt that putting Logan in such a predicament was exactly what Ralston hoped, which was why she felt especially relieved to see Logan drop his arms to his sides and take a step back.

"I feel sorry for you, Ralston," Logan said. "You don't care who you hurt as long as you get what you want. If that's the way your world works, it's a wonder that any of you want any part of it. You'll never know the meaning of the word 'honor,' and the reputation you think so highly of will never be worth a damn among the truly righteous."

Ralston stood speechless. Logan reached for Alice's hand and escorted her from the room.

Alice loved Logan more than she'd ever believed it possible to love.

Logan would have felt a great deal better if he knew that his speech had any effect on Ralston. The line had been drawn. Ralston intended to make it difficult for Alice to walk away from her commitment. Pounding the man to a pulp would have been temporarily satisfying, but it wouldn't have made the situation any better. Logan had matured enough to know that violence wasn't the answer to deter men like Ralston.

Upon regaining the power of speech, Ralston would simply have alerted the constable and let the law wreak his revenge. Or he might be the type to hire a band of thugs to take care of the situation his own way in the shadows of night. In any case, attempting to reason with the man was always the best way to go. In the event that Ralston proved unreasonable, as seemed to be the case, they had to find another way.

"He's not going to let you go easily." Logan turned to Alice once they'd reached the safety of the drawing room. "We can't give him any more reason to impugn your reputation until we find a way to force him to back down."

Alice nodded, gesturing that they should sit, making sure to take seats far apart from one another. "My reputation will survive. There are worse things than calling off an engagement. Lord Ralston thinks too highly of himself if he believes that threatening my reputation would stop me from pursuing what I want. Still, I suppose there's no sense in fueling the flames of his discontent. We mustn't be caught alone together again. I'll ring for Finch to bring tea, and perhaps he'll know where Agatha has gone. She must be our constant companion."

"I dislike the idea of needing a chaperone." Logan sighed. "I've only just returned to you."

"It's temporary. I think I know a way to convince him to release me." She smiled mysteriously.

"And you're not going to share?"

Alice shook her head. "Absolutely not. The less you know, the better. You've asked me to trust you in the past. I'm asking you to trust me now. I mean to beat him at his own game."

"If anyone can, my sweet Alice, it is you."

"I admire your restraint, Logan. If I were a man, I might have curled up my mighty fists and kept swinging at Ralston until I'd smashed him clean through one of the conservatory's glass walls."

"If you were a man, Alice, it would have been completely unnecessary. I would let Ralston fancy himself engaged to you and wipe my hands of you both."

"You wouldn't still love me if I were a man? I thought you promised you would love me no matter what." She mocked a pout.

He tipped his head. "Well, it would take some getting used to, I suppose. Perhaps if you joined me in a bottle of whiskey, and as long as you still had that glorious red hair."

She laughed. He wished he could close the distance between them and at least take her hand in his, but it wasn't worth the risk. As it was, they had all the appearance of propriety between them, her on the sofa, him seated opposite on the chair, far enough away that they couldn't be accused of touching.

Finch came along with the tea cart. "I've anticipated your needs. Mrs. Mallows included an assortment your favorite biscuits, Lady Alice."

"Gingerbread men! At last it feels like Christmas. Thank you, Mr. Finch." With childlike glee, she chose an icing-covered man, laughed at the sight of him, and took his head off with one bite.

"I will give Mrs. Mallows your regards," Finch said before leaving them.

"Remind me to stay on your good side." Logan raised a brow.

"You're safe from me, Mr. Winthrop. Unless you're crafted of gingerbread." She took off an arm with another bite before she poured the tea.

"Ah, back to formalities."

"We can't be too careful." She offered him a cup.

"Here you are." Agatha came in with Lady Holcomb. "You see, Hortense. My senses were leading us in the right direction. Oh, no Lord Ralston. Have you seen him? He must be lurking about somewhere."

"Somewhere," Alice said, pretending to be concerned. "He is sure to turn up."

"I've just given Hortense the most fascinating reading. Tea, yes please. No milk, two lumps." Agatha shuffled her tarot deck in her hands while waiting for Alice to pour.

"I've been a little afraid to attempt it," Lady Holcomb admitted, taking a seat beside Alice on the sofa. "But I told myself it was all for entertainment's sake, and do you know, I actually enjoyed it? There's great fortune in my future."

"And romance." Agatha held up a hand. "Don't forget romance. Someone might want to warn Lord Holcomb."

Lady Holcomb laughed. Logan found it fascinating that the two women were suddenly on a first-name basis. Perhaps there was hope for Lady Holcomb after all. Though, Logan reasoned, it was entirely likely the lady had gotten into the brandy early on the holiday morning.

Before long, Lord Holcomb and Lord Ralston joined them, and the parties who had gone off to the farms returned as well. They made a merry afternoon of trading stories and catching up in the drawing room until it was time to part and rest before getting ready for dinner and Christmas Eve Mass. Logan wished he could get Alice alone and lure her to his chamber, but the risk was too great. He reminded himself that they would have plenty of time to be alone when they could be rid of Lord Ralston once and for all.

He could hardly wait.

Twenty-two

ALICE'S PULSE THRUMMED WITH EXCITEMENT FOR THE evening ahead. Logan had come back for her. There was absolutely no way that she would allow Lord Ralston to ruin her chance at happiness. Somehow, she would get him to confess that he'd caused her post-accident incapacity by drugging her. Everyone who knew of it would accept that she was legitimately unable to make sound decisions for herself when she'd agreed to marry him. But why would he want everyone to know? He would be best served to back out of their engagement quietly without ascribing fault to either party.

She dressed and met with Sophia and Eve before heading to the drawing room.

"Do I meet your exacting standards?" she asked her sister, performing a slow twirl around the room.

"Alice, you look stunning. Why haven't I seen that gown before?" Sophia glanced up as she clipped on her earrings.

Alice's gown glittered with silver-edged black lace over an eggshell cream satin that clung to her figure and managed to be demure and daring at once. She'd kept it in the back of her closet, fearing it too mature for her. But suddenly, she knew she was woman enough to pull it off, and she'd chosen it for the evening. She would pair it with a more practical coat for evening Mass. "It felt festive for tonight. I'm in a good mood."

"Could it have anything to do with the reappearance of Mr. Winthrop?" Eve smiled mischievously.

"It could, but I wouldn't admit as much in front of my sister. Sophia still clings to the merits of Lord Ralston."

"I want you to be happy, dearest. Wouldn't anyone be happier as the wife of an earl?"

"No!" Eve and Alice said in unison. "You might believe having the right title is important, but the rest of us still believe in true love."

"'It's as easy to love a prince as it is to love a pauper,' Mother always said. 'But you might as well go for the prince.'" Sophia took her time looking over her strands of beads to choose just the right one to match her cranberry velvet. "Well, not if your heart really isn't in it. I don't want you to be miserable."

"Logan's not exactly a pauper," Alice defended, though she was glad to see signs of Sophia softening toward the idea of her choosing Winthrop. "Besides, he values my opinion. I need a man who recognizes my importance. If he doesn't think I'm a goddess next to everyone else on earth, what's the point?"

"I've always thought of Gabriel and Marcus as Roman or Greek gods, the gods of love and war, Marcus representing war, of course. Am I to be the only one in the family without a place in the Pantheon?" Eve wondered.

"If Marcus is god of war, he wouldn't have chosen a mere mortal as his consort. Let's see, Ares was in love with…oh. Aphrodite, wasn't it? That's awkward. Sophia has had herself painted as Aphrodite."

Eve laughed. Sophia kept pretending to ignore them in favor of dressing for dinner. "Eros, god of love, was paired with Psyche, and Psyche was a mere mortal, like me."

Alice rolled her eyes. "And Plato writes extensively about Psyche, and Lord Ralston is always quoting Plato. We're all mixed up in our mythology, aren't we?"

"Maybe not. What goddess are you, Alice?" Eve seemed to be enjoying the odd turn of the conversation.

Alice blushed. "Logan calls me his Artemis."

"If Artemis ever fell off her horse," Sophia joined in with a laugh.

"It wasn't funny, Sophia. I could have been seriously hurt."

"Yes, but you weren't. You're completely well now." Sophia dabbed her lips with rouge.

"I think I always was, but time will tell."

"Back to suspecting Lord Ralston of ulterior motives, are we? Why can't you just accept that he is a man in love?"

"Oh, I accept it. The question is…in love with whom?"

Sophia turned to Eve. "Alice has a ridiculous theory that Ralston is in love with me. Can you imagine?"

Eve looked as if she were about to laugh, and then grew serious. "Actually, I can. He rarely takes his eyes off you, from what I've seen. You might be right, Alice."

"Ha, you see, Sophia?" Alice crossed her arms.

"Don't cross your arms when you're wearing that delicate lace," Sophia ordered. "You'll crush it. We can dress you up, but we certainly can't teach you to behave. But back to your mythology, Gabriel is no Eros."

Alice giggled. "You would know."

"Because he's more of an Adonis, don't you agree? And Adonis and Aphrodite were a pair. A beautiful pair."

"Until Adonis was killed by jealous Ares because Aphrodite dared to flirt with both of them." Alice smirked at Sophia.

"We needn't worry about that. Gabriel and Marcus put all of their difficulties behind them last year. They tend to agree on just about everything now."

"Besides, Marcus would never look twice at Sophia. He prefers blondes." Eve patted the curls of her blond bobbed hair. "But Artemis, you're forgetting something."

"No. I'm well aware that Artemis falls in love with Orion, only to end up being the death of him."

Eve nodded. "She kills him by accident."

"I think it's time we stop living out the myths, then, hmm? They're not fitting to our situations after all. If there's one man I'd kill, and not at all by accident, it would be Lord Ralston. Fortunately, Agatha read my aura and deems me an orange. Apparently, I'm capricious but forgiving. It should work well in Ralston's favor."

"Provided he lives long enough." Eve laughed. "Sophia, you're beautiful. Aren't we ready yet?"

"Yes." She stood up from her dressing table. "Let's go join the men."

"And Lord and Lady Holcomb and Aunt Agatha," Alice added. "Did you see how Agatha and Lady Holcomb are suddenly fast friends? Agatha did a reading for Lady Holcomb, and now she is on a first-name basis with Hortense."

"I'm glad they're getting along. It was getting tedious trying to keep them apart when Lady Holcomb was afraid of Agatha." Sophia drifted by them to lead the way.

"Eve, there was a time that you warned me off Logan. Have you changed your mind, then? He told me that he visited you at Markham House."

"We welcomed him, of course. I know how he feels about you, Alice. You might be unaware that there was a time when I warned him about falling for you as well. It was plain to see that the two of you were developing feelings for one another."

"Then why did you warn us both off?"

Eve smiled. "You see what my warnings accomplished, don't you? You both stopped pretending the attraction wasn't there and did something about it. Well, I can't say you ever pretended all that well, but Logan did. Don't forget that I've known you since you were a little girl, Alice. Even way back then, when difficulties popped up in your way, you stomped them down until they were obliterated so that you could get what you wanted."

"There's nothing like being told I can't have, be, or do something to fire my motivation."

"Exactly." Eve patted her hand. "'The course of true love never did run smooth.'"

"*A Midsummer Night's Dream*, of course. Shakespeare, with Athenians. It seems that we have a decidedly Greek theme to the evening."

"Perhaps Lord Ralston will honor us with more Plato?" Eve smiled. "Don't worry. At least *A Midsummer Night's Dream* is a comedy, not a tragedy."

"And it's not even summer. I think we'll be just fine." But Alice's nerves began to tighten in anxiety. She was willing to pray to any god, Greek or otherwise, who could help her clear the way to be with Logan.

Lord Holcomb, Ralston's uncle by marriage, seemed to be the only man in the room who could tolerate Lord Ralston. Marcus managed a capable job of appearing amiable, as he always did. The man could charm his way out of prison. According to stories of his life as a London prizefighter, Marcus had occasionally done just that. But Lord Averford seemed to have even more reason to detest Ralston than Logan did, a fact he found hard to believe.

Averford paced near the central fireplace, under the watchful gaze of his wife's portrait. Holcomb and nephew discussed Christmas past. Apparently, at their own house, they had a Christmas Eve tradition of reciting Dickens's *A Christmas Carol*. Marcus suggested they keep up the tradition at Thornbrook Park, adding that they could all take on the various roles. But who would be Scrooge?

"Winthrop, I daresay you've got the most in common with the old man," Ralston declared.

"With Ebenezer Scrooge? I'm hardly a miser." He attempted to laugh, but was still puzzling out what insult Ralston had in mind for him.

"But you've lived a life of regret, haven't you?"

Ah, so his life of regret was to be the object of Ralston's scorn. Logan could accept it. The only man who knew how to hurt him with his own regrets was himself, and he'd put that chapter of his life behind him. He'd lived it, studied it, learned from it. "That I have, Lord Ralston. And like Scrooge, I learned that I have a chance to turn my life around. Nothing is as wounding to the soul as a life of regret. It took me too long to learn that, but I have."

Lord Averford, Logan noticed, had started pacing in sharper turns, an animal who refused to be caged. He got closer to Ralston, and more dangerously ready to snap, by the moment. What had Ralston said or done to occasion such a response in the man? Logan hoped he would get a chance to have some time with Averford later to trade stories.

Fortunately for Ralston, the ladies put in their appearance, first Agatha with Lady Holcomb, followed shortly by Sophia, Eve, and Alice. As he stepped up to take Alice's hand and compliment her on her stunning appearance—the gown did wonders for her already eye-catching figure—Logan was nudged aside by Lord Ralston.

"My Lady Alice, you are a vision."

"Thank you," she smiled as if delighted by the compliments. Logan kept his composure, even when it appeared that Alice would take Ralston's arm and let the man lead her in to dinner.

She met his gaze briefly, and the flash of gold in her hazel eyes told him that she knew what she was doing. So it was to be that kind of night? He would bear all sorts of agonies watching Ralston with her and just be expected to keep faith in Alice? To trust her? He had little choice. Trust her he did. It was Ralston who left him unsettled.

Still, he followed them all in, taking Agatha as his partner, and took his seat at the far side of the table, too far down from Alice. Agatha would be his companion. At least, she was a calming influence.

"Fate, my dear." She patted his arm. "You must believe that everything will turn out as it should. The Wheel of Fortune is the card I chose for Lord Ralston this afternoon. A change of luck is on the way for him, and it won't be a turn for the better."

Logan wondered why it had taken him so long to have an Aunt Agatha in his life. She might be full of nonsense, but she meant well and it was usually the kind of nonsense one wanted to hear.

"Merry Christmas, Aunt Agatha." He raised his glass to her. "I wish us both good cheer."

After dinner, with several hours to go before Mass, someone suggested a reading of Dickens. Alice suspected it had been Lord Ralston. Who else would torture them with Dickens on a Christmas Eve? Though, considering Ralston, she might have been surprised they weren't enacting one of Plato's dialogues. Logan had been enlisted to play Scrooge, and he willingly accepted the part until Sophia protested, thankfully so, that acting it out could take forever and why didn't Lord Ralston, with his deep, clear voice, simply treat them to a reading?

Everyone was in general agreement except for Ralston, who deferred the role to Lord Holcomb, who always read it at Holcomb House.

"But first, refreshments," Lord Averford declared. "Finch has concocted his special wassail and it's our tradition to take a cup on Christmas Eve."

"What's in a wassail?" Lady Holcomb asked. "Is it fit for a lady?"

"Of course, yes. You wouldn't expect Finch to give his recipe away." Sophia smiled. "It's cider with spices and some stronger spirits. I confess I usually have a thimbleful for tradition's sake and that's enough for me."

Alice wanted to laugh at Lady Holcomb's reluctance, considering how often she'd drained her claret glass at dinner without hesitation.

"I'll try a small amount."

"Harry, dear." Alice used his given name to increase his sense of comfort. She'd spent all of her time at dinner pretending to be fascinated with his conversation and acting as if perhaps she had changed her mind and agreed to marry him after all. She even wore the ring, gaudy as she thought it was. "If I have wassail, I'll fall asleep. Could you ring for tea?"

"Of course, darling." His eyes lit up at the idea, encouraging Alice. As the others gathered around the wassail bowl, Alice pretended to doze on the couch while Finch brought in the teapot. "You know how

I like it, Harry. Please pour me a cup. I should have napped more in the afternoon. I hope the tea perks me up."

She went back to pretending to sleep. Agatha did her part, as they'd discussed. Alice had told Agatha of her plan earlier and enlisted her help. Knowing that Ralston alternately ignored or became annoyed with Agatha, he was sure to be oblivious to her quietly watching him from off to the side as he prepared tea for Alice. She simply waited for her chance. Sure enough, he was too preoccupied with keeping an eye on Alice to notice that Agatha had kept careful watch on him.

"Here you are, darling."

She took the cup as he offered it, but she only pretended to sip. "Very good. Thank you. Come. Sit by me. I'm sorry I've been so confused. I don't know what to say but that maybe I'm still not completely well after all."

"Maybe you're not. You have been...challenging."

"Sophia talked to me this afternoon, and she made some very good points. I don't want to bring scandal to my sister. She has been so very good to me. I don't love you, Harry. I will be completely honest. But I think you're the best choice for me, and in time perhaps..."

"Love might bloom, as long as you're willing to give us a chance. Are you saying you will?"

She paused to pretend to take a long sip, and then she began to nod, and nod. "Yes. Yes, I am."

"Darling, thank you. You won't be sorry. Now I'm going to fetch a cup of wassail for myself before the reading starts." He started to get up. Agatha gestured from behind him to indicate his inside coat pocket.

"A moment. Perhaps we could seal our commit-ment with a kiss?"

He sighed and leaned in. "It would be my pleasure."

Instead of the quick peck he offered, Alice slipped her fingers inside his coat and spread them along his rib cage to urge him closer. She ran her tongue along his lips until he opened his mouth to her and indulged in a deeper, more intense kiss, the kind of kiss she would prefer to reserve for Logan.

"Goodness," he said, drawing back. "You've never kissed me like that before."

"There are a lot of things we have yet to do together, Harry. I'm looking forward to it."

In his shock at the intensity of her kiss, he hadn't even noticed that she'd reached inside his pocket and pulled out the small vial. She hid it in her hands, poured her tea into the potted plant nearby, left her cup on the table, and excused herself a moment. Agatha met her in the hall.

"Laudanum," she said, holding out the bottle. "Can you believe it? I suspected but…to have my suspicions confirmed still leaves me reeling."

"I told you he was a wizard." Agatha nodded. "But instead of a spell, he was using his potion to control you."

"More like poison. He could have killed me. I believe it's all too easy to overdo it with laudanum. And so addictive. It's a wonder I managed to clear my head at all. I spilled that last cup of tea he served me on the day I came back to my senses, and I don't recall exactly but I think I failed to drink the one previous to that, too. I recovered by happy accident. If I hadn't gotten out of the house when I did, I dread to think what would have become of me."

"He must really know what he's doing. It wouldn't have served him to kill you before the wedding. My poor little bird." Agatha patted her cheeks. "I knew I never liked him."

"Well, we must go on to the next part of the plan." She handed Agatha the bottle. "You know what to do." They'd discussed it. Agatha would slip a drop into Ralston's cup. Once he started to show some effects, she would bump into him again, and slip the bottle to the floor as if it had fallen out of his coat, then loudly call attention to it. His embarrassment would be so great that they would be rid of him.

Agatha winked and went back to the festivities. Alice waited a moment before rejoining them.

"Ah, there you are." Ralston approached her at once. "I went to fill my cup and came back to find you gone. I wondered where you'd run off to." His gaze shot to Logan across the room in hearty conversation with Gabriel, Marcus, and Lord Holcomb. Obviously, he'd made sure that wherever she had slipped off to, Logan hadn't followed.

"My head." She pressed a hand to her temple. "The buzzing has come back and I feel a tad lightheaded."

"Shall I call the doctor?" His eyes narrowed with concern.

She shook her head. "I hate to worry Sophia. Is it possible that my symptoms have returned? So long after the initial injury?"

"It's possible. The doctor warned of just such a thing," he lied cleverly. She doubted it to be at all likely, not after a week of feeling perfectly well. "Don't run off to bed just yet. Sit here. I know that being in the dark doesn't help to quiet the buzzing once it begins."

"You know me so well. How could I have doubted you? I need you, Ralston."

He kissed her forehead. "And I, you. Would you like more tea before Uncle begins his reading?"

More tea? Perhaps he *was* trying to kill her. "No, thank you. I'm going to try to regain my bearings in time for Mass. But your cup is empty. Go on and have more wassail. It's such a treat this time of year."

"It is delicious. I'll be right back at your side in a moment."

She nodded, and kept on nodding, nodding, as if she could not stop. He smiled and walked off toward Agatha, who hovered by the punch bowl.

"Lord Ralston," Agatha said. "Here, let me pour you a cup…"

Ah, they had him right where they wanted him. Alice wanted to choke him with her bare hands. How dare he think to medicate her against her will in her own home! She kept nodding as he came back across the room, thinking the whole time how she would be rid of him soon. Not soon enough!

Alice watched him from the corner of her eye as Lord Holcomb began to read.

"'Marley was dead: to begin with. There is no doubt whatever about that…'"

By the appearance of the first ghost, Lady Holcomb had got up and began to pace. "I can't sit still," she said. "Christmas is so thrilling. But read on, dear, I'm sorry to interrupt. I'm just going to stare at the tree a bit. Such pretty baubles."

"I like baubles." Captain Thorne joined her. "Let me tell you the history of some of the family ornaments. Carry on, old chap. I don't mean to interrupt."

Lord Holcomb cleared his throat and went back to the story. Within minutes of reading, he began to flub the lines, and then to laugh. "Perhaps I am old. I should be checked to see if I need spectacles. The lines are all wiggly. Someone will have to take over."

"Let's not read, then. We all know the story. Ghost of Christmas Present. Ghost of Christmas Past. Ghost of Christmas Future. Scrooge is dead. No, he's alive and reformed. Presents for everyone! They tuck into the roast goose. 'God bless us, every one!' End of story. Darling, could you play us some carols on the piano?" Sophia turned to Lord Averford.

Alice had begun to worry that Ralston was immune to the effects, until he started nodding beside her. Nodding, nodding. "Are you all right, Lord Ralston?"

"Christmas carols," he said, his voice a little drowsy. "I love them."

She smiled. "Well, you relax, then. Can I get you a pillow?"

He nodded, even as he said no. "No. I need to sit up. I have to clear my head."

"Oh, dear." She batted her lashes. "Are you feeling a little foggy?"

He gripped her wrist, apparently not that far gone. "What have you done?"

"Me?" She pulled away. "I don't know what you mean."

Unable to hold back any longer, Logan approached. "Unhand her. What's going on, Alice?"

In the corner near the tree, Marcus and Lady Holcomb began to waltz.

"Everybody dance!" Marcus declared. "'Tis the season."

Lady Holcomb began to hum loudly.

"What the devil is going on here?" Lord Averford, clearly unaffected, stood up at the piano bench.

"I wondered the same thing," Eve said, making her way to cut in on the dancing.

Alice looked at Agatha. Agatha took a seat next to Ralston on the couch and all too obviously bumped him. "Oh, my apologies."

"Your apologies?" Ralston turned slowly to look at her.

With everyone's gaze on her, Agatha none too subtly tossed the bottle to the center of the floor and exclaimed, "Laudanum, Lord Ralston. Poor thing. Do you have a cough?"

Sophia was the one to head for the center of the room and pick it up. "Laudanum? Where did you get this, Agatha?"

Agatha, never one for secrets that did not hail from the spirit world, stood and cleared her throat, cueing Alice that she was about to confess all. Alice should have known not to give her aunt too much responsibility. She buried her head in her hand, prepared for the outburst. Lending support, Logan slipped an arm around Alice's waist.

"I'm sorry, Alice," Agatha began. "I botched things. The laudanum came from Lord Ralston's coat pocket. Alice and I hatched a scheme. We suspected Ralston of drugging her."

"With laudanum?" Lord Holcomb's eyes widened.

"In our efforts to prove it, I managed to get the laudanum from Ralston's pocket and slip it into the punch bowl."

"Into the wassail?" Alice exclaimed. "No wonder everyone's gone mad. Agatha, you were only supposed to slip it into Ralston's drink."

"I know." Agatha waved her hands. "But it was too much trouble to single his out without calling his attention. I put a few drops in the bowl. Just a few. It shouldn't last long."

Sophia rang for Finch, who appeared at once as if he and perhaps some of the staff had been just behind the doors marveling at the scene. "Get Dr. Pederson on the line at once. Explain that we've had a situation with laudanum…"

"I've been following the events," Finch confessed with a sly smile. "I'll telephone at once." He grimaced slightly upon mention of the telephone, but events like these might help to convince him that such modern conveniences were perhaps a necessary evil.

"Oh dear," Sophia said. "Who has had the wassail?"

Alice breathed a sigh of relief that Lord Averford and Logan had rejected the wassail in favor of single malt whiskey. Sophia and Eve Thorne hadn't touched it. Alice and Agatha had obviously abstained. That left only Marcus, who could not resist anything with apples, Lord and Lady Holcomb, and fortunately Lord Ralston affected.

Eve took immediate charge of Marcus and Lady Holcomb, who had possibly had a little more of the tainted wassail than anyone else. She urged them to stop dancing and to sit for a moment. Once she pried them apart, she had to lead them carefully over to their seats as they stumbled a bit on their own feet. At least, they were both laughing.

"You." Sophia approached Lord Ralston, her foot tapping under her skirts. "I invited you into our home. I welcomed your help in caring for Alice. And this is how you repay me? By drugging my poor sister out of her mind?"

Alice watched with growing joy as her sister finally accepted the truth and defended her.

"No one can prove that it's my laudanum. Agatha never liked me. It's a plot!"

"That part is true," Agatha said, quite pleased with herself. "I've never liked you."

Finch returned to the room with two footmen bearing pots of coffee and more cups. "Dr. Pederson doesn't believe anyone consumed enough to be in serious condition. He recommended plenty of strong, hot coffee and said to call him back if they showed no signs of improvement."

"Coffee it is," Lord Averford said, taking cups from the footmen and helping to pass them around.

"I'll expect an explanation from you after you've had your coffee, Lord Ralston." Sophia approached Alice to offer a supportive embrace and then turned back to face Ralston. "And it had better be good."

Twenty-three

"PLEASE KNOW HOW TRULY SORRY I AM," LORD Ralston said for what Logan believed was the fourth time. Or more. He had lost count. "I truly meant well. Dr. Pederson had suggested it at first as a way to lessen any discomfort Alice had while recovering. I thought you might object, Sophia, or dislike the idea of medication, and I hated to worry you more. You were so distraught."

"At first, yes." Sophia nodded. "But later? I should have been consulted."

"And that was truly my only crime, not consulting you." Ralston, done with his coffee, put down the cup and stood. "Alice, it was all done out of love. You must believe me. I hated to see you suffering so. I would have turned to any balm to ease your pain."

Alice squeezed Logan's hand. He wasn't sure if she did it to borrow his strength or to keep him calm so that he didn't attack Ralston. Logan's other hand, curled into a fist, had flexed and tensed on a regular basis as he warred within himself. He wanted so badly to hit Lord Ralston for what he'd done. Drugging

Alice? Against her will and without her sister's knowledge? No excuse was good enough. But he knew that he wouldn't help matters by flying off in a fury, letting violence speak for him.

"But I was recovering." Alice managed to argue without becoming strident. "Recovered, in fact. You medicating me only prolonged my agony. You had to have known as much. I don't believe you did anything out of love for me, only for your own selfish interests."

"I knew no such thing." Ralston flew to Alice's side and dropped to one knee before her. "And if I am selfish in trying to win your love, so be it. I need you, Alice."

Perhaps now, Logan thought. If he dragged the man outside and beat him now, would everyone forgive him? But he stood his ground. Alice would be apoplectic if he took her right to address her tormentor away from her. He remained calm for Alice.

"You must understand," Ralston went on with his begging. "You were feeble and confused. How it tugged at my heartstrings to see you so vulnerable!"

Alice scoffed. "It tugged at something in you, but I doubt it was your heartstrings, Lord Ralston. Perhaps it was your sense of malice."

"There was no malice intended!" Ralston raised his voice in his own defense. "Perhaps, yes, I welcomed the fact that the laudanum made you agreeable. Secretly, I feared that you would turn me down. I only wanted so desperately for you to let me love you, Alice."

"That kind of love is rare to find," Sophia said, obviously touched by the scoundrel's words. "He did it all for love, Alice. Though that's certainly no way to show it. Shame on you, Lord Ralston. How can you live with yourself?"

Logan shook his head. Female sentimentality. Thank goodness Alice had more sense than her sister.

"Bollocks," Alice said from between clenched teeth. "You wanted something, Lord Ralston. Though I still can't be certain what it was."

How Logan loved her! What other woman would show such nerve, such spirit! He wanted to lift her in his arms and carry her off, to make love to her for hours at a time. Alice. His Alice. He looked at her, her dark red hair falling slightly from her chignon, threatening to spill down those beautiful white shoulders.

"By God, you amaze me," Logan said before he could stop himself. He hadn't meant to say it out loud. She met his gaze, a smile in her eyes. Looking at her, he knew that she had every idea what had driven Ralston to act, but she was holding back for some reason. To protect someone else? Sophia. She would only be so concerned for her sister or her aunt. And he doubted Ralston had any designs on Agatha. "Do you really mean to forgive this man?"

"It's Christmas." Alice shrugged. "All that is behind us now. I can afford to be forgiving, provided..." She paused to slip a diamond ring from her finger. The ring Ralston had given her. "You take this back, Lord Ralston, and never speak of our engagement again. I don't have any intention of marrying a man who would medicate me without my knowledge or permission. And go away. Go away, all of you. I never want to see you again, Lord Ralston. I should have the constable come and take you away, but I won't. In the spirit of Christmas."

"You're free, Harry!" Lady Holcomb shouted, taking a little longer to get over her intoxication. "I can't wait to tell Matilda Furbish that you're no longer engaged."

"I'm sure she will be very happy to have you, Lord Ralston," Sophia said. "I wish you the best of luck in your future endeavors."

"That's it, then? You're really willing to let me go, Alice?" Even after all that was revealed, Ralston was surprised? Perhaps he was the addlepated one after all. Logan realized that perhaps he could let the man off without beating his brains out. Ralston needed every bit of the mind that he possessed, which apparently wasn't much. "After all the tender declarations of love between us?"

"After all that. Imagine." Alice shook her head in wonder, apparently as perplexed by the man's audacity or lack of understanding as Logan was. "I'm willing to let you go. Go!"

Lord Averford looked at the clock. "It's time we get ready for Mass. Are we done here, or do I need to send for the constable? I'm willing to press charges if Alice isn't."

"That won't be necessary, darling." Sophia took Gabriel's arm. "It's Christmas. Let's just agree that Lord Ralston and Lord and Lady Holcomb will be on their way after Mass. If anyone needs the Lord's forgiveness tonight, it's Lord Ralston."

Lord Averford seemed very disappointed. "I know. But what a lovely gift it would be for me to hand Lord Ralston over for imprisonment."

"Gabriel!" Sophia had the nerve to sound shocked.

"Well, it's criminal, isn't it? The man in our home, slipping poison into Alice's drinks while the rest of were unaware."

"Not poison," Sophia said. "Medication. Unlawfully administered, perhaps."

"Laudanum is poison in the wrong hands, darling. It's easy to overdose."

Marcus, coming back to his senses, agreed. "I've seen it. One of the many unfortunate things I had to witness at war, men becoming addicted to laudanum after sustaining injuries. Not only that, but one of them was killed when a bottle was left at his bedside and he accidentally, or perhaps on purpose, took too much."

"I'm fortunate to have learned my lesson without injuring anyone, much less the woman I love." Ralston looked at Alice with large cow eyes, his attempt at remorse.

For Logan, it was the last straw. Unable to hold back any longer, he drew back his fist and let it fly, pounding it into Lord Ralston's perfect, stony jaw. Ralston reeled back, landing, fortunately for him, on Sophia's delicate sofa.

"I'm sorry," Logan said, shaking the tension out of his hand. "I was only trying to help. Consider it medicinal."

"Logan," Alice said in a chastising tone, even as she placed her hand on his arm and looked up at him approvingly.

Averford laughed and reached out to shake Logan's hand. "If you didn't, I would have. Merry Christmas, Winthrop."

❧

Alice woke to the sound of the piper making his merry music throughout the halls of Thornbrook Park. Sophia had heard that a piper woke the royal family every Christmas morning, and she had thought to do the same when she discovered that one of the footmen, George, played the pipes.

Had she actually slept? Alice realized that she had, and she had slept soundly and well. She was free of Ralston! Once she had gotten him to confess what he had done and apologize for his actions, she had forced him to take back his ring. He had no power over her now. She was free, and her next thought was of Logan waking up in his room down the hall, wearing not a stitch. Not that she had any idea what he wore, but she liked to imagine him naked beneath the sheets, his muscular hands riffling through his mussed hair as the piper's tune invaded his room.

Last night, there hadn't been much time for them to be alone and discuss what Ralston's admission meant for their future together. They'd had only enough time to get their coats and walk the short distance to Thornbrook's chapel for Christmas Eve Mass. The service had been long, but so uplifting that they all returned in joyous spirits and tired to the bone. After exchanging good-nights, they all parted for bed. Logan had held her hand in his for an extraordinary long time, though. And when he said good night, he'd called her his love and leaned in to deliver a chaste kiss on her cheek.

Alice rubbed the cheek, remembering the warmth

of his lips and the tingle that had risen inside her when she'd imagined grabbing hold of his lapels and delivering a more passionate kiss to his lips. But, of course, it was out of the question in mixed company. She'd just ended her engagement officially. She supposed they would have to wait a bit to be public with a romance.

In a tremendously fine mood, she hurried to wash and dress. Before bed, she'd told Mary that she could manage on her own and had given the maid a silver bracelet as a gift. Mary had looked delighted with the bracelet but declared that her true gift had been in hearing that Alice had shaken free of Lord Ralston. Mary confessed that all the servants downstairs had become aware of Agatha's dousing the wassail with laudanum and a few of them becoming dazed with the effects.

How they all laughed downstairs at the report of Captain Thorne dancing with Lady Holcomb—once they heard that everyone would be all right, of course. Alice laughed with Mary before bidding her good night and confessed that the scene had been rather comical to behold. Thank goodness everything had turned out for the best.

Despite rising at the first sound of the piper, Alice found that she was last to arrive in the breakfast room, where they were passing around gifts.

"Ivory knitting needles?" Sophia looked aghast at the gift from her mother-in-law but tried to force a smile. "How thoughtful. I haven't knitted in years. I guess I should take it up again."

Gabriel's mother had gifted him with a humidor. "And I suppose I need to take up smoking cigars."

"Oh dear, no." Sophia wrinkled her nose. "I can't abide the smell. But the humidor might be turned into a suitable jewelry box."

"I got the same thing last year when we were expecting Mina," Marcus said. "But I do enjoy the occasional cigar."

"And I got knitting needles last year, too, remember? Mine were onyx," Eve said.

"Oh dear." Sophia nibbled her lip. "Perhaps she's trying to tell us something. She wants more grandchildren."

The Dowager Countess also sent a silver rattle for Mina, her third, which went straight into her mouth as she cooed on her mother's lap. Eve got some cashmere yarn, and Marcus got cigars to fill his humidor.

"She's consistent, I'll give her that," Lord Averford said with a laugh.

Sophia, who must have been affected by the spirit of Christmas, acknowledged the previous gift of the lemon trees. "I'm glad she sent them now. I am looking forward to lemonade. And lemon tarts. Thanks to you, Mr. Winthrop, the trees are about to bear fruit."

"Thanks to Brian Sturridge, really." Logan was always one to give credit where credit was due. "Sturridge is the one who kept the trees thriving while I was busy attending to…other things." He cast a sly look at Alice that made her blush. She suspected that he, too, was thinking of the night they'd been out in the storm.

Next, they opened gifts from Alice and Sophia's parents, the usual muffs, mittens, and scarves. "Always thinking of keeping us warm in winter," Sophia said. "Though I suppose my mittens from last year have gone a bit threadbare. Mother does like to think that she has been useful."

Agatha held up her fur stole. "She always goes out of her way for me, our Theodora. I believe it's the guilt of casting me out that inspires her to spend extravagantly."

Theodora was Alice and Sophia's mother. "But did it have to be fox?" Alice rolled her eyes at the sight of the red and white fur, complete with a little face biting its own tail. "I'll be happy to never see another fox as long as I live."

They all laughed. The morning was for opening gifts from far-off relatives. Later that evening, they would exchange gifts to each other. Alice began to panic that she hadn't been expecting Logan, and she didn't have a gift for him. Then she noticed that he wore the cuff links she'd given him. Perhaps she needn't worry.

"Time for church," Sophia said cheerfully as she rose from the table.

"I feel like we were just there." Alice rolled her eyes.

After church, they spent the afternoon bundled up outdoors in the falling snow for sledding. The Cooper children from Tilly Meadow were out and started a snowball fight with the men of Thornbrook Park. For the most part, the women sat out the shenanigans, but Alice managed to hit Logan with a snowball after he accidentally pelted her while trying to hit Marcus.

Sophia suggested they all go skating. Alice liked the idea, though it reminded her of having been forgotten by Ralston. Of course, she couldn't be sad about something that led to better things for her. And Logan called the iced pond the Fairy Pool, which seemed so romantic. Once on skates, she was able to play at being clumsy simply so Logan would have an excuse to put his arms around her.

"I have a surprise for you," he said, as they glided over the frozen pond.

"Oh? What could it be?"

"We have to take off our skates and leave the others. Come on."

She sat on a snowbank and allowed him to help her unlace her skates. He took slightly longer than necessary, spending extra time caressing her feet and ankles.

"I can't wait to be alone with you again," she said, relishing the feel of his hands on her, even over her woolen tights and though he wore thick gloves. "Will we ever have the chance?"

"Soon." He held her hand and walked with her toward the former McGinty place.

"Logan, no." She stopped. "A family lives there now. We can't go back."

"Give me a chance," he said. "I have an idea."

When they arrived at the door, he knocked and waited. "Good tidings, new neighbors," he said when Mr. Higgins answered the door, overlooking the fact that he was no longer a neighbor. "Merry Christmas."

"And to you," Higgins said. They'd all met at Mass and at church again in the morning.

"Lord Averford would like to extend an invitation to your family to join his party at the Fairy Pool." He gestured through the woods to the pond. "It's that small pond through the trees, now frozen over. We've been skating and plan to be there a little while yet."

"Ice skating?" Higgins's wife joined him at the door. "I love to skate. What fun! I've been wondering if that pond would freeze solid enough."

"Oh, it's quite solid," Logan assured them. "We've been out a while now, and it happens that the young woman with me here…"

"Lady Alice." Mrs. Higgins nodded in her direction. "Merry Christmas to you."

"And to you." Alice smiled.

"Lady Alice doesn't do well in the cold, apparently. Might we warm up a minute in front of your fire?"

"Please, come in." Alice followed Mrs. Higgins to the small sitting room, admiring the way the furniture arrangement made the space look larger. Alice preferred it stripped down to the bare floor. With a tarp and horse blankets. She looked at the fire and back to Logan, his heavy-lidded eyes watching her. She knew he was sharing the same memory. Her toes curled at the thought of it.

"But the babies?" Mrs. Higgins said, as her husband convinced her to get ready to go skating.

"Mother will watch the babies," he assured her. "She's up napping with them now."

Too excited at the idea of skating, Mrs. Higgins got ready to go.

"You don't mind if we leave you to see your own way out?" Higgins asked at the door.

"Oh, no. Go on ahead. We'll see you back there in a short while."

Bundled in their coats, Mr. and Mrs. Higgins left

with their skates slung over their shoulders. Not a second after the door closed, Logan took Alice in his arms. "You see? Alone at last."

"Not quite alone." She pointed to the stairs. "We have to behave. We could be interrupted at any moment."

"We won't be, and I do plan to behave. For the most part." He leaned his head in slowly. Alice's heart began to beat faster. She ached for him, her nerves reacting to his proximity deep down in places that he couldn't touch with them both fully clothed. Her lips parted before his mouth met hers, and she kissed him hungrily.

"My memories of this place," she said, when he broke the kiss. "I'll never forget."

"Nor I. That's how I knew that it had to be here."

"What had to be here?"

He dropped to one knee. "It had to be here that I asked you, and here that I heard your answer. Please don't be afraid to say no. I'm willing to wait. I'm willing to give you anything you ask."

Her nerves danced with excitement. She'd never thought she wanted to be married, and now she wanted nothing more than to be Logan's wife. "Stop trying to anticipate my answer and ask me, Logan. Just ask."

He pulled an envelope out of his coat pocket. An envelope? "I've booked passage for two to India, leaving in the spring. It gives you plenty of time to decide if you would rather go on your own, but if you don't mind, I would like to go with you."

She blinked. "You want to accompany me to India." No marriage proposal? No ring? She had what she always wanted, and yet…

"Of course I would love to see India with you, Logan. Yes."

"What a relief," he said, not getting to his feet. He put the envelope back in his pocket and pulled out a small box. "Then it's not necessary, of course, but I thought it might be easier for traveling purposes if you would consent to go as my wife. Marry me, Alice."

Her knees went weak. She wobbled and found her footing. "Logan, you want me to marry you? Truly?"

"I believe I've been saying it for about a month now. Yes, Alice. Marry me. Please."

Hot tears formed in her eyes, threatening to spill down her cold cheeks. "Yes."

He shook his head. "Not if you're going to cry about it."

"I'm crying because I'm happy, Logan. I've never been so happy. I had no idea how much I wanted to be your wife until just now." He stood to take her in his arms, kissing her again. And again. She never wanted him to stop.

At last, he held out the small box. "Once, I told you that I offered my grandmother's moonstone to another woman."

"You wanted to give her the moon," Alice said. "But I believe you offered me the entire universe."

"And you shall have it, at least any part of it that's in my power to give. You're the woman I love." He opened the box. "And that's why I bought a new ring, something just for you. I saw it, and it reminded me of you. Red, like your hair. You know how I love your red hair." He stroked a tendril back from her face.

"I do." It was a solitary ruby, oval, set on a band of

tiny diamonds. "Rubies are my favorite, Logan. Put it on me, please. I want to wear it always." He slipped it on her finger.

"It's a perfect fit. Fate, as Agatha might say. It belongs on your finger."

"My grandmother's pin." She'd just remembered. "I traded it in a shop to buy your cuff links, but it's a perfect match for the ring. Grandmother believed it would bring the right man."

"We'll just have to go to that shop and buy it back again."

"Fate." She nodded. "I do love you, Logan. More than I ever thought it possible to love. I want to see the world and have adventures, but it would never suit me to do it alone now that I know what it is to love you. I want to be with you always."

"It's a good thing. I plan to be with you always, through every adventure for the rest of our lives."

Twenty-four

Back at Thornbrook Park, they all warmed up and refreshed themselves with tea. Alice and Logan exchanged knowing glances but waited to share their news. She kept gloves on to hide the ring until she felt ready to show it off. At the top of the stairs, Alice and Logan shared a warm kiss before anyone caught up to them.

"I can't wait for the day we can share a room," Alice said. "As husband and wife."

"Soon enough. But the day's activities have worn me out and I welcome a short nap. I might prove a disappointment if we shared a room."

"You will never disappoint me, Logan." She blew him another kiss as he walked off down the hall.

Later, once they were all rested and ready for the evening, they met in the drawing room before dinner. Alice didn't hesitate to wear her ring, without gloves, and she held her breath waiting for someone to notice.

"Where did you get that stunning ring, Alice?" Eve Thorne asked at last.

"Oh my goodness." Sophia came from across the

room to have a look. "I can't believe I didn't notice it at once."

"It was a gift," she said, eager to fill them all in, but waiting for Logan to say something. She met his gaze.

Eve and Sophia looked right at Logan before he needed to say a word. Agatha got up and hugged Logan at once. "Welcome to the family! I knew fate would lead you all along."

"It's an engagement, then?" Sophia's eyes darted back and forth between Alice and Logan. "For certain."

"It is," Alice acknowledged with a blush.

Logan came to her side and placed a kiss on her cheek. "I've loved her for too long to risk letting her get away again. And to my great joy, Alice has consented to be my wife."

"And I realized that I do want to be married after all, to Logan. Someone to share all my adventures."

"More than you ever dreamed." He held her close.

The rest of the evening went by in a blur. They ate and returned to the drawing room, and drank and laughed. What had started as a catastrophic holiday had turned into the best Christmas ever. The women admired Alice's ring and planned ahead.

"A spring wedding, to be sure," Agatha said. "New beginnings."

They all raised their glasses. "To new beginnings."

❧

It was late in the evening. Agatha and the Thornes had gone to bed. Logan and Alice stayed up as long as they could for the chance to spend more time in each other's arms. Gabriel and Sophia made their excuses to leave the two lovebirds alone.

"It has been such a long day," Sophia said. "I'm so tired."

"You go on up to bed, darling," Gabriel said. "I've got to clear some business downstairs with Finch. Boxing Day. I want to make sure everyone is free and able to have a day off without waiting on us. I'll meet you up in bed shortly."

"Of course," Sophia said. "Don't stay up too late, you two. And best wishes again for a wonderful life together. My apologies if I did anything to stand in the way of your happiness. I might have been overzealous in acting for what I believed was in Alice's best interest. I look forward to having you as a brother, Logan. Growing up, I always wanted brothers. Now I'm to have two of them."

"Thank you, Sophia. It means a lot to me that we have your approval," Logan said.

"To me, too," Alice added. "Thank you for coming to see things as they should be. Logan and I belong together."

"I can see that now." Sophia flashed a genuine smile. "And I'm very pleased for you. Good night."

Logan and Alice stayed in front of the fire for some time, kissing and cuddling, not quite ready to part. At last, they decided they had better go in case they were keeping the servants up. With Boxing Day about to begin, they hated to be in the way.

But as they rounded the corner to head up the stairs, they froze in their tracks. Lord Ralston had returned. He stood in the hall, his head bowed in quiet conversation with Sophia. They looked almost like lovers, which Alice began to laugh off as preposterous until he took Sophia in his arms and kissed her passionately. At first, Sophia started to push him away, but slowly she began to give in.

"Sophia," Alice breathed, unable to believe her eyes. For once, she wished so badly that she had been wrong, so terribly wrong, about Ralston's attraction to Sophia. But she seemed to have been right. Alice leaned on Logan for support.

Logan's arm was around her waist, gently guiding Alice away from the disturbing sight, when the worst of all things happened next. Lord Averford turned the corner and witnessed his wife in the arms of another man. And his face—Alice would never forget the look on Gabriel's face, a look of sheer agony. Alice watched her brother-in-law's heart break into a million pieces right before her eyes.

"Gabriel." Some sort of awareness dawned on Sophia at last, a minute too late. She looked up to see her husband watching her with Lord Ralston. "Gabriel! It's not what it seems. Please, let me explain."

Sophia left Lord Ralston standing there in the hall and ran off after her husband.

Alice stepped forward, Logan two steps behind, still holding her hand.

"*You.*" The word held all the venom Alice could muster.

"I love her, Alice. I'm sorry." Finally humbled, Lord Ralston was ready to confess. "It has always been Sophia. I finally came to admit it to her. I had to take the chance. She said I was being ridiculous, and she begged me to leave. She said she loved her husband, but I didn't believe her. I couldn't. We could be so good together. I took her in my arms and I kissed her so that she would finally understand. Clearly, I was wrong. Maybe she really does love him."

"Of course she loves him," Alice said, perhaps a little too loudly. "Are you mad? Or just daft? She loves him, you fool. Get out." She pointed toward the door. "Get out of this house and don't ever come back, or so help me God, Ralston, I'll shoot you myself."

He held up his hands, resigned. "I'm leaving. There's nothing here for me now. Good-bye. I wish you all the best."

"*Out!*" Alice yelled. Once he left, she turned to Logan. "Can you believe his nerve? That man!"

"I would have been glad to punch him again, but you seemed to have it all under control." Logan pulled Alice into his arms. "I'm sorry we had to see that. But Sophia and Gabriel have a lot of love between them. They will work it out."

"I certainly hope you're right." She allowed herself to lean into him, the man she planned to marry. She wasn't sure that he was right about her sister's marriage recovering. She'd never seen Gabriel look so broken. "Whatever the future holds, I'm so glad I have you to face it with me, Logan."

"Whatever the future holds." He kissed the top of her head. "I'm here."

Acknowledgments

Many thanks to my Sourcebooks team for helping to get my books into shape and out there. Thanks to my personal team for your endless love and support. And thank you, readers, for buying my books, commenting on my social media sites, and leaving reviews. I appreciate you all more than you could ever know.

About the Author

Sherri Browning writes historical and contemporary romantic fiction, sometimes with a paranormal twist. A graduate of Mount Holyoke College, Sherri has lived in western Massachusetts and Michigan, but is now settled with her family in Connecticut. To learn more, visit www.sherribrowningerwin.com.

Read on for an excerpt from

Thornbrook Park

September 1906

MISTY FOG DRAPED LONDON LIKE A BRIDAL VEIL, obscuring Eve Kendal's first view of her homeland in six long years. She was left to imagine the tower, the bridge, and the clusters of chimney tops merrily puffing out smoke. A dusk arrival hindered sight of the skyline, fog or no. Better to employ her time in making plans for disembarking rather than idling on deck where a fetid stench rolled off the water. Colonel Adams, who had accompanied her from India, approached her, apparently in the same frame of mind.

"I've arranged for a hansom cab, and I would be pleased to deliver you to your friend's address. No need to tempt the ruffians, a lovely young woman alone. It will be dark before we're finally off the ship."

"Thank you, Colonel. You're very kind." *Too kind.* Colonel Adams and his wife, a doting older couple, had done little else but fret over Eve's welfare in the year and a half since the colonel had delivered the news of her husband Captain Benjamin Kendal's unfortunate demise.

Six years earlier, when she'd eloped with Ben to India against her parents' wishes, making her own way in the world was something that had never crossed her mind. Now that she was on her own, she craved a chance to manage her own affairs. She'd only accepted the colonel's offer to accompany her because he had matters to attend that coincided with her return and it seemed wise to make the passage with a companion.

Her finances necessitated a return to England. Her widow's pension would only stretch so far, and she couldn't find out what had happened to their savings. Ben had spoken of investing them. Her fervent hope was that her late husband's solicitor in London would know where their money was.

That her family had disowned her for marrying Ben, an army captain instead of the earl her mother had hoped for, seemed an unhappy turn, but no crucial setback at the time. They had each other, and together they would conquer all, even life in a strange, new country. But they hadn't accounted for natural disaster. When an earthquake rocked the Kangra Valley in India, where Ben had been sent on a special mission for the magistrate, he was killed in a shower of falling rocks.

Eve had stayed in the safety of Raipur, where they'd made their home among a small community of expatriates. They'd once talked of a quiet retirement in the English countryside, their many children all around them. In six years of marriage, Eve hadn't yet conceived and she'd begun to fear that she couldn't. With Ben—and their savings—gone, it was probably for the best that she didn't have children to support.

Still, how she would have loved a child with Ben's eyes and laugh to be her constant companion. Her memories were all that remained, memories she wouldn't trade for anything, not even to win back her parents' support. Over a year later, she was out of mourning and on to a new life, the dreams she'd shared with Ben behind her.

Her parents and brother never answered her letters. Besides Colonel Adams and his wife, Adela, Eve had one friend in the world, her girlhood companion, Sophia.

All through her absence, Eve and Sophia had kept up correspondence. When Eve had written Sophia about Ben's death, she'd been touched to receive her friend's offer of the Dower House on the grounds of her estate. She was grateful to Sophia for throwing her a lifeline when she needed one most.

Standing next to her on the deck, Colonel Adams suddenly placed his hand over hers on the rail, interrupting her thoughts.

"Time heals all wounds, my dear, as they say. Or someone said. I don't recall who…"

"I believe it was the Greek philosopher Menander, as echoed by Chaucer in *Troilus and Criseyde*."

"Ah." He stroked his silver mustache. "Very clever, but perhaps best not to demonstrate that so readily. A number of suitors would be discouraged from pursuit of a bookish woman."

"Suitors, Colonel?" Eve suppressed a smile and shook her head. "Even if I wanted one, I wouldn't accept a man who shied from intelligence. You know me better than that."

"I do." He nodded dismissively. "What I mean to say is that time heals, perhaps, but it works all the faster when you're in familiar territory. As much as Adela and I will miss you, I believe being back in England will be restorative for you. A fresh start in—where is this place you go, again?"

"Thornbrook Park, the Earl of Averford's estate in West Yorkshire."

"Thornbrook Park, indeed. Nothing like the clean air of the English countryside to restore good health and spirits."

"Yes. A night at Averford House, my friend's house in town, and then the train straight to Thornbrook tomorrow morning."

"They know you at Averford House?" A bushy brow arched over inquisitive green eyes.

"No, but Sophia, Lady Averford, sent a letter ahead to the butler informing him to expect me. I don't anticipate any problems."

"Good. I'm in town for a fortnight, don't forget, at the Langham, should you need me."

"So you've told me. Three times now." Eve smiled. It was probably more like ten times. "You've no need to worry. As much as I love your company, I hope I won't need to look you up. Lady Averford's brother-in-law, an army captain, currently resides at Averford House. You might know him, Captain Marcus Thorne?"

"I don't know the name." The colonel shook his head, though his eyes brightened at the news that there was a man in charge at Averford House, an army man.

"I'm sure I will be quite safe. Give my love to Adela when you get home."

"We will start looking for your novel as soon as I get back."

She laughed. "I have to write it first. I'm not sure when I'll find time. And then, I'll need a publisher. You won't have to start looking for at least a year, and I'll send plenty of letters in the meantime."

"We have faith in you, my dear."

"Thank you, Colonel." She wished she had as much faith. As she noticed activity picking up around them on the deck, she removed her hand from under the colonel's and reached for her bag. "I believe it's time to disembark."

❧

Captain Marcus Thorne, his hands in his pockets, shouldered his way through the rough crowd gathered in the street outside the Hog and Hound.

"A fighter!" one of the lads said, gesturing to him. The boy was too young to be out late in such a neighborhood. Marcus stifled the urge to reprimand the boy, but kept his head down and kept walking.

"No, 'e's a gentleman," said a toothless old hen. "Come to watch and wager like the rest of 'em."

No one could accuse him of dressing impeccably, but he supposed his clothes stood out as fine, more befitting a gentleman than a fighter: dark frock coat concealing broad shoulders, black trousers, and black hat low over his eyes covering wheat blond hair, close cropped to be suitable for fighting, nothing for an opponent to grab. *Onward. No sense in correcting her.*

The black rage was upon him, taking him over, becoming more impossible to control by the minute. After the war, he suffered many black rages, pounding at the back of his brain like a time bomb ticking toward explosion. And when it went off, God help those around him. The only thing he'd discovered that could dismantle the rage, as he had disabled box mines in South Africa, was to hit something, someone, anyone.

During the war, he'd had steady hands, a sharp mind, and nerves of steel. Now, his nerves were shot to hell, and the rest of him was on the way there, too.

After he'd spent too many nights to count in holding cells for starting brawls, a friend had suggested Marcus put his fists to better, or at least more profitable, use and take up prizefighting. He spied the friend, Thomas Reilly, a private detective, at the bar as he entered the room.

The dim lighting and haze of smoke in the air could not disguise that the pub had seen better days. Perhaps the worn state only served to make him, and all the other miscreants, feel more at home, though the gentlemen among them seemed equally undaunted by the divots in the wood-paneled walls between prints of racehorses and pugilists, or the occasional dots of rodent droppings on the sanded floor.

Marcus acknowledged Tom with a nod and kept walking to a table in back occupied by a slim young man in a suit cut two sizes too large, perhaps to add the impression of size. Without a word, Marcus placed a note stating his intentions on the table and waited for a response.

The man did not answer, but raised his brows in

surprise, jumped up, and ran through the faded red velvet curtains to the ring in back.

"Gentlemen." Marcus could hear the man, his voice sturdier than his build. "We have a newcomer waiting. He demands a fight to the finish with the best man in the room."

The announcement was followed by silence and then hoots of laughter. The champions of all weight classes had undoubtedly been decided and declared by the time of Marcus's arrival. A challenge to take on the best, without specification of age or weight class, would be considered either a fool's mission or an outright joke.

Marcus had served in the Second Boer War, the biggest fool's mission of them all in his mind, and there could be no more ridiculous joke than sending him, a gentleman's son, off to war. Commissioned officers weren't often sent to war, and being directly involved in bloodshed hadn't been what he'd expected when he'd purchased his commission. He'd only meant to impress his father and show his brother that he, the bookish one, could pursue an active life of adventure, while his brother, the sportsman, was destined to a custodial life in charge of a house, grand though it was. Perhaps the real joke was that he had returned when so many had not; that he, a pampered mother's favorite, had faced every challenge thrown his way and survived.

He was not the same man upon his return. Memories haunted him, his conscience nagged him, and the black rages took him over on occasion, but no longer as frequently as they had when he'd got back, before he'd first stepped into the ring.

Tonight's rage had been initiated by the carriage driver who swerved and nearly killed the little urchin selling flowers at the roadside before continuing on his way without pause. *Tick*. And the lady in the bird-ornamented bonnet walking right on by, stepping over the child without a moment's hesitation to ask if she were hurt. *Tick*. And when Marcus stopped to help the girl up and gather her flowers, he could see that her eyes had the same gray-green hue as another child he'd known. His mind flew back to the South African concentration camps and a mother and daughter separated from the rest of their family by force and held against their will.

"For your own safety," Marcus had been instructed to reassure them. "Wouldn't want innocents to get caught up in the fighting." For the safety of the troops, Marcus knew. Wouldn't want opposition to grow and spread like wildfire among the civilians.

Tick. The rage had fallen upon him, ready to blow, pounding behind his eyes, throbbing in his ears, and he'd dropped his evening plans and come straight to the Hog and Hound to have a go.

Win or lose, it didn't matter as long as he got to pummel something hard and fast, someone there with the full intention of being hit and of hitting back in return. It wasn't the safest of diversions, but the money was good when he won, and even better when he had the sense to stay out of the ring and wager on the right fighters. When the rage took over, though, there was no help for it.

The slim young man returned, taking a good look at Marcus as if sizing him up. He shook his head, a gesture Marcus interpreted to mean that he'd be fighting a heavyweight, probably the biggest of them all. Marcus, six feet of solid muscle, was a match for anyone under sixteen stone, but over that he had to be fast on his feet and dodge all blows. "Come with me."

Marcus followed, any sense of impending doom deadened by the incessant throbbing at the base of his brain. Instinctively, his hands curled into fists. Without a thought to the throng of gentlemen and commoners alike assembled around the ring, Marcus forged through the crowd, climbed up, stepped into the ropes, found his corner, and began to strip down. He felt all eyes on him and let them look. If his size and the shrapnel scars dotting his muscle-bound chest made him any more intimidating, so much the better.

"Seconds?" a craggy old man with cauliflower ears known to Marcus simply as Jameson called from the ringside.

"Here." Tom Reilly appeared, the crowd parting to allow him to make his way to the ring, where he hopped up and took his place beside Marcus. Tom looked like a fighter in his own right. He stood only an inch shorter than Marcus's six feet, all of him lean muscle. His hair was short and brown with a natural curl that he couldn't seem to tame. His Irish blue eyes had an occasional twinkle that lent him an air of joviality, but they could just as often turn dark and threatening like clouds rolling in for a storm.

"Here." Another man waved from across the ring. He was as short as he was wide and swarthy enough to resemble a storybook troll. Augustus Hantz. Which meant that Marcus's opponent was none other than Smithy Harris, a formidable giant to whom Hantz might have been physically attached since they were so often together.

Harris appeared in the ring seconds later. He came by his nickname honestly, as he'd been a blacksmith by profession. His arms—thick like sides of beef from wielding his heavy hammer—bore the hallmarks of the trade, and he stood half a foot taller than Marcus, if not more. Some men might think this spelled trouble for Marcus, and no doubt the betting was fast and furious against him. But Marcus had watched Smithy Harris before and knew that his size, though unnerving, was a hindrance to easy movement and that he could tire the giant out in minutes as long as he kept bobbing and weaving around the ring.

Once stripped to the waist, Marcus followed Tom to the center where they shook hands with his opponent and the second. The blackness had taken over to the point where he couldn't think to lock his gaze on Harris, and he'd lost all awareness of the boisterous throng in the room. He did hear the whip cracking down to discourage spectators from crowding too close, and when Jameson started reading rules, he found his voice.

"American rules," he growled, and stalked off to his corner of the ring. Bare knuckles, his preference.

"Queensbury," Jameson countered, and Tom stayed center ring for some minutes arguing Marcus's case.

In the end, Tom returned to Marcus's corner and handed him his gloves. "Queensbury rules."

Marcus answered between gritted teeth, "Queensbury it is."

The time for argument had passed. He was desperate to hit something, fists gloved or no.

As soon as the bell sounded, he rushed in for Harris's head, missed him, and received a sharp body blow in return, leaving an angry mark above his ribs. He danced around, much lighter on his feet than Harris, and managed to herd him into a corner against the ropes, where he rained punches into Harris's steel-like chest and iron abdomen before landing one square to his jaw.

Unflinching, Harris returned a sound jab to the side of Marcus's head. Marcus reeled but managed to stay on his feet. His ears rang. Fortunately, so did the bell for the end of the first round.

"What's the matter with you?" Tom sponged him down and handed him a towel. "The object is to tire him out, remember? He's capable of beating you to a pulp."

Marcus grunted. His body, coated in a fine sheen of perspiration, glistened under the gas lamps. The bell rang for the start of the second round. This time, he managed to duck and weave, avoiding all blows until the bell rang again. What he didn't do was land any hits of his own, which added to his frustration. It didn't matter if he got pummeled. He needed to hit, and hit hard.

The third round delivered the satisfaction he craved. The half-minute break hadn't allowed his opponent sufficient time to catch his breath, and Harris's huge, hairy chest rose and fell while he blew air through wide nostrils like a spent old workhorse ready to be put out to pasture. Marcus didn't intend to let him recover. He sprang at him with unimpaired energy, punching, weaving, ducking, and punching again—left, right, left, left, jaw, nose, ribs, jaw, jaw. The giant staggered back and looked as if he would fall. The black had begun to fade from Marcus's mind, and his instincts of survival came back to him.

He landed one last dig to Harris's chin, and Harris recoiled and spun in a slow circle. It was all but over. Marcus's gaze swept the mob to gauge the reactions of all who had bet against him. And that's when he saw him, shaggy brown hair over soulful brown eyes wide with wonder, the very image of his buddy Cooper who had died in his arms during the war.

"Coop?" he said, but he knew it wasn't Coop. It was Cooper's son, Brandon. Brandon, fourteen years old and in need of guidance and approval, who now looked up to Marcus like the father he'd lost. Brandon, Anna, Emily, and Finn. And Prudence Cooper, widow of Lieutenant William Cooper, the best friend and best man Marcus Thorne had ever known.

"Coop!" Marcus said it again, not to Brandon, but a summons to his dead friend, as if William Cooper could come flying out of heaven to deliver his errant son safely home. The pub was no place for a boy, especially not during a boxing match, and Marcus was powerless to defend him, should something go amiss. The Coopers were Marcus's responsibility now. He'd promised his friend as Cooper lay dying, his gut ripped open from one of the box bombs they'd been sent to dismantle. "I'll look after them, Coop. Find your peace."

The last of Marcus's rage melted away, replaced by

a growing sense of urgency to see the boy from the pub and home to safety. And in those few seconds of inattention, Marcus lost sight of the glove speeding toward his face until it was too late. The slam struck with such force that Marcus staggered and lost his balance, followed swiftly by his awareness. The black returned, but this time with the deadly silence of nothingness instead of a roaring rage.

When he woke, his friend Coop stood over him. Marcus recognized him through a gauzy haze.

"Coop, brother," he said, "I'm sorry I've let you down."

"You can't win every match, hey?" A higher voice than Coop's velvet baritone answered him. "But well done!"

Marcus's vision cleared. He hadn't died and met up with his departed friend after all.

"Brandon Cooper." Marcus found his best paternal voice. "What are you doing in a pub late at night? Your mother must be sick with worry."

"She thinks I'm at the millinery. I had a feeling you would come tonight. I didn't want to miss it."

"At the millinery?" Marcus shook his head to clear it and managed to sit up. The crowd was leaving, the match over in a mere three humiliating rounds. The few who remained were collecting their winnings from wagers placed against him, insult added to injury. "Whatever would you be doing at the millinery?"

"Trimming bonnets. I've taken up some work to help Mum."

"And your mum approved?" What had Prudence been thinking? He would have to speak with her.

Their lot must be harder than she had let on. How had he not realized? How could he have been so lax in his duty to his friend? He would have to be more attentive. Brandon was at a tender age, too eager to grow up but not ready to face heavy issues. Left on his own, he could easily turn to unhealthy habits, fall prey to bad advice.

"I didn't give her much say in the matter. I am the man of the house now."

Marcus sighed. "Man? You're not a man until your whiskers come in. Now come on, no more talk of the millinery. I've got to dress and get you home."

"I have whiskers." Brandon stroked his soft, young chin. "And we're not leaving until I collect my winnings." He offered a hand to help Marcus to his feet.

"Your winnings? You wagered against me?"

Brandon had the decency to blush, at least. "Did you get a look at your opponent? Smithy Harris is enormous."

"I'm fast on my feet."

"Not fast enough." Brandon chuckled, his lip curling up at the corner like his father's used to do. His brown hair, in need of a trim, nearly hid his eyes but couldn't block the golden spark of mischief shining from them.

At least someone had made money for the Coopers tonight. Marcus watched Brandon run off to collect his winnings and bid good night to Tom.

Thornbrook Park

A Thornbrook Park Romance

by Sherri Browning

---— ❧ —---

Widowed. Impoverished. Alone.

Life hasn't gone as expected for Eve Kendal, but she has time to regroup when her childhood friend, now Countess of Averford, brings Eve to her elegant Yorkshire estate.

Can she find a refuge at Thornbrook Park?

For Captain Marcus Thorne, a return home means facing the demons that drove him to war in the first place. He's a powder keg waiting for a stray spark…until his eyes meet Eve's and the world goes quiet.

Set against the backdrop of aristocratic tradition unraveling in a fast-changing world, *Thornbrook Park* delivers all the intrigue, mystery, and grand romance fans of *Downton Abbey* crave.

---— ❧ —---

Praise for Sherri Browning:

"Delightful…fast-paced, highly enjoyable read." —*RT Book Reviews*

For more Sherri Browning, visit:

www.sourcebooks.com

It Takes Two to Tangle
by Theresa Romain

---- ✌ ----

Wooing the wrong woman...

Henry Middlebrook is back from fighting Napoleon, ready to re-enter London society where he left it. Wounded and battle weary, he decides that the right wife is all he needs. Selecting the most desirable lady in the *ton*, Henry turns to her best friend and companion to help him with his suit...

Is a terrible mistake...

Young and beautiful, war widow Frances Whittier is no stranger to social intrigue. She finds Henry Middlebrook courageous and manly, unlike the foppish aristocrats she is used to, and is inspired to exercise her considerable wit on his behalf. But she may be too clever for her own good, and Frances discovers that she has set in motion a complicated train of events that's only going to break her own heart...

---- ✌ ----

Praise for **Season for Temptation:**

"Regency romance at its best."
—*RT Book Reviews*, 4 Stars

For more Theresa Romain, visit:

www.sourcebooks.com

To Charm a
Naughty Countess
by Theresa Romain

—————— ❦ ——————

Caroline, the popular widowed Countess of Stratton, sits alone at the pinnacle of London society and has no wish to remarry. But when the brilliant, reclusive Duke of Wyverne—her counterpart in an old scandal—returns to town after a long absence, she finds herself as enthralled as ever.

Michael must save his family fortunes by wedding an heiress, but Caroline has vowed never again to sell herself in marriage. She offers him an affair, hoping to master her long-lasting fascination with him—but he remains steadfast, as always, in his dedication to purpose and his dukedom.

The only way she can keep him near is to help him find the wealthy bride he requires. As she guides him through society, Caroline realizes that she's lost her heart again. But if she pursues the only man she's ever loved, she'll lose the life she's built and on which she has pinned her sense of worth. And if Michael—who has everything to lose—ever hopes to win her hand, he must open his long-shuttered heart.

—————— ❦ ——————

For more Theresa Romain, visit:

www.sourcebooks.com

Secrets of a Scandalous Heiress
by Theresa Romain

—❧—

One good proposition deserves another…

Heiress Augusta Meredith can't help herself—she stirs up gossip wherever she goes. A stranger to Bath society, she pretends to be a charming young widow, until sardonic, darkly handsome Joss Everett arrives from London and uncovers her charade.

Now they'll weave their way through the pitfalls of the polite world only if they're willing to be true to themselves…and to each other…

—❧—

Praise for Theresa Romain:

"Theresa Romain writes with a delightfully romantic flair that will set your heart on fire." —Julianne MacLean, *USA Today* bestselling author

"Theresa Romain writes witty, gorgeous, and deeply emotional historical romance."
—Vanessa Kelly, award-winning author

For more Theresa Romain, visit:

www.sourcebooks.com

Waltz with a Stranger
by Pamela Sherwood

———— ❧ ————

One dance would change her life forever...

Aurelia wasn't hiding exactly. She just needed to get out of the crush of the ballroom—away from the people staring at her scar, pitying her limp. She was still quite enjoying the music from the conservatory. And then a complete stranger—dashing, debonair, kind—asked her to waltz. In the strength of his arms, she felt she could do anything. But both would be leaving London soon...

When they meet again a year later, everything has changed. She's no longer a timid mouse. And he's now a titled gentleman—with a fiancée. Is the magic of one stolen moment, one undeniable connection enough to overcome a scandal that would set Society ablaze and tear their families apart?

———— ❧ ————

For more Pamela Sherwood, visit:

www.sourcebooks.com

The Trouble with Harry

by Katie MacAlister

New York Times Bestselling Author

---- ❧ ----

You think you've got troubles?

As a spy for the Crown, Lord Harry Rosse faced clever and dangerous adversaries—but it's his five offspring who seem likely to send him to Bedlam. At his wits' end, he's advertised for a wife and found one, but perhaps he should have been a bit more forthcoming on certain points...

Wait till you meet Harry and Plum...

Frederica Pelham, affectionately known as Plum, spent years avoiding the scandals of her past, and is desperate for quiet security and a chance to make a family. What she finds is a titled husband and five little devils who seem bent on their own destruction, not to mention hers. And while all kinds of secrets are catching up with them, Plum knows the real trouble with Harry...is that he's stolen her heart.

---- ❧ ----

Praise for Katie MacAlister

"MacAlister's combination of adventure, thrills, passion, and humor make her a superstar. Unstoppable fun!" —*RT Book Reviews*

For more Katie MacAlister, visit:

www.sourcebooks.com

One Rogue Too Many
by Samantha Grace

From the betting book at Brooks's gentlemen's club: £2,000 that Lord Ellis will throw the first punch when he discovers Lord Thorne is wooing a certain duke's sister.

All bets are off when the game is love

Lady Gabrielle is thrilled when Anthony Keaton, Earl of Ellis, asks for her hand. She's not so pleased when he then leaves the country without a word. Clearly, he has changed his mind and is too cowardly to tell her. There's nothing to do but go back on the marriage mart...

When Anthony returns to find his ultimate rival wooing Gabby, his continual battle of one-upmanship with Sebastian Thorne ceases to be a game. Anthony is determined to win back the woman who holds his heart.

Praise for Samantha Grace:

"A merry romp... Grace captures the essence and atmosphere of the era." —*RT Book Reviews*

For more Samantha Grace, visit:

www.sourcebooks.com

In Bed with a Rogue

Rival Rogues

by Samantha Grace

— ❧ —

He's the talk of the town

The whole town is tittering about Baron Sebastian Thorne having been jilted at the altar. Every move he makes ends up in the gossip columns. Tired of being the butt of everyone's jokes, Sebastian vows to restore his family's reputation no matter what it takes.

She's the toast of the ton

Feted by the crème of Society, the beautiful widow Lady Prestwick is a vision of all that is proper. But Helena is no angel, and when Sebastian uncovers her dark secret, he's quick to press his advantage. In order to keep her hard-won good name, Helena will have to make a deal with the devil. But she has some tricks up her sleeves to keep this notorious rogue on his toes…

— ❧ —

Praise for One Rogue Too Many:

"Filled with humor and witty repartee… Grace woos readers in true Regency style." —*Publishers Weekly*

For more Samantha Grace, visit:

www.sourcebooks.com